ROGUE WARRIOR®

Domino
Theory

ROGUE WARRIOR®

Domino Theory

RICHARD MARCINKO
AND
JIM DeFELICE

A Tom Doherty Associates Book
New York

This is a work of fiction. All of the characters, organizations, and events portrayed in this novel are either products of the authors' imaginations or are used fictitiously.

ROGUE WARRIOR®: DOMINO THEORY

A Forge Book
Published by Tom Doherty Associates, LLC
175 Fifth Avenue
New York, NY 10010

www.tor-forge.com

Forge® is a registered trademark of Tom Doherty Associates, LLC.

Library of Congress Cataloging-in-Publication Data

Marcinko, Richard.
    Rogue warrior—Domino theory / Richard Marcinko and Jim DeFelice. — 1st ed.
        p.   cm.
    "A Tom Doherty Associates book."
    ISBN 978-0-7653-2540-2
    1. Rogue Warrior (Fictitious character)—Fiction.   2. Special forces (Military science)—Fiction.   3. Nuclear terrorism—Prevention—Fiction.   4. India—Fiction.   I. DeFelice, Jim, 1956–   II. Title.
PS3563.A6362R6377 2011
813'.54—dc22

                                                                                    2011007884

First Edition: May 2011

Printed in the United States of America

0   9   8   7   6   5   4   3   2   1

Dedicated to my two most significant "sea daddies," who left me this year for their final call:

Everett E. Barrett, who raised me from a wily "screaming seaman" to First Class Petty Officer, then set me on the path to OCS, where his efforts hit the first milestone.

AND

Roy H. Boehm, who frantically tried to teach me how to protect myself in the wardroom and never forget where I came from.

I hope I made their dedicated efforts meaningful!
—RICHARD MARCINKO

The Navy SEAL Prayer

Dear Father in Heaven,

If I may respectfully say so, sometimes you are a strange God. Though you love all mankind, it seems you have a special predilection too.

You seem to love those men who can stand up alone, who face impossible odds, who challenge every bully and every tyrant.

Those men who know the heat and loneliness of a calvary. Possibly you cherish men of this stamp because you recognize the mark of your only Son in them.

Since this unique group of men known as the SEALs know calvary and suffering, teach them now the mystery of the resurrection—that they are indestructible, that they will live forever because of their deep faith in you.

And when they do come to heaven, may I respectfully warn you, Dear Father, they also know how to celebrate. So please be ready for them when they insert under your pearly gates.

Bless them, their devoted families, and their country on this glorious occasion.

We ask this through the merits of your Son, Christ Jesus the Lord. Amen.

By the Reverend E. J. McMalhon, S.J. LCDR, CHC, USN

PART ONE
FUN AND GAMES

Win with ability, not with numbers.

—FIELD MARSHAL PRINCE ALEKSANDR V. SUVOROV,
QUOTED IN DANCHENKO AND VYDRIN, *MILITARY PEDAGOGY*, 1973

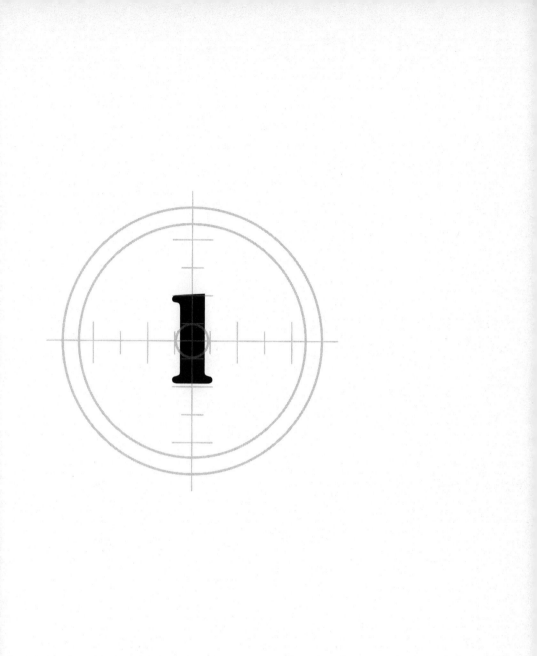

(1)

If there's one thing my sea daddies taught me, it's that life is short. You gotta grab it by the balls while you still can, enjoy those little moments of pleasure.

You know the moments I mean. Whether you're drop-kicking the butt of some tango who's dreaming of paradise while fondling his suicide vest, or maybe reaming a new orifice for a C2[1] officer, you have to make the most of the opportunity. Savor it. Life just doesn't contain that many moments of personal triumph.

But there are also moments when you have to relax and just let life flow by.

Like, for instance, when you're hurtling over the countryside in an Mi-8TV/India helicopter so close to the ground that the crew chief's spit can rebound off a rock and hit the pilot in the face.

Those tracers in the distance?

Nothing to worry about. They're not even firing in your direction. Yet.

The surface-to-air missile battery looming to the right?

What's the fuss? That's designed to shoot down airplanes, not helicopters.

The fact that you're flying over the disputed area of Kashmir, across one of the most volatile borders in the world?

Certainly a plus.

You don't think?

Then maybe it's a good thing you weren't with us.

But truth be told, I couldn't have been more relaxed if I was back at Rogue Manor, sipping a medicinal Sapphire prescribed by the good Dr. Bombay himself.

There were plenty of reasons to relax. For one thing, I had no direct role in the operation. On paper at least. I was just there to observe, a guest of the Indian government.

---

[1] Do I have to explain what C2 means? Again?

The first C is "can't." The second C refers to a female anatomy part in the most impolite language possible.

I cunt use the word because some would be offended.

Of course, we weren't in India at the time, but I'm never one to stand on technicalities. I was certainly ready to observe—watching the bullets fly out of my MP5 counts, right?

So why shouldn't I relax and let the helo toss me around a bit?

This would normally be the part where I'd explain what the hell I was doing in Kashmir. But my editor likes it when I get right to the action, so we'll save the explanation for a little later.

For now, let's just say I wasn't in Kashmir, or India for that matter, to knit sweaters.

The helo banked into a sharp turn to tuck around the mountain. Treetops scraped the undercarriage, tussling it a bit before letting go. Our Mi-8TV/India was a special demonstration version of the Russian Mi-8TV, which itself is a souped-up Mi-17 with guns, missiles, and assorted nasty shit designed to complicate the enemy's day. You can think of it as Russia's answer to the MH-60DAP, the armed Blackhawk hand-built to ferry spec op troops deep behind the bad guys' lines (DAP = Deep Armed Penetrator, or some vulgar variation thereof).

The Indians had recently purchased several Mi-17s and were reviewing the Mi-8TV/India as part of their plans to upgrade their military. Helicopters have a problem flying at high altitude, which can be a problem in the Himalayas, since even when you're low there you're pretty high. Kashmir ain't the Himalayas, but some of the *valleys* there clock in at five thousand feet, so it ain't low either. I'm happy to say the Mi-8TV was doing fine. Better than my stomach, even.

I'd mentioned tracers.

These were actually not being fired at us, even though they were in the general vicinity. They were part of a training exercise being conducted by the Indian army close to the border of the disputed area it shares, or rather doesn't share, with Pakistan. Kashmir-Jammu is claimed by both Pakistan and India, and occupied by both . . . and China. Just to keep things interesting.

China?

That's right. China controls about twenty percent of the historical demarcation of the region claimed by India. That's not quite as much as Pakistan, which I believe has between thirty-five and thirty-nine, but it's more than enough to keep things interesting.

(And complicated. The State Department used to have some good backgrounders available to the public, but you won't find them online anymore, at least not unless you have my intel and computer geek Shunt's skills. If you care for a book, Victoria Schofield's *Kashmir in Conflict* is among the better choices.)

Pakistan and India aren't at war right now, but tensions are always high between the two countries. Both armies have been known to hold maneuvers on their respective sides of the line, partly to keep their troops sharp, partly to show the other side they're not taking guff, and partly just because.

Tonight's action was none of the above. The maneuvers, with live ammo, were being staged to draw the Pakistan army's attention away from our little op. While all eyes were focused on the border area, we were dropping in on a little schoolyard roughly fifty miles behind the Pakistani lines.

Generally when you're a passenger in a helicopter, you don't measure distance in miles, or kilometers for that matter. You measure it in time and stomach acid.

It took us roughly fifteen minutes and two Maalox moments before we cleared the mountain and slid down into the valley that ran up toward our destination. It was a long fifteen minutes. Every one of the fifteen people aboard, including yours truly, felt their intestines steadily tighten with every minute that passed.

Save one.

That exception was Shotgun, aka Paul "Shotgun" Fox, one of my young bucks who was shadowing me on the mission. Besides his mandatory Twinkies and a slightly crushed package of Drake's cakes, Shotgun had brought along a huge bag of peanuts for the mission. He ate them the entire time we flew, cracking each with his fingers, pinching the nuts into his mouth, then tossing the shells on the floor. I don't think I've ever been in a helicopter that smelled just-roasted before.

One that wasn't on fire, I mean.

I have no idea how he managed to eat them. In my mind, you can't eat peanuts without a cold beer to savor the flavor.

None of the Indians we were with complained. It wasn't surprising. Shotgun stands maybe six-eight in his bare feet. He weighs three hundred pounds, give or take a side of roast beef or two. Which he'd had a particular hankering for ever since we came to India.

Not to give you the impression that the Indians we were with were small guys, much less that they were wimps. On the contrary. We were observing the inaugural mission of India's Special Squadron Zero—the rough Indian equivalent of my old Red Cell outfit. And they were about to take action against a terrorist cell that was using Pakistan as a safe haven.

Our target had once been a small farm on the outskirts of a village I'll call Heartburnville. I'm using a fake name because the village was not affiliated with the terrorists, and in fact was exploited by them. The tangos would go into town and take what they wanted from the stores without paying—not usual tango practice, I might note, and a real mistake in this case, since it stirred up feelings against them. At the time, I thought this had helped lead to our receiving the intelligence on their plans. That little ass-u-me assumption proved incorrect.

But I'm getting ahead of the story.

The helo took one last hard bank and pitched forward, pirouetting into a small field at the base of a hill. "Go! Go! Go!" yelled the team sergeant, urging the men out of the chopper.

The sergeant was Sanjin Phurem, a fortyish army noncom who'd served in Kashmir before being assigned somewhere in southern India. Like everyone else in Special Squadron Zero, he was a volunteer.

Shotgun and I followed the Indians out. There was just enough moonlight to see the rocks that littered the field. I moved to my left, looking for the unit's commander, Captain Dyas Birla.

Birla was an Indian naval officer who had been part of Marcos—the Indian Marine Commando Force or MCF as it's often called in India. You can think of MCF as a marine recon unit with SEAL aspirations. His skills were more administrative and political than actually combat-related, an unfortunate by-product of the Indian military system. Still, he did lead from the front, the number one characteristic you need in a special warfare officer.

"Good so far, yes, Commander Rick?" he asked as I ran up.

I'm not sure exactly why or when he had decided to give me the title—he must have skimmed my first book,[2] stopping about midway, then put three and two together—but he meant it as a compliment, so I grunted. Things *were* looking decent, but we had a bit of a walk ahead of us—so as not to attract too much attention, the helo had dropped us a

---

[2] If you haven't read *Rogue Warrior* yet—get your butt to the bookstore *now*.

little more than three miles from the actual target. The chopper's muffled engines would have been almost impossible for anyone there to hear.

"We will commence our operation at exactly 0300," Captain Birla told his men as they set out. "We will observe strict radio silence until this point, unless there is the necessity of communication."

That gave us two hours to walk exactly 3.2 miles, or 5.15 kilometers. Piece of cake.

Shotgun smirked at me.

"No communication until Murphy steps in," he said.

"Murphy doesn't use a radio," I told him. "He's everywhere."

"Kind of like Santa Claus," said Shotgun. "Or the Good Humor man. Want some peanuts?"

I shook my head and started walking. Shotgun's reference set is a little different from most normal human beings.

Roughly an hour later, we arrived at the fence of a madrassa—or "a Muslim school, college, or university that is often part of a mosque" as Webster succinctly puts it in his dictionary.

What Webster doesn't say is that such schools are often used as training sites and havens for terrorist organizations—most famously the organization operated and funded by a certain Saudi Arabian real estate developer known for his great love of Americans and general kindness.

Good to see you recognize sarcasm when you hear it, grasshopper. You can sit at the head of the class.

The madrassa in this case was run by a lovely group of religious fanatics and would-be mass murderers who called themselves India for Islam. When they were feeling a bit loose, they would let go of "for" and just use India Islam. Clearly a bunch of wild and crazy guys.

Like a lot of Muslim terrorist groups, India for Islam wasn't directly associated with bin Laden, at least as far as we knew. It had sent a few suicide bombers into the Indian portions of Kashmir, but had had relatively small ambitions until very recently. Over the past six months, it had recruited committed jihadists and nuts—excuse me, dedicated Islamic students—wishing to engage in a demonstration of the Prophet's peaceful intentions. It had established this school, filling it with some three dozen bright and bushy-tailed freshmen. Their study included Blowing Up Infidels 101 and Torching Nonbelievers 102.

We were about to give them an upper level class in Butt Kicking, with Ass Whipping as an elective.

Now if this had been an American operation, we would have arrived with all sorts of real-time intelligence literally at our fingertips. At a minimum, we would have had a Predator overhead, supplying real-time infrared, and more than likely a communications-stealing "asset" probing the airwaves as well.

But this was an Indian operation, and they don't have a flock of Predators, let alone Global Hawks and EC-130s straining to get into action. So the mission had been planned according to old-school doctrine. Our little group was just the advance team, scouting ahead for the main assault team, a Marine Marcos force of roughly three platoon-strength that would arrive in fifty-nine minutes.

To be honest, I kind of like the old ways. Eyes in the sky are never a substitute for boots on the ground. And intelligence is never a substitute for common sense. But then I was an old-school guy before old-school was popular.

The squad circled the perimeter of the property, observing the two large buildings at the center of the compound . . .

We'll skip ahead—you're only missing the boring, crouch-through-the-mud-and-breathe-silently stuff . . .

Within a half hour, Special Squadron Zero had determined that there were two lookouts on duty, both on the eastern side of the school facing in the direction of the border. Additionally, each building had a sentry sitting in the vestibule near the door. Our intelligence had indicated that the building to the east—one-story, flat roof, school-type structure with eight or nine classrooms—would generally be empty for the night. The second structure to the west—three stories, also a flat roof, about three-quarters as long as the first, though just as wide—was used as a dorm, housing one to two dozen "students" and at least three teachers.

The students were committed jihadists; their teachers were crazy psychos, and we should consider them all armed and dangerous. Even when asleep.

So far, so good. Intel solid, and the op was running right on schedule. The captain radioed the main assault team and gave them a green light.

Shotgun practically giggled.

"When's Murphy showing up?" he asked, shaking his head. He produced a Three Musketeers bar from his tac vest—I have no idea how he manages it, but the boy is basically a walking snack bar. If he were in the Peace Corps, he'd be a one-man famine relief force.

"Who is this Murphy, Commander Rick?" asked Birla.

I thought Shotgun was going to choke on his chocolate.

"You don't know who Murphy is?" he asked. "Murphy is the king. Murphy is the man. He makes the law."

"Law?"

"Jeez, Captain. Murphy's Law. You never heard of it?"

"Is this physics? Every action there is an opposite and equal reaction?"

Murphy's Law—whatever can go wrong will go wrong, at the worst possible moment—is indeed a law of physics, but I set the captain straight. I didn't want Shotgun choking on his food.

"Oh, yes. Plenty of room for Murphy," said Birla. "We are ready for all contingency."

Shotgun winced. If there's one thing my guys know, you don't bait Murphy. You never *ever* say out loud that you have the drop on him.

Even if, like Special Squad Zero, everything is under control. Especially then.

But you can't blame Captain Birla, really. Things were in good shape. The helicopters with the main assault team were twenty minutes away. All we had to do was wait for them to arrive.

And we would have—if that had been the plan.

A few of my most faithful readers have taken it upon themselves of late to point out that yours truly is no longer the proverbial spring chicken. Concerned about my health, they have suggested that I take a more laid-back role in my ops, going so far as to suggest that I now devote myself less to fun and games and more to mellower pursuits.

I'm not exactly sure what they have in mind. Golf with hand grenades?

In any event, I am well aware that my mortal carcass doesn't spring back as quickly from the whacks of everyday life as it once did. Further, I believe that while I have a duty to impart my wisdom to the next generation, I know full well that I don't have to get my balls shot off in the process. So, to the extent possible, I have started to delegate.

Which is why I stayed back with the captain and listened on the radio while Shotgun moved toward the house with Team Alpha.

"We're at the window," reported Shotgun, who was acting as Alpha's commo man. "Interior is clean."

"Proceed," ordered the captain.

Shotgun dropped to his knees, letting Corporal Sesha Nadar climb up onto his shoulders. Then Shotgun rose slowly, boosting Nadar to the window. After double- and triple-checking that the hallway was clear and that there wasn't a wired alarm, Nadar tried pushing up on the window to open it.

You'd be surprised how many windows in theoretically secure buildings aren't locked. But this one was locked.

Not a problem.

The corporal took out a small suction cup and placed it on the windowpane. He looped a string through the hook at the back of the cup, then twirled it around his thumb. Pulling a glass cutter from his tac vest, he cut a large, less-than-perfect circle. A gentle tap, a quick pull, and he had a hole a little bigger than his forearm. He reached in and found the two locks securing the window.

Sixty seconds later, Team Alpha was inside the building, moving down the hall toward a back staircase about fifteen feet from the window. The guard in the vestibule at the doorway was a little more than a hundred feet away, down the long, darkened corridor. If he was awake—again, you'd be surprised—his only view of the hall was through a small window at the side of the interior door. Though dim, the red light above his head made the vestibule where he was far brighter than the hallway, and the very slight glare on the glass made it nearly impossible to see through without pressing his eyes against it.

And why would he even bother? His job was to protect the interior. That meant watching the door to the outside, not the inside. The hall was the last place he expected a threat.

Corporal Nadar, on point, slipped into the staircase. Nadar and everyone else on the team were wearing night goggles.

Trotting up the steps, he tiptoed to the landing and went down to one knee, looking down the hallway.

It was clear.

The corporal counted off the doors, mentally marking their targets—rooms five, eight, and twelve, odds left, even right. Shotgun, meanwhile, went forward to the landing at the front of the building to act as a lookout there; Sergeant Phurem stayed by the back stairs. The other six men split into twos, each taking a room.

And then the fun began.

I wasn't there, but I had worked with the team during the run-throughs, so I have a fairly good notion of what happened next. The team members waited by each door, looking toward the sergeant for a signal to proceed. As soon as he lowered his arm, they entered each room—there were no locks—moving quickly and as quietly as possible.

The rooms were monklike cells, one student per room. The only furniture in each was a bed and a small chair. There were no closets or bathrooms.

The Squadron Zero members approached the beds, each taking a side. The man on the right had a small towel in his hand. He clamped it over the sleeping man's face and held it there for a few seconds. The other man was poised with his submachine gun, ready to strike the sleeper's head with its butt if necessary.

It wasn't, not in any of the rooms. The towels each contained a heavy dose of chloroform, a primitive though effective knockout agent.

Sweet dreams, dark princes.

Two of the three targets struggled initially, choking just a bit as their half-sleeping brains struggled to make sense of the strange direction their dreams had suddenly taken. Then their bodies went limp. The third man went off to a deep slumber so quickly that the Indian corporal with the towel wasn't positive he even went out. Just to make sure, he removed a syringe from his vest and supplied a shot of a Demerol-like sedative.

Trussed and slumbering, the three tangos were removed from their beds. One by one they were taken from the rooms and carried back to the staircase where the sergeant was waiting.

At this point, you may be thinking: *Why not just slit their throats and be done with it?*

Good question, grasshopper. And while there aren't always good answers to good questions, in this case there is.

Two of the men being carried down the hall were terrorists whom our sources indicated had carried out an intelligence mission in India roughly six weeks before. Special Squadron Zero wanted to "debrief" them—find out who had helped them get in and out of the country, how much they had learned, where they had stayed, etc.

Oh, their target would be nice, too. Our information was that it was related to the Commonwealth Games—not exactly a big surprise. No fewer than two dozen terrorist groups were said by various Indian intelligence agencies to be targeting the Games. Knowing exactly which venue they were aiming at and why would give us more information about what the terror groups knew of India's vulnerabilities.

The third man was a spy, planted by the ministry that had formed Special Squadron Zero.

Who was who?

Another good question—but this one couldn't be answered by anyone on Team Alpha, or Special Squadron Zero for that matter. Not even the captain knew. Nor did I.

Did I hear someone make a joke about all tangos looking the same? How un-PC.

The information wasn't given to us to help protect the identity of the spy in case things went very far south. Whether a good decision—read "bad"—or not, it greatly complicated our situation, since we wouldn't know whose throat not to slit if things went sideways rather than all the way south.

Which naturally would mean we'd just kill them all and be done with it.

The snoring tangos were carried from their rooms to the staircase. The team prepared to exit the building the same way they had come in.

Exactly thirteen and a half minutes had passed. The marine assault team, on schedule and ready for action, was six and a half minutes from touchdown. By Sergeant Phurem's watch, they were two minutes and twenty-nine seconds ahead of schedule. Getting out of the building only required another ninety seconds; they were that far from christening Special Squadron Zero with a successful op.

Then the sergeant noticed that tango number two, removed by Corporals Takin and Vasari, alias Smith & Wesson, was not one of the men they were assigned to grab.

The man had a mole where he was supposed to. But he had a scar on his cheek that didn't match the description. And by even the roughest guess at his size, he came up six inches short.

"Maybe he just received the scar," said Corporal Vasari.

The sergeant admitted it might be a possibility, but wondered about the height.

"It was just an estimate," said Takin.

Sergeant Phurem frowned, and looked at Shotgun.

"We can't take that chance," said Shotgun. "We have to look for the right guy, and take him, too."

Shotgun volunteered to go through the rooms and look. The ⟨s⟩geant had no other choice. He told his best man, Corporal Baskar ⟨⟩ to help.

"You have three minutes," the sergeant told them. "Three minu⟨⟩ and then you leave. Everyone else goes now."

"Plenty of time," said Shotgun. "Piece of cake."

Yes, that is what we call ironic foreshadowing. Glad you're keeping up.

There were twenty-four rooms on that floor. The team had gone into three, which left twenty-one to check out. Shotgun and Corporal Bhu split up. If my math is correct—and the nuns at St. Ladislaus Hungarian Catholic School were pretty much sticklers in arithmetic—that gave Shotgun and Corporal Bhu something in the area of seventeen seconds to check each room.

They gave it a good try. Shotgun was in his third room when he heard Corporal Bhu whisper that they were out of time and had to get going.

The message was followed by a gagging noise—exactly what you'd expect to hear if Corporal Bhu was being strangled.

Shotgun started to back out of the room he was in. As he reached the hall, he heard something else—the heavy *thump-thump-thumber-rump* of the approaching assault helicopters.

(II)

Unsure where Corporal Bhu was, Shotgun glanced across the hall, looking for an open door. They were all closed.

This was no time to play eeny-meeny, but Shotgun had no choice. He went to the door opposite the room he'd just been in, put his hand on the knob, and pushed in.

There was a "student" sleeping on the bed. No corporal.

Or was the student faking?

Shotgun, MP5 aimed at the figure beneath the blankets, went over to see. The terrorist-in-training was lying faceup, snoring gently.

And damned if he didn't look exactly like the man they were supposed to take out, mole and all.

Shotgun took the syringe of Demerol out, pulled aside the blanket, and plunged the needle into the man's neck. The sharp prick woke him, but a smack across the forehead settled any objection. It probably also sped the drug's effect.

"I'll be back," Shotgun told the man, leaving him to go look for the corporal.

By now, the helicopters were nearly to the roof. Someone downstairs began to shout. Shotgun went to the next door. Realizing he was running out of time, he kicked the door open.

He saw a figure standing in the middle of the room, framed by the light, gun in hand.

Shoot or be shot?

Not really a choice. Shotgun fired. His first bullets slammed into the man's gun, sending it to the floor.

The next six or seven buzzed through the man's stomach, cutting him nearly in half.

Shotgun took another step to his right and saw Corporal Bhu on the floor.

He was gasping for breath. His neck had been broken, but he was still alive.

No one has ever confused Shotgun with a nurse, but he knew enough from his training as an Army Ranger that he had to immobilize the corporal's neck before moving him. There are special neck and back braces for that sort of thing, with nifty inflatable cushions and well-designed straps that hold you tighter than Aunt Clara's hug at the family reunion. But lacking special equipment, Shotgun had to improvise—he pushed up the bed, reached underneath, and broke off one of the wooden slats. Snapping it in two, he fashioned a crude splint, which he secured with the handcuffs and tape from his vest. It wasn't very pretty, but it was enough to keep the corporal's neck from falling off his body.

As gingerly as he could, Shotgun lifted him onto his back.

"Shiva," muttered the corporal.

Shotgun had no idea what that meant, but took it as a good sign and headed for the stairwell.

While all of this was going on, your faithful correspondent was watching through a pair of night-vision binoculars as the marine helicopters came in. They were aboard four Mi-8TVs, outfitted for spec ops warfare though not quite as well armed as the one that had dropped Special Squadron Zero off.

Captain Birla was talking to the assault team's leader, Colonel Singh, theoretically providing him with complete, up-to-the-second intel on what to expect at the site.

I say theoretically, because despite the captain's loquacious nature, he did not mention the fact that eight of his men were in one of the target buildings, let alone what they were doing.

You may conclude from that that Special Squadron Zero's snatching mission was a secret even from the rest of the members of the operation. If you concluded that, you may go to the head of the class. There will be no homework for you the rest of the semester.

I'd been listening to Alpha over the radio, and knew that Shotgun and the corporal were still inside. So when Sergeant Phurem radioed the captain for instructions, I was ready for his exasperated roll of the eyes.

"Well, get out of the building," said the captain.

I broke in.

"Shotgun, what's your status?"

"Second-floor staircase, coming down with the corporal. Shit."

I heard a blast of gunfire over the open mike.

"Keep talking to the marines," I told Captain Birla. "I'll go get them."

I may have used a few more adjectives and the occasional verb to describe what I was going to do, but you get the drift.

The gunfire near Shotgun wasn't coming from the tangos on the second floor. They didn't have guns; their weapons were all locked away in the armory room on the first floor.

The burst of automatic rifle fire that echoed down the stairwell came from above. One of the marine assault teams had blown its way through the roof and entered the stairwell. Apparently they'd seen a shadow below and followed a policy I generally endorse: *Shoot first, ask questions not at all.*

Shotgun threw himself against the side of the stairwell, avoiding the bullets. He waited for another burst, making sure he was out of the line of fire, then began sliding down the steps toward the first floor.

By now, the student terrorists were fully awake and aware that they were in serious trouble. As Shotgun reached the landing, he saw two men run to his right in the direction of the window.

There was nothing to do but follow.

He took two steps. Then the hall filled with light—a flash-bang grenade had exploded nearby as the marines came into the building.

A word of advice: if you're in a situation like that, about the worst thing you can do is wear night goggles.

And don't look at the light.

Shotgun had done both. Temporarily blinded and unable to hear—even with his earplugs, the gun blasts in the stairwell had screwed up his hearing—Shotgun ran in the direction of the window where they'd come in. Unfortunately, he'd gotten himself turned around in the confusion, and was running the other way.

He realized this about fifty feet down the corridor, but by then it was too late. He kept his head low, and just kept running, trusting that the others in the building were as confused as he was.

He bumped into two or three people, bowling them over. Somehow he managed to get to the end of the hall. He opened the door and pushed into the vestibule, where the guard was spraying the nearby darkness with an AK47.

As the guard glanced behind him, Shotgun leveled his MP5 and fired, catching him in the neck and face. That took care of one problem, but left him another—the marines the guard had been shooting at.

I was about fifty yards from the building when Shotgun came over the radio with his predicament.

"They got me pinned down, inside and out," he said. "I don't want to hit the marines, but sooner or later they're going to hit me if I don't."

Shotgun was hunkered down with the corporal behind a desk in the vestibule. Glass and bits of the wall were scattered on the floor around him. He'd closed the door behind him, but there was no way to lock it from his side.

The Indian marines had practiced this assault several times a night for the past several days, and they were moving like clockwork across the campus. This was actually in our favor, because I knew exactly where the three men were that had Shotgun pinned down. I changed course and headed toward them. At the same time, I told Sergeant Phurem over the team radio to get the hell out of there with their "packages."

The marines who had Shotgun pinned down were hunkered behind a group of boulders a foot and a half high at the edge of a wide but shallow ravine flanking the building. During their dry runs, they had encountered heavy machine-gun fire from the vestibule, then been counterattacked on their left and right flanks. They'd learned their lesson a little too well, and were paying more attention to their sides than the door when I ran up.

"Marcinko!" said one of the marines.

"Easy," I told him. "What's our situation?"

"Four or five men, near the door," said the marine. "We're waiting for Corporal Presi to come up with the grenade launcher."

"Good. But some of our men are pinned down on the other side of the building. They got too close," I added, knowing they wouldn't mind hearing that the members of Special Squadron Zero had made a mistake. "Can you swing around between the buildings and take some of the pressure off? I'll wait for the corporal and the grenade launcher."

They were happy to help.

Inside, Shotgun was waiting for my signal when two of the tangos slipped into the vestibule with him. Both had been to the armory and had AK47s in their paws.

They looked at Shotgun.

He looked at them.

They raised their rifles.

He fired his submachine gun.

Advantage—Shotgun. Both men fell back against the door, sprawling into the hallway.

"How we doing, Dick?" he asked over the team radio.

29

"You're good. Come on," I told him.

I held my breath as he sprinted from the building. Assuming the marines stuck to the program, there was no one else on this side of the building to shoot him. But few plans survive first contact with the enemy, and I was worried that a wayward marine might take a potshot at the hulk running from the building.

If they did, they missed. Shotgun lumbered across the open field, legs churning, lungs double-pumping. He sounded like a bull coming across at a one-legged matador. He slid in next to me on one knee.

Corporal Bhu groaned.

"I think his neck is broken," Shotgun told me.

"Then don't bounce him around."

"I'm trying to be careful."

Shotgun explained what had happened inside, then told me the last "package" was still upstairs.

"I hit him with a shot, but I couldn't take him and the corporal," he said. "Not with his neck so bad."

"What room is he in?"

"You're not going in there, are you?"

I hate it when people ask stupid questions, especially when they already know the answer.

I got to the door without anyone in the building seeing me. Aside from the two men Shotgun had killed, there was no one in the vestibule. The tangos still fighting were either above me or in the rooms on the north side of the building, engaging the main body of the ground assault.

I went upstairs, taking two at a time.

Yeah, I huffed a little.

I threw my shoulder against the wall as gunfire erupted just outside the landing to the second floor.

A figure came around the corner. I reached my foot out as he turned and he went flying face-first.

It was a terrorist wannabe, still dressed for sleep in briefs and a T-shirt. I heard someone running in the hallway behind him.

Once again I put out my leg, and this time added a little push to make sure he landed hard. It was a marine, but I figured I was teaching him a lesson—he should have stopped and looked around the corner before proceeding.

What he *really* should have done was cleared the stairwell with a grenade. But that was in the advanced class.

Shotgun had told me the sleeping tango was in room six. I didn't have night glasses, and even with the gun flashes and flares outside I couldn't see very far down the hall. I had to get right up close to the first room to look and see how they were numbered.

The answer was . . . they weren't.

"Shotgun, which one of these is six?" I whispered over the radio as I slipped into the hall. "There are no numbers on the doors."

"Start from the north. East side is even, west is odd."

The room was on the other side of the corridor. I got about halfway when bullets started streaking through the window at the end of the hall, shattering the glass and throwing splinters of wood, metal, and cement everywhere.

I didn't really mind the mess that much.

The grenade that followed the bullets — that was a different story.

Fucking Murphy had arrived, in spades.

(III)

Most hand grenades have a seven-second delay before they explode. Now seven seconds sounds like a long time. And it can be, especially if you're looking at a grenade and waiting for it to explode. If you've watched a lot of World War II movies, you've probably come across a scene where a soldier very calmly pulls the pin, counts off to three, then tosses the grenade just in time so that it explodes after a tension-inducing bounce.

Real life doesn't quite work that way. Most people once they pull the pin realize they have 6.5 ounces of Composition B in their hand, and they do what any sane person does—get rid of that motherfucker ASAP.

Which *can* mean that the grenade sits on the ground for a whole three or four seconds before going boom.[3]

I think that's what happened here. Truth is, though, I didn't stop to count off the seconds. Instead, I spent my time diving into the open doorway to my right.

Landing on my belly in the darkness, I braced for the inevitable crash behind me.

In the next moment, I realized there was someone in the room with me. He was kneeling by the window, sighting a rifle toward the next building. He glanced over at me in the darkness, the white of his eyes glinting with a reflected light from a flash below.

Possibly he said something—most likely the Arabic equivalent of *What the fuck?* But I didn't hear it. The grenade cooked off in the hallway, the concussion strong enough to rattle the floor.

My MP5 had been in my hand as I jumped into the room, but the hard fall had knocked it from my grip. The gun was somewhere on the side, probably a few inches from my hand; if I'd been thinking, I would have scooped it over and shot the tango wannabe while he was still trying to figure out who I was.

But I wasn't thinking; I was operating on instinct, doing something

---

[3] To get around that, soldiers and marines are generally taught to toss grenades so they skip and bounce along the ground, making them difficult to catch and throw back. Easy in practice, a lot harder on the battlefield, believe me.

I've done maybe a thousand times before. I levered my arms beneath me, pulled my legs up like a sprinter's, and launched myself at the nearby shadow. My left arm became a battering ram; my right was a guided missile.

My left arm caught him in the chin, pushing his head back just enough for my right fist to connect with his temple. Meanwhile, the rest of my body crashed down on his, leaving him a wet puddle of unconscious murk on the floor.

At least that's what *should* have happened. That's what my instincts wanted to happen.

I did hit him, and as far as I can tell, I slammed him pretty hard. But rather than knocking him out, all I did was piss him off. He reared back and slugged me. I tumbled off him, then winced as he pounded my chest with his right fist.

Those were baby slaps compared to the kicks. My chest felt like it was caving in.

You've probably formed a picture in your mind of this terrorist being Shotgun's size, or maybe even a little bigger. His arms are tree trunks and his legs pile drivers. His torso wouldn't fit in a barrel. He's got one of those scraggly Hollywood beards, a couple of missing teeth, and breath that would shame a grizzly.

You're right about the beard, the teeth, and good God the breath. But the rest of the image is wrong. If this terrorist wannabe stood more than five-two I'm Wilt Chamberlain.[4] He couldn't have weighed a hundred pounds. Calling him a half-pint would inflate his size by at least a cup. But he was the most furious son of a bitch this side of Trace Dahlgren. Fortunately, my initial assault had sent his rifle down into the darkness.

As we rolled around on the floor, he punched, he kicked, he squirmed, he bit.

I hate that.

He was a regular snapping turtle. I have teeth marks on the Kevlar to prove it.

Finally I managed to get behind him and slid my arm up beneath his chin. Even then, he squirmed around so much that I couldn't quite get the leverage I needed to twist the bastard's skull off. I pulled and pulled, until finally his body went limp.

---

[4] Don't you kids know your history? Look him up. Hint: he wasn't short.

Yeah, I know he's faking—now. Not then, though. I dropped him to the floor, anxious to get my bearings and figure out where the hell our target was. Suddenly my breath was snatched away by a bowling ball in the gut. I fell back against the wall, slapping wildly at the tornado trying to drive itself through my chest.

I couldn't breathe, though given the stench of his breath that may have been a blessing. I wasn't seeing all that well either; not only was it dark, but my eyes were starting to swell from his punches.

They say hold your friends close and your enemies even closer, but that strategy wasn't helping me much here. I realized what I needed to do was hold this enemy far away. I grabbed the back of his pants, lifted, then flung with all my might. I wasn't thinking of where I was throwing him, let alone aiming, but sometimes working blind is the best strategy: he flew right through the window, still twisting and squirming. For all I know, he bored through the ground when he hit and dug a hole to South America.

I grabbed his rifle, then found my submachine gun. I literally staggered out of the room. Any suggestion that I take a less active role in the company would have been welcomed with open arms at that point.

The hall was clear. I found the room where Shotgun had left the doped tango. This time I took no chances, ducking and moving in close to the shadows as I entered. I found him passed out on the bed.

I grabbed him, flipped him over, and hauled him onto my back.

Then nearly collapsed. This guy was borderline obese, heavier than Shotgun by seventy-five pounds if an ounce.

My only choice was to suck it up. I waddled out of the room, glancing left and right at the hall.

Still clear, thank God.

Just as I started to gather steam, I saw a flash in the stairwell I was aiming at. A boom followed almost simultaneously.

It was a flash-bang grenade, a prelude to the arrival of the marine assault team.

Not wanting them to see me with my prize, I turned on my heel and headed back in the other direction. Somewhere around room seven or five, I found an open door and lurched inside. The room was empty, though at that point it wouldn't have been much of a problem if there'd been a dozen people here. I would have dumped the whale I was carrying on their heads, not only crushing them but violating five clauses of the Geneva Convention in the process.

I spun and dropped him as gently as I could on the bed. Then I ran back to close the door.

"Shotgun!" I hissed over the radio.

"Hey, boss," he chirped in his disgustingly cheerful voice. "Where are you?"

"I'm on the second floor, west side. I need intel. Where are you?"

"Heading in your direction."

"Are there marines on my side of the building?" I asked, visualizing the game plan in my head. "There should be a pair near that little cluster of bushes. Find them."

"Yeah. I see two guys."

"Get them out of there so I can jump."

I went to the window and looked out. The second story looked a lot higher than I remembered from the exercises. Suddenly my knees started creaking, reminding me that they weren't shock absorbers.

If I were jumping on my own, they'd hold. But put fat boy on my shoulders and my knees would snap like thin sticks as I hit the ground.

There was no rope handy, but there were bedsheets. I rolled Fatty off the mattress and whipped off the sheets, fashioning them into a crude, prison-break-style rope. It wasn't going to get me all the way to the ground, but a jump from six or eight feet wasn't nearly as bad as what I'd do otherwise. Worst case, I could drop Fatty from there without too much risk of breaking his neck.

Outside in the hall, the marines were going door to door, clearing each room. They used a stun grenade in each room, moving methodically, just like I'd taught them.

Methodically doesn't mean slow—I realized they'd reach me before I could get out. And there was no lock on the door. The only thing to barricade it with was the bed.

Well, I could have used Fatty, but that would have defeated the purpose of coming inside in the first place.

I hauled the bed against the door, then went to the window, knocked out the panes, and secured my makeshift line to the frame.

"How are we doing out there, Shotgun?" I asked over the radio.

"Ready for you."

I made like Atlas and pulled my overweight package onto my back in a fireman's carry. Now that I felt his weight again, I worried that he was going to be too much for the sheet. But there was no time to reconfigure it—there was a loud slam against the door, followed by a few rounds fired at the doorknob.

The sheet held much longer than I had any right to expect. I was just about even with the first-floor window when it started to strain. I reached my hand down, hoping to descend a few more feet before it gave way. But it was too late—gravity gave me a big wet kiss as my feet hit the ground. I lost hold of Fatty and shot forward, rebounding off the wall before falling backward into Shotgun.

We rolled down in the dirt, tumbling over.

"Wow, he's a big one," said Shotgun, scrambling to his feet.

"Don't tell me he's the wrong one."

"No, the face is right," said Shotgun, putting his eyes practically in the tango's nostril. "He's just a lot bigger than I thought he was. The intel was all wrong."

The intelligence we'd gotten hadn't said the guy would outweigh an elephant, but it was pointless now to worry about it.

This will tell you how strong Shotgun is—he deadlifted the guy over his head and onto his back. He barely bent under the weight as we made our way back to Special Squadron Zero's gathering point.

"Where'd you send the marines?" I asked Shotgun as we ran.

"La la land," said Shotgun.

"La la land?"

He pointed to the left as we passed their position. The two marines were slumped forward over their guns.

"I couldn't think of anything to tell them to get them to move, so I just bopped them in the head from behind," he explained.

Sometimes the easiest solution is the best.

"There you are, Commander Rick!" said Captain Birla. "We were worried that your Mr. Murphy had caused you distress."

"He was just keeping things interesting. What's our sitrep?"

Active resistance had ended; the marines were completing their room-by-room search. With Fatty in hand—or on back, to be more precise—we had recovered all of our subjects, with one to grow on.

Time to get the hell out of Dodge.

"The helicopter will meet us at the rendezvous point in ten minutes," said the captain. "Sergeant Phurem has already gone to the landing area."

"We'll join him. See you there."

Our helicopter was meeting us in a field about a half mile to the south-west—not coincidentally out of sight from the marines. We put our prize on a stretcher and with considerable help from two other squadron troopers made our way down the rocky path to the road leading to the LZ.

Sergeant Phurem was waiting there with most of the squad. The team corpsman had changed Corporal Bhu's splint, immobilizing his head. He'd also given the corporal a nice healthy shot of morphine, which may explain why he was humming.

"Indian lullaby," explained the corpsman. Just as on a SEAL team, he was a shooter with special medical training—he could sew 'em up almost as fast as he could shoot 'em up.

Captain Birla appeared as the helo hoved into view. A few minutes later, we were all safely aboard, once again zigzagging our way toward the border.

With the notable exception of Corporal Bhu, Special Squad Zero had not sustained any serious casualties. The marines, it would turn out, lost two men in the operation, one shot by a guard in the first building we hadn't known about, and another who got a gut wound from a grenade and bled out before he could be evaced back to the hospital.

Very possibly the grenade had been thrown by one of the marines, which really sucked. Naturally, that didn't make it to the obit.

Two other marines sustained injuries, one to his leg and the other to his arm. And there were the usual cuts and bruises, the inevitable pulled muscle and a dislocated shoulder, none of which are ever actually entered on the casualty report, though the guys that suffer them sure know about them.

Most are thankful for such an "easy" souvenir.

On the other side of the ledger, twenty-eight terrorist trainees, all but one of whom were from outside of Pakistan, were killed in the raid. Pakistan raised an official protest several days later, but in truth they were probably just as happy as the Indians were to be rid of them.

Among the items found during the raid were tickets for airplane and train travel into Europe and back into India, presumably for the raid they were planning. There were also documents relating to a pair of ships we think were to have been used to transport weapons into the country. Those ships never made it to port.

The accident rate at sea is simply astounding.

Among other papers found during the raid were documents indicating that the group leaders made regular trips to a part of Karachi controlled by a Pakistani political party with known affiliations to terrorists. There were also indications the group had contact with an operative the CIA believes is a Taliban "fixer" for Pakistani intelligence.

My personal favorites were the dunning e-mails to a supposed organization demanding money for jihad. They gave the slogan "Give until it hurts" a very literal meaning.

There were a number of other goodies that I won't go into because the leads were still being followed as I wrote this. The intelligence haul was solid, and all in all, the "official" part of the secret mission was a resounding success.

But I didn't particularly care about that part of the raid. It was the secret part of the mission that I'd tagged along for. And evaluating that was considerably more complicated.

[IV]

Before getting into the intricacies involving our guests, I should probably backtrack as promised and explain how it is I came to be in India.

When last we communed,[5] I was heading back to Rogue Manor, having spent a rollicking good time in the socialist workers paradise of Cuba, where the rum is heady and the girls are always willing. I'd barely walked in the door when the phone rang. I picked it up and found myself talking to a guy who sounded so much like a computer help desk that I braced myself to be put on hold.

"Is this Richard Marcinko?" he asked.

"What are you selling?"

"No sell. Dis is Assistant Minister Ahal. Please hold for the minister."

"I'm already a faithful member of the Church of No Tomorrow," I told him. But before I could slam the phone down, I heard a sexy female voice ask if she was talking to *the* Richard Marcinko, aka Demo Dick, Sharkman, and other names too dirty to mention.

"This is me."

"It is very much my honor to speak with you," she said.

When I tell you she had a sexy voice, I don't mean that she sounded like she could work a 900 number for a year and then retire a millionaire. I mean she could bring a stadium to tears by stepping up to the microphone and speaking, not even singing, the national anthem. Men don't go to war over women anymore—a damn shame, if you ask me. But if they did, this woman would have caused World War III, World War IV, and several small police actions on the side.

Her name was Minister Dharma, and she was the newly appointed cabinet minister for Interior State Security and Commerce in India.

Dharma—rhymes with "charmer." Kind of. And she was. No doubt about that. When she told me her title and responsibilities, I was ready to apply for the position of undersecretary. And very well might have, had Karen Fairchild not been glaring at me from across the room.

Karen is my girlfriend. And while she's unusually patient and rarely jealous, her eyes at that moment were sharper than the blade on the latest

---

[5] *Rogue Warrior: Seize the Day.*

prototype of my Rogue Warrior knife. Women have a special radar about these things.

"You have heard of the Commonwealth Games?" Dharma asked.

"Not really," I told her. "But I'd love to learn."

I've always considered myself something of a sports fanatic. Now granted: the sports I follow closely—ass kicking, butt stomping, and face smashing—aren't likely to be included in the Olympics anytime soon. But the fact that they haven't won favor with a mass audience yet doesn't diminish their pleasure.

"The Commonwealth Games are going to be held in India in 2010," Minister Dharma told me. "This is a very large event for us."

Background: the Commonwealth Games are the equivalent of the Olympics for the Commonwealth.

What? What's the "Commonwealth"?

The Commonwealth of Nations is an organization of some fifty-four countries around the world. Most, though not all, were at one point British colonies, part of the British empire when Britannia ruled the waves. It's not a political organization, exactly; it aims to generally encourage democracy and that sort of thing, but it's probably closer to something like the VFW or American Legion for countries than the Republican or Democratic Party.

Or Labour to Tories, to give it the British spin.

The Games are held every four years in different places around the globe, ranging from Australia to Canada to Scotland. The 1998 games were in Kuala Lumpur, Malaysia. And in the fall of 2010, they were being planned for Delhi, India.

A total of thirty-one sports ranging from archery to wrestling were to be held there, along with seven other "para-sports," which are a special subset of sports for people with disabilities. There are complicated rules about which sports member countries have to field teams for and how the scoring runs, but I'm guessing that if you're interested in any of that you already know a lot more about it than I do. My understanding of the rules is only a little more advanced than Shotgun's, who summarized the games by saying, "Girls in shorts! Hot shit!"

The minister wasn't calling to ask if I cared to compete in lawn bowls.[6]

---

[6] Note to copy editor: that's bowls, not bowling. Or lawn balls, as Mongoose liked to call it.

There had been various rumblings that the Games would provide a perfect opportunity for the likes of Osama bin Laden to demonstrate that the U.S. wasn't the only Great Satan in the universe. The 2008 Mumbai attacks were more than ample demonstration that terrorists not only had India in their sights, but could strike at will there.

The minister wanted me to help make the Games a less attractive target.

The Mumbai attacks in November 2008 got a brief amount of air time in the States. They were huge in India, the equivalent of 9/11. Say 26/11 in India, and people know that you're referring to the date of the attacks, and the attacks themselves.

More than ten separate groups—the exact number is still debated—worked together to strike Mumbai in a series of coordinated attacks beginning November 26. They hit a women and children's hospital, a movie theater—real brave pricks, eh? The action culminated in a hostage situation at the Taj Mahal Palace Hotel, a ritzy five-star hotel that deserved a much better fate.

The terrorists were eventually defeated, thanks to action by the police, the Mumbai Anti-Terrorist Squad, the Rapid Action Force, Marine Commandos, and the National Security Guards' Special Action Group (SAG).

(You can get more information about SAG's op at the Palace Hotel by Googling "Operation Black Tornado.")

One hundred and seventy-five people died in the attacks. All but a handful were civilians. Over three hundred more were injured. That's how these assholes define success—killing innocent people.

At first, Pakistan did not want to acknowledge that the attack had not only been launched from its soil, but that Pakistani citizens had been deeply involved. But that's Pakistan's usual modus operandi. The country's intelligence services have a tangled history with radicals, as anyone with even a passing knowledge of what's been going down in Afghanistan since 9/11 can tell you.

There have been *some* changes. And in fact, though the Pakistanis eventually filed an official protest against our extracurricular activities at the madrassa, they were secretly appreciative of the raid, and even offered to help Indian intelligence with future ones.

An offer viewed with appropriate jaundice, in my view. But I'm getting off the track.

The Mumbai attacks were a wake-up call not just to India but to Pakistan and the world. I don't want to build the terrorists up to be supermen or give them more credit than they deserve. But the attacks demonstrated that these Islamic radicals had tremendous discipline and patience. They made good use of cell phone technology and GPS mapping systems. They gathered considerable intelligence on their targets beforehand. They did this by working in small cells for security with the sort of organization you normally only see in the military.

Impressive, to be honest. And very dangerous.

The Mumbai attacks showed the Indians that they had some glaring deficiencies. There was a total lack of shared intelligence among the many different police agencies and intelligence units—something that's improved, but just barely.

Part of the problem is the sheer number of agencies responsible for India's national security. There are national and state intelligence agencies, police, the military, big cities. The intelligence community alone could populate several of our western states.

The attacks also showed that maritime interdiction and even basic capabilities relating to port security are another problem, though they didn't make much of a dent in the news coverage. The Indian navy is getting better, but as someone wrote recently in a private report perused by yours truly, it's "far from ready to declare a sufficient readiness posture."

Or to put it in Rogue terms—they still got big bull's-eyes on their butts.

The Indian government was rightly concerned about the Commonwealth Games being a serious target for terrorists, but it took threats to pull out from countries such as New Zealand and England to get progress on the terror front. A number of initiatives were undertaken by both military and civilian authorities. That sounded like a great idea, but it quickly became part of the problem. Take the police, take the army, take the navy, add military intelligence, the intelligence units run not only by the Indian federal government but by the country's twenty-eight states and seven union territories—add that all up and you have bureaucracy that puts our American tangle to shame. We're talking about a veritable Gordian knot of information supported by a veritable chokehold of bureaucracy. You think feuding between our CIA and FBI is a problem? Take a trip to India.

Most of these people are extremely well intentioned, dedicated to doing their jobs and dealing with the threats as they perceive them. But they're also just as dedicated to the organizations they work for, and the various viewpoints that those organizations have of the world.

Getting intelligence from point A to point B, let alone acting on, can be as difficult as getting airplanes in and out of O'Hare Airport. And failing to do so smoothly can result in a lot worse problems than chronic flight delays.

It's the boring, mundane side of the war we infidels are fighting against an enemy who tends to solve his problems by strapping a few pounds of plastic explosive to some poor schlep's chest and sending him into a crowd.

You didn't pick up this book to hear about cutting through red tape, or the necessity of banging heads together to make things work. My job—thank God—wasn't to bang everyone's heads together and make them play nice. I was brought in to replicate the original Red Cell.

In an Indian kind of way.

Being new, the Interior State Security and Commerce Ministry didn't have its own intelligence or operations unit. It was probably the only government entity that didn't. But it did have money, and Minister Dharma, anxious to advance herself politically, decided to use it to burnish her agency's standing in the government.

Or at least that was my read. Hers was that she was trying to improve the security situation for the Games. The interpretations are not mutually exclusive.

Special Squadron Zero was supposed to gather intelligence, act on it, and test the security arrangements at the Games. To do that, Minister Dharma recruited specialists from throughout the Indian military and intelligence fields, then hired my company, Red Cell International, as a consultant to help tell them what to do.

Minister Dharma kept relatively close tabs on Special Squadron Zero. I'd like to think that she OK'd the operation in Pakistan because she understood that to beat terrorists you have to take the fight to their doorstep, but I'm not delusional. Dharma was more than willing to expand Special Squadron Zero's portfolio as long as she saw a benefit to her position.

You have to understand, this was an inside-the-government game. The operations were never going to be public; no newspaper reporters were coming along as inbred embeds. She got her points in cabinet meetings, where she not only got to announce great progress in security, but could also show that her colleagues weren't doing their jobs.

Using an intelligence agency for political gain?

Gosh darn, where have we heard that before?

Since I'm doling out brain dumps here, let me give you one more on India for Islam.

Like a lot of radical groups, India for Islam's leaders were connected with several mosques throughout India. The mosques were spread across the country. The only thing they really had in common were imams who preached the need for India to return to its roots.

That doesn't sound bad at all, until you translate it according to the context that was used. If you listened to the speeches, you would understand pretty quickly that "roots" meant India during the time period when it was dominated by Muslim rulers. This was trumpeted as a golden age for the subcontinent, and even mankind in general. The imams wanted to return to that Golden Age. This could only be done by bringing back Islamic law and the dominance of the one true religion. Pure adherence to the Word of Allah would prompt a return of the moguls. Islamic India would once more become the center of the universe.

Arguing with their interpretation of history would be pointless. Religion—let's not even get started. And while some psychologist might be interested in understanding how their being bullied as kids led them to violence or whatever, the bottom line was that the imams appealed to a very small but fanatic group of people.

All young men. All capable of murder, if properly trained.

[V]

Even by Rogue Warrior standards, the Kashmir operation was a rousing success. We'd retrieved a spy, grabbed two key members of the terrorist organization that was aiming at the Games, and even picked up a bonus member to provide additional information.

So why wasn't I feeling that good about it?

Shotgun's theory was that Fatty—who, yes, did turn out to be our agent—had strained my back. But even though I did return from the mission with a little crick in my neck, that wasn't the problem. I sensed a Murphy deficiency.

Strictly speaking, Murphy's Law does not require that things *always* go wrong at the worst possible time. While that has been my general experience, it's not the *actual* math. The equation is more Einsteinian than Newtonian—the closer you get to the perfect op, the more likely the odds are that something will screw up. But just like betting on a hundred-to-one favorite at the Kentucky Derby, it doesn't always happen.

I pondered the vicissitudes and algebra the afternoon following the raid as Captain Birla and I briefed Minister Dharma in New Delhi.

About Minister Dharma: as I said earlier, she had the sexiest telephone voice I have ever heard. Ah, but in the flesh . . .

Still beautiful.

Lips, full. Cheeks, a dusty blush color. Eyes, penetrating and yet somehow soft. Brow, clear, not a wrinkle even hinted.

Breasts—*aaaaaahhhhhhhhhhhhh*.

And in perhaps the greatest cruelty of all, she was smart and had a personality that at once managed to convince you not only that she was in charge, but that she would listen to what you said and take it into account when she made decisions.

If Karen had met her, I would have been in very serious trouble.

"How long will it be before we have information from these criminals?" Minister Dharma asked Captain Birla. "This should be a priority."

"It is very hard to predict, Minister," said the captain. "To get information we can trust—sometimes this is a problem that cannot be solved. Interrogation can take a long time."

She glanced at me.

"There are some things we can do to speed the process along," I said.

"You are proposing the infamous waterboarding?"

I swear I thought she said waterbed. For once, I was short of words. Captain Birla replied.

"I am confident with our methods," he said, "we will get results."

"You must do so quickly," she said. "We need information."

The Games were coming close, but that wasn't why the minister wanted to speed things up. She needed new information to use during her cabinet meetings. Having already bragged about the raid, she now needed to present a trophy.

One thing I give her credit for. A lot of politicians in her position would have been more than happy to look at the operation and say, *Game over. We win. Everybody back on the bus and party!*

Not Minister Dharma. She realized that where there was one cockroach, there were bound to be more.

Speaking of cockroaches, Captain Birla and I went over to see Fatty right after the briefing ended. Fatty—aka Aban Numbnuts Khalid (I've translated from the Arabic)—was holed up in a hotel on the outskirts of the city.

"Holed up" undoubtedly gives you the wrong idea. The word was more like "ensconced," or maybe "luxuriating." The ministry had rented the penthouse floor of a five-star hotel to debrief him.

Or fete him. They'd stocked the bar and brought in a pair of personal "assistants" as well as a masseuse—all female of course—to help him "recover" from his ordeal.

Did I mention that there was a large hot tub on the penthouse patio? And that the government had also supplied a table's worth of Indian delicacies, and a box of cigars imported straight from *Habanno*?

We found Fatty surrounded by his "aides" on the patio when we went over. It was hard to see through the haze of smoke that hovered over the hot tub.

"Captain Birla," said Fatty, waving an opening in the haze. "Commander Rick. Have some drinks, please. Ladies, cigars for my friends."

Captain Birla passed, as did I.

"Food, then. There is very much good food." Fatty waved toward a table near the tub. It was crowded with brightly colored Indian delicacies. But neither the captain nor I was in much of a mood to eat.

"We must need to talk," said the captain.

"In good time," said Fatty, slipping a little deeper under the water. "We all have priorities."

"Adult swim time," I growled. "All of the kids out of the pool."

The girls leapt out, grabbing towels as they went. They'd been bathing without the benefit of suits.

It was a beautiful sight.

Unfortunately, it implied that Fatty was in a similar state. I stopped him as he started to get out of the hot tub.

"You stay there," I told him.

I'd have tossed him a towel, but the smallest thing capable of covering him up was a six-man tent.

"You should not be mean to me, Commander Rick. I have just risked my life for my country."

"Yeah, that looked real dangerous."

"I am speaking of Pakistan," he protested. "Among the radicals. Every day it was a danger. If they discovered who I was, my throat would have been slit."

"They'd've had a hard time finding it under all those chins," I told him.

I went over to the bar and poured myself a drink—Bombay Sapphire on the rocks, of course.

Fatty insisted on smoking a stinker while talking with us. I didn't mind the stench—it reminded me a little of the burning crocodile carcasses I'd smelled in Thailand, which brought on a wave of pleasant nostalgia. The smoke, though, was so thick that it made it hard to see Fatty's eyes.

Am I implying that I thought he was lying?

Yes.

Why didn't I trust a spy? You might as well say, why didn't I trust someone who lies for a living. Fatty's job description came down to one sentence: *lie your way into the enemy's heart*. His résumé consisted of one successful lie after another. So naturally I had to wonder what he was lying about now.

Fatty had only joined the group a few weeks before, enlisting through a mosque in Hyderabad. He'd provided very little actual information before the raid; external sources had given us the location and layout of the facility. As far as I was concerned, he still had to prove himself.

Fatty began by confirming that India for Islam was tight with certain elements of the Pakistani intelligence service.

"How tight?" I asked.

"Very."

"Did they provide instructors?"

"This, I am not sure."

"Money?"

"Maybe money."

"How do you know this?"

"I pick things up."

Not from the floor, I thought.

Captain Birla pumped him with questions. Was the group related to Lashkar-e-Taiba, the organization responsible for 26/11? Were the men we had grabbed the ringleaders? How were they planning to get to India?

Fatty gave the same answer to all.

"I am not sure."

He did describe some of the training. Most of it was fairly generic, primarily involving physical training designed to get recruits into shape. There'd been some injections—steroids, Fatty thought—and pills. Both had become standard procedure in heavy training regimes immediately before an operation, so that at least indicated the attack had been imminent. There was weapons training—AK47s—and some explosives work. They had walked through an assault on a guard post and the entrance to a building, but Fatty's descriptions were so generic that the target was as likely a condo in South Beach as a stadium in Delhi.

"You don't know what the target was?" I asked.

"I wasn't there long enough to gain their confidence," said Fatty.

I got the impression that "long enough" would have been a million years. To be fair, most of these operations would be so compartmentalized that the actual shooters wouldn't get specific information about their targets until the very last minute. There had been roughly three dozen men at the training camp; it was highly unlikely all would have been used on the operation. My guess was that the larger group would have been pared down, with the best and brightest pulled off for the mission. Only they would have gotten the real details. From the looks of him, Fatty would never have been in that group.

"I am very tired," he told us. "I need to relax."

"You look plenty relaxed to me," I told him, continuing with the questioning.

The overall program at the madrassa was similar to that followed in literally a hundred of these camps in the northern border area of Pakistan. The schools provide not only terrorists but many of the Taliban soldiers we've been facing in Afghanistan, committed Soldiers of God, ready to do whatever their supposed religious superiors tell them, whether it's murdering a police chief's infant son or strapping a bomb to their chest and boarding a bus in Kabul.

The only difference that I noticed was the lack of religious or political indoctrination classes; many of these camps devote an enormous amount of time to pounding religion into the skulls of their followers. Instead, there were classes in English and Hindi, undoubtedly aimed at making it easier for the team to infiltrate the country and then fit in.

The majority of the recruits had come from India, which has one of the largest populations of Muslims in the world. But there were a number of people in the camp from outside the region. According to Fatty, three came from Yemen, as to be expected; the place is a veritable terrorist paradise. But there was also a man from Egypt, one from Malaysia, and another from South Africa.

"They could blend with anyone," said Captain Birla.

It was a good point. With the exception of the Yemenis, all of the "students" were from Commonwealth countries. Give them fake passports, and they'd look like tourists. Dress them in sweats, they'd look like athletes. Work clothes . . . you get the idea.

"Now they will blend in with no one," chuckled Fatty, dumping the ash from his cigar into the pot of a nearby midget eucalyptus tree. "Dead, dead, dead, instructors and students both."

"How many other schools does India for Islam run?" Captain Birla asked.

"Other schools?" Fatty shook his head. "I don't know other schools. If there are others, they do not tell Khalid."

I glanced at Captain Birla. He was frowning, and I knew what he was thinking: *if we'd been able to hold off the operation for another week or so, we might have gotten much more information.*

There's always that tradeoff. Strike early, and you may not get the best information. Strike too late, and your targets may be gone.

"You think there are more people involved in this?" asked Captain Birla as we went down in the elevator after we finally concluded we'd gotten everything we could for the night.

"Hard to say," I told him. "There would definitely be support groups, but if you look at successful terror operations, they're usually carried out by eight, ten, maybe twelve people."

"Here there were three times that number," said Captain Birla. "But not all of these would have been the action people—shooters, as you say."

"Right."

"But the Games are very big, with many targets. Perhaps they are more ambitious and need more people."

Captain Birla's point was well taken. The Commonwealth Games were an immense target. India for Islam might be planning multiple hits, with different training camps for each.

From the terrorists' perspective, the Games were their own Olympics—a huge target with instant PR value if they were hit. We knew of several other plots against the Games being pursued by other agencies. (A few of them you've read about by now. Unfortunately.) Those were large operations as well. There was just no way to be sure we'd gotten this entire cancer.

"The best course is to expect more problems," I told the captain.

He nodded.

"More trouble and more trouble," he said. "That is the nature of the beast."

[VI]

Did I mention earlier that Trace Dahlgren and Doc Tremblay were also in India?

Everyone knows Trace looks good in a skirt. But Doc?

All right, so he was wearing a kilt. His knobby knees were still a sight to behold.

Doc and Trace had joined the Scottish field hockey team—Trace as a player, and Doc as a trainer. Hollywood couldn't have cast them better—Trace was practically born with a stick in her hand, and Doc just loved to get his hands on the ladies.

But why were they there at all?

To understand, you need to flash back to the 1972 Olympics at Munich. I'm sure readers of a certain age will know what I'm talking about, but to fill some of you youngsters in:

Early on the morning of September 5, with the Olympics in full swing, a group of scumbags from the Black September faction of Fattah—aka PLO—climbed a six-foot chain-link fence at Olympic Village and raided the dormitory where the Israeli athletes were staying.

By nightfall, all eleven hostages were dead. Several of the hostage takers were also killed in a heavily botched operation by the German police. (The mistakes were partly redeemed by the formation of GSG 9, a premier German counterterrorist unit formed out of their National Border Police, led by my old friend and mentor Ricky Wegner. They've saved a number of lives since their inception. The Israelis later served their own brand of justice on the people who had organized the attack in a series of aptly named operations—Operation Bayonet, Operation Wrath of God, et al. Of course, to this day, some Palestinians deny that the whole event took place, but I'm not writing a book on mass hallucinations.)

The Munich massacre is a key terrorist event studied by everyone in the counterterror community—and most likely, by terrorists themselves. Protecting athletes at events like the Olympics and the Commonwealth Games presents very unique and difficult problems. Ticking them off in detail here would be like providing a how-to list for newbie tangos, but I can say in general that athletes are used to a certain amount of freedom of movement and openness in order to train. At the same time, they're very high priority targets, in many ways a more desirable "get" than politicians.

Each of the teams coming to the Commonwealth Games were well aware of Munich, and had their own security people in place. But I knew we'd need a little more than that, which is why I'd arranged for Doc and Trace to join the team. If I could have, I would have placed someone on every team, but Red Cell International doesn't have the man (or woman) power to do that. So we focused on the teams that had come to the country early, that would be high-value targets, and that at least from the outside would look like easy pickings.

The Scots had come to New Delhi a week before to use the training facilities at a private girls school that happened to be a few blocks from Dhyan Chand National Stadium, the complex where many of the Commonwealth Games were due to be held. With the stadium still undergoing last-minute preparation work and therefore off-limits for athletes, the school was the best place available for the hockey teams.

In fact, except for Dhyan Chand itself, the practice facilities were said to be among the nicest in this part of the country. There were three full-sized fields or "pitches," along with half a dozen other large practice areas. The grass was as well maintained as any American golf course, quite an achievement in this part of India, where the weather can go from extremely dry to oceanic in a matter of hours.

The locker-room facilities were a little cramped, according to Trace, but there was a three-story dorm with private rooms for the athletes and a large cafeteria in the basement. The dorm was at the front of the campus, shouldered into an area of low-rise apartment buildings. The property swung back in an elongated L from there, backing toward an industrial area of warehouses and factories. These were separated from the fields by a wide, rarely traveled road. The large factory on the northeast corner of the property was surrounded by a barbed wire fence. The property was owned by the Indian Helicopter Company and at least superficially patrolled.

The buildings to the northwest were a motley collection of clothes manufacturers and dried food storehouses. Their yards were cluttered with trucks and old bins—a good place for a group of tangos to gather pre-raid. We'd tried getting the area secured, but had had no luck.

Two other national teams, one from Malaysia and one from Pakistan, were staying in housing nearby and using the facilities as well. Trace would have fit on any of the teams—she's part Navaho and part everything else. With the right makeup, she has passed as Chinese and Spanish; dye her hair red and she looks a bonny if sunburned lass. Doc, on the other hand, wasn't about to come off as Malaysian or Pakistani. In fact, he couldn't even do a passable Scots accent—we gave him a backstory as an American who'd been hired by the team for his skill with ankles and knees.

Fitting, since he's always been something of a leg man.

(Here's another hint: there's a rooster tattooed to his leg. The inked bird hangs by its neck. If you're ever out drinking with Doc, don't be surprised if he brags that his cock hangs below his knee. And don't bet him on it, either. Good for laughs, and more than one free drink.)

Planting them on the Scottish team made the most sense from a tactical point of view as well—it was far more likely that a team of mostly white Westerners would be targeted than Asians and fellow Muslims. The Scottish team's manager and the captain knew they were plants, but the rest of the players, coaches, and assorted hangers-on thought they were real.

If you've ever seen Trace handle herself, that's not hard to believe. In fact, when Shotgun and I stopped by late that afternoon during a scrimmage, she was single-handedly taking the Pakistani team to school.

Doc was standing on the sideline with the manager and some of the coaches when Shotgun and I ambled into the stands. Shotgun had spent the morning sleeping, and the early afternoon stocking up on snacks. He was munching some sort of Indian peanut and sugar concoction as we settled into the bleachers.

"What are you eating, elephant food?" I asked.

"That's a good one, Dick."

While Shotgun munched away, Doc came over and asked how things had gone the night before. Of course he did this with the sprinkling of the usual four-letter terms of endearment.

"Recover from your bumps and bruises?" he asked. "Or should we confirm that reservation for the Old Shooters Home."

"I'm over them," I told him. "I may have trouble with smoke inhalation. The informer we brought back likes to smoke Cubans."

"Maybe I should share some from my stash." Doc had managed to smuggle a few *puros* back from our sojourn on Cuba.

"I don't think he's cigar worthy."

"Problem?"

"I don't know. Something about him doesn't seem right. Like the fact that he weighed three hundred pounds and was supposedly doing PT and running every morning."

"Shotgun weighs three hundred pounds," said Doc.

"This guy isn't Shotgun."

Doc shrugged. He looked like he was about to say something when Shotgun spit some of his peanut concoction out of his mouth.

"Look at those guys over there," he said, pointing. "Man, they are out of place."

Two men in long coats were standing on the opposite end of the field. They were way overdressed for the weather.

And if that wasn't suspicious enough, as soon as they saw Shotgun pointing, they turned and started to run.

Shotgun jumped up from his seat and started to chase them.

"Shit," I said, looking at Doc. But there was nothing to do but follow.

Shotgun is relatively fast for a big man, and with his head start he quickly pulled away. In fact, he was so far ahead that I lost sight of him and the men by the time I reached the fence at the end of the field. I climbed to the top—it was six feet tall—paused and took a look. They all seemed to have vanished into thin air.

I went over the fence and started walking westward along the road. Every few feet I stopped, turning around, expecting to see Shotgun and the others suddenly burst into the open space in the complex of warehouses and yards to the right.

A yellow brick building stood at the edge of the road to my right about fifty feet away. It was a collection of rectangles that had grown in a crazy quilt pattern over the years. Now mostly abandoned, it had been both a factory and a warehouse over the years, growing to cover nearly two acres. I figured that the men had either kept going down the road or run inside the building.

I had just about reached it when I saw them run around its far corner, back out onto the road ahead of me. My feet tightened instantly as I started to run. But bogged down by their overcoats, they weren't running too fast themselves. Neither looked to be taller than five-ten.

The vague plan I formed in my head went like this:

Assuming they didn't stop, I'd jump on the nearest one and wait for Shotgun to catch up. Then we'd pummel the asshole and find out what he was up to.

Looking at the situation from the comfort of your reading chair, you're probably thinking: Dick, you jackass. Don't chase them. They're wearing long coats. It could be that they're wired to explode. Hang back, don't get too close. They may just decide to take you to Paradise with them.

That, gentle reader, is good and sound advice.

The truth is, though, that idea never occurred to me.

Call me stupid, call me dumb. But then I'm not the one that thought I was going to Paradise.

I was about five yards from grabbing the nearest miscreants when the other one spun around. My view of him was almost entirely blocked, and at that point I was sweating so much that my eyes were stinging with sweat, so everything in front of me was pretty much a blur.

But I could hear pretty damn well.

And what I heard was this:

"Watch out, Dick! He's got a gun!"

I did the only thing possible—I launched myself into the air in his direction, hoping for the best.

(1)

I said earlier that I wasn't thinking that either of the men I was chasing could be wearing explosive undergarments. I hadn't thought they were carrying weapons, either. In my mind, they were probably scouting the area for some later action. The Commonwealth Games were still a couple of weeks away.

Which, I have to say, was a big mistake on my part. Blame it on complacency, blame it on lack of imagination. Those two things have played a starring role in every successful terrorist attack since the dawn of the twenty-first century. So I'm not immune.

My brain finally came online while I was airborne. All sorts of possibilities occurred to me at that moment. None of them were very good.

It was too late to do anything about them, unfortunately. I spared my arms, puckered my butt, and proceeded to land full force on the man who'd pulled a video camera from beneath his coat.

Yes, video camera, not a gun.

It turned out that he and his companion were definitely scouting the practice, but not for a terror attack. They were engaged in skulduggery of a more commercial kind—they'd been hired by the Canadian team to get secret tapes of the competition.

And you thought the Canadians were all goody-two-shoes.

Our little race across the field attracted quite a crowd. Unfortunately, they didn't think it was a warm-up for the Games. School security came. Security and staff for all three of the teams practicing at the field ran over. Three Games security people on duty showed up. The city police came. I think a few meter maids also put in an appearance.

They were followed by several members of the news media, making for an A-1 circus. The trench coats were arrested for unsportsmanlike conduct and hauled off to the hoosegow. Yours truly and Shotgun faded into the background, but not before several cameras snapped my portrait. (Google "unidentified bearded man in crowd during field hockey caper arrest, Delhi, India, 2010." I'm the handsome devil in the upper right corner of the image, scowling for the camera.)

The news that someone had hired spies to check out the field hockey teams earned sixty-point type in all the local newspapers, and created a scandal back in Ottawa. Unfortunately, the images also raised my profile around the Games a little higher than I wanted. While I was never named in any of the stories, I realized that my face, even in the background, would be enough to tip off a certain subset of scumbags to my presence. That would make it a little more difficult for me to blend in with the scenery. It also could potentially endanger some of the people I was supposed to protect.

Yes, there are a number of people in the world who do not *like* the Rogue Warrior. And they're not all former commanding officers.

I'm resigned to going through life with a big fat target painted on my butt. But to give us a little more flexibility, I called home for reinforcements.

You know Sean Mako by now. He's an ex-Ranger. It breaks the heart of this old navy man to praise the army for anything, but I have to admit that the Rangers are a serious group of warriors, your basic army of one raised to the nth power. Sean's been separated from the service for a few years now, but he still retains the elite skills he learned as one of the world's premier infantrymen. Rangers like to say they lead the way, and when you work with people like Sean, you realize that's not an empty brag. He's nowhere near as big as Shotgun, nor, to be honest, as strong; he's more the narrow, sinewy type. Taciturn—as in not prone to shoot his mouth off—he's one of our jack of all trades, a weapons guy who can handle communications or first aid, and even in a pinch act as our technology officer.

And then there was Mongoose—aka Thomas "Mongoose" Yamya. Mongoose is a Filipino-American, and we've heard rumors that his grandfather's father's father was with MacArthur during World War II. If so, he certainly passed on his fighting genes, because as you'd expect from anyone who's gone through BUDS and lived to tell about it, Mongoose is one tough customer. Some of his deeds during the service are still classified, but he seems to know a god-awful amount about the geography of Afghanistan.

Mongoose and Shotgun went through our Red Cell orientation as classmates. They formed a common bond during that process—Trace, who heads our training program, tends to do that to people. Since then they've become close friends, a bit like frick and frack, thump and thud, barbell and dumbell, arts and crafts . . . you get the picture. Definitely an odd couple, but they make beautiful music together.

The Goose stands five-six in platform hiking boots. Shotgun could probably fit him in one of his pockets. Mongoose rarely eats more than a half burger in a week. Shotgun—well, you know.

Shotgun is always smiling. I'm not sure Mongoose is familiar with the concept.

People look at Mongoose and say, "His bark is worse than his bite." Me, I have a healthy respect for rabies, so I've never tried to find out.

Last but not least, there was Junior.

Junior is Matthew Loring. He was hired as a tech expert, a fill-in for our number one computer dweeb, Shunt. But since joining the crew, he's gone on to bigger and better things, surviving Trace's orientation and basic shooter classes. He's pretty much an all-around hand at the moment, a guy we can put into various situations.

Still a bit green, but he has potential.

And oh, yeah, he bears a slight resemblance to yours truly. Some people say more than slight, in fact.

That's because Matthew is my son.

I'm not going to go through the backstory here. If you're interested, you can look it up. Suffice to say that, by mutual agreement, Matt is treated absolutely no differently than any other member of the team—just like shit.

Well, truth be told, I may kick his butt a little harder than the others. Paternal love is a bitch.

While they packed their kits and caught the first plane out, I went over to an abandoned Indian air force base about twenty miles outside of town. Special Squadron Zero had taken over a small administrative building there as its headquarters. The basement had an old brig with enough rooms for the tangos we'd grabbed from Kashmir.

The accommodations would have rated five stars on the Michelin Guide to Scurvy Prisons. Most recently, the basement had been used to quarantine rabid dogs, and though that had been at least a decade before, the stench lingered. Special Squadron Zero had applied fresh whitewash on the walls and updated some of the iron bars with thick steel panels. But the place still stank of animal piss. I felt bad for the guards.

We'd quickly identified the masterminds from the photos we had. The man we'd taken by mistake had been relatively compliant; he was basically a scared and mixed up if murderous nineteen-year-old. He'd been interviewed four or five times, and his story more or less tracked with what Fatty had told us the day before. Captain Birla was just holding on to him now until he could figure out which of the country's myriad agencies to ship him to.

Our other guests were a much different story. Neither was talking. They were isolated in separate cells, hands cuffed behind their backs and feet manacled together. Blindfolded and kept in the dark besides, neither man had been allowed to sleep—some horrible Indian pop music was playing at crack-your-eardrums level when I came onto the cell block.

I don't often get to play good cop, but that was my role that morning. Cop isn't the right word, really. Good imam is a lot closer.

And come to think of it, saying that we were interrogating our "guests" may give you the wrong idea as well. In fact, the process was really more like that old television game show *Truth or Consequences*.

Our first contestant's name was Yusef from Kavali, a city on India's eastern coast. A hood was put on him and he was removed from his cell.

The guards walked him around a bit, up and down a few flights of stairs, adding to Yusef's general befuddlement before bringing him on stage. They sat him in a room only a little bigger than his cell. There were no tables, and only one chair. They made Yusef stand in front of the chair. They'd poke him when he started to sag, but otherwise didn't hit him—that kind of force is unnecessary as a general rule.

I watched him for a while through the slit in the door. We had a hidden video camera, but I like the immediacy of seeing him with my own eyes. He was about five-eight, and even in the bulky prison clothes he looked malnourished.

Him I could have carried out of the school under one arm.

I stepped aside as our interrogators went into the room. All three were dressed in plain khaki uniforms that bore no unit markings or ranks. They did, however, look *very* much like the uniforms worn by the Pakistani army.

What a remarkable coincidence.

They were also wearing ski masks covering their faces. No sense giving themselves away.

The guards left. Two of the men stood behind the prisoner, on either side; the third stood in front of him.

No one said anything for a few moments. Then, the man facing Yusef nodded. The man at the prisoner's right took hold of his handcuff chain.

"You are a failure," said the man facing the prisoner. He used Arabic first, but then switched to English. "Do you know why you are here?"

The prisoner said nothing.

"Answer me!"

When he didn't, the interrogator nodded again, and the guard on the left gave our guest a love tap on the temple.

No, it wasn't hard at all.

"Your name," demanded the interrogator.

No answer. Another slap.

"You told us it was Yusef," said the interrogator. "Was that a lie?"

The prisoner's shoulders straightened—the way the interrogator had phrased the question surely caught him by surprise. But he said nothing.

"*Naam*," snapped the interrogator. He'd switched to Urdu.

Another jerk of the shoulders, but no answer. This time the guard didn't hit him. The interrogator asked another question—where is your wife—also in Urdu.

I waited by the door, giving the prisoner time just in case he decided to respond.

Most of these guys weren't married, and we had no reason to believe he was either. But you never know. While he wasn't likely to answer verbally, his body language gave us plenty to go on for future sessions.

"When did you decide to become a murderer?" asked the interrogator.

Nothing.

"*Jawab!*" ordered the interrogator. "Answer!"

That was my cue. I slid the little panel on the door back and entered the room.

The three Special Squadron Zero members snapped to attention as I came in. They said nothing, but even with the hood covering his head, the prisoner could sense something was up. I pulled the chair over and cleared my throat.

The prisoner's hood was removed. His blindfold was undone.

He had trouble adjusting his eyes to the light. He blinked a few times, then stared at me.

I was wearing a long, gray kurta over a pair of black pants. The kurta is a shirt popular in Pakistan and other Muslim countries. It's somewhat old-fashioned, but the sort of thing someone might wear in a tribal area or even in the city if you were underlining your status as a follower of a certain brand of Islam.

It went very well with my beard. I'd let the beard grow extra long for my trip to Cuba, and by now it looked very much like the beards you saw on the Sabbath at devout mosques around the world.

Inevitably, his eyes went to the small package in my hand. It was a Koran wrapped in brown paper and covered by a silk cloth, wrapped and tied so that it could not be defiled by a random unbeliever. I held it out toward him.

He didn't move to take it. I pretended that the reason must be his handcuffs, and pointed to the guard on the left, who was holding them. He undid them quickly.

The prisoner rubbed his wrists, but still didn't reach for the Koran. I pulled back and folded my arms, glancing at the man standing beside me.

"Now, Yusef, we expect you to cooperate with us," said the interrogator. His voice was much softer, as if he were trying to impress me that he was a gentleman. "There is a traitor in your unit. We have narrowed down the suspects. You must cooperate with us. Your life depends on it."

"Who are you?" said Yusef.

"We have supported you," continued the interrogator, ignoring the question. "Given you food and clothes. We are repaid with treachery."

"I don't know what you are talking about."

Yusef glared at me. I stared back without saying anything.

In case you're wondering, aside from some useful phrases like "how much?" and "where's the restroom?" I don't speak Urdu, which is the national language of Pakistan and spoken by just about everyone there. I'm not very much on Hindi either, let alone the more obscure languages commonly spoken in India. But I didn't have to speak. The game plan was for me to sit there, a semibenevolent presence.

"You would prefer to use the language of our enemies?" said the interrogator. He switched to Hindi. "When you infiltrated to India, who did you talk to?"

Yusef pretended not to understand. At that point, I decided to ad-lib.

"Use English," I said softly. "He may be more comfortable with the devil's tongue."

"I'm not a traitor," said Yusef in Urdu. "Why am I being treated like one?"

The idea was to convince our two guests that they were questioned not by the Indian secret service, but by Pakistanis. Our story was that the terrorist training operation had been betrayed by a spy, and that the Pakistanis had gotten wind of the betrayal.

We never said any of that explicitly. The idea was to suggest just enough, and let the prisoner fill in the blanks. We figured that he would be more forthcoming if he thought he was trying to prove his loyalty. We also thought he was more likely to tell us the truth.

The big problem with an interrogation—any interrogation—is that sooner or later the subject decides to cut his losses and just tell whoever's asking what they want to hear. That was something I learned a long time ago, not from the navy, but from the nuns back at St. Ladislaus. I've never met a better group of interrogators in my life. And they never left a mark where it showed.

Yusef was extremely suspicious, and after insisting that he was loyal to the cause, he clammed his mouth shut.

"Which cause?" demanded the interrogator. "Ours or theirs?"

He didn't answer. I gave it five more minutes, then rose. I handed the Koran to the interrogator and walked out.

Good imam gone, the handcuffs and taps on the side of the head returned. But they failed to loosen his tongue, and Yusef soon found himself rehooded and on his way back to the cell.

By this time, Captain Birla had joined me in the observation room, where we were watching the proceedings on the closed-circuit video.

"I don't know, Commander Rick," he said. "They are very tough nuts to be cracking."

"They'll open up soon enough," I told him.

We went through our little game with the second captive, whose name was Arjun.

Lest you should get the impression that these guys were Boy Scouts, let me give you a little background on Arjun.

Arjun was born in India, though we were never able to determine exactly where. His family were moderately devout Sunnis. His older brother was sent to the U.S. to study. Arjun went to England. Oxford, I believe, though my memory on that may be faulty.

There he studied chemistry. He did well, graduated, and got a job. But within a year he'd quit. Apparently he had some sort of mental or spiritual breakdown. He went home, but didn't stay very long. Within a few weeks, he was in Pakistan.

Three months after that, Pakistani border guards caught him trying to sneak over the border into Afghanistan with some friends. The only problem for the border guards was that Arjun and his friends didn't want to be searched, and they made that quite clear. The border guards insisted. Arjun and the others pulled out sawed-off rifles and pressed their points home. All four of the border guards died.

About four months later, presumably after adventures we have no record of, Arjun drove a pair of suicide bombers to an open air market in Kabul.

We know this because the terrorist cell he was a member of recorded the event and posted it on YouTube. Very nice.

His little bit wasn't in the edited video. Shunt found it later, posted with some material on a relatively obscure but still public domain used to help recruit jihadists to the cause. It was the director's cut version, I guess.

After Kabul, Arjun was sent back to Pakistan. Along the way, he ran into some sort of trouble. His name and face were connected to the border incident, making him famous enough to earn bullet-point status on the alert sheets passed among international customs officials. By then, he'd joined the madrassa, no doubt aiming for a major finale to his career.

Which brings him back to our little game show. We went through essentially the same routine with him that we had with Yusef. This time, though, I had our interrogator add a little hint about our friend Fatty.

"Aban Khalid believed you were the traitor," said our interrogator about ten minutes into the show, just after we'd switched to English.

That got the first visible reaction from Arjun since he'd been brought into the room. His eyes narrowed, and I could see that he was straining not to say anything.

The interrogator saw it, too.

"Is our comrade lying?"

Arjun took one of those deep breaths you take when you're reassuring yourself that you have to hang tough.

"We know that you saw others when you were in India last," said the interrogator. He was making it up, of course. "And we know that you were not pure."

"No one is required to be a saint," I said.

Arjun lowered his head.

The interrogator's wild guess had hit pay dirt. He moved in, a lion culling a wildebeest from the pack.

"You should make a clean breast of it . . . There is no need to hold back from us . . . A way can be found to redeem yourself . . . You must not let this go too far . . . If we can stanch the blood now, there will be hope . . ."

Give Arjun credit—he didn't fold. After a few minutes, I realized it was going to take another few cycles to break him down. He was definitely going to tell us everything we wanted, but it would take a few more spin cycles before he came clean.

I rose, and handed him the Koran.

He took it.

I watched for a few minutes from the observation room as the interrogator stepped up the pressure. He wavered a bit, head shaking, sweat slipping off his brow, but ultimately kept quiet.

He wasn't exactly a weak puppy, but the flashes of vulnerability did worry me a bit. Our intelligence had pegged him as an organizer and planner; those types are generally the toughest to break. I had to consider if the long-beard godfathers who were running the show might not have seen the sort of weakness I was observing now. If so, they might have decided to use him in a way that would mislead us if he was captured and spilled his guts.

With all the high-tech gear we have available—the bugs, the GPS locators, the radio-wave snatching aircraft, the Predators, our satellites, you name it—intelligence still comes down to the gray matter between the ears. It's always a judgment call.

If it wasn't, then Naval Intelligence wouldn't be an oxymoron.

(II)

After leaving the fun and games room, I headed over to the hotel to get changed. I'd been invited to a government soiree that evening, and was expected to put in an appearance.

I know what you're thinking. What are we talking about here, Dick? A cocktail party? Beautiful Indian women in swirly dresses handing you champagne and swooning while you entertain them with stories of derring-do.

Pretty much.

It is tough work, though. Don't forget their jealous husbands plotting revenge on the far side of the room.

Seriously, while the fawning attention of some pretty young thing is always a boost to the ego, the truth is I'd rather have been sawing wood — either literally at my woodpile back at Rogue Manor, or figuratively, catching my almost-mandatory three hours of sleep.

The fawning attention of pretty young things would have been quite a relief from the monotony of the overfed bureaucrats I actually shared gin with that evening. The party was a pre-pre-pregame shindig for some of the corporate sponsors and government officials. They waddled from one side of the food table to the other, congratulating each other on the excellence of the upcoming show of athleticism. A few officials from the sports teams already in town had been invited. Unfortunately, the Scottish Women's Field Hockey Team was not among them.

I would have liked to have seen Trace in something swishy.

But there was one saving grace: Minister Dharma was there. She came in late, of course, timing her entrance for maximum effect. Actually anytime she entered, it would have had maximum effect.

You're probably picturing a woman in a tight black cocktail dress that ended well north of her knees. I'm picturing that as well. But that wasn't her style. India still has what we would consider quaint notions about women and how they should dress. Trace complained about several newspaper stories that blamed rapes on the fact that the victims were wearing dungarees. If the minister had worn anything like you and I are fantasizing about, she never would have been taken seriously as a politician.

Minister Dharma was the picture of sensible Indian womanhood, wearing what they call a sari—a velvety violet dress over an even longer dress topped by a matching scarf. There was maybe a postage stamp's worth of skin showing at her neck. But that was more than enough. There was no question that every male in the room, yours truly included, was staring at one or the other stars in the patterned dress as she came down the steps.

From the stars, most of their eyes moved north to her face, where they briefly settled on her *bindi*, a sequined red star at the center of her forehead.

What the hell are those *bindi* things, anyway?

Traditionally, married women wore a red powdered dot in the middle of their foreheads the way women in the West wore wedding rings, telling the world that they were taken. The dot also signified a third eye, and could be worn by men as well as women. These days, *bindi* are worn mostly as jewelry. They have sticky stuff on the back that keeps them in place.

Minister Dharma smiled in my direction. I smiled back, then drifted over to the table where the booze was.

India has some interesting ideas on alcohol. The country's constitution suggests prohibition.

Really.

Article 47: "The state shall regard the raising of the level of nutrition and standard of living of its people as among its primary duties and in particular, the state shall endeavor to bring about prohibition of the use except for medicinal purposes of intoxicating drinks and of drugs which are injurious to health."

Right.

Prohibition has actually been tried in various areas and in various forms—Delhi has "dry" days, kind of like the Sunday Blue Laws in that stores can't sell liquor or beer. On the other hand, restaurants can serve it—unless it's a state holiday.

Too confusing for me to follow. But fortunately the taps were running. I got a refill, then sidestepped a heated conversation about the finer points of badminton. Two members of the government sports ministry cut me off as I headed for the food.

"Mr. Marcinko, yes?" said one. "Very good to meet you."

I nodded.

"I read all your books. And I have two of your Strider knives."

"Always a pleasure to meet a fan," I said. (Of course, if he was a true fan, he'd have all *three* of my knives.)

"Can we have a picture?"

"Why not?"

I smiled and tried not to break the lens.

"Your story should be in the movies," said the other man, handing the camera back after taking the picture. "If not Hollywood — Bollywood. I have a cousin in the business."

Before I could find out whether his cousin was a producer or a ticket agent, someone grabbed hold of my arm.

It was Minister Dharma. She had a hell of a grip.

"Dick, we have to leave," she told me. "Something very terrible has happened. Two of the prisoners have escaped."

(III)

If you're wondering how in hell two men under heavy guard whose feet and hands were bound managed to escape from an army base, you're in damn good company. I wondered that myself all the way over to the old airport. Expecting to see bomb craters and spent shells by the hundreds, I was surprised when I found the fence and the building still standing. If anything, the place looked a little neater than when I had left it; the spotlights that played around the exterior gave it the luster of a used car lot.

I should have realized that the terrorists hadn't blasted their way out. Instead, they'd taken a page from my book—from several of my books. They'd out-Rogued my Indian protégé, Captain Birla, who wore a chagrined frown when he met Minister Dharma and myself outside the building.

"They had credentials from the Interior Ministry," said Captain Birla. "The guards double-checked them."

"Which prisoners?" I asked, but I knew the answer. The important ones, of course. The kid was still downstairs, snoring in his cell.

A pair of plainclothes officers had shown up shortly after a shift change, presented IDs, and asked for the prisoners. They had what looked like a legitimate copy of orders not only from the head of the Interior Ministry but from Minister Dharma as well. Even so, the guards had called both offices for verification.

"They had some way of intercepting the calls," said Captain Birla. "There was confirmation. They had no choice."

The men called Captain Birla, but he was on another call and the message bounced into his voice mail. By the time he heard it, it was too late.

A classic op. As someone who stole a nuclear submarine with only a slightly more elaborate game plan, I almost admired the sons of bitches.

Two security cameras had gotten pictures of the fake Interior Ministry men. The license plate on their car had been recorded at the gate. I was sure the plate was going to come back to a little old sewing teacher in Gurgaon, but I didn't have the heart to tell Captain Birla. He was alternating between fuming at his men and blaming himself. Every so often he would mumble something about India for Islam, complaining that the intelligence had indicated they were not nearly this well organized, let alone clever.

Minister Dharma stared at him with a cold frown. Losing the prisoners was bad enough, but now she was going to have to find a way to look for them without making herself and her top-secret organization look like idiots.

As for myself, I wanted to get Yusef and Arjun back in the fold as quickly as possible. Arjun had taken the Koran I gave him with him, and it had cost me twelve hundred rupees.

Twenty-six bucks, not counting the gift wrap.

"An alert must be put out immediately," I told the minister. "You really can't afford to wait."

"Very likely it's already too late," she said.

"We can make the alert without mentioning how the men got here," said Captain Birla. "We can leave out all details completely."

"That will not work very well, and you know it," she told him. "We will have to tell everyone why we are so fixed on these men."

"You're fixed on them because they're plotting to disrupt the Games," I told her. "You developed intelligence. You don't have to mention that you brought them back."

"Some in the government know."

"But they don't know that these were the men you brought back, do they?"

Dharma's eyes lit. It was as if the sun had come out after a week of rain.

"No," she said. "And we have the other prisoner, if necessary. We can turn him over to the Interior Ministry—that would avoid any other suspicions."

In other words—everyone would put one and one together and figure he was the source of the information that had led them to look for Yusef and Arjun.

Not exactly the way it should be done, but the minister wasn't looking for advice on proper procedure at the moment. I left her and Captain Birla to figure out the politically correct way to deal with their government.

"Where are you going?" asked Dharma.

"Bed," I told her. There was a look of disappointment when I added, "To catch up on my sleep."

I *was* planning on getting some sleep, just not then.

Shotgun had spent the evening doing important intelligence work—he hit the local bar scene. This didn't involve too much travel: our hotel featured several, including a place called Dublin, which billed itself as the most popular nightclub in Delhi. Naturally, this was a claim that Shotgun had to investigate.

There's something about Irish bars that give them universal appeal, even when translated into another country and culture. Obviously, they work in the U.S., and it's not much of a stretch to imagine them succeeding in India, which after all was part of the British Empire for quite some time. But even small towns in Italy have Irish pubs that are packed at the end of the week.

As it should be. No problem is too thorny that it can't be solved by sucking the foam off a good Irish stout.

Shotgun had turned to local India beers by the time I arrived. I found him at the bar working on a Kalyani Black Label and ogling the tourists on the dance floor. The music would have drowned out an air raid siren.

"Hey, skipper, how's it hanging?" he said, spinning around on the bar stool.

"Low at the moment. Come on. We got problems."

I filled him in as we made our way across the street to the cab I'd hired. The minister had offered me her car, but I declined because I didn't want her driver looking over my shoulder.

That was also why we weren't hanging around the hotel. The ministry had put us up at the ITC Maurya, a top class establishment favored by the diplomatic set. I highly recommend it if you're going to Delhi and someone else is paying the tab.

While incredible concierge service and fresh flowers in the room have their place, operating out of a high visibility hotel like the Maurya has definite downsides. It's hard to slip too far under the radar, especially when the local version of paparazzi are known to stake out the lobby looking for celebs. It's great when Lady Gaga is in town—she steals all the attention. But it's all too easy for spies to infiltrate the press gangs,[7] recording the comings and goings of lesser mortals.

So we'd taken the precaution of reserving rooms in other places in the city in case we needed lower profiles. We'd also reserved a floor of

---

[7] Yes, that is an obscure pun.

rooms in a hotel I'll call the Maharaja Express about a mile closer to the city center. It's a small, family-run hotel, about as distant as you can get from the Maurya. The place is owned by a friend of mine named Bali. I've known him for years, having met him at a book signing in the States before he decided to go back home and take over the family business.

Bali has a big family, with what seems like a never-ending supply of uncles and aunts. The cabdriver I was using was one of them. Urdu (like the language) drove an old black-and-yellow Ambassador taxicab that was probably old when the Beatles came to town. The interior was big—for India—and smelled like his dinner, which I take was some sort of vegetable stew with copious amounts of curry.

Shotgun stayed with Urdu and the cab while I ran up to the room in the Maharaja and grabbed one of our gear bags. Among other things, it had a GPS locator in it.

Shotgun fired it up and we went to work.

Unknown to Captain Birla, I'd taken the precaution of planting GPS transmitting chips in the waistbands and collars of the prisoners' clothes. The transmitters were operating—and they showed our two friends were headed toward the Abul Fazal enclave, an area of Delhi near the Yamuna River.

I gave street-by-street directions to Urdu as he drove. Traffic in Delhi is among the worst in the world, but it was late and we were outside the city center, so it took only a few minutes to get down to Abul Fazal. The district, or enclave as they call it, includes river marshlands as well as very densely packed rows of small houses and apartment buildings.

The area is named after a famous historian who was part of Emperor Akbar's court during the sixteenth century. At the time, India was part of the Mughal Empire.

No, I'm not foreshadowing there. At least not consciously.

"Stopping by the river," said Shotgun when we were about a mile away. "There's like some sort of causeway through the swamp. Looks like a highway runs parallel to it, along the main bank of the river."

A mile can be a long way in Delhi. We snaked through some of the narrowest residential streets I've ever seen before reaching the wide road Shotgun had seen on the GPS unit. Urdu seemed to have no problem navigating the back alleys of the area, but he balked when we reached the causeway, which forked out between a man-made lagoon and a mixture of swamp and overgrown islands. There wasn't an actual road there, and he worried about driving his ancient Ambassador over the high curb and onto the loose sand. He gave an explanation in Punjabi about why this was a problem—at least that's what I think he said, since my Punjabi is limited to pickup lines.

"You just wait here," I told him finally. "We'll be back."

"Wait, wait. Yes. I wait."

Shotgun and I got out of the cab and trotted up the dirt path. Along the way I unzipped the backpack, taking out my PK pistol and handing Shotgun his weapon du jour, a Heckler & Koch MP7A1.

The MP7A1 is a small submachine gun specifically designed to defeat body armor. It's billed as a replacement for the MP5, with its main advantage being the velocity of the 4.6mm round. It's relatively small and light—four pounds with twenty rounds—and in Shotgun's hand, it practically disappeared.

The path to the main body of the river ran maybe three hundred yards. Two hundred of those were flanked by heavy vegetation—low brush at first, then bigger bushes and trees as we moved out.

What? Do I see a hand in the back of the room? Go ahead. Ask your question.

You're wondering why we're doing this without backup? Why I didn't just call Minister Dharma or Captain Birla and have a squad of men accompany me to the water?

Think about it. A supposedly elite commando unit, handpicked with volunteers from every military service in the country, loses two highly important prisoners from its grasp.

It's not beyond the realm of possibility; elite units screw up all the time, as I delighted in proving during my original Red Cell days.

But . . .

It also seemed possible, more than possible actually, that there were loose lips inside the organization. Maybe even a traitor. So I had to assume that anything I did that the squad was aware of would get right back, maybe instantly, to the terrorists.

If that happened, yours truly would be singing out of a new airhole. So assuming I wanted to be involved at all, I had to work on my own.

And why be involved?

That actually is a good question. I have only halfway good answers.

Aside from not wanting to see all my hard work go to waste, it personally pisses me off when people I trust turn out to be scumbags. And there was the thought that these assholes might turn out to be a very serious problem down the road.

The moon was bright enough that we didn't need night-vision gear. We moved up along the southern side of the path in the direction of the river, working through the brush as quietly as possible in case there was a lookout posted.

The locator sensors hadn't moved since before we'd gotten out of the cab. Now they started shuffling around.

"Their ride must be here," whispered Shotgun.

"Come on."

I bolted over to the path and started to run. Shotgun caught up to me within a few paces, then sprinted ahead. Light glinted off the surface of the water, and I thought I heard someone moving around, maybe splashing.

I had my pistol ready.

A car sat at the edge of the path ahead, on the right. I slowed down, scanning the area nearby, ready to fire.

"Movement, right," said Shotgun, pulling to a stop and ducking down.

I slid to my knee, ready to fire. But damned if I couldn't see anything except the hulk of the car in front of me.

"Right! Right!" hissed Shotgun. "I think it's a tiger."

I stared for a few seconds before finally picking out what he saw.

"You're in the right animal family, at least," I told him, rising.

It was a cat—a domestic cat. Or maybe not so domestic, since there were no houses nearby. Cats are generally considered poor pets in India, and often thought to be bad omens or witches. This one was probably on its own, and no doubt was an accomplished hunter, preying on the birds and small mammals that lived at the swamp's edge.

We walked over to the car. It was a Maruti Wagon R—a compact Suzuki that's among the more popular local vehicles. It was about the shape and size of a bread box, though it was meant to seat four.

There was a small beach a few yards away. We could see footprints and the crease where a small boat had come in. The odd thing was that the footprints were on one side of the landing, and the crease for the boat was a few yards away.

"What do you make of that?" Shotgun asked.

"Two boats. At least." I knelt down next to the markings. There were some smudges in the mud nearby—possibly other footprints, but they were too small and faint to really make out.

Lengthwise, the Yamuna River is an impressive body of water, coursing through the Lower Himalayas all the way down to the Ganges in Allahabad. It also stinks to high heaven. The stench almost knocked me over, and even Shotgun covered his face with his arm as the wind changed. It's so polluted near Delhi that there are hardly any fish in it, which is probably a good thing, since you'd die from eating them.

The area we were in bordered a navigable canal, but I couldn't see any large boats, let alone the little skiffs that looked to have come ashore here. I stared for more than a minute, thinking that whoever had been here couldn't have gotten very far. But if they were nearby, the shadows hid them too well for me to see.

Shotgun went back to the car to check it out. One of the back doors had been left ajar. He pulled it open gingerly.

"Pants. Shirt on the floor," he said.

"Take them out, but don't touch anything else," I told him. "Maybe the Indians can get some fingerprints or DNA off the car."

I know. *DNA? This ain't America, Dick.*

Shotgun pulled out the clothes, holding them as if he was afraid of catching a venereal disease.

"Whatever they have wasn't catching," I told him. "And they deloused them in the tank."

"Says you."

He dropped them on the ground, then poked them with his gun, as if they might be alive.

"Missing one of the tops," he said.

"Where's the GPS?"

Shotgun pulled it from his pocket. Sure enough, one of the sensors was moving again.

"Maybe we should take the car to follow them," Shotgun suggested.

Before I could stop him, he grabbed the driver's side door.

There was a loud *pooof,* and suddenly we were flying into the nearby swamp, the car on fire behind us.

[IV]

I'll say one thing for the mud along the Yamuna River. It's soft.

I'll say another thing. It truly, truly stinks.

Fortunately for us, the bomb was too small to actually kill us. Or maybe we were just lucky, saved by the vehicle's frame, which took most of the blow.

Shotgun's face was blackened, his hand was burnt, and his arm was covered with little bits of glass. He was lying on his back in the mud when I reached him. It wasn't until he blinked that I knew he was alive.

And then he started to laugh.

"You think that's funny, asshole?"

"No, I think you're funny, skipper. You should see your hair. It's all up like a beehive."

Shotgun's a big boy, but I was damn tempted to put him over my knee and give him a good education.

The interior of the car was still on fire. The truth was, it probably wasn't much of a loss—the Indians were unlikely to spring for a DNA test, and even if they did, there wasn't a terrorist chromosome index handy. But the bomb was one more indication of how well organized these guys were. This wasn't your ordinary group of ragheads fresh off the madrassa.

We wiped some of the mud off our clothes and walked back to the cab. Urdu wrinkled his nose as soon as he was downwind.

"Five hundred rupee each, you sit in car," he said. "Must needs clean after ride. Otherwise, you go in trunk."

The trunk would have been a perfect punishment for Shotgun, but I'm positive he wouldn't have fit. So I paid the thousand rupees—about twenty bucks—and had him take us up to the Maharaja. From there, I called Captain Birla and told him that I'd spotted the getaway car by the water, and gave him directions.

He didn't ask how I knew, which was good, since I wasn't going to tell him.

I took a quick, cold shower—Shotgun had used up all five seconds of the hotel's weekly allowance of hot water—then went back to work.

———

Urdu was relieved not to smell us when we returned to his taxi. He'd vacuumed and shampooed the cab while we were inside, and now had so many sticks of incense going that the interior of the car smelled like a Venice, CA, head shop.

The locator signal had stopped moving in the Zakhira area of the city, south of Rama Road. As the crow flies, this was nearly ten miles from the spot where we'd found the car, and on the other side of Delhi. It was also one of the city's more notorious slums, though a good distance from the worst.

Delhi has a population somewhere around fourteen million people. Of that, four million are estimated to live in slums. These ghettos are all over the city, your basic shantytowns for the most part. Conditions vary but in general the buildings are one good huff from falling down. Depending on where in the city they are, they may be made of mud bricks or discarded wood. Mostly, though, they're collections of tin, wood panels, and plastic tarping. They usually don't have running water in the houses, and no electricity. Sometimes people cut into the city pipes for clean water, but usually they scrounge from whatever source they can find—rainwater, or the ridiculously polluted river or a stream.

Pleasant places.

The slums have long been viewed not just as breeding grounds for disease, but the birthplace of terrorists. The truth is more complex. If you look at the profiles of the terrorists who have tried to attack America and the West, most have actually come from middle class and even upper middle class families. People in the slums, at least in India, seem for the most part to spend too much time trying to eek out a living to be seduced by promises of paradise.

There's no question, though, that the slums harbor a good number of criminals, organized and otherwise. Which was why Urdu balked when I told him where we were going.

"Very bad," the driver said. "No, no, you go there."

"Why is it bad?" asked Shotgun.

"People see you, they think you rich. Take money. Maybe kidnap. Ransom."

"I don't think we'll have that kind of trouble at four o'clock in the morning," I told him. "Just take us as close to the road as you can."

"No road there, Mr. Dick. I take you to the circle. There I wait. You walk. But give me your money."

"We'll settle up at the end of the week," I told him.

"No, no, you don't understand. It is not safe for you to take money there. You will be robbed."

His concern was touching, even if it was only for his pay.

"There'll be a bonus," I assured him. "So make sure you're here."

"I be here. You make sure you are in one piece," he told me. "Do not be too careful."

It was barely four in the morning, but already the place was awake. As wretched as the houses were, the majority of the residents actually had jobs. Some had two or three. The problem was that they didn't pay much. I'm not talking about the low wages the people make in the phone centers and factories that have been outsourced from the U.S. Their wages, by Indian standards, are considered high. I'm talking about the one thousand dollars a year and less jobs—the janitor at the small factory on the other side of the train station, who's lucky to make half that. And then there are people who pick rags from the garbage, clean them, and sell them. They might net three or four hundred a year. Not enough to keep them in rice, even in India.

We picked our way through a rubble-strewn field, then detoured around a mound of garbage—there is no city pickup in the ghetto—before finding a small alleyway that took us toward the locator signal. The houses were packed tight on either side, and it was an especially good place for an ambush.

When we got within twenty feet, I was able to narrow the signal's location down to a house covered by a purple tarp. The house was a relatively solid-looking building made of scavenged bricks. It had been erected inside the foundation of an older brick building that had been partially destroyed. About half the original walls of the older building remained, so from the outside it looked as if the house was double-walled.

"Do we take them?" asked Shotgun.

"First we see what it looks like," I told him.

"We can blow their house apart with half a stick of dynamite."

I doubt it would have taken anywhere near a half stick of dynamite—Shotgun could have stood next to the wall and shouted, and half of the bricks would have fallen in.

"We want these guys alive, remember?" I told him.

"You take the fun out of everything," he answered, pulling a Twinkie from his pocket.

When I slipped around to the far side of the building, I saw that the inner walls had not actually been completed—this whole side was made out of canvas, which was stretched down from a few poles that were part of the roof structure. The fabric was patched and sewn together, and there were three separate flaps—doors to the separate apartments inside a building that was no bigger than the average toolshed back home.

The transmitter was in one of the two "apartments" on the right side of the building. Unfortunately, the only way to find out which one was to go in.

I slipped back the curtain that acted as the door and stepped inside the room on the right. Water jugs were lined against the canvas wall that separated the apartment from the others. There were two empty pails next to them. They were large, the kind that plaster comes in.

I tiptoed inside, pistol ready. The place was maybe ten feet by ten feet, and had only one room. Two figures were sleeping on a mound of blankets and cardboard to the right. To the left, where the signal would have been coming from, were a pair of boxes. Not sure whether the shirt was inside, I went over and took a look with the help of the LED flashlight I keep on my key chain. There were pots in the top box; the bottom had some dishes.

Wrong apartment. Sorry.

I backed out slowly, trying not to trip. I took a couple of breaths, then pulled back the second door.

This flap led to a hall that ran through the middle of the building. There were three more flaps on either side of the hall—a total of six different apartments, all separated by canvas. None of them could have been more than six feet square.

I froze for a few seconds, listening. If the GPS was right, I wanted the unit in the middle on my right.

I put my hand on the curtain and pulled back gently.

There was a tangle of blankets in front of me. I picked out four arms, five, six, twisted.

There was an adult on the right, sleeping, and six kids.

And a man standing at the right side of the room, holding something aimed at my chest.

One of the things we train on extensively in spec ops is differentiating between the enemy and civilians in an urban setting. It's not as easy as it sounds. You have a split second to decide, and the consequences of a mistake are a hell of a lot more severe than what happens in your average video game. You can't hit the pause button when a real-life tango unzips your chest cavity.

Even with all that training, the moment of truth depends on a kind of sixth sense as much as anything. Things happen so quickly that there's no time for your brain to completely frame the image, evaluate it, make a computation, then send the data to your fingers for processing.

Shoot, or don't shoot.

Kill, or maybe be killed.

I didn't fire.

He had a pot in his hand.

He dropped it as soon as he realized I was holding a gun in mine. I'm guessing he saw his life whiz by in front of his eyes.

"*Namaste,*" I said. That's Hindi for hello. It pretty much exhausted my store of nonfood or nonsuggestive phrases.

It didn't matter. He was as tongue-tied as a minister caught in a whorehouse.

I glanced to the left and saw the prison shirt I'd been following. There was a kid inside it, a thin rail of a thing.

"That shirt belongs to me," I said, in English.

The man didn't say anything. It was impossible to tell if he even understood what I was saying.

I glanced around the small room. Things were jumbled in different piles—clothes in one pile, cooking gear in another, some firewood in a third. There was a camp stove next to the man, and a small can of kerosene. I'm guessing he'd been planning on making some tea for his breakfast.

"Where did he get the shirt?" I asked. "Did he take it from a car? Did she see who was wearing it?"

He didn't speak English.

"I'll be right back," I told him.

I assume he was the kids' father, though to be honest he looked barely old enough to be an older brother. Outside the building, I whistled for Shotgun. He came lumbering around the side, munching on *jalebi*—a deep-fried, syrup-soaked twist of a cake that is sometimes called a sweet pretzel.

"Check it out, Dick. Guy over there sells this stuff. Costs like two rupees."

"A kid stole the shirt," I said. "Watch the building. Nobody in or out until I come back with the cabdriver."

"You sure he's gonna come?"

"Maybe on my back, but he's coming."

It actually didn't take much to convince Urdu that he should join us—the hundred-rupee note in my fist strengthened his courage.

The fact that my PK was still in my hand may have had something to do with it as well, though I prefer to believe my charm was the greatest factor.

By now it was a little after five. The sun was up and more people were awake. If anything, the place was even more depressing in the light.

"Hey, skipper! Hey, Urdu!" yelled Shotgun as we turned the corner. "Come on. Meet the family."

My erstwhile sidekick was surrounded by children, who were hanging on to him as if he were a set of monkey bars. On top of his shoulders was the kid who had snagged the shirt.

"Man, they love these pretzel things," said Shotgun, producing another from his pocket. He broke up pieces and handed them around.

"Shotgun friend to all," said Urdu, smiling.

I told him I wanted to talk to the tyke with the fancy orange shirt.

"Ask him where he got the shirt," I said.

Urdu gave me a funny look, then said something in Hindi. The kid shook his head.

"Tell him it belongs to me," I told Urdu. "And I want him to give it back to me right now."

"Excuse me, Mr. Richard," said the driver. "But the child is a girl."

"My name is Leya!" said the girl, swinging down off Shotgun's neck. "You are American?"

"You speak English?" I asked.

"English everyone knows," she told me. "All kids! You need English for Internet. Big job."

Even in the better light, it was hard to tell she was a girl. Her hair was cropped very tight, and she was skinny as a rail. She couldn't have been more than nine. I eventually found out that her hair had been shaved completely off because of lice.

"Where'd you get that shirt?" I asked.

"Shirt?" She grabbed the front. "Present."

"No it wasn't," said Shotgun. He reached down and grabbed the back of it, lifting her up.

"Let me down, Joe."

"Shotgun," he said with a mock growl, "don't like liars."

"Let me down!"

She started kicking and swinging her arms. Shotgun laughed and let go of her. She tumbled to the ground but bounced right back up, none the worse for wear.

By now we had quite an audience. I asked her a few more questions about where she had gotten the shirt. She kept claiming it was a present.

"Who gave it to you?" I asked.

"My auntie."

"Do we look dumb?" asked Shotgun, bending down.

Some of the other kids giggled, but our little Leya just became more indignant.

"The car you took it from blew up," I told her. "The man who was wearing that shirt was very bad. It would help me if you told us something about him."

"There was no man."

"I'll give you a sweet pretzel," said Shotgun.

Instantly, he had a dozen informers, ready to describe all sorts of people—old, young, tall, short, big, fat.

"Time to go," I told Shotgun. "We're not going to get anything we can use here."

Urdu was more than ready to leave. He spun around and made a bee-line for the cab. Shotgun and I took our time—him because he kept on doling out pieces of pretzel to the kids, me because I was looking to see if anyone was watching us.

We were being watched, but mostly by kids. We were a sensation—I haven't had so much attention since my last book signing. Our flock grew as we walked, until at last we had a veritable flood of people behind us. It looked like a royal procession.

Urdu had the car started and ready. When we reached it, the kids pressed in close, and he had to beep and wave to start through the crowd.

Suddenly something banged hard on my window.

It was Leya's hand.

I rolled down my window.

"There were five men," she told me. "They had a boat."

"What kind of boat?"

"With a motor."

"What did the men look like?"

She gave me a general description—two were about her father's age. Two closer to her grandfather's. She hadn't seen the last.

"I could not tell you before," she said. "My father would think I am stealing. That is very, very bad."

"It is bad," I told her. "How did you see them? Did you follow them there?"

"I was with cousin. We catch fish."

"They were probably stealing from cars in the neighborhood," said Urdu. "Little thieves."

Leya didn't deny the accusation, pretending instead that she hadn't heard it.

"One man have scar on cheek," she said. "Very dark face."

Was that worth ten rupees? Frankly, it sounded completely made-up. But what the hell. I reached into my pocket and gave the girl a coin just as Urdu found an opening in the crowd and eased away.

[V]

It was too late to go to sleep. Shotgun and I drove out to the airport and picked up Sean, Mongoose, and Junior. After exchanging the usual terms of endearment, we unloaded their luggage at the fancy hotel, secured more rooms at the Maharaja Express as a backup, then embarked on a whirlwind orientation of Delhi.

If the night before had been dedicated to the dark side of the city, the morning was spent in the light. Our first stop was India Gate, the massive sandstone monument built to honor India's war dead in World War I.

India was involved in World War I?

It's a little known fact, but India sent over eight hundred thousand troops to the Allied cause. One hundred and forty thousand served in Western Europe. A total of over seventy thousand Indians died in the war, more than any other Commonwealth country except for Great Britain herself.

The arch also holds the Eternal Flame, a memorial to the soldiers who died during the 1971 war with Pakistan.

We paid our respects, then moved on.

Delhi's version of the White House is Rashtrapati Bhawan. The president lives here, somewhere, in one of the 340 rooms. Or maybe inside the green dome that sits on the top like a giant pot cover. The building was erected for Great Britain's viceroy, and by some estimations puts even Windsor Castle to shame. Which gives you some idea of what the colonial governors thought of themselves.

We couldn't go inside, and none of my guys are much on flowers, so we skipped the Mughal Gardens that border the residence and drove past the Red Fort. This is Delhi's *real* castle, the place from which the Mughal Empire ran the country in the seventeenth century.

The Brits stormed the place after the locals rebelled in the 1857 uprising known as the War of Independence; from that point on it became a British stronghold until handed over at independence. It's a veritable city to itself, with ornate "pavilions" or buildings that are recognized as important architectural treasures. If you like ornate marble, elaborate carvings, fancy roof projections, the Red Fort is the place to go.

(Today's tourist hint: visit the War Memorial Museum, which is in

Naubat Khana, or Naqqar Khana—or to us Westerners the Drum House. Shotgun got so wrapped up in the old Mughal weaponry that he forgot to eat for several hours, probably a record for him. The Drum House is the big red rectangle made out of sandstone in the middle of the compound. If it looks a little plain, just remember that the carvings on the outside were once covered with gold.)

We weren't just playing tourist. I wanted the others to understand the size of the problem we were dealing with. On a quiet, crappy weather day, you can easily find a few thousand people wandering through the Red Fort or stopping by any of the other tourist attractions in town. So imagine how many people were going to be queuing up when the Games were on.

The Indians not only had to worry about the very high value sites related to the Games—the stadiums, practice fields, nearby hotels, etc.—but they had their national treasures to look after. Somebody blows himself up on the first floor of Moti Masjid (the Pearl Mosque), few people are going to say, "Gosh, good thing it wasn't in the middle of the badminton game. What a horror show that would have been."

But that's the whole problem with dealing with terror defensively. You can put ten thousand troops around the White House, then "lose" if the assholes blow up a telephone booth in the bus station.

Which is why you need a Red Cell mentality. You take the game to their home field.

But enough of my soapbox. You know the speech so well by now you can give it yourself.

We went around to a few more places—Qutub Minar, Purana Qila, Jantar Mantar, Humayun's Tomb, all various highlights of Mughal rule.

Who the hell were the Mughals?

Mughal = Mogul. They were an Islamic imperial power that ruled a lot of northern India and Pakistan from about 1526 to 1857 when the British formally extended their rule over the remaining stretches of independent India. At their height, the Mughals controlled nearly all of India—the island of Sri Lanka at the tip remained independent—Pakistan, and a good hunk of what's now Afghanistan.

Islam's history on the subcontinent goes back to the Islamic Caliphate, which reached Pakistan somewhere in the early eighth century. India in those days was the only place in the world where you could find diamonds, so it's not surprising that the caliphate and its successors viewed the vast south with hungry eyes. It took centuries of on and off war before the country came under Islamic rule, but well before that, traders and businesspeople had spread the word of Allah's great prophet into the Indian heartland. By the time the Mughals get going, a good part of the population is Muslim.

Practicing the same religion as the ruling class didn't guarantee you a cushy job or a bright future, but it certainly didn't hurt. However, the various forms of Hinduism remained the majority beliefs, and you had a smattering of Christianity and Judaism, mostly in the trading areas.

The result of all of this history is a pretty thick mix of religions elbowing each other. Today, Hindus account for roughly eighty percent of the population, according to the people counters at the CIA. Islam is practiced by a little over thirteen percent of the country. But in a country of 1.17 billion, thirteen percent is a humungous number.

Shunt says it's over 152 million. I didn't know he had that many fingers.

Only Pakistan and Indonesia have more Muslims. Neither country has anywhere near as many members of another religion. If you can't find terrorist wannabes here, you can't find them anywhere.

You're yawning, and so were the boys. I brought them back to the fancy hotel and put them to bed. Then I went to check in with Captain Birla.

I found the captain at his desk, staring at a disorganized mess of papers. He'd spent the night interviewing the men who'd been on duty, then talking to various people in the government and military. He didn't look so much tired as rattled. His skin was paler than normal, and he wasn't very swarthy to begin with. He rubbed his eyes as I came in. I could hear his bones cracking as he unfolded himself from behind the desk.

"A terrible crisis, Commander Rick," he said, rising. "A crisis of confidence."

"Whose confidence?"

"Mine. One of my men must be a traitor, don't you think?"

"It's possible." I couldn't lie. "But it's not the *only* possibility."

"Someone knew that the prisoners were here," he continued. "And that someone must have alerted the terrorists. They pulled off this operation. Very smart."

"Very smart, that's true."

If I'd thought Captain Birla was a traitor, his demeanor now would have convinced me otherwise. But just because he wasn't evil didn't mean that he wasn't responsible—at the end of the day, the commander has to step up and accept the blame when the shit falls through the bottom of the bucket.

"What would you do in my place?" he asked.

"Kick ass until I figured out what the hell the story was."

Captain Birla smiled sadly.

"In India," he said, "we do not kick ass."

"Then it's time to start."

Because they had been drawn from a variety of different services and agencies, Captain Birla didn't know his men well enough to really judge how loyal they might or might not be. There hadn't been time yet for him to build up the team camaraderie that would make a traitor stick out like a sore thumb.

Not that the traitor would necessarily be the guy who was complaining the loudest, or flinching at the moment of attack. Those were different problems—fixable in some cases, fatal in others.

After you've been in the trenches for a while, good commanders develop a sixth sense about who the real assholes are: who's going to be sharpening the combat knife and aiming for your balls at the nearest opportunity. It's not really something you can learn on the practice field, let alone from reading dossiers.

The ability to read that kind of loyalty isn't something you can pick up in officers' training school either. You have to have it pounded into you. I developed it in my early days in the navy. Vietnam was my finishing school. The final exam was pass or fail—massive fail, as the kids say now, with fail equaling death.

The bureaucrats forget that, in India and everywhere else. It's not surprising. These days the world is run by MBAs who can whip out a spreadsheet faster than Mongoose can unzip his pants. God bless them. Mathematics and Excel are no substitute, though, for the juice that burns a hole in your stomach on patrol at four in the morning.

"Already the papers have news of it," the captain told me, pawing through the papers on his desk. "Read this."

He pulled up a newspaper folded open to page five. Beneath the picture of the latest Bollywood superstar sunbathing on a beach was the headline "Security Scandal Brewing."

The headline was a hell of a lot more informative than the story itself, a six-line squib that stated that the government was conducting a sweep for possible terrorists in advance of the Commonwealth Games. In the process of the sweep, several possible terrorists had been picked up but "now have been released, presenting possible dangers to the nation."

I told Captain Birla that it might not even have anything to do with what happened the night before. After all, embroidering hearsay and rumors like that usually took a few days.

"You don't know India," said Captain Birla. "This would have come directly from one of the police services Minister Dharma told to look for our men. There will be more stories, angling to make themselves into a position for promotions or to bury axes in an opponent."

"You have to start testing the security arrangements for the Games," I said. "Press on with it."

He gave me a rueful look. I knew what he was thinking—any unit that was criticized for having lax procedures would now be able to throw his own unit's failures back in his face.

Our security at the gate was poor, Madam Minister? Who is making this criticism? The group that lost two important terrorists from a well-secured prison right on our doorstep?

He'd just have to deal with it.

I shared a fresh pot of Darjeeling with him, trying to buck him up. By the end of our talk, he was still pale, but a little more energetic. I'm not taking any credit. Caffeine and copious amounts of sugar tend to lift any mood.

Captain Birla was down in the dumps. Minister Dharma was fuming. She'd spent a large part of the night talking to various parliament members and government officials, working the phones to keep her political capital high. While undoubtedly the effort had paid off, she was a woman who didn't like to be deprived of things she considered vital, like sleep.

"Mr. Marcinko, I am glad to see you this morning," she said when I went over to her office. "Any news on the prisoners?"

"Nothing except for the car," I told her.

"And how did you happen to find the vehicle?" she asked.

I shrugged.

"You are sure that it is connected to the incident?"

"It answers the description."

"Captain Birla told me that it had been in a fire."

"That's what I hear."

"You didn't start the fire, did you?"

"No."

"The fire destroyed any possible evidence. There were many foot-prints, and deep tracks in the mud."

"I'm sure there were."

She stared at me for a moment, as if trying to figure out if I might have been involved in helping the men escape. I'm not sure what my motive would have been.

Suddenly she smiled. It was as if the sun had broken through the clouds on Day 41 of Noah's Flood.

"Come," she said, rising from her desk and taking my hand. "We will have breakfast."

Never one to resist the touch of a beautiful woman, I floated along behind her as she glided down the steps of her ministry building and levitated across the street to an old but swanky hotel. The lobby looked like a fronds-R-us showcase, with at least ten different varieties of frou-frou trees in copper buckets the size of wading pools. Twelve crystal chandeliers hung from the ceiling, each one with enough chiseled glass to cover the exterior of every office in downtown Dubai. The floor was made of a rose-colored marble, inlaid with black amethyst and the occasional green and red ruby.

We crossed a pair of silk rugs and reached a large door guarded by two massive ceramic beasts, fantastical creatures that looked like their purpose was to scare people's appetites away. A short man in a black suit appeared from inside. He smiled grandly and threw up his arms.

"Minister, you are here. The day is complete."

I have no doubt he was being sincere. He motioned us inside, waving his arms as if he were cutting away a barrier. Two waiters appeared, practically pushing each other for the honor of pulling out the minister's chair.

I got my own.

"Your guest, today?" said the maître d'.

"This is a friend of mine from America, Mr. Marcinko," she said.

"The Rogue Warrior we have heard so much about. An honor."

I'll take fawning when I can get it.

"An American breakfast?" he asked.

"I'll take coffee and some fruit."

He bowed and disappeared without asking the minister what she wanted. Apparently her habits were so well known there was no need to.

"You are on a health kick?" she asked.

"Not particularly," I said.

"Eating right is a wise thing. It helps you keep your strength up."

Before I could answer, the waiters returned. One had a silver platter covered by a dome so shiny I could have shaved by it. He whisked off the top, revealing two pieces of crustless toast, dry. As he set it down, the second waiter put down a cup and a pot of tea for the minister.

"Is that your whole breakfast?" I asked.

"Like you, I try to watch what I eat. When a woman reaches a certain age." She leaned forward conspiratorially. "We're not like you men, you know. Perpetually handsome."

As she said this, her foot brushed up against my pants leg.

"Some women are destined to look beautiful at any age," I told her.

"You are a charmer," she said, picking up her tea. "But that is your reputation—you know exactly what to say to a woman to make her feel good."

"I try."

"It takes more than words to win a woman's heart."

Her foot slipped off my calf . . . and reached my thigh.

I felt a tingle higher up . . . my cell phone, vibrating with an incoming call.

I ignored the first ring.

"I believe you should answer that," said Minister Dharma. "It might be important."

I pulled out the phone. I'd sensed it was Karen—and I was right.

A coincidence? I think not.

"Dick, are you alone?" she asked.

"Not exactly."

"Well, can you talk?"

I excused myself and walked back out to the lobby.

"Go ahead."

"First of all, I miss you," she told me.

"I miss you, too."

There was a sigh on her end, and some warm gushy stuff that is none of your business. Then she got to the ostensible purpose of the call.

"Admiral Jones called a little while ago. He wanted to know if you were still in India."

Admiral Jones = Director, Christians in Action (CIA).

"Doesn't he have a whole staff of people keeping track of where I am?"

"I think he was just being polite. He seemed to know you were in Delhi."

"What did he want?"

"There's a station chief he wants you to talk to, Omar Mahler. He's expecting your call."

"Uh-huh."

"And there's something up with the State Department. Someone called over to the office and left a message looking for you."

"Did you give them my sat number?"

"I wanted to check with you first."

I've done more than my share of work for the Christians in Action over the past few years, thanks to my friend Ken. He was an admiral before being blackmailed into joining the agency and becoming DCI—Dedicated Chief Idiot, or Director of Central Intelligence, depending on your perspective.

Ken sipped but never swallowed the agency Kool-Aid, so he does have moments of lucidity, which may explain why he's hired me several times. Then again, maybe that's just proof of his insanity.

The State Department was another story. Red Cell International hasn't worked for the men in the funny pants legs for roughly a decade. To be honest, I wasn't exactly looking for work either. The security business, unfortunately, is recession-proof.

I exchanged a few promises with Karen, then went back into the restaurant. In my absence, my place had been taken by a prominent member of parliament. Minister Dharma introduced him as Prince Fuzziwig, or something similar, saying he was a member of the opposition.

"The loyal opposition, I hope," he said, practically drooling on the table. He wrenched his eyes away from her—it looked as if he were uncoupling a powerful magnet—and looked at me. "You must be the famous American we have heard about, come to help us secure the Games."

"I hope I can contribute."

"These Games are very important to India," said Prince Fuzziwig. "Our prestige is on the line. We have to prove to the world that we are a twenty-first-century nation."

"I'm sure you'll do that."

"Many people do not have the highest opinion of India. We have to prove them wrong."

I'm not sure how playing badminton in the Delhi heat was going to burnish India's image, but I didn't argue. It is somewhat amazing that grown-ups believe that a few sporting contests will establish the host country as a major international player.

The prince was flanked by a pack of staff members, most of them young men who were trying to discreetly catch a glimpse of Minister Dharma's cleavage. Unfortunately for them it was well hidden under a wispy but strategically folded scarf. I wanted to talk to her about some of the politics Captain Birla had alluded to, but it was clear that wasn't going to happen now. So I told her that I had a few errands to take care of and would have to be going.

"It was so good to see you this morning," she said, rising.

She gave me a peck on the cheek to say good-bye.

A lesser man's knees would have buckled. As it was, I had trouble breathing normally until the fetid fumes of the street cleared my lungs.

(VI)

*T*he Dick Marcinko. The Rogue Warrior. Mr. Know It All. I'm surprised you could get into the building. Did you have to turn your head sideways?"

"I take it you're Omar?"

Omar Mahler, station chief of India, bishop of India in the CIA hierarchy, scowled at me. We'd arranged to meet in my hotel lobby — knowing the size of his expense account, I figured I'd rub it in.

"We have to go someplace where we can talk," he grumbled, not deigning to officially identify himself. Then again, he probably thought this was clever spycraft, having blurted my name to half the paparazzi in the city.

I suggested my suite.

"It's probably bugged," he grumbled.

It wasn't, but I didn't argue. We ended up taking a walk down the driveway of the hotel to the road. Anyone with a shotgun mike would have been able to hear what we said, but I knew it wasn't going to be all that interesting. Omar's sneer made it obvious that he was here only because his boss told him he had to be.

Most spymasters are friendly, outgoing types who can't help but make people like them. After all, their job really comes down to making friends, then screwing them. Kind of like a banker or a used car salesman.

But every so often you run into an Omar — a sourpuss who's sure that the world is out to personally screw him.

Maybe not the world. Maybe just me.

"So the rumor is, you fucked up," Omar said as we walked along the road.

"How's that?"

"You flew into Pakistan with the Gurkha squad, picked up a couple of tourists, then brought them back, figuring you'd be clever. But the tangos outthought you," added Omar. "They got away. Who'd they bribe?"

"I don't know that they bribed anyone."

"Oh, come on, Marcinko. How the hell did they get out? You think they're clever?"

"Some of them are."

"I'll tell you what the problem is, Marcinko. You're getting old. Soft around the middle."

I prayed he'd test just how soft the middle was, but he kept walking and pontificating.

"They're probably halfway back to Pakistan by now," he added. "Laughing the whole way."

"I thought Pakistan was an agency project," I told him.

"Oh, yeah, right. Half the damn Pakis are part of the Taliban. They're in Osama's back pocket. The other half are so damned afraid of him they pee in their beds at night. I thought you knew this, Marcinko."

Another thing that I didn't like about him—he pronounced my name "Mar-chink-o," like an ethnic slur.

It's "Mar-sink-o," thank you very much.

"So how come the agency knows so much about these guys, but can't find them?" I asked.

"Who said we're looking for them? This isn't our fight, Marcinko. We have bigger fish to fry. You know how many Chinese spies there are in Delhi?"

"I wouldn't hazard a guess."

"I didn't think you could."

"Did your boss tell you to give me a hard time, or was there an actual reason you wanted to talk to me?"

"I didn't want to talk to you," he said coldly. "The agency is worried about the Commonwealth Games. We don't want them screwed up."

"I hear the girls' badminton team from Sri Lanka is looking for a sub."

"Har-har. I'm offering you agency assistance."

"That's nice. But I don't need any."

"Your minister does."

"Have you seen her? I'd say she does pretty well for herself."

"You've probably gone a few rounds with her already, huh?"

No use denying something like that, I decided.

"I'll pass it along."

"There is something else," he said, his voice practically dripping with reluctance. "We're working on something, and I'm supposed to give you a heads-up."

"What's that?"

Big frown. Maybe I should have asked for a drumroll.

"Your Gurkha goons—they're modeled after your navy Red Cell thing."

"Somewhat."

"Where you went around embarrassing the brass by sneaking into Air Force One and stealing a submarine and stuff like that?"

"More or less."

There was almost a hint of admiration in Omar's smile—grudging and crooked as it was.

"These guys are planning to do the same, huh?" he said.

"They do what they do."

"There's one thing they shouldn't do. And that's hit the Banshee Armory."

"I'll make sure it's their first target."

Smoke just about poured from his ears. Curses followed from his mouth. He sputtered a bit, then ordered me not to strike the armory.

It was comical, actually. He managed to squeeze the words "treason" and "court-martial" between a dozen four-letter words. I admired him for that.

"I have no intention of hitting the armory," I admitted. "But I'm not in charge of them."

"Bullshit. From what I hear, you practically tell them when to burp."

I shrugged.

"You screw this up, Marcinko, and the agency will cut you off forever. You'll be dead to us. Deader than dead."

It was an enticing offer, though I couldn't in good faith accept it, at least not without knowing what the hell it was that I was screwing up. The Banshee Armory was not on the list of facilities that Special Squad Zero was supposed to test, and in fact I hadn't heard of it at all.

A few minutes on the Internet in the hotel business center fixed that. The Banshee Armory was the nickname of a former Indian army base about thirty miles northeast of town. Abandoned in 2005, at least according to the stories.

I was considering whether the place was too old to have a MySpace page when the phone rang. The number that came up was from Washington, D.C., though I didn't recognize it.

"Marcinko," I said, thumbing it on.

"Richard Marcinko?"

"The same."

"Please hold for Madam Secretary."

Hold what, I wondered.

"Richard, is that you?"

"Yes, Ms. Secretary."

"How are you?"

"Holding my own."

"I hope not." She laughed. "That's never been a problem for you."

You have to love a secretary of State with a sense of humor. Then again, considering her home situation, she'd have to have one.

"You make me blush," I said.

"I'll bet. Listen, Richard, I understand you're in India helping the government there out."

"More or less."

"I hope more. The Commonwealth Games are very important to us. And to the nonproliferation efforts on the subcontinent."

"I see."

"As it happens, I'm going to attend the Games myself. Maybe we can have lunch. I'll be in town in a few days."

"I'd love to have lunch."

All right, so I lied. But it's the sort of thing you have to say and anyway, she wasn't really going to invite me to lunch.

But our conversation was extremely important. Because it connected a lot of the dots Omar had scattered in the wind. Or should I say bindi.

The administration had been working over the past year on plans to reduce the number of nukes out and about in the world. Efforts to restart the START treaty—sorry, couldn't resist—with Russia had garnered most of the headlines, and everyone knew about Iran and their now-we-build-it, now-we-pretend-you're-blind charade. But the U.S. was trying to reduce the number of nuclear weapons everywhere. And frankly if there was one place in the world where cutting the number of A bombs would be a positive achievement, it was on the Indian subcontinent.

India has somewhere more than seventy nuclear warheads. Pakistan's actual number is the subject of many a barroom debate, or would be if the analysts who debate such things ever stepped out of their bunkers for beer. They're thought to have between a dozen and twenty, but you can find arguments to support just about any number you pick short of fifty.

Yes, beautifully stable Pakistan, the country whose army has regularly had its ass kicked by guys in rags and sandals.

Apparently, Madam Secretary was nearing some sort of agreement with the Indians and Pakistanis. The negotiations were secret, which was why she was coming to Delhi for the Games. Though probably as many people saw her as a rugby fan as believed she loved to bake cookies.

Actually, she makes very good cookies, but I digress.

And Banshee Armory?

Well, at first I thought it was going to be the meeting place for high-level delegations from Pakistan and India, a good isolated spot where the two sides could hash out their differences.

Come to find out, the only thing that was meeting there were nuclear warheads.

Seventy of them in fact. Supposedly all that India admitted it had.[8]

I hadn't put two and two together when I swung out to the armory that afternoon. In fact, it was Doc who really figured it out. Or at least first noticed the clues that made it obvious what was going on.

Longtime readers—and shouldn't you all be?—remember that Doc was one of the original plank owners of the first Red Cell. "Plank owners" is an affectionate navy term for the SOBs who bust their asses and risk their necks getting the kinks worked out of a vessel or a unit when it launches.

That first crew *owns* the ship. In a very real way, their experiences haunt the vessel for the rest of its days.

Doc certainly had that effect on Red Cell. One of the things I liked best about the unit was the fact that everybody involved could handle every job, and then some. You can guess that with a nickname like "Doc," his specialty, at least at one point in his career, involved medicine. And as I always say, Doc could sew you up just as fast as he could cut you up. I'm not sure there aren't a number of guys walking around with empty chests—Doc was so good he could slit open the skin, pull out your heart, then have you sewn up in a blink of an eye.

---

[8] Yes, I'm certain the Indians would hold back a few from negotiations, just on general principles. Wouldn't you?

But like the rest of the crew, he was a real Renaissance man. He could handle coms, cook, blow up anything smaller than a baseball stadium, and put a bullet into a muskrat's tail at five hundred yards.

Maybe I exaggerate. His roast beef could stand a little improvement, truth be told.

I'm buttering him up now because I was buttering him up then, singing his praises as we drove out in our rented Suzuki knockoff to take a look at the armory. Because Doc had brought up the R word.

"Retirement."

Of course, he didn't come at it straight on.

"I'm thinking of taking off for a bit, Dick, after this op," he said. "Maybe put a few miles on the RV."

"RV? Since when do you have a camper?"

"We bought it a while back. Just thinking we'll take things a little easy, me and the wife.⁹ See the world while we're still young."

"You joined the navy to see the world. And look how that turned out."

"Ha!"

Doc's got a good laugh. The car was pretty flimsy. We shook so hard I nearly went off the road.

"I'm thinking maybe I'll slow down permanently," he added.

"You can do whatever you want. You've earned it."

"Thanks. We got a lot of young bucks on board now. The company's in good hands."

"Can't argue with that."

"You oughta think about stepping back a bit yourself," he said.

I gave him a sidelong glance.

"You know, take it easier. Let Danny take up some of the slack. Trace. Junior, maybe."

"Danny and Trace, I can see. But Junior's still very wet behind the ears."

"I don't know. He's got a lot of gumption. And he's smart. There's no doubt about that."

"He's just smart enough to get himself in trouble."

"Reminds me of a young officer I knew once upon a time."

⁹ That would be Donna, aka Saint Donna. Because really, only a saint would put up with an unreformed SEAL.

Yeah, you can see where that went. It would have generated into a virtual ass-kissing contest had we not arrived at the turnoff to the Banshee Armory.

Or rather, had we not been waved away from the Banshee Armory by a very serious policeman.

How serious?

Well, he didn't smile, and neither did the assault gun he pointed at the car when he told us the road was closed.

But the true measure of his determination would have been the two T-90 Bishma tanks behind him.

We moved on, driving almost two miles before we were sure that we were completely out of sight. I took a crossroad south, then swung back to an older road we'd seen paralleling the highway south of the armory. There were rice fields on the right, and a trio of small buildings that were propped between the road and highway. One of them looked like a grocery store.

"Hungry?" I asked Doc, pulling off.

"You've been hanging with Shotgun too long," he said, getting out of the car.

Even so, he was the one who bought the pastries; I had a Coke. We sat on the hood of the car, leaning back and relaxing as if exhausted by a long day of driving. About a half hour after we stopped, a white police jeep with its red bulb light flashing passed along the highway. A few seconds later, a pair of army Mahindra MM550XDs tore up the road, canvas tops flapping with the wind.

The MM550XD is your basic jeep CJ in Indian trim, an old school throwback to the vehicle that won World War II. The pair drew a long wolf whistle from Doc, who has always been an admirer of rugged utility transportation.

While he was waxing poetic about the synchromesh gearbox, I was looking at the Stallion five-ton truck that followed, not so much because of its size but the fact that there were heavily armed soldiers perched on the running boards at the cab.

Even more interesting was the vehicle behind it—a flatbed with something tarped at the back.

Two more troop trucks and another jeep took up the rear.

"What, no helicopter?" asked Doc.

Almost on a cue, a helicopter swept up from the rear.

"Special delivery for the fort?" Doc asked.

"Let's find out."

The car complained as I cleared a small culvert, scraping its tailpipe and part of its bumper before hopping across the highway. The cars coming in the other direction weren't too happy about it either.

"We ain't in NASCAR," said Doc. "Don't get us killed."

Even Jimmie Johnson would have been proud of the way our rental accelerated. The procession had too much of a lead for us to catch it, but the helo hovering over Banshee Armory made it obvious where it had gone. I kept going just in case, trekking another ten miles before deciding the convoy had definitely gone into the armory.

"Big package," said Doc. "Think they're playing show and tell for the negotiations?"

"Has to be," I said. "Be nice to get a look around."

"You're not thinking of going in there, are you?" asked Doc as I hunted for a place to turn. "It's too much trouble for too little return."

"There's no such thing as too much trouble."

"Ah, sure there is. Remember the time in Taiwan?"

"The place you thought was a bar but turned out to be a whorehouse?"

"The *other* time."

"I do want to have a look around," I told him. "Let's see what our State Department is up to."

"All right," said Doc. "I have an idea."

"What's that?"

He pulled out his Apple 3G.

"I'll tell you as soon as I find a toy store," he said, pulling up a mapping application.

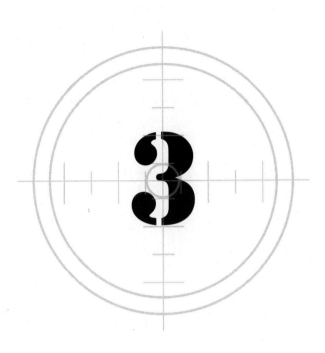

(1)

The story of Doc's conversion from a near technophobe to poster child for the connected generation is so scintillating that I reserve it for bedtime reading only—you're sure to fall asleep if I tell it. Suffice it to say that Doc, who until a short time ago thought e-mail was a creation of the devil himself, was able to use his phone and locate a toy store fifteen miles from us. When we got there, the store turned out to be a hobby shop, which was even better.

What did two grown men want with a place that sold Chinese knock-offs of Lionel trains and a hundred plastic soldiers for ten rupees?

One of the unsung heroes of the Afghanistan war—or whatever we're classifying our fun and games there nowadays—is an army weapon called Raven. Raven has seen a variety of tasks, working with the 82nd Airborne and 173rd Airborne Brigade on the front line, and even providing target intelligence for Apache gunships.

Raven is a small UAV—officially, an unmanned aerial vehicle. You've heard of the Predator and its armed brother, the Reaper. They're pickup-truck-sized aircraft that can fly for hours and hours, picking off tangos while their Air Farce pilots lounge in air-conditioned comfort halfway around the globe.[10]

The Predator family members are admirable and game-changing weapons. But like all Air Farce assets, they can't be everywhere, and getting them to where the guys on the front line actually need them can involve almost as much work as trying to get a real person on the telephone when you're calling to straighten out your local cable bill.

The Raven, on the other hand, is all about the guys on the front line. It can literally be carried in a rucksack.

The Predator has a forty-eight-and-a-half-foot wingspan. The Raven's is a touch over four feet. It weighs a little more than four pounds. It has a motor about the size of a D-cell battery or two. But it's a powerful little thing; revved to max, it can hit sixty miles an hour.

---

[10] Yes, I know there are in-theater personnel as well. Stop interfering with my story. And don't bother mentioning the RQ-15, which a number of SEALs prefer. I'm not supposed to know about it.

The Raven *looks* like a kid's toy. And it's not all that far from one, to be honest.

Now do you understand?

We bought a basic three-channel RC (for Radio Controller) battery-powered high-winged monoplane. Doc was tempted by the Sabre and Focke-Wulf models, but ultimately we went with the easier-to-control model, upgrading the engine to add flying time. The plane looked like your average Cessna, assuming your average Cessna had a forty-inch wingspan.

We did a little reengineering—gray paint to make it hard to see against the clouds—and added a small, tourist-preferred Flip video camera to the interior. And then we launched it.

There were some control issues, along with a couple of kids who came by after the plane landed who wanted to have a turn. But otherwise it was as easy as fiddling with a few joysticks and cursing when the wind gusted a little heavier than anticipated.

I took a look at the video after it landed, then gave the plane and its controller to the kids. In case anyone from the armory had seen the plane and set out to investigate, all they'd find were a bunch of ragamuffins having fun.

The video showed us everything we needed. The guard pattern inside the complex made it obvious which building was being used—a large, warehouselike armory building that would have been an obvious guess anyway. Six flatbeds were parked in a line in front. One was being unloaded with the help of an ATV and a forklift; two more were pulling in from the road.

The Indians were moving their nukes in for the negotiations.

On the way back to Delhi, I had Shunt go online and see if the proceedings were being timed according to U.S. satellite sweeps. It may surprise you to know that the track of nearly every spy satellite we have is posted somewhere on the Internet. Amateur astronomers make sport of spotting them and posting the orbits on Web pages. They've even followed some, if not all, satellites specifically designed to avoid radar and optical detection—oops.

In any event, Shunt quickly discovered that India's movements were blatantly obvious to the boys over at the National Reconnaissance Office.

I'm guessing that was intentional—the Indians wanted us to know what they were doing because they were doing it at least partly at our behest.

Just my conclusion, there. But eminently logical.

The Pakistanis must know as well. I'm guessing that this was some sort of negotiated step, some sort of tit for tat thing that the diplomats like to call "mutual understandings on the road map to peace" or some such bullshit. But they wouldn't have to take India's word for it—if I could discover them so easily, the Pakistanis surely could as well.

And so could half the terrorists in Southeast Asia.

Hmmm . . .

Granted, the Indians had a lot of troops to guard the place—which wasn't the same thing as effective security, though we'll let that pass for now. Still, I couldn't quite fathom the logic in what they were doing, though I now understood why Omar had been so adamant about Special Squadron Zero keeping the place off its hit list.

To me, that was the best possible argument to move it to the list, with big red letters, all caps. It would be a perfect test not just of the nuclear protection forces guarding the site, but of Squadron Zero's capabilities.

Or it would have been, if I wasn't worried that the spec ops team had been infiltrated by terrorists. Siccing them onto the armory might be the moral equivalent of giving away the family jewels.

It crossed my mind that Omar might have breathed his curry breath on me specifically to encourage some sort of hit there. Knowing the admiral, it was always possible that he had some sort of plot in mind that he didn't want the U.S. directly tied to. Ken's a great guy and all, a real lovable douche bag, but I wouldn't trust him with a triple-locked safe. Whatever was up, I wanted no part in it.

I saw Captain Birla later that evening. I didn't mention Banshee Armory, let alone the gathering of nukes.

"You are right, Commander Rick," he told me when I walked into his office. He was in a much better mood than I'd left him. "All we can do is prove ourselves. There will be inquiries, but I am determined to do my job."

He'd spoken to his men, reviewed the surveillance tapes, and reconsidered everything that had happened. The traitor, he decided, was outside the organization.

Whether he was right or not, it was the only conclusion he could come to that would allow him to move forward, and I didn't argue with him. I turned the subject around to the ops that were planned for the next few days.

Special Squadron Zero would test security for the Games in various ways: we'd see what we could sneak past check posts, plant a few fake bombs, take some high-ranking prisoners. It was all out of the original Red Cell playbook; easy fun and games if you're a SEAL.

In theory, the operations were all unannounced. I strongly suspect that the reality was, as they say, more nuanced: Minister Dharma had a lot of friends in government, and she had access to the target list. But even if some of the facilities knew we were coming, there were always plenty of holes to exploit.

We went over the details of our first job, then agreed to meet him the following night at Hindon air base, a military facility on the outskirts of the city that the unit would use as a jumpoff for the op. (We wanted a different starting point in case the regular base was being watched. Yes, that does happen.)

"There will be some political currents when we succeed with our tests," said Captain Birla, tapping his desk. "There will be some red faces."

"We can only hope," I told him.

〔 II 〕

The Pakistani intelligence connection to India for Islam was intriguing, to use a word that pops up in spy novels a lot.

Unfortunately, the only way to flesh it out was to travel to Pakistan and talk to some of the people I knew there, both in the capital, Islamabad, and the capital of terrorist activity, Lahore. Ordinarily, if I couldn't do it myself I'd send Doc; my network of contacts included a number of SEALs who have stooped so low as to work on a contract basis for the Christians in Action, and they're generally more forthcoming with brothers rather than cousins. But Doc had to stay with the field hockey team, and I had too much business in India as well. Danny Barrett was back in the States taking care of business there; the next logical choice was Sean.

Sean's a good kid, a Ranger veteran and possibly one of the most reliable young guys I know. He wasn't crazy about going to Pakistan, though.

"I'm going to miss the action," he complained. "This is just talking to people."

"Mostly it's listening."

"That's what I mean. I got screwed out of Cuba, and Malaysia was a picnic. I really need to get the adrenaline level up, Dick."

You gotta love these guys. But that's what the Rangers are—their motto is "Rangers lead the way," and if they're not on the cutting edge of action, they figure the world has gone completely to hell.

Not that you, or Sean for that matter, should think Pakistan's a picnic.

I gave him the requisite pat on the fanny and sent him on his way.

Mongoose and Shotgun have been like brothers ever since they tripped each other in training. They were a regular Frick and Frack, Mutt and Jeff, Abbott and Costello, cracking each other up and bailing each other out when the brown stuff hits the fan.

Mongoose had spent the past three weeks back home, working on a project of ours that Danny Barrett was heading. Danny has a background in law enforcement, and over the last year or so I've been leaning on him more and more to handle the jobs we do in that domain. He also takes up a lot of the administrative slack when I'm not around. He's the Danny Doc was referring to when he suggested I back out a bit.

Anyway, Mongoose worked with Junior on that gig, a kind of outside guy to Junior's inside. Relax, you're not missing anything—like Malaysia, the job was very routine and boring, exactly the way we and the customer wanted it to be. Bad for the books, but good for business.

During that time, Mongoose and Junior became good friends. They really hadn't had much of a chance to hang out before. At some point, Mongoose turned Junior on to a new training regime he was following. The results were astounding.

There are a million of these things out there, and I don't want to plug one over the other, especially since I wasn't the one doing it or supervising it. (At Red Cell International we have our own program, patterned after the SEAL workouts, with a few extra twists added by our resident dominatrix, Trace.) It's probable that the exact exercises weren't the real secret; more important was the fact that Junior worked hard on it every day.

He was on the skinny side when he came to work with us. In fact, that was one of his charms—all the women wanted to mother him, even Trace, who fed him protein shakes and even a few home-baked cookies. All of that food had added, oh, maybe a pound and a half to him by the time we got out of Cuba. Very likely his weight gain was canceled by the workouts Trace was putting him through.

But when he showed up in Delhi, it was obvious he'd gained weight. And it was muscle, not fat. His shoulders were wider, his neck thicker. Where I really noticed it was in his forearms, which bulged when he picked up his bags.

Muscles are one thing; physical fitness is another. It was obvious his workouts had helped both when he went out for our wake-up run the morning after he arrived.

Pride generally prevents me from finishing too far back on the morning constitutionals. With age comes wisdom: I've learned how to pace myself, go with the pack, then give it that last squeeze at the end just to keep my self-esteem up. Not that I'd finish first. All I required was to keep my companions within swatting distance when they mouthed off at the finish line—a reachable goal, especially when running with Junior, who despite his long legs and skinny frame wasn't much of a sprinter when he joined us.

But it wasn't possible that morning. In fact, he and Mongoose left Shotgun and myself way in the dust before we got out of the hotel driveway. They were so far ahead when we reached the road, neither Guns nor

I knew which way they'd gone. We turned right and caught a glimpse of Mongoose's blue sweat suit, and that was the last we saw of either of them until we got back to the hotel forty-five minutes later.

(For the record—I was two strides behind Shotgun at the end. Delhi was steaming that morning.)

We found Mongoose and Junior down in the gym, deep into their workout when we arrived for ours. Junior looked older for the first time, solid.

Older here meaning actually in his teens, which rumor has it he passed a year or two ago. (He's legal, at least according to his driver's license.)

Maybe it wasn't just his muscles. He'd proven himself in Cuba, working a lot on his own. He was more confident; you could see it in his face. The muscles were just window dressing. It made a dad proud.

I hadn't known that Junior even existed until only a few months before. I won't go back over our history, but the truth is I'd resisted the idea that he was really my son. I didn't see any resemblance, even if other people claimed they did. And our personalities were different. He was quiet where I'd been a wiseass; he was cerebral where I'd been physical.

Now I realized that some of those differences were just a matter of emphasis and circumstance. We'd had very different childhoods and educations. He wasn't Richard Marcinko, and I wasn't Matthew Loring.

Thank God, all around, right?

But who was Matthew Loring?

A good kid, intelligent, hardworking. With initiative and drive. Someone who didn't ask any favors or special recognition, but tried hard to do his job, and prove he belonged.

Not a SEAL, but not everyone in the world can be that lucky. Under the *right* circumstances, he might have been a SEAL. I can't predict how anyone would do in BUD/S—Basic Underwater Demolition/SEAL training is a personal trial no one can predict. But based on his experience with us, Matt would have had a shot at success there.

Other people, I know, had seen it earlier than I did. Trace, Doc, Karen. Me, too, I guess. But now I was willing to admit it.

To myself. And to him.

Which a lot of times is the hardest thing.

It was in the hotel gym that Mongoose met Vina. She was a cute little thing, twenty-three years old, the daughter of a visiting Argentine diplomat. She had a law degree from the States, but was here working as her father's secretary.

If she stood on her tiptoes, she might have just cleared five feet. The bar she pressed over her head looked to weigh twice what she did.

Not quite, but almost. I doubt she was more than a hundred pounds. I won't say she had no fat on her body, but what was there was very strategically placed.

Mongoose is not known for smiling, but his face lit up when Vina walked into the weight room and start racking up some of the iron. He went over and asked if she wanted some help.

Vina gave him a look that would have neutered a dog. Mongoose smiled—I think Shotgun and Junior nearly fell over from shock—then did this "*no maas*" thing with his hands.

"I'll spot you," he offered.

She said something in Spanish to the effect that he should consider carefully his body integrity.

Any other man at that point would have been a whipped cur, sleeking off to the showers. Not Mongoose.

"Oh, you speak Spanish," he said, in Spanish of course. "You have a lovely accent. Where did you grow up?"

"In a place where I learned how to deal with much more charming idiots than you."

"I'm from the States."

"I couldn't tell."

"You really do need a spotter."

"Shove it."

"You go ahead and I'll watch. If there is an emergency, Mongoose is here."

Vina looked like she was going to throw the weights into his midsection. I'm sure if she had, he would have caught them and handed them back. Instead, she jerked the weight and began doing presses, twenty-five of them, whipping them off like she was skipping rope.

Mongoose's grin grew.

Shotgun and Junior pretended to be deep in their workouts, but they were watching the whole thing out of the corners of their eyes. I just chuckled and started my crunches.

At first, Vina raced through her workout. But about halfway through—I think she was doing curls—she started to ease her pace.

Mongoose's grin grew the whole time.

My workout was done, but this was too good a show to miss. I grabbed a bottle of water and a towel and sat on one of the chairs outside the room, watching through the plate glass as Mongoose played lapdog.

Actually, he *wanted* to be a lapdog. All he got to do was stand downwind of her sweat.

And then suddenly she was done, walking out of the room. It was so quick I thought I'd missed something. But no—she'd just put the weight down and left.

Mongoose followed, trying to catch his breath.

"Hey, you didn't even tell me your name," he said as she walked down the hall. I don't think I've ever seen a person that short walk that fast.

"I'm not telling you my name."

"I'll tell you mine."

"What a treat that is."

"Thomas Yamya . . . When will I see you again?"

I'm censoring her reply, due to the sensitive nature of my audience.

Mongoose may have been in love, but he and the rest of us had work to do. Doc and Trace were sharpening their sticks and kilts. I sent Shotgun and Mongoose over to reconnoiter; after a look-around, they were to continue over to the stadium and some of the other Game sites, familiarizing themselves with the area and looking for anything, or more likely anyone, out of place.

Junior had come to India as our tech guy. He pursued his specialty by checking the various Internet shops in the city, lining up a good set of computers for us to use, freeing Shunt for other business back in the States, and giving us more immediate support. We have a system of anonymous servers that we can use to access whatever we have to access, but finding the right computer to do it from can be tricky. You don't want someone looking over your shoulder, nor do you want there to be any connection between you and the place if your foolproof anonymous methods prove less than foolproof.

No, I have no clue about the specifics involved with encryption algorithms and anonymous gateways and all that; I'm lucky I can get the damn computer to set the margins the way the publisher wants them. But that's the beauty of being the boss—I don't have to worry about that garbage.

Junior trolled the Internet kiosks in the city, but eventually settled on a set of computers at a small school a half mile from where we were staying. The school had all the usual security precautions in place, meaning that anyone who looked halfway like a student could slink in and get on the network. A few keystrokes and a stolen password later, and you could make the school's mainframes sing and dance. There were literally no barriers from there.

Indian government computers? Ha. Easier to get into than the Pentagon's. And the Pentagon's aren't that tough.

What was I doing while all of this was going on?

I'd like to say that I was engaged in another round of footsie with Minister Dharma. That was certainly my intention. But the minister was ensconced in parliament sessions, and so I got my daily update from one of her assistants, a dour-looking man named Vijay. (Rhymes with "No Way," the perfect government name.) He assured me that all preparations were proceeding as planned, the Games would not be disrupted by terrorists, and the stock market would soon reach new heights.

I'm kidding about the stock market, but I'm sure he would have said that if I asked. For all his stated optimism, his sour monotone sounded like the voice of the dead.

The members of Special Squadron Zero were a pretty quiet group when I met Captain Birla at the air base that night.

Gathering for the mission into Pakistan, they'd been quiet and nervous, but it was a good quiet and a good nervous. This quiet was not nearly so good.

It's hard to explain exactly what I mean unless you've been in that situation. It's like a sports team that's made the playoffs by a good distance, and now is heavily favored in the first round. They're anxious, a bit, and concerned that they're going to do a good job, but they're also looking forward to the contest, and pretty much confident that they can win.

That's how a group of shooters, even untested ones, are before the show. You don't want them too cocky, of course—that's about the surest way of getting your ass kicked there is. But you certainly don't want them thinking they're defeated before going into the game.

All that bullshit you see in movies where the commander gets up right before the big battle and says, "Ninety percent of you are going to die today, but what the hell—go kick some butt on the way!" Well, it's bullshit. Nobody stands up and says that.

Hell, if you're the commander and you think that, then what in God's name are you doing? Ninety percent casualties? Even fifty percent. If the situation truly calls for that—and I will grant that there are times when it must—bragging about it is the last thing you want to do.

Look, the goal of every operation is to get your guys back alive. It's not your only goal, and in fact it's often not the top goal, but getting your ass blown off sucks even when it's for a good cause. No use pretending it don't.

No, what you say before the op is what Captain Birla said that night going into Pakistan: "We've trained for this, we know how to do it, and we're going to succeed. Board the helis."[11]

He said more or less the same thing tonight, except for the heli part, since most of the team was going via truck. But the body language was all wrong—instead of seeming understated, he seemed like he was talking from a corner he'd been backed into.

His guys were the same way—slumped shoulders, gear hanging down, clothes not precisely squared away. It was a damn good thing we weren't heading for Pakistan, that's all I can say.

Our destination was the school where Trace's team was staying. Birla had chosen it without input from me—and without knowing that I had shooters there. It was a logical target: a Munich-style strike on high-profile athletes.

Most of us were going there, that is. A small group was simultaneously visiting the prime minister to pay our regards, Red Cell style.

Guess which group I was with.

There were plenty of guards around the prime minister's residence, and a well-trained security detail inside. But while I don't want to make anything too easy for anyone out there, a frontal assault would not have been out of the question. Remember, the goal of most terrorists is footage on the nightly news.

---

[11] The captain had trained with the British SAS at some point in his career, and used the British slang for helicopters.

But we weren't rolling tanks up to the front door of the palace. We went up in a tow truck.

We meaning myself, Sergeant Phurem, and Corporal Sesha Nadar, Phurem's more-or-less sidekick.

I was at the wheel. My head was wrapped to make me look like a Sikh, and I had the faded coveralls of an army grease monkey. Corporal Nadar's face was smudged with grease, and Sergeant Phurem had the universal sign of authority—a clipboard.

The sergeant sprang from the truck as we drove up to the gate.

"Where is the Mercedes we're to be working on?" he asked, tapping the back of the board on his knuckles. "What is its problem?"

The sentry looked at him as if he had stepped off a flying saucer.

"Bad gas, no doubt. We've had two other vehicles with the same problem this week." The sergeant paused, glancing at his clipboard. "We were told the car would be waiting. Should I guess that you weren't even told?"

The sergeant was speaking English, though I barely understood him. The sentry said something in Hindi, and the two of them were off to the races, discussing bad gas and car parts, complaining about bureaucracy and the fact that no one ever told the guys on the ground what the hell was going on.

And do you know about the new salary freeze they've proposed? I haven't had a raise in three years!

The corporal and I sat in the front of the truck, trying to look as bored as possible. In fact, I think Nadar may have been dozing. When Sergeant Phurem raised his left hand, gesturing as he pontificated about some intricacy involving fuel injection, I poked Nadar. He picked up his cell phone and hit one of the presets.

The phone in the guard booth rang.

What a coinky dink.

The sentry who had been talking to Sergeant Phurem went to answer the phone. The two other guards eyed the truck warily. It was hard for them to see into the cab. It was dark, we'd pulled to the side to make sure the light didn't glare into the cab, and we were a few feet above them to boot. So it would have been impossible to see the corporal, much less make out the fact that he was on the cell phone.

No, not a special phone. We hadn't even bothered with reprogramming the ID to make it look as if the call came from the maintenance office where the corporal claimed to be calling from.

The conversation was short, covering just the pertinent facts: one of the minister's bodyguards' vehicles had to be fixed before sunup, and a crew was on its way.

"Just like everything else around here, an hour and a half late," the guard told Sergeant Phurem. "And then he yells at me, like I have anything to do with any of this."

"Try working for them," commiserated the sergeant. "But I hope you have a good stomach for that."

"I would not trade jobs with you for anything in the world," said the sentry, pulling back the gate. "My job is better than most."

You almost feel guilty in a situation like that.
Almost.

We had obtained a set of IDs a few nights before by visiting a café where members of one of the government motor pools hang out. Corporal Nadar had put some real effort into the task, taking on the job of a waiter. That made grabbing the IDs off coats and in one case a pants pocket relatively easy. All the time he was hustling tea and soft drinks through the crowd.

Yours truly had a role as a diversionary guest star, a foreign visitor being fawned over when recognized by a pair of starstruck Americans out for their first Indian tea.

Trace and Shotgun made such a lovely couple.

But all that effort proved unnecessary. We didn't even need the IDs: the truck and clipboard were authority enough.

Once past the front gate, we moved around with impunity—not surprising, since generally anyone on the inside figures that anyone else they see belongs there. Because the credentials were already checked at the gate, right?

To be fair, we were attacking the soft underbelly of the security system. There was only one guard on duty at the garage. He yawned at us, and shrugged when the sergeant asked him which car it was that we were supposed to work on.

Five minutes later, we'd wired all four vehicles so that they'd work only if we wanted them to. (You know those remote start devices that let you get your car nice and toasty on a cold winter's morning? Same principle, slightly different specifics, and radically different application.)

Sergeant Phurem checked his watch. It was three minutes past five. The fun was just about to begin.

(III)

Even I can't be in two places at one time, though I enjoy creating the illusion. So my account of what happened next depends largely on what various people reported to me. It's in the ballpark, though one or two details may be slightly off-kilter.

While we were playing tow truck repairmen, the rest of Special Squadron Zero was fanning out near the dorm where the athletes were sleeping. Three shooters were already in the building, disguised as janitorial staff members, mopping up the hall on the late shift. They had more than Spic and Span in their wash buckets: all three had tear gas grenades and a few flash-bangs to add to the excitement.

This was just an exercise, and we didn't want the athletes to get hurt, either by jumping from a window or doing something really foolish like resisting. So we'd taken the precaution of printing up notices warning them what was going on. The janitors began slipping them under the doors to the individual rooms at precisely five A.M.

About five minutes later, a pair of drunken buffoons were singing loudly as they walked up the steps to the main building.

I'm not sure what the song was, but it certainly attracted the guards' attention. They both came down to shoo the drunks away.

Four team members slipped into the building behind them.

They intended on simply staring down the guard at the security desk in the front hallway, flashing their weapons, but it turned out they didn't have to—they found him sleeping. They trussed him, put a funny clown mask on his face, then left a note indicating that he was "dead" and should look forward to his further incarnation as a water bug.

Flank secured, they went back out to the front, where the two guards were still haranguing the drunks. Two passing policemen had stopped to help corral the unruly men. The guards were just helping them into the car when they found themselves both locked in the back, unable to open the doors from the inside.

As soon as the door was locked, one of the policemen gave a sharp whistle. The back door of a panel van up the street opened, and four ninjas in black garb emerged. Two sprinkled booby traps along the street, while the others ran into the building.

The upstairs floors had two guards apiece. The policemen went upstairs to question the two about the disturbance outside. Neither man had heard anything—not to imply that they were sleeping at their posts. They were asked to come down and speak to the policemen's supervisor at the sentry station on the first floor.

They shambled down the steps, into the waiting arms of two Special Squadron Zero members, who trussed them, then parked them next to the rest on the floor.

Unlike the students, the guards weren't told what was going on. There was no sense being too nice to them; their lives were going to be shit after this anyway, and nothing Squadron Zero did would make them feel any better about their fate—or the people they were going to blame for it.

The guards on the top floor were not only awake, but were actually suspicious when the two policemen came up to them. They asked questions about what was going on—*the audacity!*—and one even had the nerve to call down to the desk to see if he had been sent for.

"Yes," answered the deskman. "We have problems with the police."

He slammed down the phone. The row of captives soon had two more.

It was 0511. The operation was a little more than fifteen minutes old. The entire building was now in terrorist hands.

Over at the minister's garage, Sergeant Phurem and Corporal Nadar shared a cigarette while waiting for the next stage of our operation to unfold.

We had a good view of the back of the house. I stood by the door, arms folded, and counted off the windows to find the minister's room.

It was dark.

"Always hits the snooze button twice before getting up," I told the others, checking my watch.

Neither Trace nor Doc had been alerted to the raid. It didn't come as a surprise to either one, though, since they knew what we were up to and what the overall game plan was.

Doc was sleeping when they knocked on his door; he saw the gun, heard the explanation—"Just a drill; don't be alarmed"—and rolled back over in bed mumbling something about needing his beauty rest. But with the building secure, the ninjas had orders to round up all the athletes and team personnel so they wouldn't be harmed if things went wrong when the authorities responded. One of the soldiers shook his leg and insisted he get up. Doc grumbled, but decided to comply. He knew I'd be quizzing him on the squad's work.

Trace, on the other hand . . .

Let's put it this way: three Special Squadron Zero members were injured in the exercise. Two had broken kneecaps; the third had to have his jaw wired shut. There's a rumor that he made a disparaging and potentially sexist remark during the proceedings, though fortunately for him the video the squad made of the takeover didn't pick it up.

Trace might have worked her way through the entire squad had Doc not heard the ruckus on the floor below him. Realizing what was going on, he managed to convince a ninja to take him to talk to her; he found Trace loading one of the tear gas canisters into the grenade launcher.

"Good God, woman, show some restraint!" he yelled. "These are Dick's guys."

"All the more reason to kick them in the balls," she said. But she put the launcher down.

The athletes were taken down a back stairwell to the cafeteria, where Captain Birla was waiting. He was in his dress whites, very spiffy—the glare blew out the chip on the video camera, so all you can see is this white flash moving back and forth at the far end of the room.

"Very sorry to bother you," he told the athletes and their trainers. "We are conducting a review of the security procedures to improve protection. I realize that this is inconvenient for you, but I hope that you will agree the goal is worthwhile. We want to ensure your safety and that of everyone at the Games."

The captain then released them to breakfast, asking them to stay in the cafeteria for their own safety until the exercise was concluded. This would happen very soon, he assured them; they would not miss any of their day's workouts.

There was a bit of grumbling, but no outright protests.

The captain made eye contact with every athlete, shook all the coaches' hands, then went back to the main floor to initiate phase two of the operation.

At exactly 0523, the light in the minister's room flashed on.

I turned to my co-conspirators and told them that the minister had just woken up.

Five minutes later, a member of the Special Protection Group came into the garage, yawning and sucking down a steaming cup of strong tea.

Now let me say this about the SPG. They're the equivalent of the American Secret Service, charged with protecting the Indian prime minister and other key members of the government. Their training is excellent. The men in the Transport Wing, a subgroup of Operations, are top notch drivers, able to handle all sorts of situations.

But like any service, SPG does have its weaknesses.

We'd been comparatively gentle with the security people over at the school, primarily because we knew that they weren't going to be too hard to handle. But we didn't take any chances with the driver.

We hit him with a baseball bat.

Actually, the electronic equivalent, though at the time he might have preferred the real thing.

A lot of police departments have started using Tasers when subduing unruly subjects. They have a number of advantages in nonlethal situations, and in fact their stopping power can actually be more dependable than the conventional bullets some cops carry.

There are downsides, of course, including the goofy wires that spin out from the weapons and deliver the shock.

The Taser Sergeant Phurem used on the driver was wireless. It delivers a shotgun shell-sized dart into the target.

These aren't the darts you toss down at the pub on Friday nights. These slugs consist of a battery, a step-up transformer, and prongs that make the target a human lightbulb.

A malfunctioning lightbulb. Electricity surges through him for about twenty seconds, hitting him with wave after wave. This paralyzes his muscles and makes him tingly.

It's not a good tingly. You're left with a very serious headache. You really can't move much for an hour, either.

The dart comes out of the gun so hard and so fast that it can bowl the victim over, not to mention leave a good-sized welt. In this case, the surge threw the driver against the wall he was next to. The hot tea he was carrying spattered all over his face, which probably wasn't too pleasant either. He couldn't yell, or at least didn't, because the shock from the shell was messing up whatever mechanism it is that works your vocal chords.

We couldn't do anything about it, either. The contractor who made our gun—I'm testing it for a concern in the Midwest—advised me not to touch the target for at least thirty seconds "out of an abundance of caution."

The poor driver's eyes bugged out. I'm sure he thought he was seeing death.

"It's thirty seconds," I told the corporal, counting it off on my watch. "Put him in the trunk."

I unzipped my coveralls and took them off, revealing a suit remarkably similar to the one the Transport driver was wearing. I pulled a tie out of the pocket—clip-on; knots can be dangerous.

Even so, it had been a while since I wore one, and I felt a little uncomfortable as I drove the car around to the side entrance where the minister was waiting with two of his bodyguards. Sergeant Phurem was with me. I went up to the entrance slowly, avoiding the urge to scratch my collar, which was chafing badly. The sergeant got out and held open the back door, waiting for the minister to come out. One of the guards peeked through the inside door, then stepped back.

Out came the minister, trailed by his two bodyguards.

Just as the minister reached the car, a flash lit the night. The ground shook, and the air seemed to suck itself into a black hole.

Sergeant Phurem reacted exactly as a bodyguard is trained to act. He pushed the minister into the car and jumped on top of him.

The driver, yours truly, hit the gas.

A second explosion shook the ground as I veered away from the entrance. Corporal Nadar had gone ahead with the tow truck and was waiting a few yards ahead, just around a curve from the gate. He, too, stepped on the gas, gathering speed and momentum as he went down the driveway. One of the sentries came out to stop him, or at least see what was going on; the corporal, ducking as low as he could in the seat, clamped his foot down and rammed through the gate. We followed a second or two later.

One of the guards may have shot at us. The limo was bulletproof, and we were moving so fast that I really didn't have time to notice.

"Sorry about this, sir," said Sergeant Phurem, getting up off the minister. He pulled him up onto his seat.

"Special Squadron Zero, Prime Minister. You requested that we test the security for the Commonwealth Games? I'm sorry to say that it is not quite up to acceptable standards."

"Not quite," agreed the minister, sliding back in the seat.

[IV]

Before leaving his residence, the prime minister had been alerted to the hostage situation by Captain Birla himself. The captain had obtained the prime minister's private phone number from an overly talkative—and no doubt soon to be fired—secretary. He then made a second call to the local police, telling them where they could find their stolen squad car.

That done, he and the rest of the members of the Special Squadron vacated the building. Most of them went back to their barracks. The captain, still in dress uniform, strolled instead down the road a bit to a small tea shop for a spot of breakfast. He wanted to be in the vicinity when the police arrived, so he could evaluate their response.

We had similar plans.

I pulled into a large parking lot. Just as I did, a searchlight found the front of the sedan. The air quickly filled with dirt and grit as a helicopter appeared above the light. It was the same heli, as Captain Birla would have it, that we had flown into Pakistan a few nights before.

We got out of the car. Corporal Nadar had gone on to return the tow truck, leaving just the sergeant and me with the prime minister.

"Mr. Prime Minister, my name is Dick Marcinko. I've been helping your men work on the security arrangements."

"Yes!" he said, practically shouting. Name recognition is a beautiful thing.

"Mr. Prime Minister, we'd like you to join us in the helicopter so you can observe the response to the hostage taking, both at your residence and the school. But we're concerned that there might be some danger when the units realize that you're gone and begin responding. We can drop you off at your office, or anywhere else you want to go."

"Where exactly are you going?"

"We're going to fly over the school and watch the response. After that, it will depend on what the response to your kidnapping is."

"Mr. Marcinko, I would very much like to be with you when you do that."

"Absolutely, Mr. Prime Minister. Would you like to stop back at your house and pick up the rest of your security detail?"

"I feel much better with you men, thank you just the same."

The prime minister put on a safety belt at our insistence. I had him come over to the door and watch as we pulled over the school. The first policemen were just responding to the front; two men got out of the car.

"If the building had been taken over by terrorists, those guys would be dead right now," I told the prime minister. "They're acting way too nonchalant."

"A big deficiency," he said, shaking his head.

We saw many other big deficiencies over the next few minutes as the response built. The prime minister's head nodded up and down so much as I pointed them out that I started to think he was a bobblehead doll.

I have to admit I was feeling pretty damn good right about then. We'd just pulled off a highly successful op—there is no better way to start a morning. I had the ear of the country's most important leader, and was giving him a firsthand lecture on what needed to be done to toughen up his country's war against terror. This wasn't a home run; this was a grand slam.

But, to mix my metaphors in a way that will surely drive my copy editor back to the bottle, into every bright day must come a dark cloud.

And sometimes a little fire and smoke as well.

"Interesting and dramatic," said the minister, pointing out the door of the helo. "Is that explosion part of your exercise as well?"

Explosion? *What explosion?*

I looked over his shoulder just in time to see a very small puff of smoke erupt from a building across from the athletic fields.

The small puff was followed by a much larger flash of red, which in turn was followed by an angry furl of black, which gave way to an exceedingly orange sheet of fire.

I've run out of adjectives to torture, but you get the idea. The building beyond the fence of the athletic center was in the process of blowing up. Fireballs shot straight up from the north end, while black bits of building and other debris spat from the south with a force Old Faithful would have been proud of.

I took out my sat phone to call Doc and find out what the hell was going on. He had the same idea, and I went straight to voice mail. I clicked off; before I could redial, Trace was on the line.

"What the hell is going on?" she demanded.

"I'm trying to figure that out myself. Get out to the field."

"I'm out there. Dick—*Helos!*"

I looked down in time to see two large pieces of shrapnel being ejected from the turmoil. As I stared, the jagged pieces of rubbish grew into the shape of two small helicopters.

"Land the chopper!" I yelled over the helo's interphone circuit. "We need to let the prime minister out."

"Then what?" asked the pilot.

"Then we have to follow those helicopters. They're being stolen."

Yes, I did jump to conclusions. Yes, I was right. No, don't be impressed. It's not hard to put two and two together when you see red flashes of gunfire directed at the corner of the property where there's a security post.

Had I realized the helicopter factory was a target a few days before—now *that* would have been impressive.

Our pilot dropped the Mi-8TV down on the practice field directly behind the dorm. I helped the prime minster out as the team security people ran over, then nearly fell over as a hurricane whipped nearby.

Hurricane Trace Dahlgren, to be exact.

I scrambled back into the aircraft.

"Go!" she was yelling. "Get this piece of shit off the ground! Follow them."

The pilot had already started to do just that. He lifted the craft up at the end of the field over the goals, then banked sharply to follow the track of the two helicopters. They were flying to the northeast.

Roughly in the direction of Pakistan. China's over there as well.

A cacophony of confusion filled the radio airwave. Our pilot alerted the Indian air force, but of course they didn't have a fighter patrol nearby. Interceptors were scrambled to the north and west; in the meantime, they "hoped" we could keep the choppers in sight.

Our captain was certainly trying. He had the throttles at max, and even strained forward against his restraints as if that might give his bird some extra momentum.

The purloined helicopters had a reasonably good lead, but they didn't seem to realize that we were chasing them. Within two or three minutes we spotted them ahead, two little black dots at the right side of the forward windscreen.

"Faster!" urged Trace. She's become a fairly good helicopter pilot over the past year or so, and I could tell that she was itching to take the controls.

The little dots started to grow. As we closed to roughly three miles, the copilot called the Indian air command on the radio, giving the approximate location and heading.

He'd no sooner clicked off his mike when the other helos began pulling ahead. They were monitoring the frequencies.

Which gave me an idea.

"Tell the air force you have them in your sights and you're ready to shoot them down if they don't land," I told the copilot.

"But, Commander Rick, they are out of the range. And even so, we do not have the missiles with us today."

"We don't have to tell them any of that," I explained. "They're going to get away if we don't do something. This way we might be able to get them to surrender."

"A bluff?"

"That's right."

The copilot made the call—several times. Each time, the transmission was overrun by a number of other pilots on the circuit, all talking over each other.

"Shit," muttered Trace. "They'll never hear it."

I looked up and saw one of the helicopters peeling to the left.

"Which one do we follow?" asked the pilot.

"Whichever is closer," I said.

"They're not splitting up," said Trace. "They're attacking."

She was right. Whoever was in the helos had heard the transmission and was in no mood to surrender.

The chopper on the left banked into a one-eighty. Something flashed from its chin.

A thirty-millimeter shell, which sailed far to our left.

The next twenty or so were considerably closer, all coming within two or three feet of us.

Except for one that grazed the right underside of the helicopter.

You'd think that a shell running along the bottom of a helicopter doesn't really amount to much. A light flesh wound, barely more than a paper cut.

But when you're traveling at 150 knots in a sardine tin, even a paper cut hurts like hell. The helo bucked, pitching hard on its axis. The tail jerked to the right while the nose tried to push itself higher, probably to avoid the acrid smell of burning paint and metal.

Our pilot held us in the air. Even better, he kept the helicopter from tearing itself apart, and began a sharp bank away from our approaching enemy.

The stolen helicopter whipped past. It looked like an artist's dream of an Apache attack helicopter, a sleek collection of triangles topped by a tornado, with stubby wedge wings and double cannons mounted beneath the hull.

Nasty.

Something started popping behind me. I turned back toward the crew cabin and saw Trace at the side gun mount, blasting away at the gunship as it passed.

"Those are blanks!" I yelled. "We're not carrying live ammo because of the exercise!"

She gave me a look that said, *you dumb shit.*

Not that I disagreed at that moment.

The stolen attack helicopter spun around behind us. The pilot shouted a warning as he began pirouetting through the sky, ducking left and right and firing flares to decoy our adversary. Shells burst all around us; the side of the helicopter took some light shrapnel, but the maneuvers were enough to keep the big blows away.

We were lucky—had the attack bird been carrying heat-seeking missiles, things would have been different. But at that moment, we weren't exactly counting our blessings.

The Mi-8TV suddenly yawed hard on its keel. Trace fell against me as we both tumbled toward the other side of the hull. I looked up and saw the attack chopper passing within two or three meters.

Trace pushed down, coiling her body for a leap across space. I grabbed her just in time.

"Easy, Geronimo," I said, collaring her. "Don't do something stupid. You can't fly and this isn't worth dying for."

She probably cursed, but if so, I couldn't hear it over the rush of wind. Our helicopter jerked hard to the left, sending us back across the cabin. It bucked a few times, and we lurched against the bulkhead.

"Prepare for a landing," said the pilot. "Emergency landing."

I realized I heard him clearly, though his voice was rather soft.

The engines had stopped. We'd run out of fuel.

PART TWO
TROUBLE AND MORE TROUBLE

Victory smiles upon those who anticipate the changes in the character of war, not upon those who wait to adapt themselves after they occur.

—GENERAL GIULIO DOUHET, *THE COMMAND OF THE AIR*, 1921

[1]

I remember reading an article somewhere that claimed that helicopters are a hell of a lot safer than airplanes, because if they have engine problems or run out of fuel, they're easy to land. The author made it sound as if they just flutter on down to the ground like a butterfly, settling without a care in the world.

He must have been referring to some other helicopter.

The Mi-8TV did have good forward momentum, but the pilot was basically guiding a brick to an abrupt stop. He got the helicopter into what is called autorotation: basically, he traded momentum and altitude for enough wind energy to spin the rotors, which acted like a giant wing.

More like a wing with holes. We came down in a rush, not quite a belly flop but not a gentle glide either. My ears popped and my stomach tried to float upward.

"You will brace for impact!" the pilot yelled.

We braced away. The ground kept coming.

We'd flown about seventy miles from Delhi, to an area north of Dhanaura filled with small farm fields and trees. Lots of trees. Which was all Trace or I could see out of the side as we came in.

We scraped the top of one of the trees, then flopped hard onto the ground, pitching forward then rearing back, all in seemingly the same motion.

There was a moment of silence, as if the chopper were paying tribute to its pilot.

"Well that sucks," said Trace, letting go of the spar she'd grabbed. "They got away."

Some people just never know to look on the bright side of life.

The two crewmen in the back began securing the helicopter. I went forward and checked on the pilot and copilot, who were calmly going through a post-flight checklist.

"Dick!" shouted Trace from outside. "Dick!"

I went to see what all the shouting was, stepping out of the side hatchway.

Into muck up to my waist.

"Be careful!" yelled Trace. "We landed in a mud hole!"

She was still laughing when we got back to the capital a few hours later. She was probably the only person in Delhi who was, though. The government was in an uproar, and of course the Indian media was having a field day, talking about the daring daylight attack on the Indian defense industry.

The two helicopters had gotten away clean. Because of their design, they had no trouble eluding air control radar, and by the time the Indian air force was able to get its fancy new Su-35s into the area, they were nowhere to be found. You can imagine how overjoyed the government and military were about this.

Pakistan was suspected of having stolen the aircraft. This was a rather logical assumption, and not just because relations between the two countries were permanently strained. Clearly, the operation had been carefully planned, and it seemed obvious that only a highly motivated foe could have pulled it off.

China was also a suspect. Not exactly an Indian ally, the Chinese have been extremely active in the realm of industrial espionage as well as military spying, and this caper combined both. On the other hand, the Chinese lately have been generally trying to buy what they want. They have plenty of U.S. Savings Bonds, after all, to do just that.

The argument against China as a suspect went like this: if they were really after an attack helicopter, China could have worked out a deal with Eurocopter for one of their Eurocopter Tigers, or with the Russians for whatever version of the Mi-28 they were willing to part with. Both helicopters are basically Apache knockoffs, with a few little spiffs here and there. India had actually taken the same approach, surveying prototypes from Eurocopter and others while working up their domestic solution.

The stolen helicopters were the first two examples of that solution. Known as the Ahi, the model was said in the media to be the equivalent of the American Comanche, the so-called stealth helicopter developed by Boeing Sikorsky but canceled during the Bush administration because of costs elsewhere.

The Comanche was designed as a scout—fast, less detectable on radar than normal helicopters, it would have been only lightly armed. The Indian Ahi, however, was conceived of more as an attack bird than a scout, able to pound as well as sneak.

Whatever. The bottom line was, someone had stolen two of India's real military prizes, and there was hell to pay.

The fact that India had been conducting training exercises to test its response to terrorism at the time of the attack just added to the general uproar.

I don't know that the prime minister actually blamed us for the military's failure to prevent the theft, but he really didn't have to. Opposition parties were screaming and making all sorts of wild accusations, and with so much excrement in the air, it was inevitable that some would fall on Special Squadron Zero. Though still officially secret, its existence was now a matter of open speculation.

Minister Dharma spent most of the day in damage control mode, making phone calls and attempting to charm fellow cabinet members. Captain Birla, who should have been celebrating a decent operation, was even glummer than he had been after the prisoners had escaped.

It had been a hell of a week. Seven days before, he'd been at the pinnacle of success, the founding commander of one of the country's elite counterterror squads. Now he was on the verge of becoming the punch line of every joke about intelligence and covert agencies.

"There's only one thing for you to do today," I told him when I saw his long face hanging over his desk at headquarters. "You have to go see the good Doctor."

"The Bombay cure?"

"Known to fix nearly every ailment plaguing man," I said. "And a few that bother women as well."

He nodded. I rounded up Sergeant Phurem and a few of the captain's other trusted noncoms and sent them out for gin therapy.

I would have joined them, but Omar, the friendly Christian in Action station chief, phoned and requested a personal briefing from yours truly on the helicopter fiasco. He was pretty nasty about it, but since I was wondering what was going on myself, I agreed to meet him at the embassy. He invited the deputy chief of mission[12] — the number two guy at the embassy — along with two other spooks. We all went into the secure area for a little confab.

It was your typical CIA conversation, a cross between an inquisition and a pep rally, where I was supposed to genuflect and kiss their rings in the name of patriotism.

Omar thought I had arranged the entire caper as a cover to steal the helicopters.

---

[12] He's not a spook. Believe me.

Why?

"Let's face it, Dick," he told me, leaning across the table that sat at the center of the bug-proof room. "You're not getting any younger. You don't have much in the way of savings. You pull off something like this, you can retire in style."

"Much as I like the idea of commuting to work in an attack helicopter," I replied, "I don't quite see how it would be a real money-making proposition."

"Come on," said Omar. "You sell it to the Chinks, the Ruskies—that's quite a payday."

"I'm not exactly a great friend of the Chinese premier. I embarrassed one of his protégés not too long ago."

"Boeing would be willing to pay," said one of Omar's sidekicks. "And you wouldn't be betraying your country."

Looking back, I realize that maybe that was an offer, very cleverly worded. If so, it went over my head at the time. I glanced at the deputy chief of mission, who looked like he wanted to be somewhere else, like maybe strapped to a log in a sawmill.

"You don't really think I had anything to do with this, do you?" I asked. "If we were going to steal something like this, I sure wouldn't have hung around Delhi to be called over the hill by some shit-for-brains pencil-dicked spymaster."

I know, I know—calling Omar a spymaster damned a long line of honest, hardworking spies.

"We're not questioning your patriotism," he said. "We just want to know what happened."

"So do I."

I know an exit line when I utter one, and I left without further ado. Or *adieu.*

I made it back to the Maharaja Express for an afternoon briefing and skull session. Everyone was there—Doc, Trace, Shotgun, Mongoose, and Junior. They'd spent the last few hours monitoring the various news reports on the helicopter theft.

There was one bright spot: Trace's exploits had been noticed by the bookmaking community, which had moved the Scottish field hockey squad from long shot to odds-on favorite.

Other than that, not so good.

If you like conspiracy theories—and who doesn't—linking the escape of the prisoners, the theft of the helicopters, and the nuclear warhead negotiations was child's play. All of us in the room could supply any number of theories, twisted and otherwise, to show that they were linked. But there was no evidence that they were. On the contrary, everything suggested they weren't—if, for example, terrorists had stolen the helicopters to attack the nuclear storehouse, wouldn't they have just gone straight there? Why fly in the opposite direction?

Even linking the exercise with the helicopter theft seemed unlikely. It was almost certainly just a coincidence.

Bad luck wasn't much of a consolation, though.

"End of the day, all of this makes the Indians look bad," said Doc. "But it doesn't really change anything as far as we're concerned. Two more tangos running around in India aren't going to change the basic equation. The damn country is a recruiting paradise. And it's a wall-to-wall hideout. That hellhole you were in the other morning is exhibit A, Dick. You can't tell your tango from a ragpicker without a scorecard."

Doc was just getting started.

"Let's say they took the helos, and not the Pakis or whoever," he continued. "Stealthy attack birds? Hell, they're shitloads easier to stop than some poor schlep who's got C4 taped to his scrotum. And with all due respect to the secretary of State, nuclear proliferation treaties are all very well and good, but they're not worth jack when it comes to dealing with a dirty bomb in a train car, or a couple of containers in a ship sailing into Bombay. Hell, this stuff is great television fodder, but it has nothing to do with our jobs here."

He rose from his chair.

"If you'll excuse me," he added, "I have to get back to work. I have a couple of wrenched knees that need to be taped."

It was vintage Doc, and a good lecture.

But our aim, if not our job, wasn't *just* to help train Special Squadron Zero to test the Indian defenses at the Commonwealth Games. We wanted to prevent a strike. Every training exercise could go off without a hitch, and if some jackass with a bomb under his headdress blew himself up at the closing ceremony, our op would have failed.

Yes, that's a very high standard. But when you're Red Cell International, it's what people expect. Never mind the political shenanigans. Or the money that was currently being wasted on contracts with people who had no business being allowed in the country, let alone giving its military any advice. Forget about the screwed up efforts to coordinate intelligence. Ignore the choked arteries of the government and military bureaucracy. The bottom line was results, not excuses.

And Doc's main point was indisputable: it was time to get back to work.

The one person whose perspective we didn't have on the two escapees was Fatty's. Since it was just about teatime, I decided to pay him a visit.

Urdu was half a block from the hotel, polishing his car, when I went down. He wiped off the dried polish with a smile, then threw the rag in the trunk and hopped in the car.

"Hot day, Mr. Richard."

"It's always hot in Delhi, Urdu."

"No, we have winter."

"When is that?"

"One week. December."

It was hard to believe, given the sweltering heat and shirt-soaking humidity, but Delhi does have a winter, and it can get all the way down to eight or nine degrees Celsius . . . which works out to about forty-eight Fahrenheit. A typical day in February would see the mercury hit twenty-one C, or about seventy.

That's balanced out by the sand storms of summer, when the temperature can touch forty-four C—in the area of 112 F.

"It gets so hot you wish for the monsoons," said Urdu as he navigated through a series of chokepoints, bringing us through the early afternoon traffic. He had heard of the helicopter theft; everyone in Delhi had. As far as he was concerned, it was clearly the work of the Pakistanis.

"They have sworn blood to have our throats," he explained. "They encourage the terrorists. And then there are the outlaws in Sri Lanka and Bangladesh. Do not forget the Maoists."

"Who could forget them?" I said.

Far from being a remnant of the Cold War, the Communist Party of India was formed only in 2004 from the merger of two other parties. They had vowed to violently overthrow the government. While they don't get as much ink as Islam nutjobs, these guys were responsible for more than two dozen murders and bombings since their creation.

"So what would you do?" I asked him.

"We take the fight to them. We attack these terrorists in their beds at night. No hold back."

Cabdrivers. If I were president, I'd replace my national security advisor and half the CIA with them.

With the political fallout continuing, Minister Dharma had transferred our remaining prisoner to the Interior Ministry. This wasn't a big loss. We'd gotten everything we could from him. He hadn't been pals with the two escapees, and aside from saying that Fatty was the laziest terrorist he'd ever met, hadn't done more than confirm things we'd already known. I'm not sure what the Interior Ministry did with him; for all I know he's a passport clerk in Mumbai.

Fatty, meanwhile, was now under protection of a plainclothes detail from the NSG, the National Security Group. The NSG's Special Action Group (SAG), the people who pulled off the counterterror raid in Mumbai I mentioned earlier, wanted to talk to him. Through some sort of backroom handoff, military intelligence apparently "owned" him, to which I say . . .

Never mind what I say. The important thing was that his bar bills were no longer being paid by Special Squadron Zero, but we still had access to him. We went over to get his thoughts on the most recent developments.

Obviously, the organizations in question were under the misunderstanding that Fatty was an effective spy and didn't want to blow his cover. The unit watching him had been told to be ultra-discreet. They had two men outside the hotel in cars, two in the lobby, and two more on the floor directly below Fatty's suite. Another pair was in the hotel suite. They rotated at irregular intervals.

When I arrived, they were about ten minutes from a planned shift change, and decided to go through with it a little early. I went up in the elevator with the two men who were going into the suite. The elevator had been locked off so that it had to stop on the floor below the suite; there the two plainclothes guards would check visitors out before letting them proceed.

The first sign of trouble was the empty chair across from the elevator when the door opened.

The two NSG men I was with exchanged a look. The one on the right patronizingly put his hand out to keep me back while the other drew his weapon and went out into the hall.

The two guards had disappeared. There was no sign of struggle, nothing out of place that we could see—the hall was just empty. There were no guests on this floor, no restrooms, not even an ice machine—nothing except the stairwell, which was clear.

The NSG men wanted me to stay there while they went upstairs, but I wasn't about to do that. We called for backup, sent the elevator down, then began trotting up the stairs to the penthouse level.

The stairwell opened at the side of a small foyer that consisted of the elevator door and the door to the suite. There was another empty chair near the suite door. It was knocked over.

One of the NSG men reached for the door handle. I stopped him and pointed to the carpet. There were small spots of blood leading inside.

He said something in Punjabi—a curse I believe—then reached into his pocket for a handkerchief, putting it over the knob so he wouldn't disturb any evidence.

The door was locked. He took out his passcard, buzzed the lock open, then pushed the door cautiously.

He called Fatty's name, then for the agents who'd been inside.

No answer.

Two more NSG men came out of the elevator behind us. Everyone looked at each other—not a word was spoken—then began moving into the suite, guns out, two to a side in mutual support. I was at the rear.

The main suite room was empty. But there were blots of blood on the floor here. We followed them around to the bedroom, then to the bath.

Both NSG bodyguards were lying in the whirlpool, facedown. The tub was full of blood. They'd been shot in the head, at close range with small caliber bullets.

Fatty was out in the hot tub. He'd been garroted. His tongue, swollen, was sticking out of his mouth.

They found one of the girls who'd been with him in the service area near the air conditioners; she'd been thrown to her death.

The other was in the bushes nearby. They both appeared to have been raped before they were killed and tossed over. Apparently the killers had decided to mix a little perversity with business before taking their leave.

(II)

Give the bastards credit—in less than half a week, they had managed to embarrass, befuddle, and bamboozle some of India's finest counterterrorist groups. To use the politically correct term, they had kicked the good guys in the balls.

The worst part of the fiasco was that no one could agree on who exactly it was who'd been doing the kicking.

We have a tendency in the West to see our enemies as something like a mirror image of ourselves, with maybe some long beards and AK47s. We think of them as organized along the lines of an army, with a commander-in-chief at the top of the pyramid: Osama bam Lambfuk, or whatever sociopath mass murderer happens to be au courant. The generals take orders from him, passing them on to colonels and captains and on down the ladder, until some dumb schmuck of a pimple-faced eighteen-year-old virgin turns himself into an exploding shitbox in the middle of the city.

But that's not an accurate picture.

Some organizations that use terror as a weapon are highly structured. Think of the PLO in its prime, Hamas at present, the Viet Cong, or even the early Nazi and Fascist parties if you want to stroll down memory lane. In cases like that, the groups' goals are usually pretty specifically political. Often they're related to a specific geographic area or grand cause—take over a country, exterminate a people.

Those are the sort of goals that require a large political organization, and the groups use terror as a weapon because it helps them achieve them. Or rather, they think it does, which is something else again.

But not every group that practices terror is organized, or even wants to be. If you just *hate* someone—nonbelievers, for example—then there's no need to elect a chairman to achieve your goal. You just go kill them.

These groups tend to be small, even a few dozen. When viewed from the outside, their organizational principles may look chaotic, even schizophrenic. But they're not usually. And the ones that are use that to their advantage.

Small means hard to infiltrate. Small means, potentially, disciplined.

It doesn't mean not capable of big things.

Some of the most dangerous groups operating today are very small cells of like-minded terrorists who have little if any formal connection to larger groups, or Osama bin Goatherder. Many have had contact with al Qaeda, bin Goatherder's favorite charity, but others just look at it as a model of inspiration.

Al Qaeda has directly sponsored a variety of terrorist actions, as we all know. But just as importantly they have acted as a financial seed organization for many. They take the CARE idea to the opposite extreme, providing money and training.

Al Qaeda isn't the only one—Iran has what is essentially a rival organization seeding its own brand of psychotic dickwads throughout the Middle East, and there's an Arabic dictionary's worth of groups willing to pass expertise and the occasional euro to anyone willing to take it.

All of this support has created a hothouse environment for terrorists. Many different groups, with different goals, are thriving. The one thing they have in common is—they like to kill innocent people.

In a way, it doesn't matter who exactly the group is, or even what their motivation is. It's the end result that concerns the general public. Murder sucks, it's got to be stopped.

A few years ago, the Virginia/Washington, D.C., area was terrorized by a nutcase and a teenage sidekick who decided they were going to snipe people for the hell of it. Were they any less effective because they didn't shout "God is great!" after every murder? Would we have been more concerned if they did?

Actually, we might have had quicker media coverage and a better response from law enforcement if they had, but that's more about us than them.

If you want to stop a murderer, mass or otherwise, you have to start by knowing what or who the hell it is you're up against. If you're looking for a sniper, you don't want to waste a lot of time analyzing who buys strychnine in the metro D.C. area.

Or to put it in biblical terms:

Know thy enemy, so that you may smote the motherfucker before he smoteth thee.

You'll find that in the Old Testament, Book of Marcinko, Chap. V, lines 32–33.

———

Not knowing who to smote, the Indian security forces went about smoting whatever the hell they could. Literally thousands of people were arrested all around the country.

I'm not saying that some or even most of these people didn't belong in jail, or that checking on them was a complete waste of time. But it wasn't the best use of resources, and there was a good deal of collateral damage. To take one example—the overnight doubling of the prison population in one of the states led to a riot, which led to a prison escape. Among the prisoners who escaped were two men who had organized a terror cell within the jail. That cell ended up perpetrating a series of terror incidents several months later—but we'll save that, and the danger of prisons as terrorist breeding ground, for another book.

Meanwhile, the politicians and press screamed that Pakistan was organizing and harboring terrorist groups. True statements, even if in this case they were made by people who had no idea what the hell they were talking about.

What you had was a massive domino effect—one terrorist action setting off a reaction, encouraging another, etc., etc. In a perverse kind of way, the reaction helped the terrorists: all of Islam is under attack, their arguments went. We need a holy war to end the persecution.

Start in India, move on to the Middle East. Eventually, all of Islam would rally to their brothers' cause. Islam would be reunited as a grand world force.

That may or may not have been anyone's actual plan, but it was hard to argue that events weren't leading in that direction as the cabinets in both countries began meeting around the clock and their armies were put on high alert.

How do you run a disarmament conference in the middle of that sort of crisis, let alone host a world-class sporting event?

Short answer: you don't.

But our State Department didn't figure any of that out. On the contrary, disarmament was now even more important.

Which made me suddenly a very popular person at the Foggy Bottom. Everyone wanted to get my perspective on the crisis.

It's nice to feel wanted.

Ha.

I did take *one* call, naively believing that maybe there was one person[13] in Washington who actually wanted an honest appraisal of the situation. It took all of sixty seconds for me to realize that the only thing the caller really wanted was some sort of cover for a position he'd already decided on.

My sat phone suddenly lost its signal. Quaint, but effective. I didn't bother taking any calls from Omar, either, or his lackeys.

I spent a few hours with NSG's investigative staff, reviewing what I knew and what I'd seen. I felt sorry for the guys I met with. Neither man had apparently known the dead agents, but you could tell the murders had affected them.

I know what that's like. When you're in a war, everyone you work with is a brother. "Do not ask for whom the bell tolls" isn't just the name of a famous novel or a line from a seventeenth-century poem, it's a statement of fact. We're all connected in battle.

After that, I headed back to my state-paid posh digs, figuring I ought to put in an appearance for whoever was watching my comings and goings there. My cab was blocked by several cars from a high-level African diplomat, who apparently had decided to bring half his family along for his official visit. I got out near the end of the driveway and trekked toward the entrance, still working over the different threads of everything that had happened during the day.

My guard was down—or, more specifically, up, as I was looking at the plainclothes security people accompanying the diplomatic delegation. Because of that, I missed the real threat—a miniature torpedo that struck my right knee and nearly knocked me over.

I looked down to find the urchin I'd chased into the slums a few mornings before. She was still wearing the prison shirt, now adorned with a variety of beads and buttons.

"There you are, U.S. Joe!"

She gave me one of those smiles they use to get money out of people in UNICEF ads.

"Let go of the leg, ragamuffin," I growled.

"My name is Leya, U.S. Joe! Don't you remember?"

She was a chirper. She had a bright voice to go with bright eyes. If you're in the business of outsourcing wake-up calls to India, she's your girl.

---

[13] Given that I don't want my passport revoked, I'm not using his name.

I reached down and unhooked her from my leg. She grabbed on to my hand with both of hers. The stuff they use on mousetraps is less sticky.

"Aren't you supposed to be in school?" I asked.

She laughed. It was the sort of laugh an IRS agent gives you when you ask if he's here to lower your tax assessment.

"What do you want?" I asked.

"You have a candy bar?"

"No, I don't have a candy bar. Go home."

"I know a lot about the boat."

"What boat?"

"You asked about a boat. I have answers, Bozo."

"Do I look like a clown to you?"

She giggled. It turned out she didn't actually know who Bozo was.

"Give me a candy bar," she said, "and I will tell you all about the boat."

You could look at it as extortion. Or a business deal. In my mind, though, it was charity—the skinny rail of a brat had to be at least ten pounds underweight.

I'd noticed a candy machine in the hotel lobby, around the corner from the desk. I took her inside and got her a Cadbury Crunchie Bar—ninety-nine cents anywhere in the world *except* for a ritzy hotel, where it cost five hundred rupees, a little more than ten bucks.

Then again, the stares from the hotel staff were probably worth twice that in sheer entertainment value. They looked at the kid as if she were a vampire child. They kept their distance, probably afraid of getting cooties if they got too close.

"Good work, U.S. Joe," she said, biting into the candy bar. "This is good candy!"

"You can call me Dick."

"You got it, U.S. Dick."

"So tell me about this boat," I said, leading her over to a couch at the far end of the lobby.

"Boat is train."

"Boat is train? What language is that?"

"You speak English, right, U.S. Dick? Or I can speak Indian for you."

She said something in Hindi.

"No, I speak English. Tell about this boat train."

"Boat becomes train."

147

She shrugged, and pushed the rest of the candy bar into her mouth. It cost me two more, but I finally got enough words out of her to realize what she was trying to tell me: the escaping prisoner had gotten onto a boat, which had then ridden down the train tracks to a hiding place not far from where she lived.

An absolutely brilliant piece of deduction on my part.

Which is not to say that it was anywhere near correct.

I had the desk call a taxi, which they were only too happy to do. Then, with the promise of more candy bars, Leya and I went for a ride.

She thought this was a fantastic idea; she'd never been in a cab before. The taxi driver gave us an odd look—God knows what he thought—but he didn't object to the address, and about a half hour later he dropped us off on the outskirts of her slum.

"Now take me to the place where this boat train is," I told Leya.

"Candy bar first, U.S. Dick."

"No, first I see the boat. Then we get something to eat."

She pouted, but took my hand and led me down a narrow alley not far from her hovel. I was beginning to smell a rat—among other things—when she suddenly let go and ran inside a squat yellow building.

Doom on Dickie.

I turned around, bracing myself for an ambush. But there was no one behind me. I backed against a nearby wall—gingerly; I didn't want it to fall over. A minute or so later, Leya reappeared with two other kids, a boy and a girl about her age.

"U.S. Joe take us for candy!" she yelled.

"You have the wrong idea," I said. "I'm not Santa Claus."

"They will tell you about the boat and train."

The others started talking really quickly.

"I want to see the boat," I said. "If I don't see the boat, no candy."

"Boat went away. Took the train."

"Who took the boat?"

"I rode the boat, U.S. Dick," said the boy.

More jabbering and bickering. I finally decided the best way to sort this out was on a full stomach—mine as well as theirs—and with brood in tow headed for the nearest food stall. Four helpings of *roti, murg,* and *dal* (bread, chicken, and lentils) later, I pieced together what they had seen.

The boy's name was Uma. His mother worked as a nanny in a house in the Abul Fazal enclave. He'd gone there to bring something to her, catching a ride on a city bus. He was supposed to go straight home, but, kids being kids, decided to go exploring instead. Apparently he had a habit of catching frogs or turtles in the swamp area there; he would sell them and use the money to buy candy or soda. He was by the water with a bag of critters when the car with the terrorists drove down.

Uma watched from the side of the swamp as they got out of the car and walked over toward the water. There were four men, and they were waiting for someone who hadn't arrived. Being curious, the boy slipped back to the car and looked inside.

Had he opened one of the front doors, he would have been burnt to a crisp. But Uma looked inside first, and either because he saw the clothes in the back or he was lucky, that was the door he opened.

He was just climbing inside when he heard a shout. He grabbed the shirt near him—he wasn't sure what it was at first—then slipped back into the shadows. Two of the men came running back to the car. Possibly they had seen the light inside the car go on, or heard something. In any event they searched around the area for a few minutes. Uma moved into the shadows, waiting for them to go. He'd left his bag with the critters by the water, and was working his way back toward it to retrieve it when he heard two boats approaching. One of the men by the water yelled to the others, and they all got into the boats and left, going south.

I must have arrived a minute or two later. By then, though, Uma had discovered that his bag of frogs was gone. He thought the men had stolen it, and started walking along the riverbank, determined to get it back.

"Were you crying?" asked his sister Bha.

"I never cry."

"I know you," insisted his sister. "You were bawling. Look—your eyes are even now still red."

He gave her a good punch and continued the story.

Uma made his way home, eventually getting a ride on the back of a truck, presumably without the driver's permission. Leya and his sister were friends; they'd been looking for him and scolded him severely when he returned. How Leya ended up with the shirt wasn't clear; he seems to have given it to her either in payment for some sort of debt, or because he believed she was his girlfriend, though when I suggested that, both Leya and Bha made faces.

The shirt was a trophy, but Uma wanted the frogs he'd left behind. The next day, he went in search of them. He didn't find them, but he did see the boats, tied to the edge of the river near some train tracks about a mile, he said, from where he had seen the men get in.

When he started looking around the embankment, a scary man with a submachine gun chased him away.

The boats turned out to be more like three miles from the Abul Fazal enclave. But the area the kid described was exactly as he said, a run-down industrial quarter downwind of one of the worst-smelling sewer plants you ever wanted to sniff.

I didn't see the boats when I visited there after dark. But I did see the scary guy with the submachine gun.

Two of them, in fact, standing outside a rusted steel warehouse.

The other two guys had AK47s. Even terrorists have to economize somewhere.

(III)

Convincing Captain Birla that we ought to raid the warehouse wasn't as hard as I thought it would be. Fatty's death had actually lifted his spirits—if the bad guys could get the better of NSG, well then Special Squadron Zero didn't look quite so bad.

Minister Dharma, however, was an entirely different story. She told Captain Birla that the unit was to lie low for the foreseeable future. The political shit storms rocking the country would magnify any failure, no matter how slight, and the resulting fallout would effectively kill the group.

I'm all for success, but you can't succeed by being afraid of failure. You have to be able to make mistakes. Canceling an operation because you're afraid that something will go wrong—or worse, someone will *think* that something went wrong—is surrendering before you even play the game.

Captain Birla agreed, and invited me to make that argument with the minister. And I would have—if she'd taken my calls. But the woman who had been playing footsies with me a day or two before now refused to acknowledge my existence.

And people say I have a way with women.

If you can't run an authorized op, then your only choice is to run an unauthorized one.

Which explains how I came to be crouching in the darkness near the train tracks that ran next to the warehouse at 0300 the following morning, holding my nose against the stench of the nearby river, waiting for a train.

A freight train that is. Not that I was planning on moving anything anytime soon, much less taking delivery of the garbage this particular train generally hauled. We were planning on using its sound as a cover to move in on the warehouse.

"We" consisting of Shotgun, Mongoose, Junior, Yours Truly, and several strangers who may or may not have had some association at some point with Special Squadron Zero.

I didn't ask who they were. They were wearing fleece masks, the sort a spec ops soldier would wear during cold weather to keep the snot from freezing in his nose. Everyone knows it can get awful cold in Delhi at night in the spring.

Wherever they came from, they certainly knew their business. Besides the cold-weather gear on their faces, they were also well equipped with submachine guns, armored vests, and even a shotgun or two. You gotta like strangers who come prepared.

"I hear a train a comin'," said Shotgun over the team radio.

I won't say he was singing, and I won't say he was doing a Johnny Cash imitation. As I just said, everyone needs the freedom to fail.

"Somebody coming out of the building," hissed Mongoose over the radio. "Heading in your direction, Dick."

Wasn't that special? We'd been watching the warehouse for almost two hours now, and no one had moved from inside. Now, just when the train was coming, someone came out and walked toward me.

Coincidence, probably. That and a straining bladder.

He assumed the position on the side of the building. The train, riding the rails about ten feet from the side of the building, gave a long wail.

"Go!" I said over the radio.

The diesel's whine and ground-shaking rumble covered my footsteps as I sprinted toward my target. He was just buttoning up when I hit him across the back of the head, sending him flying against the wall, right into the work of art he'd left there.

War is cruel sometimes.

I gave him another shot to make sure he'd stay down, then put my knee in his back, pulled his arms together, and ziplocked him like a trash bag. Another set of ties took care of his legs. I spun him over, then checked for a weapon.

Avoid the dirty jokes, please.

He had an old Walther PI combat pistol in his belt. Under other circumstances, I might have waxed poetic about this simple but sturdy German gun. But I had some ass to kick. I grabbed the weapon, slipped it into my vest, then moved around to the side of the building, where the team was preparing a new doorway.

There's nothing like some strategically placed plastic explosive to create a door in a hurry. It's a great technique—spec ops units use it all the time—but there are certain precautions you should use when employing this method.

Such as not using too much explosive.

Of course, for some people, there is no such thing as too much explosive.

Mongoose, who handled this one, is one of those people. The charge he set not only blew a wide hole in the wall; it took out part of the roof.

"Inside, inside," said one of the men[14] who were with us. Several of the team members rushed in, working the room so precisely they looked like an advertisement for a Discovery Channel program. Mongoose, Junior, and Shotgun followed. I brought up the rear.

The interior of the building was one large open space, divided by piles of boxes and lit by two or three small oil lamps. The area where we'd gone in was a sleeping room, with mattresses and blankets spread around. There were two men, though there would have been space for at least a dozen more. Both men had apparently been dozing when the wall blew out, and to call them stunned would be to understate their confusion by a factor of ten. They were quickly corralled by two mask-wearing team members while the rest of us went through the building.

The boxes made things interesting, but the strangers I was working with went about things very expeditiously. We found two other tangos in the warehouse. One was hiding in the clutter at the far end of the building. He put up his hands as soon as he was spotted, offering to surrender.

The other cowered in the corner not far from the sleeping area. He was hunched over, looking like a scared rabbit when we saw him.

"Up!" commanded one of the mask-wearing strangers.

The man in the corner complied. It was then that I saw the grenade in his hand.

Doom on Dickie. And everybody else in the damn building.

Four or five of the masked strangers fired simultaneously. They were good shots; the grenade-carrying rabbit fell straight back into the corner.

His grenade bounced out onto the floor.

Pinless.

Something flashed before my eyes.

It wasn't my life. It was Junior. He dove down at the grenade.

Of all the stupid, idiotic, dumb things he'd ever done, that had to be the most moronic.

---

[14] He had an Indian accent, but otherwise I have no idea who he might have been.

I could have kissed him.

Junior didn't throw himself on the grenade, as heroic as that would have been. He did something much more practical—he scooped it with his hand and tossed it up through the space where the roof had been. The grenade flew up in the air and arced just outside the building, where it exploded.

Not entirely harmlessly, however. The force of the blast crumbled what was left of the front wall of the building. Those of us who weren't already covering our private parts waiting for the grenade to blow covered our heads to keep the wall from shattering our skulls.

Fortunately, the wall was more loud than heavy. The pieces clattered down with a rumble that sounded like a thunderstorm, but aside from some bruises, they did little damage. I pushed my way out from under one of the panels, then helped Mongoose pull two of the strangers out.

"Shit," grumbled Shotgun. He started to run.

It looked for a second as if he were chasing the train. Then I realized that the man who had surrendered earlier had taken advantage of the confusion to run off.

I joined the chase, as did Mongoose and Junior.

"Stay with the rest of the Squadron Zero boys,"[15] I told Junior. "Make sure they round up the others. I left one in back."

Junior probably said something in protest, very likely adding a few insults about my alleged lack of sprinting speed. But I didn't hear it. I was too busy trying to catch my breath as I hustled after the others.

The train whose passing had initiated our attack was very long, with eight engines at the front and what had to be two hundred cars behind them. They were all what we used to call coal cars, but what my erstwhile copy editor claims are properly dubbed hoppers or gondolas, depending on whether they open at the bottom. I can't say definitively which choice was right, though I will admit that they were not coal cars, since they weren't carrying coal.

What they had in their large open bays was garbage. Lots of it.

It wasn't bagged in nice big Heftys either.

I had known it was a garbage train from the research we'd done earlier setting up the operation. But for some reason, that information hadn't

---

[15] So I lied about not knowing who they were. Arrest me.

really sunk in until, having grabbed the ladder at the side of one of the cars and climbed up, I sank into the contents.

I've been mired in worse swamps, but I don't care to relive those memories. I climbed, pushed, and slid my way above the junk and pulled myself to the next car.

"He's going toward the back," yelled Shotgun over the radio.

My first instinct was to turn around. Then I realized that I'd jumped onto the train after the others, and that I was at the back. All I had to do was wait.

Better than swimming in more garbage, believe me.

"I'm about five cars from the caboose," I told them over the radio. "Flush him back to me."

A poor choice of words.

I managed to get my feet on top of something solid and waited. Finally I saw a shadow of something ahead on the train. We were going around a curve and the cars leaned slightly to the right. I ducked down, hoping to blend into the general darkness.

Whatever you want to say about the guy we were chasing, he had a strong stomach. He was literally swimming across each car, pushing his way through mounds of rotted food and the worst possible detritus of everyday life. Indians tend to be rather poor and get the most out of everything they have. That means that when they throw something out, it's pretty far gone.

I was just about ready to hack my nose off when I saw my target emerging from the swill at the end of the next car. He pulled himself up on the lip of the compartment, steadied himself for a moment, then did a full gainer past me into the mound of rot at my right. I leaned and swatted my arm into the morass, hooking the back of his shirt. Hauling him up out of the debris, I grabbed the side of the car as leverage and I leaned over, intending to snap him against the metal and knock him out.

Murphy, who'd been teasing me all night, decided to take a more direct hand in the proceedings. The tango's shirt gave way, and my arm smacked against the hard ridge of the train car so hard it went numb.

Murph wasn't taking sides, though. Without my arm to hold him up, the terrorist dropped straight down into the swamp of garbage.

Another man might have leaned over and grabbed him. But I'm far too cruel for that—I leaned over and pushed the bastard down farther into the pile of crap he'd fallen into.

There was a flutter of garbage, then the surface calmed. I reached under, got a fistful of hair, then hauled him upward. He was gasping for air.

By that time, Mongoose and Shotgun had reached the car. I threw the tango over to them and leaned over the side, trying to clear my nasal passages.

"I don't think I've ever smelled anything this bad," said Mongoose, joining me after our prisoner had been hog-tied.

"I don't know," said Shotgun. "Kinda makes me hungry."

Not a normal human being, that boy.

[IV]

We de-trained a mile and a half later, as the train went up a grade. With his arms tied behind his back and his legs manacled together, I'm afraid our friend didn't take the fall from the car too well.

Life's like that sometimes.

The strangers sent a truck to retrieve us. We smelled so bad that the two men who'd been riding in the rear walked rather than ride with us.

Back at the base, we were doused with fire hoses before entering the building. A half hour in the shower later, we all smelled . . . like dog plop. Unfortunately, that was an improvement.

While we were taking in the smells of India, Junior had supervised a thorough search of the warehouse and its ruins. The cartons contained two dozen AK47s, a few Uzi submachine guns—oldies but goodies—and some Russian grenades so caked with grease and dirt that they must have dated from before World War II.

In the stacks of assorted clothes, he found two police uniforms, both freshly laundered. He also found a small stash of well-worn rupees, enough to buy everyone on the raid Chinese takeout for a week.

No papers, though, no computer. No obvious trail to the people who had set these guys up.

And no escaped prisoners.

There were, however, two cell phones.

Hold that thought.

Junior and the others repaired the warehouse as well as they could, setting pieces of the wall back in place so it didn't look quite as demolished as it really was. Then, with the help of some small, inexpensive video cameras and a Web feed, they set up surveillance on the area. A group of men were posted nearby, well out of sight.

In the meantime, Captain Birla went about trying to get information from the men we'd grabbed. This time the interrogation procedure was direct and immediate. The prisoners were not allowed to rest, much less sleep.

The results were mixed. Two of the men were actually cooperative, or at least willing to talk. They claimed to have been recruited for jihad three years before.

Both were residents of the Punjabi area of India, close to the Pakistan border. Disillusioned with life, they had been recruited at the local mosque by a fellow worshipper who claimed to know how people could make a real difference. Eventually, they made their way to Pakistan, where they were educated at a school similar to the one we had raided. After that, they had gone farther north into the tribal lands bordering Afghanistan, and done time with the al Qaeda–supported Taliban.

This was an apprenticeship, a testing time to see how loyal they'd be. Once they passed, they were brought to a finishing school—a training camp where they learned somewhat more advanced ways of blowing people up.

Both men had gone to college; one had an engineering degree, the other had majored in comparative literature. In many cases, a recruit's specific skills are exploited by terrorist groups, but at least according to their narratives, these weren't.

What? You understand how the engineer's skills could be used—if you can put things together, you can learn how to blow them up. But how does a lit major use his ability?

Language can be an invaluable skill in a place like India. Being comfortable with English can be a passport not just into the business world, but government as well. Embassies need locals comfortable with the language to function.

Proficiency in language isn't just a matter of knowing nouns and verbs, and when to use a participle. A man or woman who can understand idioms is a rare commodity in many places. Take our tango and put him in Kenya, say, where an Indian would be almost above suspicion, and he could practically run the place inside six months.

Fortunately, whoever was calling the shots in this case didn't do that. Instead, they sent both men here two weeks before to await further orders.

Neither man knew who had sent them. To hear them tell it, they had not been part of the operation to free our prisoners. In fact, they seemed to know very little about it. The night of the prison break, they had seen several men they hadn't seen before at the warehouse. But the men had left the next afternoon.

So why were they in Delhi?

They claimed to have no idea.

Captain Birla was convinced they were holding back.

"We will use more aggressive tactics, Commander Rick," he assured me. "We will find the information."

I wasn't so sure. Everything we'd seen indicated that the people we were dealing with were on the extreme side of the organizational scale.

In fact, they were so tightly organized, it seemed a wonder that any intelligence had been developed on them at all.

The third man refused to even give his name. He was the swift one who'd bolted into the garbage train. I guess if you could stand the strain of the refuse, you could deal with anything Special Squadron Zero threw at you.

Captain Birla wanted to waterboard him.

I said we should let him go.

"This is crazy talk," said the captain, shaking his head. "Rogue Warrior gone soft? Are you crazy?"

Crazy, yes. But there was a method to the madness. We had no leads. If we let him go—and followed him—the odds were that he would take us to more members of the cell. That might be back in Pakistan. Or it might be here in Delhi. In either case, we'd have a lot more information than we had now.

"To follow a man in Delhi, not easy," said Captain Birla. "If we lose him, a great scandal."

"First of all, you're not going to be in any more of a scandal than you already are," I told him. "There can't be more political pressure on you than there is now. Second of all, no one in the government knows you took these guys yet. We turn over two rather than three? Who's to know? The prisoners have been isolated from each other. They saw this guy run. The don't know that we grabbed him. And even if they did, who would believe them?"

Captain Birla was pretty troubled by the idea. Beating the asshole to a pulp, maybe scraping the skin off his scrotum layer by layer with a rusty razor blade—that would have been OK. But letting him go and following him through Delhi?

Too risky.

"We'll plant a bug on him that helps us follow him," I explained. "He won't get far."

Captain Birla frowned. I hadn't told him about the bugged prison clothes; that would have been a good argument against my plan. But in that case, the bugs had been planted as a precaution so the men could be tracked through the Indian prison and intelligence system. I was thinking of something much more effective.

"Where would you put a bug that he could not undo it?" asked Birla. "Or it would not be discovered?"

"Plenty of places, if we had the time," I told him. "But since we don't, we'll have to improvise."

"I do not like improvising."

"Trust me."

The captain sighed. "I am in your hands," he said finally. "What do we do?"

"First thing we do is step on his foot."

Actually, crush his toes.

I did the honors. I owed him something for that stroll through the garbage.

We played it very straight. He was fetched from his cell and walked down to one of the interrogating rooms. He was wearing a hood, mostly so he couldn't identify anyone later on, but it also added to his general disorientation.

One of the Special Squadron interrogators started barking at him as soon as he was in the room. The prisoner did his usual silent act. We let that go on for a few minutes, pretty much following the routine already established. He was standing, not allowed to sit—there were no chairs for him to use anyway.

Tired, he started to slump. I went over to him. The interrogator demanded to know if he was going to answer. When the man didn't, I planted my boot on his shoeless big toe.

It hurt. It had to. Hell, it hurt me.

Give the bastard credit. He didn't whimper. He started to fall back, but the guard shoved him straight up. He stood, ignoring the pain.

He was brought back to his cell. A few minutes later, the overhead light that had been on ever since he arrived was turned off. The blaring, hideously obnoxious Indian rap music that had been pounding the cell walls went silent.

Another half hour passed. A kindly doctor arrived. He removed the hood, examining the prisoner with the sort of gentle hand and easy bedside manner you can only find on obscure reruns of *Marcus Welby, M.D.*

He asked, in English, if the man's toe hurt.

The prisoner frowned, but then nodded.

"For the pain," said the doctor. "Morphine. See? You'll sleep."

Finally, the man showed fear. I don't think he was worried about being brain-washed—I think he didn't like needles.

That's fear we *all* understand.

He winced, but the shot was easily administered. The doctor positioned him back on the cot, then began to clean the outrageously stubbed toe.

The bottle was morphine, but what had been in the needle was a double dose of Demerol, and the fatigued prisoner quickly fell asleep. The doctor administered a dose of Novocain, dulling the nerves in the toe, then took out a scalpel.

I had to turn away from the monitor. Something about toenails sends shivers up my spine.

It was over in five minutes. Doc came out of the cell and met me at the end of the corridor.

Yes, our Doc, aka Al Tremblay. One of the last medical people in the world to still make house calls. Or cell calls, as the case may be.

"Planted it right under the toenail," he said. "It's working."

"Is it going to last a week?"

"Not my department. Talk to Shunt. Or Junior."

The tracking device was about the thickness of a nickel card and the size of a quarter. It wasn't exactly something you'd miss if it was implanted in your body, but under the battered nail it just looked as if the entire toe was bruised. Glued back, the only way to get it out would be to operate. As another precaution, Doc had layered the foot with bandages, and applied more local anesthetic.

Using the body as a kind of antenna, the device transmitted a pulsing signal through a radius of about two kilometers. The bug's greatest limitation was its battery, which had to be relatively small. According to the specs, it would last fourteen days, but I knew from experience that if we could get a whole week out of it we'd be doing well.

(The tracking bug wasn't *quite* state of the art—I'm told the CIA has better ones—but it was as good as the techie people at Law Enforcement Technologies in Colorado could do, which is damn high praise. Yes, I'm well acquainted with their work. Being on their board has certain advantages.)

The second phase of my plan began a few hours later, when our guest was woken from his slumber by two men in police uniforms and told to come along. He complied groggily. Only his hands were bound, and the police officers even asked if he wanted a wheelchair.

He declined. By now we had given him a nickname—Igor. Given the way he stiff-legged through the corridor, it seemed pretty appropriate.

The two other prisoners were also being moved. Their legs were chained, and unlike Igor, they were wearing hoods.

Two police cars and a van were waiting for them. Igor reached it first. One of the policemen put his hand on his head and started to duck him into the back. As he did, a bomb exploded nearby.

Shouts, confusion, cursing followed. Then more shouts, more confusion, more curses.

Gunfire. Lots of it.

Igor kept his head down. He started to crawl away. One of the policemen saw him, grabbed his legs, and began pulling him back to throw into the van. But before he got very far, a stream of bullets hit his chest. Blood spat everywhere and he tumbled to the ground.

It was a dramatic death. Sergeant Phurem was a bit of a ham, I'm afraid.

Two terrorists with AK47s ran up from the side building, spraying the area with lead. Igor managed to squirm to his feet and ran to them. The terrorists, who were wearing Arab-style scarves as masks, pushed him behind themselves and continued their suicide attack.

Then the van blew up. A giant fireball shot into the sky, flashing red and black in a pyrotechnical display that would have put many small-town Fourth of July celebrations to shame.

"You *really* have to cut back on the Semtex," I told Mongoose as we watched from our truck.

Igor, seeing no one at the gate, made his break. He ran straight out the front entrance, down the access road, and disappeared into a large field.

Disappeared from view, I should say. Mongoose and I were watching his progress on a laptop computer screen. Shotgun, in a truck with Doc on the other side of the field, was doing the same.

He got about fifty yards into the field and then stopped moving. I guessed he was trying to undo the ziplock handcuffs behind his back.

"Maybe we should have undone his hands for him," said Mongoose.

"Then we'd rob him of the great sense of achievement that he'll feel when he frees himself," I said.

Surveillance is a mostly boring, generally thankless job. You sit around waiting and watching, hoping something will happen and generally praying that it won't. So let's skip the afternoon and evening's worth of surveillance, during which the boys and I played follow the roaming tango, and skip over to see what Junior was up to.

When last we'd left Mr. Matthew Loring, he was examining two cell phones found in the terrorists' lair. Everyone knows that cell phones can be tapped and tracked. The trick is to avoid having that happen to you and, if it does, to minimize the risk that any one single episode will signal your downfall.

There are a variety of ways to do this. One of the most common is to buy prepaid or so-called pay-as-you-go phones or their sim cards, use them for a bit, then toss them. (Sim cards are the little chips that are like the phone's brains. They're tied to a specific phone number, so losing them is the same as losing the number.)

But prepaid phones are not a panacea. They, too, can give away a lot about the people using them—if you know where to look.

Junior went back to our private hotel and went to work. The first thing he did was check and see if the phones had been used. Phone A hadn't. Phone B had been used to place a call to another phone with a Delhi area number. That gave him one lead.

He then went to work tracking down where the phones had been bought. Over the last few years, many countries have adopted laws that require some form of identification to be given when phones or sim cards are sold—they're trying to cut down on the phones' use by criminals and terrorists. That's met with mixed success. There are plenty of places to get phones without showing any ID or having to pay with a credit card or something else that could be traced.

These phones, as Junior expected, had been purchased at one of those places. But he was able to track them to a wholesaler who had apparently supplied them.[16] Interestingly enough, though I guess not ultimately surprising, it was a legitimate wholesaler in Delhi.

There were a few ways Junior could have gone at that point to develop further information. He decided on a direct approach. He went to the wholesaler and told him he needed a dozen untraceable phones.

The operation was a smallish warehouse near the airport. It wasn't set up for retail, but it did have a receptionist, who gave him a cross-eyed look when he told her what he wanted.

"We do not do that," she told him. "We are not a retail store."

"You're very attractive, you know," he told her.

The girl furled her eyebrows.

"I know you can help me," he said. He bent over the desk, smiled, and gently took the pad from in front of her. "Have someone call me at this number."

He wrote his cell number on the pad. Then, after an exchange of significant eye contact, he walked out.

A half hour later, his phone rang, and he was instructed to return to the warehouse to meet a Mr. Joad. Junior thinks it was his flirting that got the receptionist to prod her boss; more likely it was the hundred-dollar bill he dropped on the counter as he turned around. In any event, he was soon back at the warehouse.

The girl, to Junior's disappointment, was gone. In her place was a large, smiling man in a flowered silk shirt. He smiled as Junior came in, nodded, then raised his arm to reveal a Beretta.

"Your money and your passport for your life," said the man.

"I must be in the wrong place," said Junior. He took a step backward, but found his way barred by another man, not quite as big as the first, though his rifle was twice the size as the other's pistol.

"You are definitely in the wrong place," answered the man behind the desk, rising. "That is why you will hand over your wallet and your passport."

"And if I don't?"

The man in front of him smiled. The one behind him swung his rifle butt first toward Junior's head.

---

[16] I think it's better that I don't give his actual methods here.

If Junior were telling this story, I imagine what happened would go something like this:

> *I heard a rustle as he swung the gun up. I ducked quick, spinning at the same time. I caught him in the gut, flipped him over my shoulder, and grabbed the gun.*
>
> *I could have plugged the prick behind the desk with a few rounds, but I needed them both alive. So instead I just shot the gun out of the asshole's hand, then gave him a good smack across the mouth to show him who the hell he was dealing with.*

But Junior's not telling the story, I am. And I like to be somewhat accurate. So here's what really happened:

The thug behind him swung and connected, smacking Junior halfway into next week. He somersaulted across the room, crashing into a stack of phones that had just arrived from assembly in Bangladesh. At that point, the two men hauled him to his feet and began wailing on him, taking turns smacking and punching his dazed frame.

This could have gone on for quite some time, had a shotgun blast over their heads not gotten their attention. The goons turned around to see Trace Dahlgren standing near the door, a shotgun packed with birdshot in her hand.

"Next round takes your balls off," she promised.

Unfortunately, the man on the left didn't believe her.

He took a step, then crumbled to the ground as Trace fired point-blank into his midsection. The shotgun had been loaded with rock salt—it wasn't going to kill him, but it sure didn't feel good. He whined and whimpered in a very high-pitched voice.

Junior pulled himself off the floor where he'd been dropped.

"You sold a bunch of phones to a terrorist group a few weeks ago," he told the other man, who was now shaking. "You're going to tell me all about it."

The man said something in either Hindi or some other local language that Junior couldn't understand.

"We're not fucking around, asshole," said Trace. "You tell us what we want to know, or we plug you like we plugged your friend. And then we'll call the cops."

The man and his partner ran a thriving black market operation, and I'm sure he didn't want to let the local police in on it. But odds are that the threat of that buckshot in his groin had a little more to do with his willingness to talk.

According to him, they never sold to terrorists—not directly, anyway. Most of their illegitimate business was carried on directly with the Indian underworld. There were, however, a few stores where the phones might have been obtained.

Prompting from Trace got the most likely one—a place not far from the slum where little Leya and her friends lived.

"If you're wrong, we'll be back," said Trace.

"I swear it on my mother's head," said the man.

"And your gonads?" She aimed the gun at his privates.

"On those, too. I swear."

He looked sincere. Trace gave him a whack anyway.

"If there's a next time, I'll be packing buckshot," she told them as she left.

[V]

Meanwhile, our friend Igor had found his way to a junkyard on the other side of the field. There he got a piece of metal sharp enough to slice through the thick plastic binding his hands. He cut his arm to hell, but given everything else that he'd been through, that was a minor consideration. Waiting until dark, he crossed into the nearby residential area and stole some clothes. Changed, he began walking in the direction of the city.

We took turns following, one car going ahead, the other trailing, as he slowly worked his way toward the heart of the city.

By ten P.M. he had arrived at a squatters slum not far from Deer Park, a large preserve intended by the city planners to provide some green space in the dense urban gray. The park is a beautiful place, with wildlife and an art gallery, a skating rink and sports facilities. There's a shopping area nearby that tourists visit, and, yes, even a place for deer, who are fenced in so as not to bother the visitors.

And then there's the slum. It's basically the same sort of place that Leya lived in, nicer in some spots, worse in others. There were a few more alleys, and the largest huts might have been a little bigger and arguably in better shape, but *Better Homes and Gardens* wasn't going to be doing a photo shoot there anytime soon.

We mapped the place with the help of some satellite photos off the 'net. We stayed out of the slum itself—we would have stood out like pimps at a church social.

Igor went to a hut about fifty yards from the entrance to the slum. That distance is as the crow flies. The convoluted path he had to take to get there was five times that. The hut turned out to be visible from the roof of an office building about a half mile away. Within an hour, Special Squadron Zero had a team with an infrared scope there; they could see anyone coming in or out of the house.

Igor's sensor had stopped moving, except for the occasional shudder; he had gone to sleep.

Sometime around then, Junior and Trace came to update me on their cell phone adventure. This earned Trace a tongue-lashing—she was supposed to be with the field hockey team.

"What?" she asked. "I hit some balls with a stick. Wasn't that my assignment?"

Everybody's a wiseass.

With things under control, I told Doc to take Trace back to the school. Then I had some of Captain Birla's men swap out with Shotgun and Mongoose, who'd been working nearly nonstop for the past few days and needed a break.

Junior and I hung out with Captain Birla for another hour or so, getting a tour of the area in the process. Then I had him drop us off at a restaurant a few blocks away, telling him we'd join his relief in the morning.

While the goal of our little operation was primarily to gather intelligence about India for Islam's local network, I did have an ulterior motive: find the traitor in Special Squadron Zero, assuming there was one. Someone had told the terrorists where their people were, and the main suspects were still the members of the squadron. Just because Captain Birla didn't think any were turncoats didn't mean they weren't.

And yes, he was a suspect, too.

We had supplied the team radios and had the encryption codes as well as the frequencies, so eavesdropping on the radio circuits was child's play. The units also had an always-on feature. Under normal circumstances, that allowed you to talk to everyone on the team without having to press a talk button, obviously convenient during an operation. With a little engineering—very little, though that's easy for me to say since I didn't do it—Junior had programmed the function so we could use the radios basically as bugs, listening in on everyone on the surveillance team. I'd also planted a few bugs back at the headquarters building.[17]

All of these sources gave us a tremendous flow of audio—far too much for one or two people to sort through. Then there was also the problem of having to translate the conversations that weren't in English, as most weren't.

We partly solved the problem of information overload by using Junior's computer network to send the data streams to Shunt, who was working from New York. He managed to turn out near real-time transcripts of mostly remarkably dull conversations.

---

[17] You may think that this means there is a way to get around the standard sweeps for electronic bugs that Special Squadron Zero and others use. I have no comment on that.

I assumed that Shunt had concocted some sort of computer program until I checked in with him.

Uncharacteristically, he had taken a low-tech though admittedly modern approach to the problem: he'd outsourced the real-time translation to a company in southern India.

"Isn't it great?" he asked. "These guys do ticket sales for the World Series and stuff. This is their downtime."

I could have kicked his ass.

"How fuckin' secure do you think that is?" I practically shouted—and I have to say, I've removed most of the four-lettered words here.

"I told them it's for a TV show. No worries, Dick."

"Shunt, when I get back to the States, I'm going to put your head under a magnet and pull your skull apart."

"Won't work," he said cheerfully. "Everything inside is aluminum or plastic now."

"Cut the translators off right *now*," I told him. "And find another way of figuring this out."

"Oh." There was a tone of deep regret in his voice, your puppy after it's peed on the rug. "Sorry, skipper."

A thorough review of the transcripts to that point revealed that most of the discussion was about getting something to eat. Igor was mentioned once—and called Igor—and the context gave nothing away.

Luckily for Shunt.

Junior and I had a little time on our hands. We got something to eat, checked back with Shunt, who was in one of his Asian moods: "Translator still offline, boss. Very sorry."

With things slow, I decided to pay the phone retailers a visit.

The store was a narrow wedge of space in a one-story building made of what looked like a sampler collection of every brick known to man. Every conceivable size and color was represented in the walls. The only thing they had in common was that all were rectangular, after a fashion. They ranged from about two inches by two inches to eighteen by twenty-four. The mason who had assembled the place must have been a killer on jigsaw puzzles.

The store—Muwhat & Sons—had a glass door reinforced by a metal grid. The floor and nearby shelves were lined with old appliances and gadgets, radios, toasters; there were even a few crates of old shoes. A small sign on a cluttered table near the front proclaimed that they could "fix U while U wait."

The place was closed, not surprising given the late hour. We took a walk around the block and found a back entrance. I proposed a reconnoiter. To my surprise, Junior objected. And not without reason.

He pointed out that we were unlikely to come away with any real information. It was doubtful that the proprietor was keeping records.

"Even if we find a bunch of phones, that's not going to tell us anything," said Junior.

"If we go in now, it'll help us know what to expect when we come back and pay the owners a visit during the day."

"Oh, I don't mean that we shouldn't go in," he said. "I just think we should do more than look around."

"Like what?"

"I think we should bug the place. Better yet, we should bug the phones."

Damn bright kid.

Bugging the store was easily accomplished—we'd just return to the Maharaja Express, grab a few goodies, then come back and put them in place.

Tapping into the phones, however, was a more ambitious project involving special sim chips[18] that, unfortunately, we didn't have in India.

Special Squadron Zero didn't have them either. I wasn't sure, in fact, whether any of the Indian intelligence agencies did.

I knew the CIA did, though. It was just the sort of technical assistance the Christians in Action loved to provide.

So I gave Omar a call.

You would have thought I asked for a million dollars. Actually, getting a million dollars would have been easier.

It wasn't that Omar didn't want to help. On the contrary, he sounded almost pleasant—for Omar, at least. But as soon as he mentioned that he had to talk to "home base" first, I knew there would be trouble.

Home base being a euphemism for CIA headquarters at Langley, I assume.

He called me back a half hour later, saying that he had preliminary approval to proceed.

"Good. When can I pick up the chips?" I asked.

---

[18] There are several ways to tap into cell phones. The method we're talking about here would have created what you might think of as a "party line"—we'd be on the same circuit as the caller.

"Whoa, hold your horses. I didn't say we got an OK. I got approval to put in a request."

I won't waste your time with the tortured trail of approvals he needed before he could actually requisition what we needed. I'm going to guess that a dozen lawyers were involved in the process, each vetting a different aspect. There was a political officer who would weigh in on the political ramifications, a PR officer who would decide on what the public relations angle would be, a parking officer to figure out where we would park . . .

I'm exaggerating. I'm sure they would have let us park where we wanted.

It was a moot point by then anyway. Junior had come up with an alternate idea.

We didn't necessarily need to use special sim cards. As long as we knew what the numbers were, we could use our connections to get into the lines.

Of course, the fact that the numbers had not yet been assigned was a problem. But that, too, could be easily solved—all we needed were the serial numbers. Once they matched, bingo.

Except that the numbers were protected by a scratch-off strip. Once the strip was gone, anyone paying attention would realize that the number had been recorded.

I'd have been willing to bet that ninety-five percent of the people who bought the phones wouldn't realize that. But we had to worry about the other five percent.

Junior's solution was easy—we'd have Special Squadron Zero go to the Indian phone company and have some new cards made. Then we'd slip them into the store. No high-tech wizardry—the Indians could do this all on their own.

The only problem was knowing which service provider to use. Unlike the U.S., India has a lot of providers—I stopped counting at two dozen.

The only way to find out was to take a look. Which brought us back to my original plan.

There were three locks on the rear door. While Junior went to work picking them, I went and had a look in the nearby window. A light was on in the back, just bright enough for me to see inside.

When originally built, the architect had made the stores of medium size, forty or sixty feet across. This had proved much too large, and the individual spaces were gradually partitioned smaller and smaller. Some of the partitions were standard walls, all the way to the ceiling, as the wall on the right side of the shop was. But the wall on the right side at the back had apparently been built as a temporary structure, and stopped a good two feet from the ceiling.

A lot of people lock their doors but forget their windows. Muwhat & Sons' neighbor was a case in point. I was inside the building before Junior got the second lock picked. I pushed open the door and ushered him inside.

"Where do you think they keep the phones?" he asked.

I was about to answer when I heard footsteps charging in our direction. Or should I say, paw steps?

I made it to the doorway to the interior just in time for a set of fangs to snap onto my arm. I'm not sure what kind of dog it was, but it was big. The jaws felt like a tiger's.

Yes, I have had the unfortunate pleasure.[19]

Junior kicked the mutt in the side while I pushed it out of the room. The bastard refused to let go until we were able to wedge the door closed against its snout.

I must've tasted better than its usual dog food. The damn thing was so determined to get another piece of me that it threw its head against the door, yapping and barking, scraping its paws against the thin wood. The door had obviously been built by the same carpenter who'd fashioned the low partition—it shook violently, threatening to give way.

I'm sure Murphy's Law has a whole set of corollaries regarding ferocious dogs and the whereabouts of items protected by them. Suffice to say that a quick search failed to turn up the sim cards or the phones. The dog huffed and puffed the whole time.

"He must be hungry," said Junior.

Good guess.

"Go down to that Chinese restaurant we spotted," I told him. "Get some chicken. I think there was a drugstore near there—get some child's cough syrup with lots of antihistamines."

"Not a tranquilizer?"

"If you can find a tranquilizer, go for it," I told him. "Get the strongest thing you can get."

Junior came back in a half hour. He had persuaded the druggist to give him twenty-four pills of a generic Ambien drug, your basic sleeping pill.

I had no idea whether it would work on a dog, but we decided to try

---

[19] See *Holy Terror*, et al.

it. Junior ground the pills into a fine powder and mixed them with kung fu chicken. Getting the door open without letting the dog into the office was tricky, but once the mutt had its snout in the container of takeout, he was a changed animal. He practically inhaled the food, then tore the cardboard apart and chewed it up as well.

He gave a few growls in our general direction, took a few steps toward the front of the store, then promptly collapsed. Within seconds, he was snoring peacefully, undoubtedly happily chasing cats in his dreams.

The interior of the store was Martha Stewart's worst nightmare. There were layers of grime that had been old when the British first reached the continent. Boxes of everything from razor blades to toothpaste lined the shelves.

"I'll work from the front back," I told Junior. "You start here."

There were old fans and baby carriages that had more rust than metal on them. Some of the shoes looked like they had been made in the eighteenth century.

I did find a nice pair of winter gloves.

"We interested in AK47s?" asked Junior. "How about grenade launchers?"

A half-dozen Russian-made RPG-7s were stowed in a pair of metal footlockers beneath a pile of Indian porn magazines. The AK47s were across the aisle with canned goods.

We found the phone section near the iPod knockoffs. There were sim cards with keys for eight of the country's largest cell providers. Right next to the phones were radios that featured encryption as good as the units I used.

"This place is a Wal-Mart for criminals," said Junior. "We just going to leave it all here?"

He had a point—the items weren't exactly going to be used to cure cancer. But blowing up the place wasn't going to help our immediate goal. We had to leave the goodies in place.

We did compromise in one area—I undid the grenades and modified the fuses so they wouldn't explode.

I was just finishing the last grenade when a foul odor nearly knocked me over.

"Not me," said Junior. He glanced at the mutt, slumbering peacefully back by the office partition. "It's Chinese food dog farts."

"Don't light a match," I said, quickly finishing with the grenade.

[VI]

Captain Birla came up with cards for two of the country's largest cell phone providers; Junior made the swap the next morning while one of the Special Squadron Zero members pretended to be in the market for some gravy boats.

He remarked later that the place smelled like the best Chinese food he'd ever eaten.

The two days that followed were a mixture of surveillance, frustration, and dead ends. The cell phones stayed unbought and silent. Igor remained in his little hut for twenty-four hours, then went to an even smaller house on the other side of town. Special Squadron members tracked him across the city, and now we had two houses under surveillance.

The first house held six people in a single room that couldn't have measured more than ten feet square. The sole adult male—we figure he was the father—picked rags at a local dump and brought them home; the oldest woman, his wife, cleaned them in fetid wastewater outside their hut, then sold them. One of the children helped the father get the rags. She was about eight. The others, none older than six as far as I could tell, stayed with the mother while she worked.

We spent a lot of time trying to figure out the family's relationship to Igor. We eventually decided that he had chosen them at random, so exhausted he simply took the nearest open door. He may have told them a story about having been beaten up by robbers. Or maybe he had managed to find a few coins in the clothes he stole, and paid them for the night's stay.

However it worked, it turned out to be a big mistake. Their possible link to the terrorist network was passed on to the state secret service after we left the country. The unit promptly took all of them into custody. Mom and Dad were questioned and eventually got prison sentences for helping a terrorist. The kids went to an orphanage. I'm not sure how any of that made India safer, but I'm sure some local politician there made the claim.

The second house Igor went to was a legitimate terrorist safe home, a "squat" in a slum not too far from where the Commonwealth Games were to be held. He arrived around eight at night, and stayed until the following afternoon. The family circumstances at the second house were almost exactly the same—this father had a slightly better job sweeping a factory at night, and the wife cleaned toilets, but I would have been hard-pressed to tell the difference between the two families. It was only when we followed the father to his job at the factory that we discovered the terrorist connection.

To a group called People's Islam.

Sounds sorta kinda like India for Islam, except it's not.

And that was where things became even murkier.

Which is to say, the muddy details I'd been trying to decipher blurred into solid black nothingness.

I'm trying to skip as much of the boring intel and blind alleys we took as possible. But if you're playing along at home, this quick dossier might help make things a little clearer:

The full list of terror groups active in India could fill a telephone book. Throw out the pseudonyms and unintentional duplicates, and you still have several pages. Put the Maoists to one side, and add the people involved in Sri Lanka and Bangladesh, and the list will be a manageable dozen or so pages.

Alphabetically, India for Islam hits just about page four. It's relatively new, though with the Pakistani connections it certainly had its potential.

People's Islam is over on page seven, about halfway down. It has some potential as well, though no connections (known, anyway) to Pakistani intelligence or its political parties. It doesn't have bases in Kashmir to draw soldiers from, another drawback. It has ambitions, though, and at least according to rumor, contacts with al Qaeda.

You'd think from the title that there was something communist associated with them—any country with the words "people's democratic" in it almost inevitably has a communist dictatorship. It's partly true here. One of the founders of People's Islam had been a communist before undergoing an Islamic "rebirth." As he pulled like-minded nuts together, he kept "People" in the title of his group.

There were apparently links to the larger Maoist party, but it's unclear how strong that connection was. No matter, because it seems to have ended completely when the leader conveniently blew himself up while trying to make some bombs to celebrate a religious holiday.

The group soldiered on. Over an eighteen-month period in 2008–10, they took credit for three terrorist bombings. Two killed only the bomber because of problems with the equipment; the third killed three people including the bomber.

From the distance, it would look like India for Islam and People's Islam were just a couple of identical bad apples in a very rotten bunch. But that's our point of view. From their point of view, the two groups were rivals for funding and affection from a variety of sources, most especially Osama bin Goatfuckin'. And even more importantly, they were competing for followers and fans.

I didn't know this at the time. When I saw the name, I thought it was just another nom de terror for the assholes we'd been dealing with.

Captain Birla and his G-2 man put me straight.

"Very surprising here, Commander Rick," said Captain Birla. "They are working together. An ominous development."

Ominous because two very different groups, with no known connections, had worked together in an elaborate operation to free our prisoners.

The intelligence agencies started working on that idea full-bore. In no time at all, they had pieced together mountains of evidence that showed that not only were India for Islam and People's Islam working hand-in-hand, but a whole bunch of other groups on that list of alphabetically sorted terror organizations were teaming up. Maoists and jihadists, Sunnis and Shiites, Yankee and Red Sox fans.

The Commonwealth Games were going to be Armageddon.

A few hours after they reached that determination, one of the government ministers issued a statement saying that the terrorists who had struck the helicopter factory had probably had an "Indian handler" who helped guide them. It was a classic chapter in the book of *Utterly Unhelpful Political Statements Issued by Politicians Who Know Jack About What's Going On.*

It probably didn't seem that significant to the minister at the time. It echoed another statement made a few months before by the home minister who said that the Mumbai attacks—known in India as 26/11—had been facilitated by "an Indian handler whose true identity has yet to be ascertained."

Or someone who looked like an Indian. Or could have looked like an Indian. Or might have thought he looked like an Indian.

But in a tense India, the statement was a lit match. The reaction was immediate:

Real Indians would never be involved in terrorist acts. How can you say such a thing!

The uproar drowned out his real message, which was that local police should be better integrated into the security network.

Americans shouldn't feel too smug. We have a hard time facing the truth as well, even when it's presented with a paragraph's worth of qualifiers.

The swirling political storm was weighing on Minister Dharma. Finally taking my calls—it felt like the first day of spring—she asked that I brief her on the situation in her office. She gave me one of her thousand-megawatt smiles, but she seemed only mildly interested in my suggestion that People's Islam be targeted by Special Squadron Zero the same way India for Islam had been.

"You are very persistent, Richard," she told me, arms folded across her bosom. "But we are not in America."

"Just giving you my advice," I said. "That's what you hired me for."

"Maybe that was a mistake."

Oh, ouch.

She stared at me for a few seconds. A beautiful woman's glare can be an intimidating weapon, and I'm sure she had castrated dozens of men with hers. I just smiled. At that moment, her stare reminded me of my ex-wife's.

"I can resign if you want," I said.

I wasn't really thinking of resigning, but the offer wasn't a threat either. While we'd lose a certain amount of revenue, there was no sense continuing to work for people who didn't want me.

"No. That's all right. Of course you must stay on and help us. You are invaluable."

The daggers in her eyes changed to tulips as she turned on the charm, talking about how I must come to the party she was having in a few days. Before I got a chance to decline, there was a knock on her door. Two of her aides came in, and her manner made it clear I was dismissed.

The reason for the blow-off was soon pretty obvious. The intelligence Special Squadron Zero had developed was shared by the minister with the Indian intelligence establishment. Rather than focusing on either of the two groups, there was a fresh cycle of arrests. None of those brought into custody, alas, were members of either India for Islam or People's Islam.

What are the odds, huh?

Well, at least the entire Indian military, intelligence, and security apparatus was now focused on a massive threat, alerted to the most serious problem and danger facing the country.

Dream on. You clearly haven't been paying attention.

It was Junior who raised the most serious objection to the theory of an India for Islam–People's Islam alliance.

We were reviewing our days at a debrief/bullshit and beer session at our safe hotel three days after letting Igor "escape." He was now at yet another safe house several miles outside of Delhi. Special Squadron Zero had just officially turned him over, and was concentrating on the Commonwealth Games.

No questions had been asked about how the information had been developed regarding Igor, but it was known that he was connected to the two prisoners who had disappeared and were still at large.

"If these groups were getting together," said Junior, swigging from his beer, "wouldn't there have been a hell of a lot more intelligence before all this happened?"

"That's not how it works," I said. "They're not going to send out Twitter updates every ten minutes."

You'd think he'd be impressed that I knew what Twitter was, but no.

"There should have been *some* communications traffic," insisted Junior. "Look at everything we got on India for Islam."

"Most of it is worthless," I told him.

"Sure. But there was at least some volume. No Such Agency[20] should have reams of intercepts and other shit connecting these two groups."

"They could have met in person."

"You still have to send some sort of notice back and forth."

"Maybe the NSA has the intercepts," said Doc. "They're just not sharing with the Indians. Who aren't sharing with us."

That was a good point—except that I thought the admiral would

---

[20] Also known as the NSA = National Security Agency. They gather electronic intelligence. If your toaster's bugged, blame them.

have mentioned something along those lines when we spoke. And whatever else you wanted to say about the Christians in Action and the No Suchers, they did tell each other what was up.

Four or five times out of ten.

"Dick always says life follows the KISS principle," Junior countered. "Keep It Simple, Stupid."

"I see the Stupid part," said Shotgun. "Where's the rest?"

"There has to be a simpler explanation," said Junior. "To us, these groups are all basically the same. But if that were really true, they wouldn't be forming so many. They were rivals up until now."

"The enemy of my enemy is my friend," said Doc.

"The first murder was between brothers," countered Junior.

"Maybe they were recruiting them," said Shotgun.

"That's a possibility," said Junior.

"Under that theory, they kill Fatty because why?" asked Doc.

"Because he was a spy."

"How'd they know?"

"We have a traitor inside Special Squadron Zero."

"A traitor who let the mission proceed? We nailed over two dozen of them there."

"My head hurts," said Shotgun.

"Have some more beer," said Doc.

You have to admit, the man knows his medicine.

Neither Mongoose nor Trace were at the meeting. Trace had a competition the next morning, and making the meeting would have meant blowing a bed check. Since we didn't want her banned from the team, she stayed at the dorm.

Mongoose, however, was officially AWTTMO—Absent While Trying To Make Out.

He'd gone back to the gym several times to work out or meet Vina, depending on whether you believe his official story or his hormones. After quite a bit of work, he'd managed to convince Vina to go to dinner with him. Dinner was followed by an evening at one of the hotel's clubs, where they danced and necked for a few hours.

I'm not sure what else they did, but Mongoose's butt dragged pretty low at PT the following morning. I even beat him on the run—put a star on the calendar for me.

Sean wasn't making much headway in Islamabad. The connection to People's Islam gave him another excuse to talk to our contacts, but all he got were blank stares.

With one exception.

"Very ambitious," said a contact in the government passed off to us by a former SEAL who does some contract work for the CIA from time to time. "Trying to prove themselves with the jihadists because of the commie connection. But I'd keep my eye on them."

"They work with India for Islam?"

"Not a chance. India for Islam is hard-core Muslim. They're to the right of Osama bin Laden. Way, way, way to the right. That's how they got their funding."

Sean nodded.

"India for Islam is hurting," added our informant. "They got their clocks cleaned a week or so ago. You wouldn't know anything about that, would you?"

Sean shook his head sadly. "I've been missing all the good stuff lately."

I was just coming out of the hotel gym headed for the shower the morning I finished ahead of Mongoose when two members of Special Squadron Zero met me in the hall.

"Commander Rick, the captain needs to see you now," said the senior man, a corporal who I remembered as one of the team's best shots.

"Soon as I hit the shower, boys," I told him. "I'll wash off, grab some clothes—"

"Commander Rick, please," said the corporal. "There is an operation under way."

"What sort of op?"

The corporal glanced around, making sure he was alone.

"They have found the helicopters," he whispered. "Please. Time is of the essential."

Who am I to argue about fractured English? If they could brave the b.o., so could I. I tossed down my towel and followed them out to their car.

(1)

The two helicopters had been traced to an area about 150 miles northeast of Delhi. The area was extremely rugged.

Pull up Google Earth and make a line at about two o'clock straight out from the city, and all you'll see are swirls and squiggles. A few highways tread through the mountains, cutting back and forth with the terrain. They're narrow, and have more curves than the Miss America Beauty Pageant. Villages cling to the sides of the roads like rats climbing up a rope.

The helicopters were said to be located in the yard of a building at the outskirts of one of these villages. The building had once been the center of a small fortress outpost, held during the Mughal times but abandoned well before the British moved in. The Indian air farce had spotted the choppers on the ground after a series of painstaking reconnaissance flights. The location wasn't exactly on a straight line from our flight, but it was well within the helicopters' flight capabilities.

Since it found them, the air farce got to put together the welcome home party. Special Squadron Zero had not been invited—originally. But as the air force pooh-bahs began drawing up their plans, they realized they didn't have enough ground troops in that area to grab the aircraft that night.

Rather than waiting several days—I have no idea why it would have taken them that long, or why they didn't have a suitable force in Delhi to begin with—they decided they would share some of the glory. Of course, they were pretty selective about who they wanted, choosing partly on the basis of whom they figured would be least likely to try and steal the press, and partly on the basis of political connections.

Whatever.

The upshot was that Special Squadron Zero had been assigned to cut off the road near the compound, isolating it from a village about two-thirds of a kilometer away.

You're thinking:

What the @#$#$ does the Indian air farce know about ground operations?

The air farce actually does have a capable special operations unit—the

Garud Commando Force. There are somewhere in the area of fifteen hundred men in the unit, all trained in various facets of force operation and spec ops warfare. Some of them were in the Congo recently, and earned good praise there. They've worked with Indian army special forces in Kashmir. A few of their officers have trained with our air farce units in the U.S.

I won't hold that against them.

The Garud members are pretty dedicated. There should have been more coordination among the officers of the different units working with them, but that's probably more of a quibble, really, and frankly something that could be said across the board.

More critical were the limits on the operation imposed by their helicopters, which were being pushed to their operating limits because of the high altitude. They solved that problem, but things would have been easier if they'd had up-rated ships like Special Squadron Zero's.

Chinooks wouldn't have hurt either. But I'm not in charge of procurement.

No, the problem with the operation had nothing to do with the commandos assigned to it, or even the officers. The politicians—they're a different story.

I rode with Captain Birla in Pangong 1, the Mi-8TV/India helo we'd taken into Pakistan. Shotgun and Mongoose, fighting off his hangover, were in Pangong 2, an Mi-8 with up-rated engines just barely able to make the climb.

Our assignment was simple—we would arrive at a spot north of the village exactly two minutes ahead of the main assault team. We'd rappel onto the highway, stop traffic, and act as reinforcements for the main team, which was hitting the compound with Hinds.

Trees were scattered throughout the area, and there was no suitable place for our aircraft to land, so they would have to pull donuts nearby. Once the compound was secure, they would go off and refuel, then return before picking us up.

Things started out fine. All the helicopters got off without incident and rendezvoused in the air about thirty minutes from the target. So far so good. They flew together for some period of time—it may have been twenty minutes, may have been less—then split up for their assignments.

There were several other non-Garud elements in the task group. Some army special ops guys were taking the other side of the road, another unit was heading north to a building they thought might be a related safe house, etc.

Anyway, we were five minutes from our drop zone when Captain Birla's radioman turned to him with an odd expression on his face. He handed the captain a handset he had, his eyes almost crossed.

"We scrubbing?" I asked after Captain Birla handed the phone back.

"No. We're on television."

He didn't mean that literally, but he could have. Someone in the Indian government had leaked the information that the helicopters had been found, and that an operation was currently under way to recover them.

I'm proud to say that I have been involved in many SNAFUs, and more than my share of goatfucks and FUBARs. But this was a new one on me. I can't think of an American operation that was compromised by a politician while the assault force was en route to its target.

Of course, now that we know it's possible . . .

There was nothing to do but play it through, hoping that the terrorists weren't paying attention.

We reached our target about twenty seconds ahead of schedule. We rappelled down to the road, set up a roadblock, and waited.

We couldn't see the target building from where we were, but we were plenty close enough to hear the helicopters, and the RPGs and machine guns that greeted them.

Raise your hand if you're *not* familiar with the Russian Hind.

Who's that in the back?

All right, nugget, we'll give you an info dump. Rest of the class—smoke 'em if they're legal.

The Russian-made Hind is a combination gunship troop transport that the Russians perfected in the 1970s after watching how we had used helos in Vietnam.

It comes in several varieties. There's the Mi-24, which was the first and, unfortunately for its crews, flawed version; the Mi-24A, which took care of most of these deficiencies; the Mi-24D/Mi-25, which tends to be used more as an assault ship than a transport; and the MI-35 Hind E, which brought destruction to admirable levels.

All of these aircraft share the same basic layout—gunner in the nose, pilot above him, crew area in back. As a general rule, they can carry eight troops, unless they're all Shotgun's size. Exact weapons depend on the version and the crew chief's felonious tendencies, but among other goodies there's a four-barrel 12.7mm machine gun, a twin 30mm, and your basic assortment of rockets, Gatlings, antitank missiles, and small bombs.

In short, one nasty son of a bitch.

The advantage of combining a gunship with a troop carrier is that your assault team is never without shitloads of firepower. One of the disadvantages is that it's tough to carry out two jobs at one time.

Another disadvantage is that if one of your attack ships goes down, you lose part of your assault team.

The helicopters began by suppressing the ground fire, but the barrage of RPGs and shoulder-launched surface-to-air missiles that met them was pretty ferocious. One of the Hinds crashed at the edge of the compound. Only one man was killed—the aircraft gunner in the nose—but everyone else aboard was injured, most seriously.

The other helos took out their frustrations on the house, where most of the tangos were holed up. Within two or three minutes, it was a burning wreck.

It would turn out that the majority of the enemy was dead by the time the commandos reached the ground, but there was still some sporadic gunfire coming from the hillside above. The Garud units spent several hours chasing them down.

Captain Birla and I were listening to the play-by-play over the combat frequencies. Within a few minutes, we both realized that the helicopters weren't in the compound.

Had it been a false alarm?

Or had the helos managed to escape?

The answer came over the frequency used by the air force fighters monitoring the area.

"We have two contacts at low altitude flying north. They appear to be helicopters," added one of the pilots. "Are they part of the assault group?"

Duh.

"We should follow those helos," I told Captain Birla.

"The air force—"

"They're either going to get shot down or they'll land somewhere," I explained. "We ought to be there to grab whoever's flying them."

Captain Birla rubbed his forehead. The battle was still going on at the compound. Following the stolen helicopters might have other consequences, such as allowing some of the tangos to escape, or permitting them to be reinforced from the village.

"Leave most of your men here," I told him. "Shotgun and Mongoose can come with me. We only need one helicopter."

"Yes, this is an idea," he told me, bowing his head.

The Mi-8TV is a relatively fast helicopter, but it's not in the same league as the Ahi. There was no question about catching up to the helicopters, but I didn't think that was an issue—the air farce, after all, had a pair of MiGs to do that.

Sounds easy, right? And if we were talking about F-15s, say, or F-16s or F/A-18s, it would have been no problem. But India gets most of its aircraft from Russia, an arrangement that dates to the Cold War. And being Russian-made planes, the Indian MiGs apparently lacked the advanced look-down radars that would have made it easier to find the helicopters.

It's not that they didn't try. Or that they were totally incompetent. In fact, one of the planes got close enough to the helicopter[21] to get some footage of it on its gun camera.

Why didn't the pilot shoot his gun rather than his camera?

Because his ROE—rules of engagement, or Rape Orders preceding Enema—dictated that he get clearance from his unit commander first. And the unit commander had to check with his division commander before clearing the shot. And the division commander had to talk to the group commander before clearing his underling. And the group commander had to get the OK from the minister's office.

There may have been a janitor in there as well.

While all of this was going on, the helicopter snaked through the mountain passes, literally diving behind trees and pirouetting around canyon faces. The MiG had all sorts of advantages compared to the helicopter. The one thing it couldn't do, though, was go very slow. The helicopter pilot managed to slip away by dropping to the ground, letting the MiG fly overhead, and then changing direction.

The jets kept up the chase. They continued getting fleeting radar con-

---

[21] Note the use of the singular here. It will be important in the pages that follow.

tacts. By now they were close to the Pakistan border, and it was obvious that that's where the helos were heading. The chain of command cranked out an order: destroy the helicopter. The MiGs armed their missiles, ready to fire—but no longer had any targets.

The last contact they saw was three miles deep over the Pakistan border. It wasn't clear where the other helicopter was or even that those were *the* helicopters. But everyone assumed they were.

Pakistan fighters scrambled as the Indian MiGs closed on the border. There was no point crossing over, let alone engaging the Pakis.

The MiGs turned back for base.

The operation was officially FUBAR: Fucked Up Beyond All Recognition.

By that time, we were only about ten minutes from the border ourselves. Our pilot suggested we check around the area where the helo had apparently stopped. It was a good idea; we banked south and spent some time tracing the route in the hills before fuel concerns forced us to break off. Needless to say, we didn't see the helicopters, or spot any wreckage thereof.

"Ol' Murphy kicked ass tonight," said Shotgun as we headed back to the barn.

(II)

I don't know how much credit Murph really deserves for that fiasco.

After all, the biggest contributor was really plain old human stupidity. Let's assume that the air farce was right and the operation had to proceed immediately that night, rather than waiting until they had more assets in place. That was a judgment call, and I personally am prejudiced toward doing things sooner rather than later.

And let's not worry about the antiquated equipment in the Indian jets, though frankly that's a little harder to forgive, given that the Indians do actually have some planes with better radar; they just didn't deploy them for this mission.

(Yes, there are reasons. Mostly the air farce doesn't want its toys getting broken. Air farces the world over are like that. They clamor for cool toys, then hide them in the garage where they won't get wet.)

Using gear from Russia rather than Europe or the U.S.—we'll give them a dumb pass on that.

But the politician or government staff member who leaked the news of the operation?

He or she should be crucified. That wasn't chance, or even human error. That was stupidity to the nth degree.

You can't fix stupid. That's beyond even Murphy's abilities.

Another media firestorm followed. The Indian press was unmerciful.

They were also screaming for revenge.

It appeared that Pakistan had the helicopters—there were the radar contacts, and they'd certainly been flying in that direction when they disappeared.

The Indians wanted them back. The Indians told the Pakistanis that if they didn't get them back, they were going to take them back.

The Pakistanis claimed not to know anything about the helicopters.

"Helicopters? What helicopters?" was, I believe, the prime minister's official reply.

You can imagine how well that went over.

There was some back and forth, but pretty much the conversation was a spitting contest. Both sides mobilized their armies. A shit storm seemed imminent.

Once again, I found myself very popular with the secretary of State, or rather one of her intelligence flunkies, who pressed me for a "face-to-face" to discuss developments. Madam Secretary would have talked to me in person, he assured me, but she was in Europe doing whatever it is secretaries of State do when not conjuring world peace or banging shoes at the UN.

I didn't particularly want to brief the State Department official, mostly because it meant that I had to go over to the embassy and risk spending time with my good friend Omar, whose aftershave caused my nose to stop up. I needn't have worried, though—Omar came to pick me up personally.

"You really got things in an uproar, Marcinko," he told me as I stepped into the car. "Is this on your Rogue agenda—start World War III?"

"I don't start wars. I finish them."

"How are you going to finish this one?"

"Send you to Pakistan and call it a day?"

"What happened to those damn helicopters?" he asked. "Did you steal them?"

"I have them in the hotel parking garage."

"I've heard about the shit you've pulled. This would be a perfect Red Cell operation."

It would have, actually.

We traded insults all the way to the embassy. Once there, I went into the cone of silence room and briefed the ambassador and chief of mission and the aforementioned State Department aide. I didn't tell them anything you haven't heard already.

They were actually grateful. Well, the aide and deputy ambassador were. Omar . . .

We appreciate your cooperation, Mr. Marcinko.

You've been very informative, Dick.

You're a peach of a guy, asshole.

It's so nice to be loved.

"No way that was the helicopter."

"And good morning to you, too," I told Junior. I wasn't sure what the hell he was talking about. He'd been waiting at our fancy hotel for me to return from the embassy for more than an hour. I had them meet and drop me off there because I didn't want the Christians in Action knowing where we were; they're such blabbermouths.

"It wasn't the helicopter," said Junior. We were outside under the canopy area, a few feet from the door. "Come on over to the airfield and look at the tape."

"Let's go inside first," I told him. "We're surely being watched."

We went upstairs, threw some things around the rooms for a few minutes, then went back out.

Captain Birla had obtained a copy of the video from the MiG's HUD or heads-up display showing the helicopter. It was, as you'd expect, a murky collection of shadows moving across the screen.

Junior freeze-framed it.

"Look at that," he said. "That's a Bell JetRanger. It's got some fancy paint on it, and panels on the side to make it look like a gunship."

He might have been right. Then again, he might not have been. What it mostly looked like was a collection of shadows.

"And, it's only one helicopter," he said. "We were looking for two."

"The other one was farther ahead."

"No. Check this out."

He showed me a blurry reconnaissance photo that had also come from the air force. There was one helicopter on the ground, under heavy netting.

"Where's the other one?" I asked.

"They think it's in this shadow," he said. "But there's no way—the shadow is here later on. Look."

He produced a photo taken by our helicopter during the mission.

"There were two radar contacts," I said.

"Their radar is for shit. There was so much ground clutter, they couldn't follow it."

I'll admit that each one of Junior's objections had a point. But taken together—it just seemed like he was stringing too many objections together to come up with an alternative theory.

Which was?

"I don't think that helicopter left India," said Junior. "I wonder if it was ever at that compound to begin with."

"The satellite photo," said Captain Birla. "There were definitely helicopters there."

"One. And it's under the tarp and netting," said Junior. "Sure, you can see the back end and some of the rotor. It's roughly the right size. But it could be a Jet Ranger. Seriously. Look at it."

We did, for several minutes. Junior had a point. You couldn't really tell what was under the tarp. Only the tail of one helicopter was visible, and it was partly obscured by a tarp. It did look like the Ahi, but even with a magnifying glass, we couldn't be positive.

"We should check the compound," said Junior. "That's the only way to be sure. We should see what kind of evidence is there."

Captain Birla shrugged. "This is no longer our problem."

"I want to have a look, Dad."

Did he just call me dad?

No way. If he had I would have smacked him right across the face.

I may be prejudiced against air farce types, with whom I've had mixed experiences, but it seemed to me they were the ones who had logic on their side here. Still, Junior was so adamant that I felt I almost owed it to him to let him go. We weren't getting anywhere here. The worst that would happen would be that he'd learn a lesson in how not to be so dead sure about things.

"If you can find a way to get up there, go ahead," I told him. "Go in the morning. Be back by tomorrow night."

Captain Birla shook his head.

"Better to let him get it out of his system," I told Birla when Junior left. "He's still young."

"Our next operation is tomorrow night."

"He'll be there, his butt dragging on the ground. That's the only way he'll learn."

We went back to planning for the next operation, a mock attack on the soccer stadium.

There was a much simpler way to find out what the helicopter or helicopters in question had been: ask one of the terrorists who'd been there.

As far as we could tell, there had been nineteen tangos at the compound where the helo or helos had been. Only two men had survived, and both were in very serious condition. The military hospital where they were being held wasn't that far away, and I stopped there after finishing with Captain Birla. The Garud guards wouldn't let me in. It turned out that their commander was a fan, but even that didn't get me anything.

Besides drinks, of course.

"These men are potentially as big as Ajmal Kasab," he told me, naming the terrorist who had been captured during the Mumbai attack in 2008. "For us, there can be no chances. Not even with a famous hero as you."

"You flatter me."

"Even so, you cannot go in."

He did share what they had found at the site, but it wasn't that much. The building had been leveled in the battle, and they were only now picking through the ruins to see what they could recover and make sense of. The villagers claimed to know nothing of the place—your basic lie, obviously, but one that would take weeks if not months to unravel.

The commander and I had a nice dinner, and a few drinks afterward. He told me stories about parachuting: he'd had chute failures not once but twice during training sessions, yet lived to tell about it, both times miraculously finding another jumper before biting the great beyond. Once was unlucky; twice smacked of recklessness: sabotage was suspected, but the culprit never found.

I told him the story of my Fulton system recovery, sort of like parachuting in reverse: I stood under a clear balloon I had launched from the Skyhook kit. It lifted the basket weave tubular line five hundred feet in the air. The line was a specially configured C-130 that flew directly into the line. A special contraption on the nose trapped and locked the line. With the line snagged, I flew *higher* than the plane. The line fed back to a winch, which eventually reeled me in. Think fifteen-minute freefall trailing behind the plane. A great kick in the balls.

It was all sorts of fun, windsurfing into the rear of the cargo plane to the consternation of a hardtack navy chief, who knew I was being a wiseass but couldn't quite figure out how.[22] I was the first person to use the system without a parachute—not that the damn thing would have done anyone any good if there was a screwup anyway.

"Flying without wings is interesting," said the commander, nodding solemnly as the check came. "But it is always a good idea to have a sturdy parachute."

"A seat inside the aircraft is a hell of a lot better," I told him.

---

[22] See *Rogue Warrior*, p. 47, under flying without wings for fun and profit.

The air farce's reluctance to let me question the men is probably under-standable; I wasn't Indian, and I had no official standing with them.

But they also refused to let anyone else question the men for more than two weeks. Supposedly, they had their own experts extracting in-formation in the meantime. Based on the results, they got bupkis.

You're tired of the whining about interagency bickering and political interference, so I'll let it go.

Our friend Igor was still on the loose, staying in the safe house outside of Delhi. With the pressure now ratcheted to violin string levels, the intel-ligence operatives at the state security office who'd taken over as the lead agency in the case decided it no longer made sense to watch him. Igor, they reasoned, was a valuable source of intelligence. Ten minutes in the backroom and he'd be singing like a bird.

As either a thank you for turning him over, or an f-u to show how much better at this game they were, the unit "invited" Captain Birla and me along as observers.

The word "invited" is in quotes because we were told about the raid twenty minutes before it happened.

Some people want company, and others don't. It was going on mid-night, and Captain Birla was at home sleeping. It would have taken him nearly an hour to get over to the raid site anyway, so he demurred.

I, on the other hand, happened to be only five minutes away, just leaving my post-dinner briefing session with the Garud brass. I found the command post with plenty of time to spare.

It was a panel van parked up the hill a block from the house. Incon-spicuous, except for the guys who kept climbing in and out of the back.

Just as I got there, I saw a white flash at the bottom of the street. This was followed by a loud boom.

Flash-bangs, I assumed—they're moving in.

A second or two later the night turned red. The ground rumbled beneath my feet. I got two words out of my mouth—"Oh, shit"—before I felt myself being thrown backward by the shock of an explosion. When I got to my feet a few seconds later, I saw that the entire block was in flames.

Igor wasn't going to be singing for anyone now.

Twelve members of the security force lost their lives in the explosion and blaze, so there's little sense in berating them about the decision to go in. Apparently they used tear gas grenades as well as flash-bangs, and a spark from one of the grenades had ignited a store of gasoline bombs in the house.

Or not. Maybe it was rigged to explode if attacked. Maybe Igor pressed the detonator himself.

The place was such a mess that I don't think it was possible to say exactly what happened. There was gasoline and kerosene in the place, but whether it had been fashioned into bombs or stockpiled for some other reason, I couldn't say. There was plenty of fertilizer, which was the main ingredient of the boom. Plastic explosive was recovered—the stuff doesn't ignite in fires, though I wouldn't go hitting it with a hammer. So at a minimum the house was used as a weapons depot, if not an actual bomb factory.

The nearest neighbors had been quietly evacuated just before the action, so there were only minor injuries among civilians, but needless to say it was another low point in a series of low points. The tangos were theoretically on the run, yet it sure looked like they were kicking ass.

The house that blew up was definitely connected to People's Islam; its founder's cousin had bought it several years before. The compound where the helo had been seemed also to have been a People's Islam property, though that connection was less clear. There were a few other circumstantial links as well, making it seem pretty clear that the helos and the escape from Special Squadron's jail were both People's Islam projects.

Where was India for Islam in all this?

Funny you should ask.

According to everything Sean was hearing, our raid into Pakistan had killed two of the group's leaders and sent those we hadn't killed scurrying under the biggest rocks they could find. Pakistan was now monitoring their communications. Most of what they had heard since the raid were brief messages aimed at trying to ascertain who was still alive. But right after the explosion of the safe house, one of the surviving India for Islam members sent an e-mail to another:

God's wrath is just.

Now, I suppose that could have been meant as a generic rah-rah-rah statement, praising the death of infidels. But the news reports of the incident—the explosion and fire were far too large to go unnoticed—all followed the government line that claimed a major terrorist site had been destroyed. The reports claimed four men had been killed, all members of People's Islam.

(Why or where they came up with four dead I have no idea. As I said, the only terrorist actually killed was Igor, who had been alone in the building for at least twenty-four hours.)

None of the stories included any information about casualties among the Indians.

So why was Islam for India crowing about it?

Because they hated People's Islam?

It was the only thing that made sense.

"What we need to do is review the intelligence we got on India for Islam," I told Captain Birla when I saw him after talking with Sean. It was the afternoon following Igor's immolation. "Everything that led up to the raid in Pakistan."

Captain Birla blinked at me. He'd been trying to catch a nap in his back room, grabbing some bunk time before the stadium operation we had planned that night.

"That is a lot of data." He rubbed his eyes. "Why do you want it?"

"I want to see some of the sources."

"Well. OK. But it will take time and the Games are only a week away. The athletes are already arriving and—"

"I can do it myself. I just need your OK to get into the files."

Captain Birla agreed, and I started going back through the files. I'd seen most of it before, and it would have been ideal to have someone else go through it with a fresh eye. But Doc was busy with the team, and the other likely candidate—Junior—was off in the hills on his wild goose chase.

It wasn't really a wild goose chase—there are no geese in India. But Matt had set off without knowing what he was looking for or what he wanted to find.

Check that—he knew what he wanted to find: something that would say he was right about his hunch that the helicopter or helicopters we'd chased weren't actually the ones that were stolen. What exactly that proof would be, though, he had no idea.

Not necessarily a bad thing. Youth needs space to recon.

Shotgun and Mongoose accompanied him on the trip. They rented a Land Cruiser and headed out early in the morning. Getting out of Delhi took more than two hours; after that, they didn't have much traffic until they ran into a herd of sheep a few miles from the compound. After some wrangling with the local police helping guard the place, they got out and had a look around.

The ruins of the main building were still smoldering. The Garud commander had made it clear that they weren't to disturb the ruins, but I doubt his orders would have stopped them if they really wanted to poke around.

They didn't need to, Junior claimed, because he found "a clincher" right away.

What could follow here is a long technical discussion about helicopter undercarriages and weights. I know how excited you are to read several pages worth of charts and graphs, so I'll substitute the layman's version:

The Bell JetRanger sits on skis. The Ahi rests on wheels that are folded up during flight.

Junior found a set of impressions where the helicopters had sat before taking off. According to him, these could only have been made by a JetRanger, or a very similar helicopter.

He took photos. I've seen the photos. Maybe the lines in them were made by helicopters, and maybe they weren't. There were a lot of marks in the small field there, not only from explosions, but from the helicopters that had brought the assault teams.

For the record, though, the Hind lands on wheels.

"Very distinctive pattern," said Junior when I pointed this out. "Very different from the Ahi. Let me explain . . ."

You'll have to wait until he writes his own book if you're truly interested in double-tire nose wheels and undercarriage spans. The bottom line is, in his mind he had evidence that the helicopter(s) we had chased were not the right ones.

So, you're wondering, where were they?

I'll let Junior explain. This is from his after-action report:

I could understand why the terrorists had dressed the other helicopter up—they wanted to confuse the Indians and throw them off the trail.

It seemed to me that with all the reconnaissance going on, the helicopter had probably been in place for a while. That fit, really—the guys we were dealing with had obviously been planning this for some time. So this place was all a blind or a deek, a ruse they would use if they were followed—as it turned out they had been.

Obviously, they must have had some other way of getting out of the country. Or not getting out of the country. Because as Mongoose said, it's usually better to do the opposite of what everybody is expecting you to do. That's pure Red Cell think, and SEAL philosophy as well.

In my mind, though, the heist of the helicopters was related to the Commonwealth Games. If they were hiding the helicopters, it was because they were going to use them during the Games. It would be a spectacular assault. I closed my eyes and saw it: sixty thousand people in the stadium, gathered for the final track and field competition. The camera follows a javelin as it flies upward. Then all of a sudden, it lingers—there's something else in the air.

The helicopters. They begin their assault. They could wipe out the stadium in a few minutes. Then they could fly across town and crash into the government buildings for an encore.

Good creative theory, with sound reasoning and a novelist's imagination—throw in his purple prose, and no doubt he'll be writing these things someday.

But there were problems with Junior's theory. Most obviously—if the helicopters hadn't been taken to the site, where did they go?

Junior, Shotgun, and Mongoose started trying to figure that out as soon as they left the compound. The nearby village had no other place suitable for a helicopter landing, but they looked around anyway just to be sure. Back in the SUV, they took out the satellite photos and maps of the region, examining different spots as possible helicopter landing areas.

In theory, you can put a helicopter just about anywhere. They don't need all that much space to land. Here in the States, the parking lot of a small mall or even a large front lawn will do nicely.

But there were no shopping malls in that part of India, and the larger fields were regularly checked. That's not to say it wouldn't have been possible to get in, but if they landed in one of the fields, they would have had to hide the aircraft pretty quickly. Which meant they needed either a large building nearby or some way to get the helicopters away from the field by truck.

Starting from the area where the Mi-8TV had run out of fuel, Junior diagrammed a large semicircle where he figured the helicopters could have gone before they, too, would have run out of petrol. The area was 150 miles long and pretty damn wide. But he decided he could cut it down by eliminating a lot of the area very close to the Pakistani border, since the air force had had planes there very quickly. He also assumed that it wouldn't include the area the air farce had raided, since why would you lead anyone near your hideout?

In the end, he came up with two dozen places where he thought the helicopter could be. Then they set out to check them.

Trace in shorts is a beautiful thing, but Doc in a kilt—very rough on the eyes.

They both showed off their knees that same afternoon as the Scottish field hockey team scrimmaged against Pakistan. Security was heavy, and we were on serious alert.

Yes, Pakistan was part of the Commonwealth and would be at the Games. So why would Pakistan want to disrupt them?

The answer was that they didn't. While Pakistan had backed many radical groups in the past, it was generally an expression of the old "the enemy of my enemy is my friend" theory. But as Pandora learned, the forces of evil once unleashed cannot be controlled.

Pakistan had slowly been waking up to this. They cooperated, albeit reluctantly, in the Mumbai investigations. They had been somewhat cooperative with the intelligence efforts before the Commonwealth Games. They have cooperated with the U.S. against the Taliban. Maybe if things go along without further complications, they might even become an effective counterterror force . . . say, two hundred years from now.

But the day of that scrimmage, tensions were pretty high. Newspapers and blogs were accusing them of having stolen the helicopters, and being behind what was called The Terror Bomb House where Igor had checked out.

Which made the atmosphere at the field hockey game absolutely rabid. The crowd adopted the Scots, knobby knees and all.

They were backing winners. Trace scored two goals in the opening period, and the Scotsmen never looked back.

When the Pakistani team was called for a raised stick early in the second period, the crowd began throwing things onto the field. It looked for a moment as if there'd be a riot. Trace took matters into her own hands—she raised her hands to calm the crowd, then stepped up and took the penalty stroke, flicking the ball past the diving goalie for the score.

That settled things down somewhat, but the Pakistani team still had to run a gamut of abuse to reach their bus at the end of the match.

"If something happens at the Games," Doc warned me later, "there'll be a bloodbath. People will lynch the Pakistani athletes. And that'll just be the beginning."

Or the end, depending on your point of view.

Later that evening, just as the sun was about to set, Junior and the others pulled into the lot of an old train siding about a hundred miles northeast of Delhi. They'd already searched more than a dozen spots where Junior thought the helicopters could have landed without finding a trace.

This looked like one more. It was an asphalt parking lot serving a building that was no longer there. Strewn with glass and small rocks, it had been abandoned for at least a decade. The macadam, though old and broken up, was still plenty strong to hide any evidence that an aircraft had landed there.

A train passed as they were walking back to the Land Cruiser. It blew a long, wistful wail from its horn. Shotgun turned and watched it.

More from Junior:

I realized that something was wrong, out of place, but I wasn't sure what it was.

I saw it as soon as I pulled out the satellite photo, which had been taken a few days before, by the commercial service we subscribe to:

There had been two large freight cars parked on the siding. Now they were gone.

Bingo!

When we drove back to Delhi, I double-checked the area with Google Earth. Their satellite photo, which had been taken the year before, showed no cars at that siding. Based on that, I went to our service's archives and started paging through. They had images roughly every twenty-two days. The cars were not in any of the photos.

That's when I started looking into the possibility that the helicopters had been moved by train.

The tracks that Junior had found belonged to a small line. The siding was not used that often—which made it easier for him to track the records down.

Two cars had been left there a week before. They'd been picked up the night that the helicopters disappeared, transported to another line, and then delivered to a train yard in Delhi.

The train yard near the slum our little friend Leya lived in.

And, according to the railroad records, the cars were still there.

[IV]

Junior gave me an info dump on the train cars about two hours before Special Squadron Zero was scheduled to deploy on its stadium operation. I decided to check the cars out myself.

We met at the traffic circle just outside the slum. By the time I got there, Shotgun had detoured over to one of the food vendors and bought what looked like apple turnovers. They were actually samosas, vegetable mini-pies, a meal for some, a two-in-the-mouth-at-a-time snack for Shotgun, who tossed them down like M&Ms.

"Hey, skipper," he said, crumbs falling from his stuffed mouth. "Hungry?"

I shook my head and asked Junior where the trains were.

"They ought to be in that siding over there, on the other side of the houses," Junior said. He pulled out a printout of the satellite image.

I was just looking at the page when a pint-sized cyclone jumped onto my back.

"U.S. Dick! You have come to visit!" yelled Leya. The little monkey slid off my back and hung down from my neck.

Cute kid. Did I ever mention I hate cute kids?

"Hey, little thing," said Shotgun. "Hungry?"

"I *am* hungry, Mr. Mountain," she said, jumping up and snatching a samosa from his hand. She wolfed it down even quicker than Shotgun could have.

The boys bought her and some of her friends food while I studied the images. The cars were parked on a siding right up next to the slum. There were several places they could be watched from, both inside the housing area and in the train yard itself. We'd have to check for lookouts first.

That was a problem, since we didn't exactly look like we belonged there.

But the children did.

We went at it systematically, working over the spots where the lookouts might be point by point. Leya or her friends would run by the spot quickly while we watched. If nothing happened, we moved in and made sure the place was empty. Then we moved on to the next spot. It took about a half hour before we were sure that no one was watching from the slum side of the yard.

The kids thought it was all great fun. By the time we were done, it was obvious that we were looking at the train cars, and Leya declared that she would run and climb on top of them to tell us if there were any "bad boys" as she called them.

"No, pipsqueak." I gave her my best growl, then channeled my inner chief, conjuring a crusty seadog snarl. "This isn't a game."

"Oh, yes, fun game, U.S. Dick."

"You oughta be sleeping," I told them. "Don't you have school tomorrow?"

This was apparently the funniest joke in the world. All the kids nearly bent over with laughter.

Shotgun came up with a solution.

"Before we play the train game," he said, "let's get some ice cream."

The kids all thought this was a great idea, though they weren't sure where the nearest open vendor might be.

"The farther the better," I told him.

We approached the cars from the slum side, working out from a stack of rusted steel drums used for drinking water. A deep set of shadows covered most of the approach. Mongoose took point; Junior was behind him and I trailed.

I tried not to huff too loudly as I ran the last twenty yards to a small stanchion where the others were crouched waiting. No matter how much you run during PT, sprints during combat are always ten times as hard.

I think Junior might have smirked when I caught up to them, but if so he was smart enough to hold his tongue.

"Weapons ready?" I asked when I caught my breath.

They were both set. We pulled on our night goggles and took a last look around. The closest train car was fifty yards away.

"Mongoose, you go to the door. Junior and I will cover you. Don't trip."

Mongoose said something in Spanish that I didn't catch. Probably he was saying what a genius I am.

Then he ran off. I could hear his breath over the team radio.

Kid huffs and puffs, and it's because he's working hard. A veteran huffs a little . . .

Mongoose slowed as he reached the train car. He practically glided against it, putting up his hand and leaning gently against the base. He put his head against the wooden side, listening. He didn't hear anything.

I swear he tiptoed to the door. It had a big lock on it. He looked around, up, down, then he waved us forward.

We checked the other side. Same thing.

While Junior climbed up to the top, Mongoose ran to the second car. Once again, he found the doors locked, and no one around.

"You sure these are the right cars?" I asked Junior.

"Serial numbers match," he said. "The records show they just came here. Do you remember seeing them the last time you were in the yard?"

I didn't, but that didn't mean they hadn't been here. I hadn't been taking inventory.

"Let's have a look inside," I said. "Bend over, Junior."

Hold the jokes.

I retrieved the long-handled wire cutters from the back of his vest where we'd strapped it, then climbed up so I could reach the lock, which was mounted high on the car to make it harder to tamper with.

Cutting the lock off was easy enough. Now we had to ask ourselves, was the car booby-trapped?

I had a small device that checked for electric currents in my tactical vest. I ran it over the area near the door. There was nothing. But that only ruled out a battery-powered device. There were plenty of ways to rig something simple, like a hand grenade, so that pushing the door open would set it off. And given what we'd seen of People's Islam so far, nothing could be taken for granted.

We rigged a line to the handle, then moved back about thirty feet. If something blew, we might catch some splinters, but not the full force of the blast.

"Pull," I told Mongoose.

He tugged. Nothing budged.

"And you've been working out?" I said.

He tugged again. The door stayed closed.

"Maybe it's time you tried steroids."

Junior grabbed the line. Both of them pulled. Nada.

"All right, you sissy boys," I said. "Let's get a man on the rope."

They welcomed me with an assortment of tender endearments—which became a virtual shower when I, too, couldn't pull the goddamn door back. All three of us tugging together, and the thing stayed closed.

"I say we blow the mother up," said Mongoose.

He said a lot more than that, but I don't want to offend your tender eardrums.

Besides, reproducing them all would take up three pages.

"I say blow the mother," he insisted.

"We aren't blowing anything up, at least not tonight," I said.

"We could hook a truck or something to it," said Junior.

"I don't think that will do it," I said. "Let's go have another look."

I went back and took a look at the door. It had a metal frame with wheels that rode on a set of rails at the bottom. I expected to see the wheels rusted in place, or something blocking them. But when I studied it, I realized the problem was more permanent.

"They welded it shut," I said. "Somebody doesn't want anyone getting in."

The other boxcar had been sealed the same way.

Until now, I'd had only a lukewarm feeling about Junior's theory. It had all sorts of holes. Why bring the helicopters back to Delhi? If you were planning to use them, it would be a lot safer to fly from outside the city. And hell—if you had another helicopter or, Allah be praised, two, why go to the trouble of stealing two more?

Terrorists aren't like air farce procurement officers, who have never seen a piece of expensive equipment they didn't want. As a whole, they're cheap bastards—they take what they can get and do the most with it. Whatever else you think of them, you gotta love their frugality.

But finding the doors welded shut put things in a whole new perspective.

"What we need is a Sawzall," I told Mongoose. "Preferably a battery-powered one."

"Where are we going to get that?" Mongoose asked.

"Does our fancy hotel have a maintenance department?"

They did. And they had a Sawzall—two of them in fact. Unfortunately, both were corded models, and the nearest electrical outlet was some one hundred yards away in the slum. And it wasn't exactly UL tested, either—it was a wire hacked into the overhead power line.

Junior managed to get us connected without either frying or blacking

205

out all of northern India, a minor miracle. In the meantime, Shotgun returned with the kids. We put them to work as lookouts on the road, telling them to watch for bucket trucks—we were more worried about the local electrical company than tangos at that point.

There's something about cutting into wood that does a man good. Rip away at a board with a ten-inch blade and you really feel like you understand the universe.

We had to work around a few metal straps, but otherwise the job was easy. It took Mongoose and me all of five minutes to cut a four-foot-by-four-foot hole in the side of the boxcar. I gave it a good slap with the saw, cringing at the last second just in case there was a booby trap.

No worries. No explosion. The only thing I could hear besides my pounding heart was the occasional snap of a spark back at our electrical connection.

I leaned toward the hole, then fell back, practically knocked over by the stench.

My time in India featured many exotic smells, but this one may have been the worst. The train car, and its companion, were filled with potatoes that had been left to rot.

Judging from the stench, they'd been in the car for at least six months. Temperatures inside had, I'm sure, reached well into triple digits. The smell was so bad it even curbed Shotgun's famous appetite.

"Never really liked baked potatoes anyway," he claimed after he caught a whiff. "Fries. That would be a different story."

[V]

Junior will eventually live the infamous potato car episode down. Assuming he lives to be three hundred years old.

We razzed the shit out of him, as he so richly deserved. This was a tiny payback, given the damage to our lungs.

"Definitely an al Qaeda plot," said Mongoose. "They're using friggin' germ warfare on us."

Let me tell you something, though. I went back there the next day, just to see if we'd missed something. Every one of those damn potatoes was gone—eaten, I'm sure, by the people who lived in that slum.

There are days when I just get down on my knees and thank God I was born in America, and that was one of them.

Mongoose and Shotgun went to see the doctor at Dublin, the Irish bar at our fancy hotel. Junior, licking his wounded ego, said he was going back to the Maharaja Express to go to bed.

I said sure, even though I knew that wasn't what he had in mind. Not that I blamed him.

Pissed off at his failure, he did what we all should do when life kicks us face-first into a shit pile. He rolled up his sleeves and got his butt back to work. He went to one of his computer hideouts—probably one of the colleges he had scouted, though I'm not sure—to try and figure out what the hell he had done wrong.

I had my own work to do. I shooed Leya and the kids back to their respective hovels, then went over to the stadium[23] to see how the Special Squadron Zero operation was going.

Following in the tradition of KISS—the plan was simplicity itself.

Sergeant Phurem and several accomplices detained two of the night guards at their homes just as they were about to leave for work. Taking their clothes and IDs, they reported to the stadium in their place. The stadium security force was so large and relatively new that no one noticed.

---

[23] Part of my contract with the Indians required me not to name the facilities we were testing, for fairly sound reasons. If you're curious though, you can probably figure it out from the description.

Ten minutes into the shift, there was a disturbance near one of the gates. An alert was sounded, and the security teams began deploying. As they did, a dozen Squadron Zero members infiltrated through another gate manned by the two imposters.

The disturbance turned out to be nothing more than a fight between two drunkards, who were quickly packed off to the local hoosegow. The security teams returned to their posts.

Special Squadron Zero began picking them off one by one and two by two. Within an hour and a half, the entire stadium was under Squadron Zero's control.

This was just an exercise—or maybe more precisely a demonstration—so we couldn't actually slit any of the guards' throats, even if they did deserve it. On the other hand, just tapping them on the shoulder and saying, *"You're out of the game, sweetie,"* wouldn't have quite driven home the point of the operation.

If we had been terrorists, they'd be dead. Period. A lot of other people would have been dead. Period. We wanted them to understand and remember that.

So each guard was gagged and maced, then shot with a fluorescent pink paintball before being taken to the holding area, a pair of stuffy rooms under the stands where they were locked in for the night.

That pissed some of them off, and it didn't please their supervisor either.

Ain't life a bitch?

The protests amused Captain Birla, who was smiling when I arrived at the stadium. I hadn't seen him happy since before our night run into Pakistan.

"I expect the minister will be getting many phone calls today," he said triumphantly. "There will be many complaints about how good a job we are doing."

I laughed. Captain Birla would undoubtedly face a political shit storm, but he was finally developing the sort of attitude he needed to deal with it.

The exercise was essentially over, but the captain couldn't leave the stadium without protection. He sent most of his men home, leaving six men to guard the gates and wait for the morning shift to arrive. Then he had two of his bomb experts begin a sweep of the facility to make sure that there were no IEDs embedded anywhere that the regulars had failed to find.

Nada.

When they were done, he sent them home as well, then went up to the main security office at the top of the stadium to relax and wait for the morning crew to arrive.

I went up with him, thinking I'd take a look around the place and maybe scout a good seat for the Games. After the semifiasco in the train yard, not to mention the series of setbacks over the past few days, it was good to see something working right.

Captain Birla took me aside about halfway up the ramp.

"Commander Rick, I have a desire to tell you something," he started, "but I hope it doesn't offend."

"Fire away."

"With respect, Commander Rick. You stink."

I guess I'd picked up a little potato scent and couldn't shake it. I went off and hit the showers, using half of Delhi's supply of hot water to wash the stink away.

Nothing like a good shower to put you in a good mood. And the stadium's facilities were top-notch in that regard — perfectly placed ceilings to give maximum acoustics as you sang.

I'll spare you the song.

Fully refreshed, I shut off the water and realized I had neglected to properly preposition my gear prior to embarking on the operation — in other words, I'd forgotten a towel.

Sacrifices have to be made in wartime, and modesty is the last resort of scoundrels. If that's not a quote in Bartlett's, it ought to be.

I went into the locker area to look for something to use to dry off. I'd been in the showers so long a warm, wet fog filled the air, misting over everything, and making it hard to see more than a few feet in front of me. I had to feel my way across the row of lockers, pulling open the doors and fishing around inside.

The problem was, the lockers were all empty. The stadium had been built for the Games, and not yet occupied. Finding a towel in them was going to be harder than finding a hamburger in a Hindu temple.

I was just about to turn back to the shower room where I'd left my clothes when I heard a noise in the hall. Thinking it was Captain Birla or one of his men, I was just about to yell that I needed a towel when I heard something else:

An AK47, rattling in the hallway.

Through the mist, I saw two figures run into the locker room, heading for the shower. They were dressed in black, with red rags around their foreheads. They grunted directions at each other as they ran.

They were speaking a language I didn't understand, with the exception of one word—"Marcinko."

I don't think they were complimenting me on my singing.

(1)

Standing naked in a locker room with a couple of guys going crazy with AK47s a few feet away is not exactly my favorite after-shower occupation. I also don't think it's a great way to spend the wee hours of the morning. Any morning. But I didn't think I was likely to get a time-out if I asked.

I moved back between the lockers and hoisted myself up on top. They were double-banked, back to back against each other, making roughly a twenty-four-inch-wide top. Unfortunately, the tops were angled down the way a house roof would be. I had to straddle it on my hands and knees.

I'll let that image sink in for a minute.

Yeah, I get a weak feeling there just thinking about it myself.

The gunmen shot up the showers, either because they couldn't see too well with all the mist, or because they felt like wasting ammunition. Meanwhile, water dripped off my hairy carcass like rain falling from a summer cloud burst, and I was worried that the puddle below would tip them off. The lockers were spaced too far apart for me to easily move to the next row without getting down. Instead, I moved in the only direction I could, toward the showers, gingerly trying to keep my balance.

The gunfire stopped, and the two tangos started talking again. I have no idea what they said, but when they came out of the room, they split up, one going to my right, the other going to my left. They moved down the aisles, looking for me.

They were on the lazy side. Rather than opening the lockers, they simply shot through them. The bullets flew through the thin doors like paper, rattling the metal and filling the room with the lovely smell of cordite and burning steel.

Bastards had a lot of ammo. Some of the bullets ricocheted wildly. I was hoping they'd shoot each other, but no such luck; apparently Murphy was off in bed somewhere.

They worked down the aisles methodically, shouting to each other every few steps, no doubt proclaiming what brave SOBs they were to be taking on all these unarmed cubicles.

The tango nearest me came down the aisle on my left, shouting and firing. I waited until he was just passing, then pushed up and swung around to jump on his back.

I've made tougher jumps, but given the circumstances, this one really was incomparable.

Did I say Murphy was sleeping in bed?

My bed.

The son of a bitch reached up and grabbed my leg as I jumped, pushing me off balance just enough to make me slam into the side of the opposite locker as I fell.

Damn, that hurt.

I'd intended to grab the asshole around the neck and twist it off, but I was lucky just to get my arms out and push him down as I landed. I spun up, intending to swing my leg around in a kung fu-style kick—I had been making a lot of guest appearances at mixed martial arts matches lately before coming to India.

Unfortunately, I hadn't counted on how wet and slippery the damn floor would be, and my leg shot out from under me. Instead of kicking the asshole, I flew into his gut, slamming him against the lockers and sending his gun to the floor.

His face was next to mine. There was a look of horror on it. I guess he'd never seen a naked infidel before.

Two good elbows to his nose later, I glanced over my shoulder just in time to see the other tango turn the corner ahead, automatic rifle in his hand.

I'd like to say he saw us grappling and didn't fire, fearing that he'd hit his companion.

That would be giving him too much credit. He pressed the trigger, sending a burst of bullets into the wall behind us. By the time he corrected his aim, he was out of ammo.

For that magazine. He dropped it, fishing another from his pocket.

I launched myself at him just as he slammed it home. Bullets sprayed from the gun as we slammed against the lockers.

My eardrums felt like they had been hit with a hammer, and the rest of my body wasn't much better. But I didn't pause to take inventory. There's nothing like fighting for your life to knock the rust of age off your bones. I was damned if either of these punks was going to make retirement mandatory.

I punched, I kicked, I kneed—I did everything but throw up on the bastard to subdue him, and I would have done that if I'd had any food in my stomach.

He fought like a madman. Blood poured from every visible orifice. Finally I managed to get my hand under his chin and gave it a good snap as I pulled up on his neck with the other from behind. He crumbled, game over.

The other tango was lying dazed. I put the AK47 against his forehead and pushed the trigger.

Nobody screws with me when I'm taking a shower and lives to talk about it.

My first step out of the locker room was the longest I'd taken in days. I wasn't sure what I was dealing with.

I did, at least, have my clothes on. There was a lot to be said for that.

I'd also tied one of the bandannas the tangos were wearing around my head. I figured they'd put them on for identification—you see someone in the hall wearing a red band around their head, and you don't shoot him. Everyone else gets terminated.

The stadium was a big place. Had it been completely taken over? How many other people were involved? A dozen? Two dozen? There was no telling.

The two men in the locker room were wearing black ninja clothes, which was the squadron's standard uniform, but I didn't recognize either one as a member of the squadron. Still, not knowing what was going on, I wasn't about to trust the members of the squadron.

I couldn't even call for help, though I did have my phones with me. Neither my cell nor my satellite phone could get a signal, either because I was so deep in the stadium that the signals were blocked, or because the security blocking system had been activated.

I held my breath and sprung out, spinning in both directions, finger gently against the trigger.

Sprung is an exaggeration. I was feeling pretty beat up, all the energy from the shower gone. Fortunately for me, there was no one watching the hall.

I sprinted to the end, pausing near the doors. There was no one there either. I started to think that whoever had taken the place over had vacated. That notion was dispelled a few moments later as I heard voices ahead. I ducked into a room at the side of the hall, leaving the door open a crack so I could listen. Two men came trotting down the hall, running past before I could jump them. Unsure whether my gunshots might alert someone else, I decided to let them go rather than try to chase after them and shoot them down.

I waited a few seconds, then continued down the hall in the direction of the rooms where we'd locked the security team.

Like all stadiums, there were several levels to the building below field level. The rooms where I was heading were two stories down, reachable by a freight elevator or one of two staircases on either end of the building. My preference was the staircase at the north end of the stadium; the door was only a few yards from the rooms. But I heard voices as I neared it. As I pushed back against the wall, I noticed a wire on the floor. I followed it with my eyes down the hall to an exposed girder that formed part of the arch over the hall.

The bastards were wiring the place to explode.

The voice got a little louder, and I had to backtrack—there was no place to hide in the corridor.

Suddenly I heard a shout from the direction of the locker rooms. Fearing that the two men who had passed earlier had found my friends and were sounding the alarm, I ducked into the nearest room, hoping to hide until they passed. But as I stepped into the darkness I bumped against a set of ropes that were next to the doorway, and realized I'd gone into one of the shops.

Besides the athletic events, a fair amount of pomp and ceremony was planned for the Games, and the organizers had already started working on the stages and the assorted displays that were going to be used. This was done in the workshop area that I had just entered. It was a maze of half-built sets, ladders, carts, and piles of material.

It was also a way down to the basement, since the freight elevator opened onto the field here. The elevator was noisy as hell—half the stadium shook when it moved—so I didn't want to turn it on. But I figured I could use the shaft to get below.

It wouldn't be the first time I got the shaft, no?

And then?

Breaking out of the stadium clearly was going to require some assistance. And I had a ready reserve in the basement—the guards we'd locked in the two rooms.

I had a destination, motivation—staying alive—and a plan. Can't ask for more than that.

Except for a warm, curvy body and a cold beer, of course.

I walked through the room like a blind man, stumbling and trying desperately not to knock too much over. Disoriented—I'd only been in the shop area once—I walked into a workbench. I reached around the surface and shelves, hoping to find a flashlight, but all I could come up with were some screwdrivers and other assorted hand tools. Finally I found my way to the elevator, bumping my knee on the pipe rail that guarded the perimeter to prevent accidents. I climbed over and started searching for a manhole or something else to get down below through.

A hinged hatchway sat at the far end. I had trouble figuring out how to open it—you had to turn two large lugs in recessed compartments—and then nearly fell through.

My balance restored, I located the ladder and started working my way down. It wasn't until I reached the first-floor opening that I realized I had another problem—the large panel doors to the elevator were closed.

Well, duh.

I know there are typically emergency levers and other mechanisms to open the damn things when there's a problem, but in the dark I wasn't about to find them. I climbed all the way down to the lowest subbasement, hoping there was no elevator door on that level.

But there was. I patted the walls, looking for a release or some other way out, and eventually found an access door to the elevator pit a few rungs up, just to the right of the ladder. This put me in a room the size of a phone booth, where I stumbled around cursing until finally I found a light switch. I held my breath, then turned the light on, figuring I might just as well see where the hell I was trapped before I died.

It was a maintenance closet. Somehow I'd missed the doorknob opposite me.

A locker was recessed into the wall on the right. I found a pair of flashlights on the top shelf. I doused the overhead light, undid the lock so I could get back in if I had to, and went into the hall.

I'd slung the AK47 on my back while climbing down. I left it there now, walking slowly through the hall to get my bearings. I made nearly a full circuit before realizing the sentries were locked one flight above.

Assuming that they were still there—at this point, I couldn't take anything for granted.

I used the south stairway to get up to their level. I could hear someone talking at field level, two flights above where I was going. I tiptoed, and moved as silently as I could, forcing myself to breathe as quietly as possible.

I mentioned earlier that the sentries had all been sprayed and marked before being locked in the rooms. They were in a great mood when I unscrewed the locked door and let myself in.

Let me say this: I now know a lot more curses in Punjabi than I did before I went into that room.

Eventually I calmed them down and found the supervisor. I told him that I thought the stadium had been taken over by terrorists. They'd apparently overpowered the people who had overpowered them—which meant they could win back their pride by retaking the place.

Maybe my pep talk rallied them. More likely they were so ornery from the pepper spray that they were itching to tear someone, anyone, limb from limb.

We had eighteen men, not counting myself. I split them into three groups. I left one group at the bottom of the south staircase, telling them to charge up once they heard us attacking from above. Then I led the others back to the elevator shaft.

I went up the ladder first. Marut, a guard who spoke good English and knew his way around the shop, came with me. Armed with the flashlights from the closet below, we checked out the workshop, hoping to find some sort of weapons. But I couldn't find anything more lethal than a hacksaw.

"Could we use the pyro?" asked Marut.

Pyro as in fireworks.

Hell yeah, we could, depending on what they were. We found a bunch of Roman candles, some cherry bombs, and M60 firecrackers: quarter sticks of dynamite. Nasty stuff if it explodes in your face.

What we didn't find were fuses. They were all rigged to go off by electrical charge, and the ignition devices were not yet in the stadium. Without time to figure out how to deal with the wiring, I stuffed some of the M60s in my pocket and left the rest.

Marut went back to lead the others up the ladder. I snuck out to the hall. I paused by the door, listening, but couldn't hear anything. So I slipped out into the corridor and began walking to the staircase.

Nothing.

Then I spotted the explosives.

The wire I'd seen along the wall earlier was connected to a small gray box filled with plastic explosives and taped against the girder. I undid the tape and pulled the wire gently from the assembly, hoping like hell the damn thing wasn't arranged in such a way that doing that would set it off.

Unlikely, but not impossible.

It wasn't, fortunately. I followed the wire back to the stairs, around a corner, and up into the fire alarm system. The tangos had used the alarms as their wiring backbone. Pulling an alarm anywhere in the building would blow it up.

I was about to conclude that they'd gotten the hell out of there when I heard footsteps in the hall behind me. I got to the corner and saw two ninjas with red bandannas running toward me with a wire reel between them.

I took them out with the AK, both shots through the head. Only one of them was armed—he had a Beretta handgun in his waistband.

Marut and some of the others came up while I was grabbing the gun.

"We feared the worst," he said.

"You any good with a rifle?" I asked him.

"I am not bad. Not too good, not too bad."

That wasn't the answer I was hoping for. I gave him the rifle anyway—I'd have a better chance of hitting something with the pistol than he would.

"Where's the master panel for the fire alarms?" I asked.

Marut didn't know. The shift supervisor said it was in the main security office one level above where we were.

"They're probably there, waiting for the wiring to be finished," I said. "Is there another panel as a backup? Something to disable the entire system?"

If there was, the shift supervisor didn't know where it would be. The main circuit breakers were on the basement level where they had been kept prisoner; there were backup generators there as well.

Would cutting the power to the fire alarms disable all the bombs? Or would it ignite them?

Unfortunately, the only way to find out was to try it.

[II]

I told Marut and the supervisor to take the tangos out, post by post. It was possible that some Special Squadron Zero people were holed up somewhere, perhaps by the entrances, but everyone with a red bandanna was the enemy.

Except me, of course.

I was still optimistic that some Special Squadron Zero people were in the building alive somewhere. I shouldn't have been optimistic, but I was. So I told the guards to simply arrest anyone who seemed legitimate, as long as they were willing to surrender peacefully.

"Try and get them to surrender," I said. "But don't risk your life for it."

There were a few nods. Mostly there was a look of evil in their eyes—these guys wanted revenge for the humiliation they'd just suffered.

Which was a good thing, as long as they didn't decide I was the easiest target.

"When I cut the power, the lights in the whole place will go out," I continued. "There won't be backup either."

The supervisor shrugged. I didn't trust his English, so I had Marut explain it to him in Hindi. He shrugged again.

"We have been through so much this evening," he explained. "One more hardship is nothing."

I nodded. There was no sense telling him that killing the power might also bring the house down.

I went straight down the staircase, taking the steps two at a time. I ran, not walked, to the power room. I didn't stop to turn on the lights . . .

. . . dropped the damn flashlight fumbling to get the door open . . .

. . . picked it up and saw someone coming down the hall from the other direction.

The light behind him framed his silhouette in the hall. He had a roll of wire in his left hand, and an AK47 in his right.

Doom on you, Rogue Warrior.

No, he didn't fire at me. At that particular moment, I didn't know why. I thought it was just luck. I held the flashlight in his face, but he kept on running toward me, squinting.

Then I realized why—I was still wearing the bandanna.

He raised his hand, waving at me with the wire to stop shining the light in his face. I pulled the flashlight away, then swung it hard against the side of his head, knocking him out.

So hard, in fact, that I busted the damn flashlight. The lamp snapped off, ricocheting down the hall. I lose more flashlights that way.

I grabbed his gun and put a round through his skull. Then I went back to work on the door.

The fact that he'd been coming down with the wires probably meant that the explosives hadn't been wired in yet, but I wasn't about to take any chances. I killed the backup power unit first, ripping out the long cable that snaked from the generators into the large steel boxes where the circuit controls were. Then I found the master switch and pulled it down.

Instant darkness.

If the flashlight were still working, getting back upstairs would have been easy. But once more I stumbled around, knocking into the wall and bruising my knee before finding the hall.

It was just as dark in the corridor, but the wall gave me something to use as a reference. I went back up to the stairwell and started climbing up toward the security office on the upper level.

The stairwell was lit by skylights at the roof, and while it wasn't exactly bright, the dull gray was easier to navigate than the halls below. Once my knee stopped throbbing, I took the steps two at a time.

I heard gunfire as I neared field level. Two bodies lay on the stairs near the landing. Both were wearing bandannas. I stepped over them and kept going.

The next two bodies weren't wearing bandannas. One was a Special Squadron Zero private I remembered from our training sessions.

The other was Captain Birla. Both men had been shot from behind, and some time before—the blood around them was already sticky, starting to dry.

At least I knew he wasn't a traitor.

I continued up the stairs to the top floor where the administrative offices were, walking now instead of running. There was a ripple of automatic weapons fire as I reached the landing. I slipped into the corridor and joined two of the guards crouching by the wall near the main office.

The guard next to me turned around and jerked back, startled.

"You all right?" I asked.

"Marcinko?"

"Yeah, it's me. What?"

He tapped his forehead and pointed to me. I was still wearing the bandanna; he'd thought at first I was one of them.

The main office had a set of long windows separating it from the hall. Most of the glass was gone, and there was just enough light for anyone inside to get a good view of the hall. There were at least two tangos inside the room toward the back barricaded behind some desks, with what figured to be plenty of ammunition.

Right then I decided I was getting them out alive. I wanted to find out what the hell was going on, and shooting up the bastards, though satisfying, wouldn't help. And I wanted to get them out myself—waiting for reinforcements to help would probably mean that I'd never get a chance to interrogate them.

My bandanna gave me half an idea.

Just then, Marut and the shift supervisor came up on the other side of the hall, two guards behind them. That gave me the other half. I waved at them to stay there, then got down on my belly and started crawling across the glass on the floor to tell them what I had in mind.

I was about three-quarters of the way past the office when whoever was inside fired a few rounds. That gave me a burst of adrenaline and I just about flew to the other side.

"I want you to shout to the others—say they've got people coming up the stairs behind you and you're going to evacuate the floor," I told Marut. "Then shoot up the front office and fall back."

He nodded, but even in the dim light I could tell he had an expression on his face that said I was nuts.

"One more thing," I said, spotting some more of the wire they used for charges running along the baseboard. "Give me your flashlight."

A few moments later, the hall began crackling with gunfire. I waited a few seconds, then fired off a burst myself. Marut, at the end of the hall, yelled something, then screamed as if he were dying.

It was an Academy Award performance.

I made my move, jumping toward the shattered glass at the front of the office. I dove down, rolling beneath the wall.

They'd seen my bandanna, but whether it was that or the shock and awe of someone flying at them from the side, nobody fired.

A second later, there was a loud explosion at the back of the office: the M60s going off.

I saw a figure on my right, framed in the flash. I threw myself on him, just as Marut and the shift supervisor came in from the other side, guns blazing.

When it was over, the three men who'd been at the back of the office were dead. Two had already been severely wounded, possibly dead when we attacked. An ocean's worth of blood pooled around the third.

The man I jumped on had taken some glass shrapnel in the forehead. He was dazed, but alive.

Oh, yeah. The estimate on how many were there was off by one hundred percent. Par for the course.

I could hear the police sirens as I hauled him down the street to one of the Special Squadron Zero vehicles. I threw him in the back and drove over to the Maharaja Express, determined to find out what the hell was going on.

(III)

Mohammad al Jazra was a member of People's Islam. He'd been born in southwestern Afghanistan toward the end of the 1980s. His father had been a poppy farmer whose complicated relationship with the local Taliban waxed and waned depending on their changing views toward his crop of choice. By the mid-nineties, the family had moved to Pakistan, settling in Karachi.

The Taliban's military defeat after 9/11 drove many to Karachi, where they renewed old friendships and ended old animosities. Mohammad's family was never part of the inner circle, but they weren't total strangers either. By 2005, Mohammad took up the call as a devout believer ready to wage jihad against the devil scum Westerners. He journeyed to the northwest territories and began his education.

Skip forward a year or two, during which he seems to have had some doubts about what he was doing. He hated India, which he was taught discriminated against Muslims at every turn. At the same time, though, he saw a need for social justice and fairness lacking even in the Islamic societies around him.

Some of the ideas of Marxism attracted him. But it was an old and discredited philosophy. No one with as much intelligence as Mohammad could really feel comfortable with it.

A chance meeting with a man on his way to join what became People's Islam changed Mohammad's life. Here was a combination of strict religious observance and social justice influenced by Marxism.[24] He joined the cause, and began praying for the day when he would find revenge against the nonbelievers who had persecuted his religion.

Persecution is a theme you hear a lot from people who have come through these camps, whether they're from Pakistan, Europe, or even the U.S. You can look at any number of statistics or studies or what have you that indicate the society they've been part of is among the most tolerant in the world. Doesn't matter. To a man they feel as if their religion is being persecuted, and that they are, too.

---

[24] The scholars who really study this and similar groups will quibble with how much influence Marxism really has, but this is what Mohammad believed.

I'm not saying that there's no such thing as religious persecution or discrimination in the world. But a psychotic paranoia infuses these camps. It lives in the minds of the people who literally pledge their lives to the cause of death. You could make the world a perfect place, and these folks would still want to blow it up. So while I'm all for improving society, when it comes to dealing with terrorists, it's beside the point.

Having adopted the name Mohammad al Jazra — I'm not sure why he was claiming to be from Jazra, and I don't remember his actual name, assuming he was telling the truth — our friend joined a small cell that was being trained for demolition work. Various adventures followed, most of them almost comically boring. The group was in disarray when its leader died. Then, about a year before our meeting, a new set of leaders emerged. Mohammad never met them. In fact, he hadn't even seen them, except once from a distance. But his training resumed. His religious commitment was reignited.

Finally, he was shipped to Belgium, where he was given credentials indicating he was a British national. He then made his way to Great Britain and flew into India from Pakistan via Greece, arriving in Mumbai a few days before the operation at the stadium. He had not specifically trained for the operation, and thought it had been decided on at the last moment, but since he wasn't involved in planning, he really couldn't say.

Aside from his knowledge of wiring explosives, which was fairly extensive, that was the sum total of what he knew. The group's leaders compartmentalized the operation pretty damn well. Mohammad said he didn't even know the name of the on-scene commander, claiming to have only met him the night of the operation. He used the Arabic word for "Red," clearly a temporary *nom d'operation*.

Was Mohammad telling the truth?

I guess that there were lies here and there, but the overall pattern fit. I suspected he knew a little more about the group's leadership, but he had no reason to lie about not knowing the man who'd led the operation, since he had died next to him. Once you're dead, they get the word out about you, erecting verbal monuments to your supposed heroism. Mohammad had every reason to be honest about how well he knew him.

In any event, it was as close to the truth as I was going to get.

I turned Mohammad al Jazra over to the state security forces around noon the next day, literally leaving him on the doorstep. Urdu drove up to the ministry with me and al Jazra in the backseat. I opened the door, kicked him out, and Urdu hit the gas.

The six men who'd been with Captain Birla at the stadium had been killed. Two were shot from a distance through the head at their posts, probably by snipers; we figure that's how the tangos got into the stadium.

Everything beyond that point is a guess. From what I saw and what al Jazra had told me, the terrorists intended to plant explosives around the stadium, wiring them to the alarm system so they would go off when the alarm was pulled. The initial idea was to sneak in through the south entrance, where they believed the guards would be sleeping—something that happened during our exercise, I should note.

But the guards had been replaced by two Special Squadron Zero members, who resisted, of course. At that point, the operation went to hell. The leader assumed the entire stadium had been alerted, though this proved not to be the case. After taking care of the token Special Squadron force left, they went ahead and wired the place, probably intending to wait to blow it up when the next shift of guards arrived.

My theory is that the leader was debating whether they should all commit suicide or not, since it would have been the only way to blow up the place. But Mohammad claimed that hadn't been mentioned.

Was it just a coincidence that they picked the night Special Squadron Zero was running its exercise?

I don't believe in coincidences.

On the other hand, just because I don't believe in something doesn't mean it doesn't exist. The yeti, world peace, Santa Claus—you never know.

The way the story *officially* came out, it looked as if Special Squadron Zero had broken up a major terrorist attempt. Carefully worded accounts and even more carefully crafted leaks made it appear that Special Squadron Zero had arrived during the terrorist takeover, and a gun battle ensued. In this version, the regular security people had been rounded up by the terrorists, then managed to free themselves and turn the tide at the end.

I suppose it wasn't *that* far removed from reality. Or what everyone would have preferred was the reality.

The story gave people the comfort of seven dead heroes, including Captain Birla, who in death became twice the man he was in life. And I mean that with respect. Stories were written about him that would have made even *moi* blush. At least his family got a full pension out of it.

Despite the stories, Special Squadron Zero itself was in shambles. They'd lost their leader and some of their best men. Morale was, to put it delicately, in the shit hamper.

Sergeant Phurem was now in charge. He had missed the stadium portion of the operation, overseeing the team that had grabbed the two guards for their IDs and posts. So he didn't know the entire story when I arrived that afternoon.

His frown grew deeper with every word. Finally, he shook his head.

"No more details," he said. "My heart is heavy as it is."

Under other circumstances, state funerals would have been held for Captain Birla and the men who had died in the operation. But with the Games now less than a week away, the government was afraid that doing so would add even more attention to the terrorists, upsetting the athletes, and maybe encouraging other groups to try their hand at an attack. I can't say I fully understood their logic, but the upshot was that the funerals were private affairs.

Minister Dharma came to Captain Birla's. She stood so close to the funeral pyre at one point I thought she was going to throw herself on—a custom reserved for Hindu wives, and now officially banned.

There was absolutely no danger of that. Dharma wasn't about to sacrifice herself for an underling—or anyone.

She gave me a strange look at one point in the ceremony, an accusatory, this-is-all-your-fault expression. So what she said afterward wasn't particularly surprising.

"Your contract now has been fulfilled," she told me. "Your duties are no longer required."

"My contract has another week to run," I told her. There was also an option for further engagements, as well as some provisions for additional training work, though there was no sense mentioning those.

"Your further efforts are no longer necessary," she said. "Special Squadron Zero's tasks are fulfilled. And the unit's status will be reviewed following the Games. Thank you for your service."

And with that, I was dismissed.

That's gratitude for you, right? Whatever else had transpired, Special Squadron Zero's press was further enhancing Minister Dharma's position in the government. I wasn't exactly plugged into the Indian political scene, but I have no doubt that her name was now being whispered around in connection with a run for prime minister. She was exactly the sort of selfish, self-aggrandizing, opportunistic, cutthroat politician who'd be perfect for the job.

Minister Dharma's treatment was downright jubilant compared to Omar's. He met me at the funeral as well, supposedly by accident—which of course meant that he had moved heaven and earth to make sure he'd run into me.

To debrief me?

No. To gloat.

It's possible the agency had a vague notion of what had really happened. But it's also possible that Omar had put two and two together and come up with twenty-two.

Whatever. He didn't lose a chance to berate me.

"Special Squadron Zero, huh? It is a zero," he said, walking alongside me as I went to my car. "The unit couldn't fight its way out of a paper bag."

"That's real original, Omar."

"You know why it stinks so bad, Marcinko?"

"All the curry in the food?"

"It stinks because it's based on an old idea. Face it—Red Cell is yesterday's news. You're tired, Marcinko, and trotting around the city in gray sweats before the sun comes up is never going to change that. Your time's gone, old man. Go home and cash in your IRAs."

He deserved a good punch in the mouth, don't you think?

Not that I would do that to anyone.

I didn't trip him either as I got into my cab. Or gut punch him as he went down. He slipped on the pavement somehow, mysteriously doubling over before rolling flat on his back.

Now there's a coincidence you can believe in.

I had a war council with my people that evening at the Maharaja Express. The question was put to a vote:

Is native Indian pale ale of the same quality as that brewed in Great Britain?

The jury was undecided.

The decision to remain in India for the Games, however, was unanimous. Our contract said we would stay, and that's what we fully intended to do. No one wanted to miss the chance to see Trace in shorty shorts, stick or no stick in her hands.

There was also another matter, as Doc put it between his second and third beers:

"Everybody's looking at this operation by People's Islam as if it was a coincidence that it happened the night that Special Squadron Zero took over the stadium. Maybe it was. But I was raised not to believe in long-shot horses that miraculously show life around the last bend. Or coincidences."

Sean, calling in from Karachi, pointed out that it wasn't a neat fit. And there were plenty of elements missing from the picture. We still couldn't figure out what had happened to the two men we'd snatched in Pakistan at the madrassa. The helicopters seemed to have nothing to do with this attack. If there was a traitor, why hadn't he done more to destroy Special Squadron Zero itself?

"You have a theory on that, Mako?" Doc growled.

"No, that's my point. I'm not hearing jack about it up here."

"You're not listening well enough, maybe," said Doc.

"I'll gladly trade places with you."

"You're doing all right, Sean," I said. "Just hang in there."

We knew we didn't have the whole picture. Whether we could get enough pieces to flesh it out was an open question.

[IV]

Junior was missing from our meeting. He wasn't precisely AWOL, though he had taken a fairly liberal interpretation of his orders.

Stung by the infamous boxcar caper, he had gone back to work, hacking his way into the records of the railroads that operated on the lines that ran through Delhi. He started with the assumption that the serial numbers of the railroad cars had been switched.

We all know what happens when you ass-u-me something, but in this case, he had to start somewhere. It was a relatively obvious deduction, and rather than biting him in the butt, it led Junior to discover two other cars that had moved through Delhi in the time period after the theft of the helos.

The cars had gone to Mumbai. Our satellite service showed they had been sitting at a yard near the water there early that morning. (The latest images available.) He went to investigate on his own, grabbing a flight just about the time I was tossing my firecrackers into the security office at the stadium.

Yes, he should have checked with me before he did that. I owe him a good swift kick in the seat of his intelligence for that.

Mumbai is India's largest city. You may know it as Bombay—yes, the namesake of that glorious liquid refresher and instant cure for all that ails you. The name "Bombay" is associated with the foreigners who once lived in and built much of the city, so it's generally not used, though for a surprising number of Indians the name has an almost nostalgic ring.

Mumbai is actually a collection of islands, connected over time by development. The British East India Company leased four of them back in 1668, and things have never been the same since. Over fourteen million people now live in Mumbai, making it the second biggest city in the world. It's India's largest, and despite its size, a recent poll found it the second best place in the country to live—after Delhi, by the way. A quarter of the country's manufacturing happens there; seventy percent of its banking is either done there or related in some way. It's the Indian heartland *and* its economic engine at the same time.

Mumbai represents much of the best of modern India, but it's also a target for much of the worst, and extremely vulnerable. The attacks of

26/11 were not the first time the city has been struck by terrorists. In fact, more people were killed in a 1993 bombing spree that left the city scarred. Those attacks—thirteen bombs were exploded on the same day, March 12—followed riots between Hindus and Muslims in the city and the destruction of the Babri Mosque. Mumbai has been victimized by terrorists in major ways at least eight other times since then, most of the attacks occurring in 2002–2003.

Junior landed in the city just before the morning rush. This gave him a lot of time to think—the traffic in Mumbai is about as bad as you can imagine. He eventually got into the city and found a hotel in a slightly seedy area, the sort of place where young Indians on a tight budget might stay. He was the only American in the place. With a tattered backpack slung over his shoulder and iPod headphones sticking out of his pocket, he looked like a student on a shoestring world cruise. It wasn't a bad cover.

He went over to a nearby university and talked his way into the computer lab. After running a quick check to make sure there wasn't a keylogger lurking in the memory somewhere, he pulled out a headset and fired up Skype, placing a call to Shunt. They didn't actually talk—the call was just a pre-arranged signal for them to connect via another private Internet communications service with much better encryption and anonymous server addresses[25] to make it harder for anyone to track the calls.

The two began speaking geek to each other. Shunt had taken Junior's search of the train records a little further, and had a line on the bank accounts that had paid for the cars to be transported.

"A little more work to follow the money," he told Junior. "In the meantime, the cars are still in the yard by the ocean. The satellite made a pass two hours ago, just after dawn."

Junior downloaded a few maps of the city and the water area into his iPod, then went to one of the local student hangouts for breakfast and additional intelligence gathering. He emerged with directions to a cheap but dependable bicycle renting agency, where he got a heavy framed two-wheeler that was the bicycle equivalent of a tank. He stopped at a store to pick up a tourist guide, a goofy hat, and a cheap camera, then went to do some sightseeing on the waterfront.

---

[25] Apparently this is the wrong technical term, but I'm damned if I can understand Shunt's explanation.

The two boxcars sat at the edge of a jetty bordering a shipyard. The shipyard was surrounded by a twenty-foot fence topped by razor wire, but the siding was wide open. The tracks ran out along a crumbling concrete pier. Half a dozen fishermen sat along the edge, throwing in homemade lines when Junior went out.

He asked a few annoying tourist questions to establish his bona fides, then pretended to wander aimlessly around the track area, checking to see if the cars were being watched. While he couldn't see a lookout, Junior realized that any of the fishermen could be watching him surreptitiously, and there were plenty of places in the shipyard and the buildings opposite the track area for someone to perch. So he decided he'd have to wait to check the trains out when it was dark.

If you've followed any of my recent adventures, you're undoubtedly aware that Mongoose has been downright jolly during his time in India, certainly compared to his usual cranky self. It's not that he lacked material—on the contrary, India was chockful of Mongoose's top bitches: muggy weather, incessant mosquitoes, and people who would just as soon steal your wallet as give you the time of day.

But it also had a beautiful woman: Vina.

Ironically, she was Argentinean, but Mongoose was never much on geography. Or maybe I should say that the only geography he was interested in was of a very personal nature.

He spent his small amount of free time trying to—well, you know what he was trying to do.

Mongoose left our staff meeting early to accompany her to a reception for one of the arriving Commonwealth teams. During the course of the evening, he met a few fellow mixed martial arts enthusiasts and wrangled an invitation for the next day to check out the athletic facilities where they were training. It was at a facility we hadn't checked before, and I agreed it was a good idea for him to take a look at the security arrangements. His only disappointment was that Vina couldn't go along because of other commitments.

That was counterbalanced by another invitation to accompany her to a diplomatic reception planned for the following evening at the British ambassador's residence. This was a high-level to-do, with all of the government's big shots and even some Bollywood superstars expected to attend.

Vina really wanted to attend, and in fact undertook a special shopping mission to obtain just the right dress. Mongoose wasn't exactly looking forward to it, to be honest, since it was black-tie formal. But as a show of true love, he went down to the hotel tailor and had himself fitted with a rental tux.

Amazing what nookie can do to a guy.

More from Junior's after-action report:

> I knew from my recce during the early afternoon that the area where the boxcars were was exposed to observation from all sides. So rather than trying to sneak in unseen, I decided to make it obvious that I was there, creating a pretense that would explain my presence.
>
> During the morning I'd met some international students at the café. Some of them had mentioned a party that evening in a building on campus. That gave me an idea—why not have a party by the water?
>
> I started spreading the word immediately after returning from my trip to the water. It was going to be a great party—you name the substance, it would be there.

> My plan worked even better than I had hoped. I got down to the waterfront around 2300. There must have been five dozen kids milling around in the area. There was a very sweet, herbal smell in the air, and a few girls were showing off some yoga poses on the rocks.
>
> It was hard to tear myself away from that, but I did finally, grabbing a free beer from a cooler someone had brought along and meandering over to the boxcars.
>
> Remembering our experience in Delhi where the boxcars had been welded shut, I had taken along a battery-powered Sawzall with an extra battery pack and a case of blades. I also had a heavy-duty lock cutter. But the tools turned out to be unnecessary. The door on the first car I checked wasn't locked. With little difficulty, I pushed it open and went inside.
>
> It was empty. No helicopter.
>
> The car smelled like fuel. Something had leaked onto the

floor of the car. I thought it was jet fuel—the Ahi runs on JP—but I couldn't be sure. I dug out a few pieces of saturated wood with my knife and stuck them in my backpack. Then I went and checked the other car. That one also wasn't locked. The floor was marked with black, as if something had been pushed inside and moved around. Naturally, I was convinced the marks had been made by a helicopter's tires, but I had no proof.

I started looking at the walls and noticed that they had been scraped as well. There was black paint in one of the marks. By my calculation, the helicopter had been a tight fit, and when it was pushed in, the tail had scraped along the side.

I had no proof though. This was all speculation. And I knew I had to be careful with that.

Junior went back to the first car and found similar scrapes. But that was all he found. If the helicopters had been there—and really, he had no proof of that—they were now gone.

Junior spent the next few hours trying to figure out where they had gone. At first glance, the plant next door seemed like an obvious choice. And yet, there was no easy way to get there from the train tracks. The razor-wire fence had no opening on that side.

The property belonged to a small wire factory. There were two small-ish buildings and an open-sided shed, along with acres of storage area where spools were collected. There was also a dock area where ships and barges unloaded scrap metal and took on the large spindles.

A close examination of satellite photos of the yard proved that the helicopters weren't there when the satellite passed overhead. Junior, thinking they might have been disassembled, looked for large parts as well, but couldn't find any that looked like they might belong to a helicopter. It was a pretty crowded place, and everything in the yard was exposed to the satellite. A comparison of several days' worth of images seemed to prove that, except for a half-dozen spindles and scrap metal near the dock, nothing had moved.

But Junior couldn't see into the shed, or the buildings for that matter. So he decided he would have to go inside. Since it was already dawn by this time, climbing the fence unseen was no longer an option. Besides, the front door is always the best solution.

He arrived at seven in the morning on his bicycle. There was a small crowd of workers near the entrance, and for a moment he thought he could just slip in. But as he slowed down, he saw that there were security people at the gate, checking IDs against names on a clipboard. More importantly, all of the workers were dark-skinned and clearly Indian. A white boy would immediately stand out.

That didn't rule out the possibility of getting into the factory; it just changed the way he'd have to do things. Junior rode off on his bike, heading toward a shopping district. It turned out to be way too early for him to buy what he wanted there, so he diverted to a large western hotel complex that featured a number of shops on the first and second floor.

Expensive shops, I should add. Our bookkeeper is still howling about them.

An hour later he emerged equipped with an overpriced suit and a new briefcase. A quick detour to a stationery shop later, he arrived at the wire factory as an American businessman looking to buy ISO 9001 certi-fied zinc aluminum wire, or "zincal" as they call it in the trade.

That wasn't the factory's specialty, which was just fine as far as Ju-nior was concerned.

"What's your best material?" he asked. "I have other clients . . ."

He got a full tour, including a walk-through of the shed area. He learned a hell of a lot about wire—but about helicopters, nada.

If the helos had been brought into the factory, they had gone into a smelting area and been made into steel rods, and were now wrapped around spindles destined to hold slats of wood together when they were bundled and shipped halfway around the world.

Unlikely.

Junior left his card with the vice president and went back to work.

Back in Delhi, I'd grabbed my reading glasses and headed over to Special Squadron Zero's headquarters to continue my review of the intelligence gathered prior to the Pakistan raid. I never got the glasses out of my pocket, however; I found myself barred at the gate by two apologetic but nonetheless burly members of the squadron.

"Sergeant Phurem gave us explicit orders, Commander Rick," they apologized. "You are not allowed on the property."

"What?"

"It's the minister," said the taller of the two guards. "You are persona non gracious."

"Persona non grata?"

He nodded solemnly. At least it was a title I was very familiar with.

"Go get the sergeant," I said. "I want to talk to him."

They called him on the radio, but could just as well have held their breaths. I could see by their frowns that he wasn't coming long before they passed on his excuses.

"Let me use the restroom, at least," I said. "Breakfast didn't agree with me."

"Sorry, sorry," said the taller guard. "But you are not allowed. It is our jobs to not let you in."

"The gas station across the road has a clean restroom," offered the other guard.

"You're really not going to let me in?"

"You are not permitted. There is no way you can come in."

It's not every day you get a challenge like that. After some appropriate gestures of my appreciation, I made a strategic retreat to the gas station, then went to equip for the operation.

Many are the ways one can break into a military facility. I'd lectured Special Squadron Zero on many, and since they knew me pretty well by sight a number of choices weren't available to me.

That still, however, left me a variety of choices. I suppose I could have been flashy and made a HALO jump. But as I said a few pages ago, the front door is always the best.

About a half hour after I was ceremoniously kicked out, an ambulance drove up to the gate. There were two men in the front seat—a driver with a thick black beard, and the attendant with an even thicker gray one. Both men were wearing long robes and fancy cloth hats, and could be said to bear at least a passing resemblance to Richard Marcinko.

The vehicle they were driving, though it looked like a legitimate ambulance, was several years old, and in fact its registration indicated it had been put out of official service more than eight months before.

The guards quickly ordered the ambulance to the side and began a careful search of the men and the vehicles.

They were in the middle of the search when a garbage truck drove up for its weekly pickup. After a precursory glance, the truck was waved through.

Fifteen minutes later, having changed out of the protective coveralls and sprayed a bit of eau de parfum around my shoulders, I was in Sergeant Phurem's office chair, smiling as he came through the door.

"I should have known," he said, shaking his head. "Did anyone see you?"

"Many people saw," I told him. "They just didn't realize what they were seeing."

He laughed, then closed the door.

"It is the minister's orders, not mine," he said sadly. "If you are found, I am off to a post on the Bangladesh border, for sure."

I started to get up to give him his seat, but he insisted I stay where I was.

He admitted to being in a poor mood. He'd lost his commander and some of his best men, and now faced the likelihood of a reassignment that would end his career. The minister had claimed that the unit would be revitalized after the Games and some of the current controversy died down, but he had been in the army long enough to know that "revitalize" meant "reassign the NCOs," especially those who were closely identified with the now out of favor commander.

I commiserated.

"There is nothing more to be done," he said sadly. "But, Commander Rick, what can I do for you?"

"I want to review all of the intelligence relating to the Kashmir raid," I told him. "I'd started to the other day."

"Why?"

"I'm wondering if we were set up."

He didn't quite understand what that meant, so I spelled it out for him: were we spoon-fed intelligence so that we would conduct that particular raid for some ulterior purpose?

"What would the sense of that be?" he asked.

"If I knew, I wouldn't be here."

"I'm afraid I cannot help. It can't be permitted. And besides, you know that we didn't conduct the intelligence ourselves. We were given only the summaries, and then only what was relevant. So if there is something interesting, it would be with the military intelligence unit. That is where you should conduct your search."

"You won't help me?"

"I can't." He shook his head grimly, and stared at the ground. Puppies that have peed off their papers looked more cheerful. "My hands are bound. I'm afraid I can't help."

I had suspected he might say something along those lines. Which is why I had copied the computer access codes, key words, and encryption keys to the USB memory chip in my pocket while waiting for him to come in.

Yes, I'd taken the precaution of installing a keylogger when our troubles began, as part of the effort to see if we had a traitor in our midst. Not that I didn't trust anyone.

I know Shunt or Junior would have done it much, much quicker, but a few hours later I found my way back to the intelligence files on India for Islam. I wasn't so much interested in what they said—I already knew a lot about the group, obviously—but how and where the information had been compiled.

Most of the information on recent activities had come from a single source labeled F5. He had pinpointed the madrassa, and forwarded information about the group's intention to strike at the Commonwealth Games.

Who was F5? The files of course didn't say. The most logical guess was that he was Pakistani—the group's connections with the intelligence agencies there were well known. But if so, he wasn't an official contact, or even a "turned" agent—those exchanges were handled in a different manner, and weren't coded as sources.

He also didn't come up in the cross-reference indexes, meaning that he hadn't supplied any other intelligence, at least none good enough to make it to any of the files that were used to prepare the pre-Commonwealth Games briefings. There was no record of information from him older than two and a half months.

In other words, F5 had existed only to pass on information about this group, where it was located, and why it should be attacked.

There were many possible explanations; the most benign was that the Indian military intelligence agency had compartmentalized their operation, dividing the information from a single course in neat little envelopes depending on who he was ratting on: F5 for India Islam, F7 for Free Kashmir, etc. But that wasn't the way the agency normally worked.

I was predisposed to smelling rat, and I certainly smelled one here.

What else was useful?

The file on India for Islam contained images that had been made by

Indian reconnaissance flights prior to our attack. Yes, I had seen them before our raid; we'd used them to plan the assault. We had good images of the grounds and the tangos going through their exercises, and even working through a mockup raid. Looking at them now, I realized something I hadn't earlier.

The mockup appeared to show them doing a simple run-through of an operation, taking down part of a command post. It was clearly part of a much larger plan, a practice run on a difficult segment.

I'd assumed[26] the first time I saw it that it was an attack on the stadium, which would have posts behind concrete barriers similar to the ones in the photo. Looking at it now, I realized it wasn't the stadium at all. I'd just spent a great deal of time there, and knew that the layout was very different. The mockup had double guard posts, and even what could be interpreted as gun emplacements nearby. There was none of that at the stadium.

But I had seen something very similar just a few days before: the main gate at the army complex where the nukes were being stored.

---

[26] What did we say about ass-u-me? But why is it my ass that's always getting bitten?

(V)

We last left Matthew Loring playing Junior Achievement businessman at the wire plant in Mumbai.

Having discovered that was a dead end, he checked in with Shunt and began exploring other possibilities. Shunt had broken into the railroad company's computers and taken a look at its billing system, trying to track down who had ordered or paid for transporting the cars to Mumbai. Unfortunately, the company's record keeping left a great deal to be desired. It was a jumble of invoices and work orders that had no relation to the transport or traffic files.

There's no doubt that the train cars were deliberately switched somewhere, most likely in Delhi, but you could never prove it from the records, and not just because someone had carefully covered their tracks. Even regular train runs showed wide discrepancies between what was billed and what the manifests claimed was transported—discrepancies, I should add, that didn't necessarily favor the company. Whoever had picked them had chosen carefully.

The bank it dealt with, however, was a different story. The bank kept good records of deposits made into the company's accounts. After getting into the system—using a technique Chinese hackers have since been excoriated for—Shunt discovered that most of the rail company's business came from a dozen large firms. Most moved handcrafted items out of the Punjabi area down to Mumbai or elsewhere along the coast for shipping. They did this at regular intervals, paying with commendable frequency and in very consistent sums.

This made it easier to find the company that had paid an amount that seemed to correspond with the charges for taking train cars to Delhi, and then from Delhi to Mumbai. (I say "seemed" because the books were so screwed up, and there were no customary costs.)

The company's name was Greater Sterling Ltd.

Nice, English-sounding name, common not only in Great Britain but in places once dominated by Great Britain, where the hint of a link to the former colonial power implied stability and substance. But names are easy to manufacture. Shunt realized the connection was probably spurious, even as he started to trace it back. Sure enough, Greater Sterling had no link to Great Britain.

It did, however, have a link to a Hong Kong shipping firm known to have been used by the Chinese two years before to ship spare aircraft parts to Iran.

"Hey, Dad."

"Junior?"

"You know they can sew a whole suit down here in three hours?"

"Down here where?"

"Mumbai. I didn't buy the suit though. There was a jacket that was pretty good, so I went with that, right off the shelf. You should check this place out."

"*Junior*—"

"I'll bet you're wondering what I'm doing."

Junior and I didn't have a lot of father-son bonding time when he was growing up, mostly because I didn't know he existed. Which means he missed a lot of chances to get on my bad side, and I missed a lot of opportunities to kick his ass.

Maybe he was trying to make up for it. Let's put it this way: he was damn lucky he was in Mumbai and I was in Delhi.

After I reamed him out for not telling me where he was headed, I made him give me an info dump on what he was up to.

"The train cars arrived two days after the helicopters were stolen," he told me. "What I figure happened was this: they were taken up north to that rail siding, and packed into the cars there. That night they were picked up and taken down to Delhi, where the IDs were switched. From there they were taken to Mumbai. They came in at night. Either that night, or the next night, the helicopters were taken out of the cars and driven out to the jetty where they were loaded onto a barge. From there, they were taken out to sea."

"Why the sea?"

"I'm getting there. They were loaded into a cargo container. It's the *Han Li*."

"That ought to be pretty easy to check."

"Thanks, Dick."

"Whoa! Whoa!" I yelled into the phone, but he'd already hung up.

You gotta beat them when they're young, or they never learn.

I found out what he had in mind a few minutes later, but only because Mongoose had the good sense to ask me if I had approved Junior's plan.

Which I had not. Although on review, it did meet certain requirements for audacity and gumption. So after a number of minor adjustments, I raised my hand and gave it the one finger blessing.

Among the minor adjustments was my contacting the Indian navy to let them know about the container ship, which was now sailing south in international waters.

One of the advantages of getting a few hash marks on your sleeve is that you accumulate contacts in high places. I'd first met Admiral Inay Yamuna when he was a young buck lieutenant trying to make a name for himself in the Indian navy. His political strategy was somewhat flawed at the time: he believed that the quickest way to the top was to take on a contingent of Indian soldiers single-handedly.

This was in a bar in Portugal. I can't entirely remember why we were there; it was during my early SEAL days, so I was probably ordered to forget it anyway.

I do remember why I got involved—a chair came crashing over my shoulder, knocking not only my drink but an entire bottle of gin to the floor. Somebody had to pay for that gin, and it wasn't going to be me.

Like most barroom disputes, the actual outcome that night was murky, though I can assure you that I did not pay for that drink or any drink. The lieutenant and I eventually found our way to a different bar, where we discussed important naval matters such as how to find the best bar in port, and whether blondes really are more fun.

I'd spoken to him occasionally over the years as he made the climb to admiral. He stopped pressing his luck in the barroom and distinguished himself on the bridge. Now he happened to be commander of the naval detachment in Goa, the Indian state whose shore the cargo vessel currently was steaming off of.

One thing about friendships forged in battle, they endure. He came right on the line when I called, and after an exchange of the usual terms of endearment—I believe he used the words "shit-faced," "green balled," "angstrom dick motherfucker"—I filled him in on the situation.

Admiral Yamuna would have loved nothing better than to take credit for getting the helicopters back, and the fact that he didn't particularly like the Chinese made him all the more anxious to cooperate.

But the Chinese ship was in international waters, and the Indian navy couldn't intercept it without quite a bit of proof, and even then he'd need an order from the prime minister that, the admiral predicted, would take weeks if not months to arrive.

"I thought that would be the case, dung brain," I told him. "So I have another idea. Or rather, one of my men does."

"I'm all ears, donkey face."

Actually the plan that Junior came up with wasn't nearly as good as what the admiral suggested. Junior wanted to lease a speedboat, go out, sneak aboard the *Han Li*, find the helos, then return with evidence.

"A speedboat would be expensive to lease," said the admiral. "And getting it back in one piece might be difficult. What you need is something more dependable. I cannot give you a navy warship, but I know where you could steal one."

[VI]

The vessel Junior and Mongoose ended up using—my lawyers dislike the word "steal"—was not an Indian navy ship.

First of all, it was more like a boat, especially if one considers the traditional definition of a boat being a vessel that can be lifted onto a larger vessel.

And second of all, it actually belonged to the Tamil Tigers, although they were in no position to reclaim it, having had it confiscated in a raid by the Indian navy some months before.

The Tamil Tigers—who the hell are they?

Another entry in the Terrorist Hall of Fame, Indian division:

Full name—Liberation Tigers of Tamil Eelam.[27]

Aspiration—the liberation of northern Sri Lanka.

Occupation—Depending on your point of view, either full-time freedom fighters or unconscionable terrorists. Or both.

The Tamil Tigers were founded in 1976, I believe, in hopes of establishing a Tamil state in Sri Lanka. Sri Lanka is the big island off the coast of southern India, formerly known to us in the West as Ceylon. If you look at a map, it's the football about to be punted toward Malaysia. Like India, Ceylon/Sri Lanka was once ruled by the British. And like India, there are many Hindus and Muslims there. But even taken together, they're a minority; something in the area of seventy percent of the population is Sinhalese. A sizable portion of the remainder are Tamil. As you might imagine, there are frictions.

I'm not going to get into the ethnic back and forth. Take it for granted that I'm oversimplifying here.

Basically, after independence the majority Sinhalese declared their language the official language, and then passed laws limiting the rights and government job opportunities for people of other backgrounds. The Tamils, who are mostly concentrated in the northern provinces of the island, didn't particularly like that and eventually rebelled. Hence the Tamil Tigers.

---

[27] I'd give the Tamil script but the typesetter would surely take up drinking again in response.

The actual civil war is usually dated from July 23, 1983, when the Tamil Tigers launched an attack on a Sri Lankan military base. But the conflict had been simmering for years, and was always running hot and cold during good times and bad. At their height, the Tamil Tigers controlled a large portion of the northwestern corner of the island. They had armored vehicles, airplanes—and yes, attack boats.

Small attack boats, but sometimes that's all you need.

India's attitude toward the civil war gradually changed. At first, and for quite a while, the government secretly helped many Sri Lankan rebel movements and dissidents, including the Tamil Tigers. But the Tigers weren't particularly easy to love. They had a well-earned reputation for terrorist acts, and their goals weren't necessary those of the Indian government's.

In 1987, the Indians came to terms with the Sri Lankan government. Part of the agreement saw India sending peacekeeping forces to Sri Lanka. That helped Sri Lanka escalate its war against the Tamil rebels in the north, since they no longer needed their own troops to protect the south.

Things got real complicated after that. The Indian troops were so unpopular at one point that the Sri Lankan government armed rebels to fight them.

Eventually, India pulled out. But the Tamil Tigers were still pissed, and so they decided to make their own strike against the Indians, sending a suicide bomber to kill Rajiv Gandhi (the former prime minister) in 1991.

What? You thought suicide bombers were only in the Middle East? And that Osama bin Goat-turd created terrorism?

Read up on your history, grasshopper!

But I digress.

Almost twenty years of civil war followed, with so many different phases that you could spend months sorting through them all. The Tamil Tigers had their own public relations teams, and quite a number of people came to admire their spirit and their audacity. Their tactics were, at times, relatively inspired. If you're interested in asymmetric warfare, they're not a bad group to study.

However, they weren't exactly model citizens. One of the features of the Tamil Tigers armies were children soldiers, recruited at the point of a gun. Then there was the fact that Tamil Tigers would rather shoot civilians than allow them to flee to government-controlled areas. More than a few times the Tigers used civilians as human shields. And they weren't shy about using terrorism as a weapon of choice.

The war ended in 2009, a little more than a year before I got to India. At that point, the Tamil Tigers had been crushed militarily, their main leaders mostly killed. How long peace will last is anyone's guess. Perhaps more ominous for the rest of the world, there have been consistent rumors that "soldiers" trained by the Tamil Tigers have gone elsewhere to share their training. Terrorism is a lot like VD—it keeps spreading, and keeps getting you in the privates.

Info dump over. Back to our regularly scheduled mayhem.

The Indian navy had, at times, done battle with the Tamil Tigers' sea branch, the Sea Tigers. That campaign had resulted, among other things, in the capture of several of the Sea Tigers' vessels.

Much of the Tamil Tigers' success depended on their audacity and courage—SEAL traits, to be sure. But they were also very clever not only about leveraging their equipment, but adapting seemingly innocuous gear to deadly purposes.

The Tiger boats were a case in point. They were commercial boats adapted to military use with the addition of cannons and other weapons. Among the most potent—or at least coolest—were small speedboats outfitted with gun mounts for RPGs and heavy machine guns. Painted in a sharp camo, the speedboats were the Tamil equivalent of SEAL insertion craft.

Two of them were sitting at a dock in Goa, where they had been taken for evaluation after being captured by the Indians during the conflict. Rumor had it that said evaluation included several sorties of water skiing, but I have no hard information on that.

(Just in case you're not using Google Earth to follow along—Goa is quite a distance and on the other coast from Sri Lanka. So there was very little chance of these vessels making their way back there if some former members decided to mount a raid for old times' sake.)

Ordinarily, the docks where the boats were kept was guarded by members of Marcos. But for some odd reason, the watch was ordered to stand down that evening and attend to other duties.

What a shocking coincidence.

Junior picked up Mongoose at the local airport and they drove over to the dock, stopping to fill a few jerry cans with high-test boat juice. That turned out not to be necessary—both boats had been topped off at some point earlier that day.

The coincidences just keep multiplying, don't they?

They took both boats out, slipping past the shore lookouts, which were curiously quiet. The cargo vessel was fifty miles out to sea and a little south of the Indian naval base at Mormugao. The speedboats ate up the distance, and the dark hulk of the cargo carrier came into view a little more than an hour after they set off. The boys headed south about fifteen miles, roughly the distance they calculated the cargo carrier would cover in two hours. They left one of the boats there, engine idling, then headed back to pay the *Han Li* a visit.

I've written several times about the tactics SEAL teams employ to board ships, a rich variety of possibilities that include everything from lightweight aluminum ladders to suction cups that turn you into Spider-man.

My personal favorite? Being invited aboard, of course.

In this case, the boys planned on using a harpoon gun. Rather than a harpoon, the warhead was a grappling hook attached to a line. The plan was simple: they'd draw up alongside the cargo area where it was unlikely anyone was posted. The line would be fired. When it stopped playing out, they would pull it back, secure it against the rail or whatever obstruction it caught on, then scramble aboard.

Simple to explain, much harder to do. You're moving, they're moving, the line is wet, and it's an awful long way up.

Surprisingly, though, detection is generally not much of a problem. Today's cargo carriers are very big ships mostly run by automation. They don't have many crew members, and those who are aboard have plenty to do that doesn't involve examining the rails for odd-looking pieces of metal. The ship has its own peculiar sounds, and the clunk of a twelve- or eighteen-inch grappling iron rarely registers above the engines and general loud shush of the ocean.

Once you're on the vessel, it's not hard to get into the cabin or the container area without being seen. There are plenty of shadows and unlit areas to hide in. And few if any watchmen think it's possible for anyone to come aboard outside of port. Their eyes may see something, but their brains quickly explain it away.

The big problem in this case would be identifying which of the 160 or so cargo containers aboard might have the helicopters. But Junior had considered that problem already, and with Shunt's help, had narrowed down the possibilities to four containers that had not been on the ship in the last satellite image they had before Mumbai.

In their waterproof, rubberized rucks—similar to standard SEAL issue, though ours are a little fancier and I'd guess less expensive, since I do the buying myself—they had acetylene cutting torches and small digital cameras. They'd cut the locks, take a peek, photograph what they saw, then get off the ship.

I keep saying "they."

Ideally, one of them would have stayed aboard the speedboat while the other did the onboard recce. Makes a lot of sense, right? You want the boat there when you're done.

The problem was one of youthful ego. Junior wanted to go onboard himself. Mongoose, who after all was a former SEAL, figured that he should be the one to do it.

I would have chosen Mongoose myself. But I wasn't there. And rather than argue about it, they decided they would tie the boat to the line so they'd be sure it would be with them when they were done. And if it wasn't—well, they had that other craft waiting farther south. They could bail out, inflate the little survival life rafts they had with them, then drift and/or paddle over to it.

Way too macho, frankly. But there's no use second-guessing them now.

They caught a big break as they took the boat in toward their target. Circling in from the stern, Mongoose spotted two lines trailing from the quarterdeck. That's a sign of very poor seamanship—but it's also very typical, and was something he'd been trained to look for in this situation.

They cut their motor, cruised in, and tied up. Then, like a pair of rats in search of booty aboard a fat ocean cruiser, scurried up the lines.

I missed out on the fun and games because I had other things to do in Delhi:

Namely, take Mongoose's place at the black-tie reception.

Not that I was moving in on Vina. She was an extremely attractive young woman, but as I've said several times now, my thoughts may roam and my eyes may wander, but my heart and carcass belong to Karen.

Right, hon?

If Vina was disappointed by the substitution, she didn't let on. Mongoose had already explained the situation, and while I suspect that she may have thought he'd been a little too eager to accept the assignment, she never mentioned it.

I know the women want me to explain exactly what it was she wore. I'm afraid that's not my best department. It was a kind of beige white, it came all the way to the floor, and it made her look like an angel floating above the ground. It had straps and a daring yet tasteful décolletage, which is French for *ooo la la*. Her hair had been pinned back with a pair of silver combs. With the exception of Karen and Trace, I can't recall taking a prettier girl on my arm.

We arrived at the ambassador's residence about an hour and a half after the soiree was officially scheduled to start, which made us among the earliest guests. I escorted her in, then gave a fatherly glance toward the row of young swains who were looking her over from the edge of the dance floor.

You could hear the shriveling loud and clear.

The band struck up and I escorted her to the battle zone. My dancing may have been a little stiff—it had been a while since I'd danced the light fantastic in the name of duty—but Vina was so light on her feet that I could have worn leaded diving boots and still looked good swirling her around. I did my manly duty as a sturdy partner, then left her to greet some of her friends while I went in search of some refreshments—and the people I'd come to see.

First up on the list was Madam Secretary of State, who was supposed to be here taking a break from the intense round of peace talks trying to stave off the latest escalation of good feelings between the neighboring enemies. Alas, Madam Secretary was in the middle of a group eight or nine deep, and as things worked out I never got a chance to ask if she'd care to dance. But east of the scrum was an old acquaintance of mine who worked in State intelligence.

I was surprised to see Jerry D.[28] there, but now I realized why the secretary of State had deigned to call me for my impressions in the first place. Before joining the State Department, Jerry had been a SEAL. He retired and, either through boredom or temporary insanity, defected to

---

[28] Not his real name or initial.

the National Security Council as a weapons analyst. Now instead of blowing things up he was trying to stop other people from doing so.

There's nothing like seeing two men in monkey suits cheerfully cursing each other out as they make their way toward the booze.

"Let me buy you a drink," he said, following our lively exchange of the usual terms of endearment. "Bombay Sapphire?"

"Is there a drink more appropriate to India?"

"If there was, you wouldn't drink it." He raised his glass. (Scotch, neat.) "Thank you for your help."

"Are things going well?"

He moved his head back and forth, a little like a speed bag when it's being given a sturdy workout. "They could be better. They could be worse."

"How long have you have been working on this?" I asked.

"Oh. Well, in a serious way—six months. We realized that things were getting closer about three months ago."

"That's when you started moving the chess pieces around?"

The comment, an obvious reference to the warheads, took him by surprise.

"Same old Dick," he said, recovering. "Always with the ear to the ground."

"It makes it easier for people to step on me that way."

Jerry laughed.

"Is that an important question?" he asked, sipping his drink.

"The answer might be. I need a ballpark."

He looked down at his glass.

"And if something were to happen that made it very important," he said, "the secretary would find out?"

"You'd be the first to know. Where it goes from there, I have no idea."

"Ah, you don't have to lie to me."

"It's not a lie. An exaggeration. But you would be on the list. Sooner rather than later."

"Three months, the planning started," he said. "The timeline was always a bit theoretical, but it's pretty much followed along as predicted."

Let's connect some of the cookie crumbs here:

Three months ago, India started planning on moving its nukes to a central location. Very soon thereafter, a terrorist organization begins planning an operation that seems intended to strike at that base.

About as much a coincidence as the marines leaving their posts near the Tiger boats, I'd have to say.

We exchanged some further small talk before I wandered off into the farther recesses of the reception hall. I had suspected that Minister Dharma would be among the guests, and I wasn't disappointed. There she was, as radiant as ever, standing with a group of foreign dignitaries who looked as if they were preparing offers of marriage.

I could hear the flutter of hearts breaking as I approached. Minister Dharma kept her gaze locked ninety degrees from me, a sure sign of interest.

A British foreign service worker whom I knew slightly approached and began making conversation. We talked a bit, giving me a chance to observe the minister without being overly obvious about it.

What does a traitor look like?

Like everybody else. They usually don't have horns, or multicolored auras rising over their heads.

"A man may smile and smile, and be a villain," said Shakespeare.

"Not all scumbags smell like puked milk," says Richard Marcinko.

"Richard, how good to see you here," said the minister, deigning to notice me standing right in front of her.

I got the royal treatment—air kisses on both cheeks.

Naturally I had to return them, sans air.

"I didn't know you were coming," she said after I planted the second wet one.

"I was a last-minute replacement."

"I see. I thought you were on your way back to America."

"I'm sticking around for the Games. I'm due for a vacation, and I love sports."

A very slight look of displeasure passed over her face—a lone cloud on an otherwise perfect summer day.

"Maybe we can have lunch sometime," I said pleasantly.

"I'd like that," she said, with just enough eye contact to make it seem as if she meant it.

"We really didn't have a chance to get to know each other," I added. "And that was a shame."

"Mmmmm, yes. That was. It would be . . . interesting."

Further flirtations were ended with the arrival of Vina, who curled her hand proprietarily around my arm.

"There you are, Dick," she said. "I was afraid I had lost you."

Most likely she gave the minister a flash of green eye, for Dharma's gaze narrowed a bit. I introduced them.

"Very pleased to meet you," lied Vina. She turned to me. "Dick, you promised you would dance."

"I did."

I told Minister Dharma that I would definitely call and find some time for her before going home.

"Please do," she said. "Lunch would be most . . . nutritious."

While I was finding my rusty way through a fox-trot, Junior and Mongoose were doing their own dance up the line to the *Han Li*.

Climbing wet ropes at night with the spray of the sea in your face is more an art than science, especially when the waves rise and the line slackens just enough to tug your stomach.

There's a point about halfway up when you think, *My God, is this mother ever going to end?* Then about three-quarters of the way to the deck you're sure it's not going to end. You glance down, even though you realize that's the absolute last thing you should do, and all you see is a yawning black pit. Letting go is not an option, but your curled fingers can't take much more, and your thigh muscles—climbing ropes requires a surprising amount of leg action—are ready to implode.

You keep going. Partly because of pride—you don't want to fail. Largely because you know if you don't, you are never going to make it home.

Mongoose made the rail, took a quick peek at the deck to make sure they were clear, then turned back and waited for Junior to arrive. One thing I'll say for Junior—I doubt he could have climbed that rope a year before. He had busted his ass getting himself into better shape, adding bulk and a lot more upper body strength, and it paid off that night.

They went over the rail one at a time, resting in the shadow of the cabin to recoup their breath and strength. The cargo containers they had to inspect were far forward, at the top of a row nearest the bow.

Getting there wouldn't be too difficult. There was a run of about twenty yards where they might be visible from the bridge, but otherwise the deck gear and containers gave them pretty good coverage.

"Ready?" asked Mongoose.

Junior nodded and began to step away from the bulkhead.

Just as he did, the forward deck area lit with searchlights.

I'd gotten what I'd come for at the reception, but Vina wanted to stay awhile longer. I had no objection to that, as long as I could fortify myself for the long haul. I deposited her with a group of friends and made my way to another of the portable bars stationed around the large ballroom.

The British do colonial decadence particularly well. The ambassador's house was a veritable monument to the lost Age of the Viceroys, with intricately patterned marble tile on the floor and walls, grandiose columns at the side, and crystal chandeliers whose bulbs could have lit half the city. Even though they were all native Indians, the servants were the stoic, stiff upper lip types you see in posh London clubs.

"Bombay Sapphire," I told the man working the bar. "Give me an extra helping of rocks. I'm feeling a little warm."

"Hot flash?" said a familiar scolding voice nearby.

Omar.

"I didn't realize they were so desperate for guests," I said, taking my drink.

"I was going to say the same to you."

"Well, have a nice life," I told him, starting to make my exit.

"Rushing off to your latest defeat?"

I would have thought his accident at the funeral improved his manners, but obviously he needed a refresher. Even so, I would have left that to others had he not added something along the lines of, "Everything you touch goes to shit eventually, old man."

As mild-mannered and even tempered as I am, I couldn't let a remark like that go. I took him by the elbow and gently steered him toward the nearby French doors, which led to a small, private, and thankfully empty, patio.

Maybe I applied a little pressure to his elbow. The precise details escape me.

"Don't screw with me, Marcinko," he said, with all the ferocity of a pussy cat that's just been neutered.

"You're going to have to work on your manners," I told him. "You're at an ambassador's residence."

"At least I'm not a failure."

"That's a matter of opinion."

"Only because I can't puff myself up like you."

"That's all I do. Puff myself up."

"You're a dismal failure. You've been a disaster here. You even screwed up in Kashmir."

"What the hell are you talking about?"

"You didn't make a dent in that cell," he said. He didn't name India for Islam, though it was obvious that's who he meant. "That madrassa? Pppph."

He was trying to spit, but all he did was dribble down his shirt.

"They're still active, you know. All sorts of comm traffic in the past twenty-four hours." Omar smirked. "Your time is over."

"What kind of traffic?"

"Lots of traffic." He got a worried look on his face, realizing finally he'd shot his mouth off when he shouldn't have. "They're planning something."

"When?"

"How the hell do I know?"

I grabbed his elbow again. Or maybe it was a different body part, more strategically located and more sensitive to pressure.

"God only knows what they're doing," he squeaked. "But soon. Soon. Twenty-four hours. Twelve. Everyone's going on alert. Like I said, you're washed up. Your time is over."

PART THREE
DOMINO THEORY

A fundamental principle is never to remain completely passive, but to attack the enemy frontally and from the flanks, even when he is attacking us.

—Major General Carl von Clausewitz, *On War*, 1831, tr. Howard and Paret

[1]

Junior and Mongoose froze on the side of the ship, unsure what was going on as light flooded over the deck. They had their weapons out and at the ready.

"I don't think they saw us," Mongoose whispered. "The lights are up near the bow. There's something going on up there."

They waited a few minutes, making sure Mongoose was right. Worried that someone would come aft and spot the line and, more specifically, the boat tied to the other end, Mongoose made a tactical decision to cut it.

"We can always swim to it," he told Junior.

Junior nodded. I'm going to guess a bit grimly.

Reasonably sure that they hadn't been spotted, they began slinking forward, hugging the bulkhead of the superstructure. They were on the port side of the ship. The hatchways and doors that they could see were all battened down, everything snugged against the sea and what little there was of weather. The air was calm, and the heave of the ocean gentle. The moon, about three-quarters full, peeked between a few high-level clouds. Under other circumstances, it would have been a very pleasant night.

As they reached the forward corner of the superstructure, they realized that the light was coming from a set of floods that were focused on the forward cargo area. The ship had slowed, its speed gradually falling from the five or six knots it had been making when they boarded to closer to two.

A lifeboat was tied to its davits about ten yards from the edge of the cabin area. The way the lights were arranged, it was in shadow. Lying flat, Mongoose crawled out two or three feet, twisting around to try to see if there was anyone nearby.

Nope.

"I think we can make it to that lifeboat without being seen," he told Junior, pulling back. "We can climb up on the assembly and get a better look at what's going on."

"They'll be able to see us from the bridge," said Junior.

"If they're looking at us, sure. Odds are, though, they're not."

"But they might be."

"Might be."

"I say we run."

"Walking makes more sense," Mongoose told him. "Somebody sees us, we look like crewmen."

Junior was dubious. They were dressed in black, wearing dive suits. And they had rucks. It was one thing to pass through a shadow, where they'd more or less blend with the darkness. Out in the light they were going to look as out of place as rottweilers in a cat show.

But Mongoose was the experienced hand and senior man, so they walked—quickly, nervously in Junior's case, but walked nonetheless.

No one saw them, or if they did, didn't raise an alarm.

Ships like the *Han Li* typically sail with a small crew. The ships are designed so that they can be handled with numbers that would have shocked captains and warmed the hearts of owners a generation ago.

But when Junior climbed up the davit and gazed forward, he counted at least eight men scrambling over the stack of containers near the bow. That represented more than three-quarters of their estimate of the ship's crew size.

More of a problem, two of them had assault rifles.

Chinese army issue QB2-95s, to be exact. The little bullpup jobs with the magazines where the trigger should be.

They were standing on top of the middle row of containers, gazing forward toward the bow. The rest of the men were setting down large metal planks over the forward row of the containers. It looked . . . strange.

I don't know how long it took Mongoose and Junior to figure out what was going on. Mongoose climbed up a ways behind Junior, and he claims he realized what was up the second he saw it. Junior, who tends to be somewhat more modest, said they watched the proceedings for a good five minutes, and it was only when they opened one of the containers behind the platform created by the planks that they could guess what was up.

"They're going to fly the helicopters off the ship," he told Mongoose. "Holy shit."

The smart thing to do, at that point, was to use their satellite phone and call the Indian navy. Taking pictures of what was going on also made a hell of a lot of sense.

They did both.

But boys being boys, they didn't stop there.

By that time, I'd hustled Vina from the reception and was on my way out to meet Shotgun at the installation where the warheads were being stockpiled. I'd sent him over to keep watch from the highway just to the south where he could see the entrance that was to be assaulted according to the India for Islam plan.

When I'd sent him that afternoon, I thought it was only a long-shot precaution. Now I realized from Omar's remark about the increase in radio traffic that something big was brewing.

More ominous was the content of some of the intercepted messages, which I had Shunt access for me using the sign-ins I'd purloined from Special Squadron Zero.

"They only encrypted one message," Shunt told me when I checked in. "It was a PK encryption, not too hard to break. I have the text, but I'm not sure what it means."

"Tell me."

"100210."

"That's it?"

"Complete."

"It's a date," I said.

"It's tomorrow," said Shunt.

"No. It's today," I said. "You're a day behind."

I had my sat phone out to call Doc for more backup when it lit with an incoming call from Junior.

"Dick, this is Matt."

"Yeah, I got that, Junior. What's up?"

"The Chinese have the helicopters. They're on the ship."

"You're sure?"

"Damn sure."

"Get pictures and get out of there."

"Listen, they're going to fly them off the ship."

"What?"

"No shit, Dad. They're pulling them out of the containers as I speak. Damn."

"All right, listen. Take pictures. Then I want you—"

"I called the number you gave me for the admiral. I can't get a response."

"I'll take care of that."

"We think some of the guys aboard are PLA," he said, using the

263

abbreviation for the Chinese People Liberation Army. "They have army issue weapons, and—"

"I'm sure you're right. Listen to me. Get your butts out of there. We didn't sign up to get involved in any war."

We didn't sign up for any of this, as a matter of fact. Pro bono work for the U.S. of A. is one thing; working for free for the Indians or anyone else is quite another.

"What'd you say?"

"I said, get your butt off of that ship." My tone was a few decibels louder than the one you use to tell your teenager he can't borrow the car Friday night to go out drinking. "Leave the boat. Now."

"Sorry, we're having transmission troubles. I gotta go."

The line clicked.

Transmission troubles, my war-bruised butt.

Let's join the boys, shall we?

"That rig over there looks like a pump," Mongoose told Junior, probably a few seconds after he hung up. "I'll bet they're going to use it to fuel the helos."

"We could blow it up."

"That's what I was thinking. But I can't see the gas tank from here."

"We could if we could cross the deck somehow," said Junior, "and get up along the starboard side."

"Let me think about that."

The deck area immediately in front of them was covered by a light from above the bridge. The middle of the ship was also fairly well lit, not to mention visible from both the bridge and the top of the containers. The guards had their backs to them, but it was a long way across. Mongoose decided that the easiest and safest way to the other side of the ship was to go belowdecks.

"Only one of us should go," he told Junior, clearly meaning that he should be the one.

"All right." Junior started to climb down.

"No, no, I'm going to go."

"Screw that, I'm faster."

"I'm a better shot."

"Bullshit on that."

Actually, Junior *is* the better shot.

"When was the last time you shot on a ship?" asked Mongoose. "You gotta adjust for the swell. I'm doing it."

"We'll both go," said Junior finally.

They went back to the superstructure, once again walking quickly across the lit area. By now they were probably feeling invulnerable. You slip in and out of the lion's den often enough, and you start to think you're invisible and maybe even invincible. Adrenaline gets the better of you. Your heart is pumping and your head starts swelling with blood. It's a super amphetamine rush, without the drugs.

One of the unsung benefits of SEAL training is the very lessons in how to keep that rush under control. Being brave is important, surely, but being able to use your head *prudently* in battle is critical. And just because people aren't firing at you in any given instant doesn't mean you're not right in the middle of a shit storm.

There were three doors on the port side of the superstructure. Mongoose reasoned that the forward one, which sat roughly under the bridge area, would be the one most likely to be used by any crewmen detailed to go out on the deck. So he went to door number two.

It opened on a passage that ran along the side of the superstructure area. The corridor was narrow. The interior lights were low, but obviously anyone seeing them would know in an instant that they didn't belong. Both had their submachine guns ready.

Mongoose led the way to a ladder that ran down to the next deck. There, he spotted a hatchway into the hold. They climbed down quickly and found themselves on a metal catwalk that crossed above the forward portion of the engine room. The engines themselves were to the right; there was a control area just forward of them, maybe thirty feet away. A man sat at a panel there, watching the board like a kid staring at Saturday morning cartoons.

Take him out, and maybe the ship's captain would realize that something was up as soon as he asked for a bit more speed.

Leave him, and maybe he saw them and raised the alarm.

Judgment call either way.

Mongoose leveled his gun.

Flit-flit went the MP5, barely audible over the hum of the power plants.

The engineer dropped against the panel.

"I told you I'm the better shot," said Mongoose, moving forward across the catwalk.

"You needed two squeezes to get it done," said Junior. "I would have nailed it in one."

II

I had Admiral Yamuna's personal phone number, but he wasn't answering that either.

So I called another number he'd given me, though he'd warned to use it only in the "most dire emergency."

A woman answered. She sounded sleepy, and a bit younger than his wife.

Not that I could tell.

"This is Dick Marcinko. I need to talk to the admiral. It's very important. I have his helicopters."

The admiral was wide awake when he came to the phone.

"It's possible they're getting ready to fly," I told him. "You want to move in as quickly as you can."

"I owe you very much for this, scum-kisser," he said.

"Payback's a bitch, asshole," I said. "Don't forget that."

With the Indian navy steaming to the rescue, I put my thoughts and priorities back on the warheads. As soon as Urdu and his taxi dropped me off, I sent him back to rendezvous with Doc at the outskirts of the city, where he was waiting after being dropped off by another cab. I left Trace sleeping in the dorm with the rest of the Scottish athletes. I knew she'd be pissed, but I didn't want to leave them completely on their own.

Shotgun hadn't noticed anything unusual since taking the watch.

"Well, except for the fact that my last batch of Twinkies are stale," he said when I arrived. "That's pretty out of character."

The Indian army had a good-sized contingent guarding the base. They sent over helicopter patrols every twenty or thirty minutes, moving men around the perimeter at irregular intervals. They were doing a lot of things right. And frankly, if the tangos followed the game plan they seemed to have been rehearsing, then in all likelihood the assault would fail miserably. There were several armed vehicles just inside the gates, so even if the tanks that blocked the way were somehow defeated, there was no way an assault on the main gate was going to succeed.

But most terrorists are savvy enough to realize that they don't have the firepower to take on an army on its terms. The few who don't generally become ex-terrorists as soon as the fur starts to fly.

Given that India for Islam had survived our raid, these guys by definition fell into the wiser camp.

That would indicate that the front assault was just a bluff, something to take the army's attention away from the real action. But what was their real game plan?

I get a lot of credit for figuring out what terrorists are up to; I've always prided myself on trying to think the way they do. But my success really has depended a lot on the people I've worked closely with over the years. You couldn't find a better bunch of slimeball scumbags than the bastards I fought with in Vietnam, unless maybe you're counting the shit-tards who formed Red Cell with me. Over the years I've been blessed with subordinates who have made me look good, even a whole lot better than I should.

Assholes.

And I say that with the greatest affection.

So it's not surprising that it was Doc who came up with what had to be the terrorists' game plan a few minutes after he arrived.

"You have the main attack here," he said, pointing at one of the satellite images we were using as a map. "What happens? Everyone rushes to their battle stations. You begin to respond. The reinforcements come in, yada yada yada. You secure the perimeter. The helos are in the air, the tanks are moving up. What do you have? A donut."

"But just two," said Shotgun. "Otherwise I'd share."

"I mean that you're vulnerable inside, shit for brains." Doc has grown more tolerant of Shotgun in general, but there are still times when he'd like to give him a few reinforcing shots to the seat of his intelligence. "It also means that the tangos are inside already."

"So, that's where we gotta be," said Shotgun.

"There's hope for you yet," said Doc. "Now give me one of those donuts before I kick your butt into next week."

Junior and Mongoose, meanwhile, reached the port side of the ship, but were still belowdecks. The passages inside the superstructure were not arranged symmetrically. They had to move aft before finding a ladder that would take them topside. They were just about to start up when a crewman came down from above.

Mongoose, who was at point, swung around the back of the steps. Junior retreated down the corridor. There was no way of knowing which way the man was going, or whether he'd been sent to check on the engine room, but they couldn't take a chance. The sailor came down whistling, completely oblivious to the danger he was in, not even looking where his feet were landing.

Mongoose reached to grab his boot as he passed, but somehow missed. The sailor, still blithely unaware, skipped on out into the passage, where his stomach met the butt of Junior's submachine gun.

Swing one, horizontal—into the gut.

Pull back. Lift.

Swing two, in a downward motion, being careful to apply full force to the vulnerable area above the neck.

Angling the stock slightly helps, though you must be careful here, since it is easy to miss as your subject falls forward and strike only a glancing blow.

Finish with a timely shot to the temple or whatever other vital area is handy.

In other words, bend, fold, and mutilate.

They hauled the fallen sailor back behind the ladder. Junior pulled off the man's shirt to mop up some of the blood, then got a better idea—he dropped his ruck and pulled the shirt over his chest. He'd never pass any sort of sustained scrutiny, but even a moment or two of delay might be handy.

"Let's get out on deck," said Mongoose. "The longer we screw around down here the less time we have before they take off."

They scrambled outside without any other encounters. Pausing near the rail, they got their bearings and made sure they weren't being followed.

Junior, who's been a landlubber all his life, was starting to get a queasy stomach. There's nothing for it, really, except to push on. Eventually you get a good set of sea legs that never leave you, but until then, you just have to be willing to accept the fact that your stomach no longer slots properly in your body.

Or as Mongoose said later, you have to be ready to puke in the face of danger.

The shadows were a little thicker along the port rail, and there was an oblong cutout in the metal deck bulkhead that blocked the view fore and aft. As long as they were willing to crawl along the pipes that ran parallel to the side, they'd be invisible.

So that was the way they went, all the way up to the edge of the area where the containers were stored. A large housing for some of the unloading equipment sat at the edge, giving them a covered vantage of the men working near the bow.

But they still didn't have a shot on the gas equipment.

They could see the helicopters, though. In order to fit in the train cars and then the shipping containers, part of the helicopter tail sections had been disassembled. The crewmen who'd set up the launch platform were now engaged in lifting the helos upward, using a block and tackle mounted on a boom near the bow. They'd already lifted the tail sections.

A pair of portable generators were running near the helo parts, powering the air tools they needed to bolt the sections back in place. A small tree of work lights was mounted on one of the generators. The lights shone in Mongoose and Junior's direction, casting a long shadow across the nearby containers—a help or a hindrance, depending on how they used it.

"I'll have to climb the boom mast," said Mongoose. "I can't get a shot down here."

"We can go out along that container there," said Junior.

"Nah, they'll see us."

"You think they won't see us there?" asked Junior. He pointed straight up.

"They won't be looking there."

Mongoose went up the mast while Junior covered him from the nearest container. Parked in the well closest to the mast, the container was only a few feet away, and Junior had no trouble clambering up, crouching at the edge where he was partly hidden by shadows.

By this time the first helicopter had been fully assembled and loaded with fuel. The platform where it had been lifted was relatively small, able to accommodate only one of the helos once the rotors started spinning. As Mongoose readied his shot on the fuel tanks, a pilot climbed into the Ahi cockpit.

The rotors began whirling. It wasn't the casual cough that you see in movies; these suckers spun right up as if propelled by a giant spring. Obviously the Indians had gone for the high-grade instant-on option.

Wind from the helo wash swept across the deck. The effect was so severe that a few of the workers fell down; the others had to duck away and grab on to anything they could.

Mongoose, with impeccable timing, fired into the tank and pump machinery, working his spray so that the last bullets in his gun struck the gas tank.

You do remember, of course, that it is standard Rogue Warrior practice to load tracer rounds into the end of the magazine, alerting the shooter to the fact that he's almost out of bullets and should reload.

Tracer rounds—another way of saying little incendiary devices that would just love to set escaping gasoline fumes on fire.

The tanks exploded with a violent burst of red, orange, and black. At more or less the same moment, the helicopter lurched upward. The pilot flew directly through the fireball. Perhaps blinded, his forward wheel bumped against the top of one of the containers. The helo lurched around, spinning so that its tail was now pointed at the bridge. The force of the fire made it back up a few yards before finally the pilot steadied it, lowering its nose and starting to bank off to the right.

It was at that moment that Junior did the stupidest thing he ever did in his life.

He leapt up, jumping at the winglet of the helicopter, trying to get into the empty cockpit seat.

I guess. Sometimes impulsive stupidity is hard to explain.

(III)

You and I know that was a foolish and even idiotic move. I think even Junior knew that at the time—or at least somewhere after his feet left the top of the container he'd been standing on.

But once you're in the air, there's no turning back. Junior grabbed on to a bar on the winglet—it was designed as a foothold for the mechanics working on the engine—and tried to pull himself up to the cockpit area. Overwhelmed by the forces of gravity and momentum, he failed miserably, slipping and dangling from the bar like a trapeze artist who suddenly lost his nerve.

He hung there for a good five seconds as the helicopter banked sharply right and twisted around. The pilot would have been oblivious to him—he was concerned with the fireball that had erupted unexpectedly at the forward area of the ship.

That, and the small finger of fire at the nose area of the aircraft. Flying through the flames, he had inadvertently ignited grease smeared there by the workers or during transport. The fire flared, then turned into an inconspicuous yet even more ominous finger of blue, trickling around the nose and climbing in accordionlike threads toward the engine and fuel tank above his head.[29]

Mongoose, watching from the mast where he'd climbed, didn't realize what was going on. A series of unconnected images flashed in front of him—the fireball, Junior on the cargo container, the helicopter, something dangling off the side of the helicopter, Junior on the narrow winglet . . .

He stared in disbelief, too stunned even to curse his companion.

Then he saw something drop into the ocean from the helicopter.

His first inclination was to hope it wasn't Junior.

Then, as the helicopter exploded into a fireball, he changed his mind.

"Please God," he said as he dropped to the deck. "Let that be Junior."

---

[29] The explanation of what happened is based on Mongoose's descriptions and a subsequent examination of the wreckage. Frankly, as far as I'm concerned, God looked down and kicked them all in the butt for being assholes, Junior included.

[IV]

I was blissfully unaware of all this excitement, luxuriating in a warm if pungent bath many hundreds of miles to the north.

I would not go so far as to say I was enjoying myself. Swimming in a sewage lagoon is never a particularly good way to have fun.

The lagoon was the last lap—excuse the pun—in our journey into the base. Doc, Shotgun, and I had walked through a large storm sewer, then followed the piping from the abandoned sewer treatment plant that once served the installation.

When the base was shuttered, the sewage plant was abandoned. Before reopening it, a pair of barracks were renovated and their sewage shunted to a cesspool and large septic system near the barracks. A second septic tank and leach field served some temporary trailers used as command buildings. But the storm drains still connected into the treatment plant and the associated piping. This kept the pond full.

I'm being generous by describing it as a treatment plant, since all existing evidence was that the treatment consisted of pouring the shit into a big bowl and letting water run through it. Once in the pipes, the effluent flowed into a tributary of the nearby river. The outlet was patrolled by a guard and watched over by a pair of video cameras. Defeating the video cameras in the dark wasn't hard—we got up close, then used a bowl-like blackened mirror to cut down their image area, in effect blocking the camera's view. This wouldn't have worked during the day, or even on a very bright night, but the occasional clouds overhead made it relatively easy, even if they did require us to be a little more patient than I would have liked.

The guard was a little trickier. We could have taken him out, but I didn't want to leave the place completely undefended, in case the tangos hit on this route themselves. So we made our way along the rocky jag above the pipes, crawling on our bellies and waiting to cross into the lagoon as he swung on his foot patrol back and forth behind a wired fence.

Again, it took a lot longer than I would have liked. It also meant that we had to slide gracefully into the murky swamp of decades-old sewage, rather than simply closing our eyes and jumping in.

Yes, we were wearing diving gear. Nuclear protection suits would have probably been more appropriate.

Delicate stomach?

I'll spare you any more of the slimy details. Instead, close your eyes and imagine us snorkeling through the pristine waters of the southern Pacific reefs, ogling schools of brightly colored fishlets and scantily clad tourists, whiling away the hot hours of the day in the cool waters. Visions of a decadent beach luau, pig on the spit and buckets of cold beer, play in your head. An errant bikini strap or two falls southward, there's a gentle breeze and calypso music in the air . . .

Got the vision?

Do a one-eighty and you're about where we were.

We snorkeled up to a large concrete block where a large pipe entered the lagoon. Using a wrist lamp to light the way, I paddled through about three feet of stagnant muck into the treatment plant itself.

The large cement tunnel that led to the pond opened into a large box made of grating on the south side of the building. The grate was at the end of a trenched pool. The trenches ran lengthwise and had once been used to collect sediment before it went out into the pipes. Now they were simply filled with sediment, a kind of shitty quicksand.

We weren't sure whether there might be a guard posted inside, or even if the building was used as a shelter or getaway by bored guards looking to grab a smoke while escaping their NCO's glare. I doused my light and stared through the bars across the scummed surface of the shallow pool.

I couldn't see anyone, nor did I hear anything. So I swung my rubberized ruck up out of the muck and removed the battery-powered Sawzall.

The bars of the grate were so corroded that they practically fell away as soon as the saw blade touched them. I cut a half dozen, just enough to pass into the pool.

I stood and felt my left foot sinking, sucked into the thick sediment. I had to struggle and spin to get it out.

"Be careful where you step," I told Shotgun and Doc, pointing out the trench. Then I pulled myself up onto the concrete ledge.

We could all have used a good shower at that point. But by now we'd been breathing in the stomach-turning smell for so long that we'd become immune to it. This was probably because the caustic fumes had burned our noses completely, but we weren't in a position to analyze it. (Here's a trick if you find yourself in a similar situation—stick some Vicks VapoRub beneath your nose. Then all you'll smell is menthol-flavored crap, rather than the real thing.)

While we had escaped the outer defenses, we still had a long way to go. The sewage plant lay at the northwestern corner of the facility, some two hundred yards from an interior perimeter fence that surrounded the area where the nukes were being held. A motor pool sat between us and the fence, and while it was very lightly staffed, it was well lit, and threading our way across its perimeter took almost twenty minutes.

There were gas and diesel pumps on the western side not far from a gate connecting the parking area with the inner part of the base. Our plan was to sneak over the fence near that entrance.

It was close to a guard post, but I figured that the proximity was actually an advantage—the guards would be watching the gate, not expecting someone to go over the fence right next to them. But as I hunkered down near the pumps, I got another idea. A truck had pulled up to the gassing area. The driver was topping off the tank. The truck would give us mobility and a good base of operations inside the area where the nukes were. There were plenty of vehicles there already, so it wouldn't look out of place.

"Shotgun, up," I said in a low stage whisper. We had radios, but we were so close we didn't need them.

"Skipper?"

"I'm going to grab the guy pumping gas. You cover me. Anyone comes out of the cab, clobber them."

"Got it."

"I have to circle around. Watch me."

"No problem."

I slipped back and trotted around the edge of the fueling area. My breath started to catch in my chest. As I turned the corner to come around the truck, I saw two guards walking in my direction.

I dropped to my knee. There were some stanchions and a light pole between us, but primarily I was relying on the darkness to keep from being seen. Dressed completely in black, with my face the color of anthracite fresh from a mine, I was just part of the black night.

Or so I hoped.

The two men walked forward about five paces, then suddenly stopped. They looked at each other, and began to practically moan.

"What? That smell," said one.

The other answered in what I guess was Punjabi.

"I don't understand," said the first. "Use Hindi or English."

"Something died," said the other. "It must be that truck. It came up from the south."

"They're all farmers there," said the first, in a way that implied anything but a compliment.

The two soldiers turned and began walking quickly in the other direction. Proof positive that stepping in shit does have its occasional rewards.

I waited a full minute, then continued around to the truck, where the driver was just finishing filling it. He returned the nozzle and hose to the machine, then came around the driver's side to climb back aboard.

I smacked him on the neck with my trusty blackjack. A whistle brought Shotgun lumbering from the shadow. Together we hoisted him into the back.

"We better tie and gag him, just in case," I said. "I don't want him waking up and screaming while we're in the middle of something."

Shotgun felt bad for the soldier—he figured that he was going to be in trouble for losing his truck.

"Better that than his life," said Doc, who by now had joined us.

I promised Shotgun that if we had a chance later on, we'd cut the soldier's binds and just stick him in the driver's seat when we left. That seemed to make him happy; I sensed that there was a dark incident in Shotgun's past involving a first sergeant and a snooze fest in the back of a truck, but I didn't probe.

Clearing the worst of the muck and black off my face with a few splashes of water, I got behind the wheel and started up the truck. It was a Russian-made Ural transport, a six-by-six five-ton combat support vehicle roughly equivalent to our old M44, though its petrol-fired engine couldn't quite match our six-by-six's reliability or toughness.

We weren't putting it to the test, however. I drove around the service area and through the gate, slowing but not stopping as I neared the guards. One of them put up his hand, as if he was going to wave us over—Shotgun and Doc were poised in the back in that eventuality—but then quickly waved me by.

He was one of the men who'd reversed course earlier. I had the windows down, and he'd undoubtedly caught a whiff on the wind.

Like I say, sometimes stepping in shit is the best way to proceed.

The truck brought us right into the lion's den. The center of the compound was dominated by a row of three brick buildings, each two stories high. These had been the center of the installation at one time, command post buildings used for various offices. Empty now, they stood at one side of a large open square where several tanks and about a dozen Land Rovers were parked. Some tents were pitched at one end of the square; these were used by guards as rest areas when they took breaks or came on or off duty at the armory building that sat opposite the buildings on the other side of the square.

The armory was our target. It was essentially a large warehouse, a mustering area whose interior was probably the size of Madison Square Garden. Relatively plain, the only architectural flourish was a narrow second roof that ran down the middle on top of the first. Nestled atop a row of narrow-slit windows, this top layer of the building worked like the cupola in a nineteenth-century barn, drawing hot, stale air out in the summer. Maybe not as effective as the air-conditioning units, but a lot cheaper.

About a dozen guards circulated in and out of the building, keeping watch.

I parked in front of the empty administration buildings, then went around the back to get Shotgun and Doc. Rather than staying in the truck as I'd planned, I took them around the side of one of the buildings where I'd seen a fire escape while passing. We climbed up and got on the roof. There were guard towers on the perimeter, but the men inside were watching the fence line, not the middle of the fort.

"Now what do we do?" asked Shotgun.

"Now we wait for something to happen," I told him.

"How much you figure those bombs would be worth?" he asked.

"Why? You thinking of buying one?"

"Just askin'."

"If you could find a buyer, one would be worth millions. A hundred million, easy."

"Yeah, but you'd never find a buyer," said Doc. "Who the hell's going to buy it? For one thing, the people who really want one—North Korea, Iran—they already have programs of their own. The U.S., Russia—they're not going to buy secondhand weapons. Israel? They've got plenty."

"You don't think Saudi Arabia would pay for a nuke?" I asked. "Just to have them in case Iran explodes it?"

"I guess," he admitted. "But really—if they did want one, they could buy it themselves. Hell, they could go over to India, cut a deal for oil. Don't give us a bomb. Just give us technology. Because we don't want to be pushed around by Iran. And it's in your interest. If Iran decides to play nuclear chicken, your energy prices are going up, and you're going to get screwed."

It was decent logic. I didn't make the argument at the time—we had a few other things to concentrate on—but if you really wanted to play devil's advocate, you could suggest that the most logical technology seller in that kind of calculus was the U.S. We wanted oil, we hated Iran, and if we didn't do anything about Iran's nuclear program—which at the point this was all taking place, we hadn't—we'd have a real incentive to keep things balanced in the Middle East.

You want to be a real cynic? Think about this: when our antimissile system is perfected, we could make ourselves essentially immune to threats from nations that could "only" launch a few dozen ballistic missiles. In that case, we might even *want* a war in the Middle East, or between countries like China and India. Let them duke it out while we wait in safety on the sidelines.

Maybe that's not even a bad idea.

Of course, you and I both know that ballistic missiles from Iran are probably the least of our troubles. Put a nuclear warhead on a medium-sized coastal freighter, *chug-chug-chug* into the harbor of one of our major cities, or one of our less major cities . . . 9/11 looks like a picnic by comparison.

Put it in the back of a tractor trailer, drive right into the heart of the city . . . not a pleasant afternoon.[30]

We spent about a half hour watching the armory, getting a feel for the sentry assignments. I'm not sure that Shotgun wasn't fantasizing about what he might do with the money he could get if a weapon ever did fall into his lap.

Buy a lifetime supply of Twinkies, no doubt. He'd brought along

---

[30] Yes, I know that nukes are actually designed to do more damage when exploded at a certain altitude. But why quibble over ten or twenty thousand casualties? Port watches, border control—how long have I been talking about those things?

several bags for the mission. They were squished and bruised, and God knows what they tasted like after our trip through the *merde*, but he ate them merrily, munching away while we watched the armory.

"I don't know, Dick," said Doc finally. He looked at his watch. "It's past midnight. Nothing's going on. Maybe Shunt screwed up when he decrypted the message. For all we know, it says something like lick your f'in' balls."

"Shunt's a better speller than that," said Shotgun.

Doc shook his head but said nothing.

"Easiest way out will be to take the truck and go through the front gate," said Doc a few minutes later. "We should go at four-thirty or so, before it gets too light."

I agreed. It was beginning to look like I'd jumped the gun on the alert.

Which, frankly, wasn't all bad. Aside from our stroll through the lagoon.

But one of the things you learn early on in the special warfare racket—actually, in *any* warfare—while there are an intense four or five minutes in every day, most of what happens *between* those four or five minutes is . . . nothing. Dealing with that nothing may determine how you deal with those four or five minutes of high octane excitement.

Then again, they may not. Impossible to predict.

Hanging around on a roof overlooking the third world's biggest collection of nukes is like hanging around on just about any other roof. You try not to fall asleep.

"Say, Dick, you think there's a place in Delhi where I could get a real McDonald's hamburger?" asked Shotgun. "With real beef, you know?"

"Vegetables aren't good enough for you?" asked Doc.

"I'm not against vegetables. Just not in my food."

"God forbid."

"Maybe I'll ask Urdu when he picks us up," said Shotgun. "You think that would offend him?"

"No idea," I said.

"What's wrong with eating cows, anyway?" asked Shotgun.

"It's against their religion," said Doc.

"What the hell," said Shotgun, "is some god going to like strike them down with lightning or something?"

At that precise moment, a shell streaked across the sky, arcing down in a flashing blaze of white light, and exploded behind us on the roof.

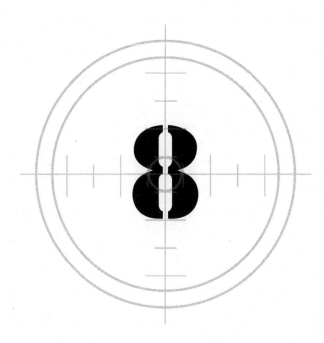

(1)

Junior was last seen dangling from the wheel of the advanced Indian attack helicopter seconds before it exploded in a fiery ball of incandescence over the Indian Sea.

Mongoose, the person who had seen him, cursed under his breath as the helicopter augured in. He didn't have time to do much more than that—the fire on the containers at the forward end of the ship began to expand exponentially, fed by the drums of fuel the Chinese seamen had been readying for the other helicopter.

Some of the shrapnel from the tank that had exploded broke through one of the nearby containers. The heat and flames ignited cartons of furniture inside the container. Within seconds, a hundred Queen Anne dinettes, carefully packed in foam and lacking the odd screw, were burning. The blaze ate away at the thin metal sides of the container, actually melting the walls on several others. More dinettes caught fire.

A container of fake Persian rugs went next, the nylon-based threads melting into a liquid inferno of raging flames. At that point, the fire went out of control.

The sailors hadn't seen either Mongoose or Junior, and must have believed the explosion had been a malfunction of the equipment. In any event, they were too busy trying to grab fire hoses and muster a defense to worry about intruders.

Mongoose slid down to the deck area, grabbed the rucks, and ran to the side. A sailor with a fire hose loomed on his right, running forward with the hose.

Mongoose didn't see him. They collided. The sailor and hose flew over the rail and into the ocean. Mongoose, slightly dazed, stumbled back, took a deep, smoke-filled breath, then jumped over the side.

Whatever else you do when you are a SEAL, you swim. You swim in the morning, you swim in the evening, you swim at night. You swim when you're strong. You swim a lot when you're tired. You swim in pools. You swim in the ocean. Basically, whatever else you learn, you end up in the water.

But not even all that can prepare you for a blind dive off a ship in the middle of the night. No matter how calm the sea is, she is a mighty mistress, and she will have her way with you no matter how well prepared or tested you think you are.

Bitch.

Mongoose broke water pretty quickly. He dropped one of the rucks right away, then while treading water, tried to grab the blow-up raft package out of the other.

The sea that night was about as calm as you could want the sea to be. If you were sitting on a beach in San Diego or Miami, you'd probably have said it was smooth as glass.

But this glass had very sharp edges. They poked and pushed at Mongoose, turning him around as he tried to get the raft out. His fingers, suddenly cold and stiff, fumbled. Finally he got the bag out. He wiggled his fingers against the handle that worked the auto-inflator.

Murphy chose that moment to pluck Mongoose by the scruff of his neck and tug him back under the waves.

The raft slipped out of Mongoose's hand. So did the rest of the ruck.

Resurfacing, Mongoose shook the salt from his eyes and began cursing. He worked through a long litany of things that were no f-ing good. He started with zippers—the zipper on the ruck had seemed to stick—and worked his way eventually and inexorably outward to gravity and the greater universe.

Finally, the Mongoose we all know and love.

In the midst of this catharsis, he started swimming back in the direction of the ship, which was a few yards away.

Mongoose was not actually thinking of getting back aboard the ship at that moment. He was hoping to find the Tiger boat on the other side somewhere. He figured he would swim around until he found it, then climb aboard and look for Junior.

It was a plan, give it that.

We'll never know whether it would have worked or not, for as he neared the stern he saw a line dragging down into the water. Mongoose is a powerful guy, every bit as strong as anyone you could imagine. I'd never want to arm wrestle with him; he'd make me use all my tricks and I still might not beat him. But it had been a very long day. He was exhausted, and his arm muscles were burning with enough lactic acid to upset a hundred stomachs.

His first thought was that he would grab the line and rest for a while.

Then he wondered if he might not use it to climb back aboard and grab one of the lifeboats.

When he reached the side of the ship, he saw that the line was actually the fire hose he had knocked over with the crewman a short time before. He tugged at it, worried that it might pull off whatever it was attached to, if it was attached. It would be just like Murphy to pull such a stunt.

But the master of mayhem was elsewhere employed. The fire had spread on the foredeck, and was now raging in crimson glory against the backdrop of the black sky. Murphy, darting between the containers, pushed flames this way and that, seeking out the most flammable contents. Then he went to the pumps, where a crewman was trying desperately to get some water for the sailors battling the flames. Murphy gummed up the mechanism—though here perhaps the bribes taken by the inspector to insure the parts were in working order played as big a role in their failure as Murphy's machinations.

Shortly before the fire broke out, the captain realized the engine room was not responding to his calls, and sent someone to find out what was going on. On discovering the man dead, the baffled sailor took matters into his own hands and increased the engines. Fully engaged, the ship spurted forward. We're not talking speedboat velocity here, but the resulting jerks were enough to knock the men fighting the fire off their feet. One rolled into the flames. A friend tried to help him and caught fire himself. Both men jumped over the side.

Somewhere in the ship's stack of containers were several stuffed with ammunition from Ukraine. It was en route to a port in Africa—illegally but happily accepted by the vessel's Chinese masters, since the payment of the shipping fee would easily cover most of the transit costs.

Heated to a temperature that a thick porterhouse steak would envy, the ammo in the crates started cooking off. A series of explosions began rocking the ship. Within minutes, the bow was edging downward.

A very bad trend, Mongoose realized, starting to climb the hose.

(II)

We're all guilty of the occasional mental disconnect, where what we say or do is completely at odds with what should be said or done; it's just a question of how often that happens. If you're a politician, the ratio is going to be somewhere close to one hundred percent. If you're a SEAL, you train and you train and you train to get it down near zero.

But human nature does win out every so often.

"Wow. Look at the meteor," said Shotgun as the white light arced over our heads at the nuke base.

He will *never* live that down.

"Incoming!" yelled Doc as the shell hit. We threw ourselves flat on the roof as a second and then a third shell flew threw the air. These over-shot the roof by a few feet, but the air shook with the explosion.

"Mortar shells," said Doc, maybe explaining to Shotgun that it was men, not gods, trying to kill him.

"Maybe they're trying to blow up the nukes," said Shotgun.

"Warheads don't explode that way," said Doc. "If they did, you'd never be able to risk launching them on a missile."

Doc was right, but the continuing barrage did make it seem as if that was their intention. The flashes grew in intensity and number, just like the finale at a Fourth of July fireworks show.

No, I did not make that metaphor idly.

I pushed myself up off the roof and stood, watching the shells as they came in.

"You nuts?" asked Doc from the roof.

"Hey, I'm with you, Dick," said Shotgun, rising.

"You guys are gonna get killed," said Doc.

"I don't think so." I folded my arms, staring in the direction the shells were coming from. It was beyond the sewer plant where we'd come in.

"A diversion?" said Doc, getting up.

"Definitely a diversion," I said. "The question is, for what?"

"Hey, Dick—nothing's exploding when these things land," said Shotgun.

"They're firecrackers," explained Doc. "Big ol' firecrackers. A lot of boom and flash, not much else."

More likely they were training rounds, or maybe specially prepared pyrotechnics, but Doc was in the right neighborhood.

"What's their plan?" asked Shotgun.

"Let's look at the effect," I said. "They fire mortar rounds into the middle of the compound. Everyone there takes shelter."

"Except us," said Shotgun.

"We're not here. We don't count."

I scanned the area between the buildings.

"There should be a team running right across here," I told the others. "Any second now."

We waited a minute. I could hear gunfire coming from the eastern side of the complex.

It didn't sound like blanks.

"Maybe they're already inside," said Shotgun. "Maybe they snuck in like us, and this is the signal for them to attack."

"It could be," I said.

"Or maybe they infiltrated the guard force," said Doc. "And they're working on the fuse to one of those bombs. Now if there was a nuclear explosion in the middle of all those weapons . . ."

He didn't finish his sentence. He was too busy trying to catch up to Shotgun and myself as we clambered down to the ground and headed to the nuke armory.

Three black-clad maniacs who look like avenging angels and smell like creatures from the underworld burst through the front door of a heavily guarded armory shouting. What would you do?

If you were assigned to protect the nukes, you'd shoot first and ask questions when those assholes were good and cold. And if you were the bad guys, you'd shoot first and skip the questions. So there was no way we were going in the front door or the side one I passed as I ran toward the back of the building.

The guards who'd been outside had gone back in as soon as the shelling started, buttoning up so they weren't hit by shrapnel. Obviously I couldn't see them, but I'm guessing they were crouched a few feet from the portals, fingers all too heavy on their triggers, waiting for someone to come crashing against the door.

"Up to the roof," I said, grabbing on to the metal drainpipe that ran down the back corner of the building. "Doc after me, then Shotgun."

"Don't worry," said Shotgun. "I'll cover you guys."

I wasn't worried about us getting picked off—the compound was still empty, and was likely to remain so as the barrage continued. The metal drainpipe didn't seem all that sturdy, and I thought Shotgun's weight might be too heavy for it. But it stayed in place as he climbed up after us.

From the ground, the windows that ran in the rectangular cupola above the first roof looked barely taller than a cigarette carton. But they were nearly six feet tall.

Unfortunately they were mostly dirty as well, the glass thick with years of exhaled crud. Breaking them would alert whoever was inside that we were here, so I took out my knife and worked it gently against the frames, trying to find one that wasn't locked or would give way easily. I tried four or five before realizing that the panes actually swung upward rather than sideways.

Duh.

Once I knew that, they were easy to open. I picked a pane from the back of the building, reasoning it was not a likely place for anyone to be looking, then opened it and leaned in.

I thought I'd have an unobstructed view of the interior of the building, but that wasn't the case. A metal framework ran directly below the long cupola. It was a raceway for the hoists and chains used to move the bombs and other equipment around. It was just wide enough and close enough to the ceiling to keep me from seeing much of the floor below.

But what hid the floor would also hide me.

"I'm going inside," I told the others. "Quiet. And remember, even the good guys are going to think we're not on their side."

Doc grunted.

I slipped down through the window, swinging my legs toward the centerline of the roof to make sure I landed on the runway. It was only six or seven feet from the peak of the roof, but I couldn't afford to miss.

The grating shook when I landed, but not as much as I expected. It was supported by heavy rods inserted into the roof members every four feet.

Crouching down on the gridwork, I moved over to the edge and took a peak. The room was lit by a few lights from above, a yellowish cast flowing toward the floor.

The nuclear caskets were arrayed along the back two-thirds of the room. Aside from the bombs and some machinery used to move them around, the space was empty. A set of walls and partitions at the front separated the room from the forward part of the building. Some of this space was covered with ceilings, I imagine for offices. The forward area nearest the front was open; I peered down and saw the guards hunkered behind sandbags, heads forward, no doubt waiting for an attack.

I made my way back toward the window. I was debating whether the guards might be stationed in a corner I couldn't see when I heard something fall below. I leaned over and saw a man in a pair of coveralls pick up some sort of tool from the floor near the middle of the room. Another man stood a few feet away, shaking his head. They'd either been in the shadows when I'd come in or entered through one of the doors on the side, which connected to a hallway of offices flanking the center of the building. They moved to one of the stacked caskets, attached it to a chain, then started up a winch.

"Shotgun," I whispered through the window, "come down here, quietly."

Shotgun eased in through the window. He was just tall enough to let himself down without jumping.

"What's going on?" he asked.

I pointed out the two men. They'd pulled the crate off the other and set it down on the ground. They were unscrewing the locks—they looked like large T handles—getting ready to open it.

"Think they're going to blow it up?" Shotgun asked. "Or steal it?"

"If I had to guess, I'd say they were going to blow it up. Come on."

I led him all the way to the back, where several rows of chains hung down to the floor.

"Why don't we just shoot 'em?" asked Shotgun.

"Because we don't know what they're doing," I said. "And we might miss."

"Doc says the bombs can't go off."

"Is Doc a nuclear scientist?"

"Uh—"

"Let's go, Guns." I started climbing down. "It's a rhetorical question."

"I knew that."

Once we were about halfway down, we could no longer be seen from where the men were working. They were talking to each other in a kind of hushed whisper, but it was in Hindi or Urdu and neither Shotgun nor I could figure out what they were saying. I circled around the back end of the stacks, then moved up the side along the wall. Along the way I spotted a fire extinguisher and grabbed it. Shotgun took the next one.

We crept through the rows of caskets, angling in the direction where the men were. They'd stopped talking, but the hoist they'd used was still overhead, so it was easy to gauge their location. Finally we got to within five yards of them, at the corner of one of the large caskets across from where they were working.

They had removed the top part of the crate, exposing what looked like a black garbage pail. The front skin of the garbage pail had been stripped away, and I could see some wires and circuit boards beneath the metal frame. The men were bent over, examining what looked like a small oscilloscope they'd perched atop the body of the warhead.

They glanced over at the bomb, looked back at the scope, adjusted something on the bomb, and then started the whole process over again.

I turned to Shotgun. "You're left. I'm right."

I pulled the pin to the extinguisher and sprung to my feet. I hit the trigger on my third step.

The blast from the fire extinguisher was so fierce it knocked both of the men over, and caught me off balance as well. I stumbled, but stayed upright, dousing both men with the powder from the extinguisher.

Shotgun was right behind me. He gave a short burst, then put his extinguisher to more practical use, slamming the body into the head of one of the men as he started to rise. The other man threw up his hands in surrender.

We hadn't been exactly quiet, and I expected the guards from the front to come running in. But they didn't. It's possible they didn't hear us, but my theory is that they were so focused on the direction they thought the threat would be coming from that they were oblivious to everything else.

"Up," I told the other man, dropping my fire extinguisher. I pulled my MP5 from off my shoulder. "Stand over there, away from the warhead."

The man complied, hands trembling. Shotgun, meanwhile, pulled the other man away, sitting him up against the top of the crate. He was out cold.

"Who are you?" I said to the man who'd surrendered. "And what are you doing?"

"Bhavata," he said. "I am a technician."

"With India for Islam?"

"Islam?"

"You're a terrorist."

"No, no. No terrorist. No."

He started to reach into this coverall. I put my foot against his chest quickly, stopping him.

"Shotgun, check what he's fishing for," I said.

It was ID, showing that Mr. Bhavata was a member of the Indian Nuclear Commission.

"I am making sure the weapon is safed," he said.

"Is it?"

"Yes." He nodded quickly. "We had four more to check. We had planned to do them tomorrow, but now with the attack we had to hurry."

A likely story.

But it turned out to be true.

I used my satellite phone to call the nuclear ministry, and when I finally got someone—it took more than a half hour—I confirmed that the two workers were indeed legitimate employees, and were assigned to the storage project. That of course told me almost nothing, but a call to my friend at State got me connected with the security supervisor.

"Why are you implying that we are endangering our country?" he said, pretty damn huffily. "Where are you coming from?"

His tone pissed me off.

"I'm not coming from anywhere. I'm sitting in the middle of your family jewels. I suggest you get over here before somebody else figures out how to get around your guards."

Consternation followed. There was the usual spitting and empty threats. The building was surrounded and a SWAT team moved in.

It was all very amusing, or would have been if we'd stayed to watch. By that time the mortar shells and gunfire on the perimeter had ended, and I figured that our energy could be put to better use elsewhere—say, at the fancy Irish bar at our fancy hotel.

After securing the workers just in case, Shotgun and I climbed up to the roof while Doc went around and got the truck. We drove out the front gate just as the first SWAT team vehicle responded.

We blinked our headlights as a salute and headed into the city.

III

Out in the Indian Ocean, Mongoose was scrambling up the side of the Chinese container ship, doing his best to ignore the increasing list to starboard. His plan was simple: he'd climb up, drop one of the life rafts into the water, and look for Junior.

It was a decent, workable plan, and remained viable even as explosions began tearing the bow to pieces. The rapid movement of the aft end in the direction of heaven was not a positive sign, however.

Mongoose pressed on with a perseverance born in BUDS, and a stubbornness Douglas MacArthur would have admired. He walked up the side of the ship, bending forward and moving sideways, even as it began to roll under him. The ship leaned so badly that by the time he reached the rail, he was practically horizontal. The metal was making loud groaning noises, grunting as it worked to tear itself apart.

Mongoose was just considering how to alter his plan when he heard the blare of a horn behind him. It sounded like the horn of a diesel train, and he thought at first that he was having an aural hallucination.

He ignored it, trying to climb along the rail toward the stern that was now rising like an eighteen-year-old's erection. It wasn't until a flare shot overhead that he glanced over his shoulder and saw a boat in the water behind him.

Not just any boat. It was one of the Tiger boats. Junior was at the helm, loading the flare gun for a second shot.

Mongoose literally ran off the side of the sinking ship and jumped into his arms, knocking him to the deck of the heavily modded speedboat. They got up, cranked the engine, and headed away, barely escaping the giant suck that followed the sinking of the ship.

WTF? How did Junior do it?

About a quarter of a second after Junior grabbed on to the wheel of the helicopter, he realized he'd made a serious mistake.

It was a bit too late to back out. The helicopter swept aft, over the deck of the ship, just barely missing the bridge as it veered over the port side and banked westward. Junior decided that his only real option was to keep going—climb up the wheel strut and force his way into the cabin.

There's no question in his mind that he would have made it. There's no question in mine that he wouldn't've. But the point is moot, because Murphy stepped in, prying Junior's fingers off the slippery wheel strut as it began folding upward.

Oh, you don't believe it was Murphy? You think Junior just slipped? Or maybe just got tired?

I'd be inclined to agree, were it not for what happened next. As Junior began to fall, he glanced down, worrying about how hard the waves were going to be.

To his left, he saw the Tiger boat they had set adrift earlier.

A hundred-to-one shot? More luck than *anyone* has a right to experience? Or just very good planning?

Take your pick. All I can say is that Murphy works in mysterious ways.

One of Newton's Laws of Motion dictates that once in motion, a body tends to stay in motion, until acted on by another power. In Junior's case, the other power was gravity and water, which smacked him for being so foolish. He got a good smack on the seat of his brains, and took a bit of salt water into his nose for good measure. He surfaced, shook his head, then turned around just in time to avoid being clocked by the hull of the Tiger boat. He worked his way around to the side and climbed aboard.

Better to be lucky than smart: a motto to live by.

The Indian navy had sent two destroyers out on a *quote* routine *end quote* patrol. One of those destroyers just happened to be close enough to see the fire from the cargo container ship and rushed forward to its aid. It arrived too late to prevent it from sinking—not that it could have in the first place—but did manage to save most of the crew. Meanwhile, a helicopter from the other destroyer and several jets from a shore base caught up to the helo Junior had jumped from and offered the pilot a choice—instant, fiery death, or a nice warm bed in the clink.

The pilot,[31] to much surprise, turned back toward shore.

So where was it and its companion, which never got off the ship, headed?

---

[31] He was later traded in a diplomatic deal for two Indian "tourists" who had wandered over the border into China while hunting for snow leopards. Their story made about as much sense as his claim that he was testing the helicopter for an oil drilling company, so I guess the two countries were even.

It's hard to be sure, but a pair of Chinese navy vessels were sailing about 150 miles to the west—less than an hour's flight time for the Ahi. They would seem to have been the logical destination. Interestingly enough, when a helicopter from one of the Indian vessels flew in the ships' direction, the helicopter decks on the ships' fantails lit up.

The Indian helo hailed the Chinese ships, asking if they were conducting nighttime operations. The lights went off, and the ships changed direction, heading farther west.

A coincidence, I'm sure.

"What an incredible turn of luck," said Admiral Yamuna when we talked later that morning on the phone. "We managed to recover one of the stolen helicopters. And we are reasonably sure that the other will not fall into our enemy's hands."

"Well, that is lucky," I said.

"We found one of our little Tiger boats out to sea," he added. "Apparently it slipped from its berth and the tide pushed it out into the ocean."

"Amazing."

"The other was right where it belonged. And a funny thing—its tanks were filled to the rim. The day before, only halfway."

Always return the car with a full tank—somebody taught those kids well.

"Just one piece of luck after another," I said.

"I hear you have had some luck as well," added the admiral. "I understand the al Qaeda tried to strike an important base last night. You broke it up."

Well, not exactly, but I saw no point in correcting him.

"This Mr. Murphy you always speak of," added Admiral Yamuna. "He is not interfering with you much of late. Maybe he is losing his punch."

Ol' Murph was still throwing monkey wrenches left and right, but I wasn't about to tempt fate by saying anything on the subject.

Recovering the helicopter made the Indian navy the hero of the day, but I wasn't doing too poorly myself. In fact, I was getting incredibly positive spin from the press following the adventures out at the armory. Which was a bit of a puzzle.

Even before I'd managed to soap away the last of the sewage stain from my toes, the story was circulating inside the Indian government that I had personally stopped a team of terrorists from detonating a warhead. Not the worst thing that's ever been said about me behind my back, I'm sure. But given how far it deviated from reality, and how quickly it began circulating, it was pretty damn interesting.

Even Omar brought it up. In fact, he delivered the official American version in person.

Following our return to the swanky hotel and requisite steam bath to remove all external toxins, the three of us headed to Dublin—the pub, not the city—to restore our internal stasis with assorted medicinal elixirs. We'd just ordered our second round when Omar loomed around the corner.

"I thought I'd find you here," he said.

I'd say he sneered, but that would be overstating his enthusiasm.

"Have a seat," I told him. "There are plenty across the room."

"Har-de-har. The ambassador is impressed. He'd like to talk to you tomorrow, at your convenience."

"What's he impressed about?" asked Doc.

"Whatever the hell it is you did at the armory. Apparently bailed the Indians out." He scowled. "You're a lucky man, Marcinko. Always stepping in shit at the right time."

"That's my middle name."

Over the next hour or so, I fielded a bunch of congratulatory calls. Even Minister Dharma called, asking when we were going to "debrief."

No, no, you read that wrong.

Dee-brief.

Try it again.

Deeeeeeee-brief.

She was still the most beautiful woman this side of Karen Fairchild. And maybe the other side of Karen Fairchild.

"Debriefing you will be a pleasure," I told her. We made an appointment for the following evening.

Leave it to Doc to bring the reality-based world back into the picture. He took some cocktail napkins and laid them out on the table, sketching out the operation that we had allegedly foiled. According to the Indians, an unknown number of tangos had engaged in a brief firefight along the eastern side of the facility after the mortar shelling. They withdrew without casualties, and without inflicting any.

"Bogus mortar attack," said Doc, holding up a finger—no, not that one.

"Wimpy assault on the strongest part of the base." Another finger.

"No attempt on the main gate, which was the original plan espoused by India for Islam."

Finger number three. Of course Doc used the same finger each time.

"Number four." This earned two middle fingers for some reason—must have been that new math. "We're the heroes of the hour. Why?"

"I smell a rat, too," I said.

"Don't look at me," said Shotgun. "I was in the shower for hours."

What? Demo Dick looking a gift horse in the mouth?

Could it be because most of my acquaintance with horses comes at the other end?

Let's review what we know, or rather what we knew then. Because I'm sure by now at least a few of you are confused.

Don't feel bad. I was ten times more confused. You're seeing this after the fact, with a few red herrings and false leads removed. (Sean's fun and games in Karachi, for example, which while entertaining turned out to be entirely unrelated to our story here.) I was in the middle of it; I felt like I was trying to count confetti in the middle of a hurricane.

Let's reduce what we know to bullet points. You can count them off with your saluting finger, if you like:

THE TERRORIST GROUPS
1. Red Cell International was hired to help a new Indian special operations unit prepare the country for the Commonwealth Games.
2. In the course of said preparation, Red Cell International traveled with said spec ops unit north of the border to kick some terrorists' butts, specifically butts belonging to a group called India for Islam.
3. At the end of the operation, four individuals were returned from Pakistan. One was a low-level recruit who offered very little of value. Two, co-targets of the operation, were supposed to be the masterminds of the attack. They turned out to be members of a rival organization, People's Islam. They were sprung from jail in a well-planned and possibly rehearsed operation. The fourth—an Indian spy—was killed before he could really give much useful information.

THE HELICOPTERS

4. Shortly thereafter, an unknown group hijacked two high-tech helicopters from an Indian development lab.
5. Said hijackers appeared to have been connected to People's Islam, the same terrorist group whose spies had been captured by the Indians and then sprung.
6. The helicopters were later located on a Chinese ship.

THE NUKES

7. At roughly the same time, an attack was made on an armory where most of India's nukes were being gathered. Said attack was one of the wimpiest ever launched by a terrorist organization.

    An exaggeration—we usually give terrorists more credit than they deserve—but you get the general picture.

So what did all of that leave us?

Let's start with our two terrorist organizations—India for Islam and People's Islam.

We hit India for Islam because they were planning to disrupt the Commonwealth Games. We knew this because of intelligence that had been gathered beforehand.

During the raid, though, we discovered no clear evidence of a plan to attack the Games. What we *did* find was that the group's assault target bore a remarkable resemblance to the base where the nuclear warheads were being gathered.

So was the initial intelligence wrong? Misguided?

Those things happen, more often than anyone admits. There are many reasons. In this case, though, it seemed to me that the intelligence had been passed along from sources who wanted to hurt India for Islam and help People's Islam.

The first part is obvious, based on the results: the intelligence about what they were planning was wrong, but the location was absolutely right. And that was the key to the result—India for Islam had been busted up pretty badly.

But what about the second part? How did that help People's Islam?

Well, first of all, it brought two of their operatives into the country very conveniently, at a time when Indian security had been heightened. Now it's possible that any of a dozen other methods might have been used to bring them here, but at the end of the day, the bottom line is that the pair were in India.

What I'm saying here is that People's Islam ratted out their competitors, and used Special Squadron Zero as a taxi service. A slight leap from the evidence, perhaps, but it does fit.

What didn't fit was the attack on the nuke base. Because although it appeared that India for Islam was aiming at that base and not the Commonwealth Games, the attack that had been made did not match the plans we'd seen. It also seemed designed to fail.

Ah, you say, but there was an increase in radio traffic. Maybe the attack was carried out by the second or even third string.

Shotgun made that point to Doc as well. And it was a good argument—good enough to get me to call Shunt.

"Shunt, can you still access the Indian intelligence network with Special Squadron Zero's codes?"

"Does the pope shit in the woods?"

Ask a stupid question, get a ridiculous answer. Before I was finished with my second Sapphire, Shunt had reported back on the increase in traffic.

"Mostly e-mail and text," he said. "Interesting."

"Why?" I asked.

"They're using a real sissy encryption, and these e-mail addresses are all a few months old."

"Maybe that's all they have working now."

"Then how come they used a better encryption to gloat about the demise of People's Islam? They rotate to new codes and contacts every few days. They've never gone back."

If you were a terrorist, even a stupid one, and you knew your comm system had been compromised, would you still use it?

No, I said you're a terrorist, not a high-ranking member of Homeland Insecurity.

So maybe the idea wasn't to actually threaten the base, but to generate headlines about an attack—the kind of headlines that hit the Internet, newspapers, and television news?

Hmmmm, you say.

But why would India for Islam do that?

Hold that thought.

Now let's look at the other major thread of the story so far—the helicopters. Those were pretty clearly stolen by People's Islam, which may or may not have been taking advantage of the turmoil over the breakout of the two prisoners.

We know People's Islam was behind it because of the raid to the north, where the dead were all members of the group. The Chinese were also clearly involved—that was their ship where the helicopters were taken, and their destroyers waiting for them.

Let's make a guess here—the Chinese paid People's Islam to get the helicopters.

Were they working together because of the Maoist legacy? Just for the money? Just by chance?

Maybe all of those things. Let me be very careful how I phrase this; after all, I wouldn't want to anger our Chinese masters, since they hold billions of our debt. But here, in politically correct language, is what I think happened:

The slimebag Chinese commies hired scumbag terrorists to steal high-tech weapons from their neighbors, not really caring that in the process they were probably enabling the slaughter of thousands if not millions of innocent civilians.

Just saying.

It would be nice if there was a little more backup to that charge. Like, for example, a large piece of money going from a Chinese account to a terrorist account.

Would that satisfy you?

I hope so, because during the afternoon following our fun and games at the armory, I put a call in to the CIA to fill Admiral Jones in on what had happened over the past few days.

In exchange, the admiral cleared me to talk to one of his analysts, on the condition that I not bitch about Omar. The analyst straightened me out on a few things; I pointed him in the right direction on People's Islam.

The interesting thing is that it took him literally a matter of seconds to find the transactions between the Chinese and the terrorists, even though they were using front companies and a pair of banks in Eastern Europe. Yes, grasshopper, it turns out that our government knows about a lot of these transactions, and is supposedly powerless to stop them.

I won't share my opinion on that.

How much money was involved?

"Four million two hundred thousand in this transfer," said the analyst. "Probably it's just an installment, though."

"Why?" I asked.

"From what you're telling me about that helicopter, it would have been worth at least a hundred times that. These guys may work cheap, but not that cheap."

No matter how much the pay really was, it was a hell of a deal for a weapons system that cost well over a billion to develop. But I digress. The bottom line was this: China had hired People's Islam to steal the helicopters.

So what was People's Islam going to do with the money?

"Something big," said the analyst. "But what? Who knows."

You could argue—as Doc did—that it no longer mattered to us. The Indians had now signed off on our contract—and paid in full.

"Best thing for us is to kick back, admire Trace's stick work, and cut for home," said Doc when we reconvened that afternoon for lunch near the school. "Quit while we're ahead."

But for better or worse, the quit-while-you're-ahead gene is missing from my DNA.

(IV)

Speaking of butts, Trace's was in top form the afternoon following the attack as she and the rest of the Scottish team took on New Zealand in the last pre-Games scrimmage. Trace was a demon, racing up and down the pitch, doing what she does best, whacking balls.

I'm not a sports reporter, and I can't pretend to know anything about field hockey. It looked to me like Trace was dominating the field—she scored two goals in the first few minutes while I was watching. But she didn't look very happy about it. She frowned and growled and stared and kicked the ground. At one point, she looked like she was going to spit—an extremely un-Trace-like action, as she's always been a bit of a priss when it comes to personal hygiene.

More than normal competitiveness was at work here. If I had to guess, I'd say she was angry that she had missed out on all the fun and games we'd been having in dear old India. She'd missed the helicopter assault into Pakistan, she'd missed Junior's water sports, our troll through the sewer—well, that she might not have resented missing. Still, I'm sure the cumulative effect was wearing down her normally sunny disposition.

Not in a million years would she admit that, of course. And if you just heard the sound of a book crashing through a window, you'll know she just read that passage.

I was standing behind her team's bench during the scrimmage, trying to learn the fine points of the game in between fielding calls on my sat phone. Junior and Mongoose had checked in, and after being summarily spanked for putting their bodies in gear before engaging their brains, were awarded with forty-eight-hour passes and upgraded rooms at the overpriced hotel they'd collapsed in after their foray. They were planning on coming up the following morning so they could catch the opening of the Games; whatever debauchery they were hatching in the meantime I didn't want or need to know about.

Among the other calls were several from Indian journalists, who by now had heard the rumors of my exploits inside the base.

Never one to turn down free publicity, I gave them all the same reply: *No comment.*

This had the effect of making them even more interested in me.

Eventually, one enterprising cub reporter found me at the scrimmage. He cringed as he walked toward me — it definitely pays to have a reputation.

"Excuse me, sir," he said, coming up to me. "Are you Richard Marcinko?"

"Who the hell wants to know?" I growled.

"I am Kenyon Ganesh from the *New Delhi Delhi Times.*"

"What is that to me?"

"I am a reporter, Sir Marcinko."

"*Delhi Delhi Times*?" I asked. Secretly, I liked the fact that I'd just been knighted, but I didn't let on. "What the hell is that?"

"Very good newspaper, Sir Marcinko. *New Delhi Delhi Times.*"

"Are you stuttering?"

"It is the name of the paper, sir. A very interesting history indeed."

"Not to me."

"You are the famous Rogue Warrior we have heard so much about."

"No."

"Well, very good, Sir Marcinko. I am wondering, when you were at the base . . ."

It was like having a conversation with a telemarketer. He either had an answer for everything, or just ignored what didn't fit into his script.

"I'll tell you what, Kenyon," I said finally, "I'll answer a question if you answer a question."

"Oh, this would be very pleasing, Mr. Rogue Warrior."

"How did you get the name Kenyon? It's not Indian."

"Oh, this is an easy question. My mother is a great admirer of America . . ."

Apparently, his mother had named him after the Grand Canyon, but messed up the spelling.

Fair enough, I told him. What's your question?

"Do you think this attack on the armory is part of a combined terrorist movement?"

He was wondering if this was part of a wave of coordinated terrorist attacks on India, and if they were being orchestrated by Pakistan.

"It's more like a domino theory," I explained. "Terrorists don't necessarily work together. The people on the ground — the small groups that actually do the dirty work — they're usually isolated. They have their own beefs with each other. Sometimes those are just as murderous as the ones they have with you. But you have to look at the entire effect."

All these little groups are working in the same direction. They're helped directly by ideologues—another word for crazy maniac murderers—who are giving them money, resources, and religious and intellectual cover, if you want to call it that. The best known of these umbrella groups is al Qaeda, but it's not the only one.

They're also helped, directly and indirectly, by countries that can use them for their own agenda. In our case, China saw People's Islam as a means to an end—getting India's new secret attack helicopter. China didn't necessarily endorse the terrorist's methods and certainly didn't share their immediate goals, but that was irrelevant.

Pakistan had also been involved, helping India for Islam and probably providing the location of the nukes. The benefit to them was more direct, even if the game was more dangerous.

All of these forces tend to align. One attack encourages another, weakening the system. A strike in India leads to a fresh round of recruiting in Great Britain, which helps a group flourish in Brooklyn, New York.

It's a new kind of domino theory: whether planned or not, coordinated or not, the effect of all these attacks would eventually threaten not just Indian society, but the entire West as well. You have to think like a terrorist: after India falls, Great Britain will be next, then the U.S.

Do all terrorists think this way?

The people strapping the bombs to their chest at the India for Islam level almost certainly don't. They're wrapped up—literally—in their own paranoid and murderous delusions. Farther up the ladder, though, there's quite a lot of thought going on. Whether you and I would be horrified by it is immaterial. So is the question of whether it should be classified as rational or not.

It's critical for us in the West to understand what the nature of the threat really is. We have to deal aggressively with what seem to be small, isolated groups because of the cumulative effect. And we have to help countries like India and, God really help us, Pakistan, because they really are on the front lines. They are the first dominos that will fall.

I realize it's a tough metaphor for anyone who's lived through the Vietnam era, but it becomes self-evident when you step back.

"God, that was some lecture you gave that kid," said Trace after I finished with the reporter. "What are you, getting ready to write another book?"

"Just setting him straight."

She smirked.

"Hey, Gorgeous," said Doc, zipping his trainer's bag. "You were a terror out on the pitch today."

"Wait until the Games open tomorrow," she said.

"I hope you have something left," Doc told her. "I'm putting five hundred rupees on your team."

"What is that, fifty cents?"

"I figured you're worth it."

I suggested they join me and Shotgun for an early dinner. Doc was up for it, but Trace declined.

"The team is eating together tonight. It's a morale building thing. And we have an early curfew. We have to be up early in the A.M. for the opening ceremonies."

"You're going to bed early?" asked Shotgun, who'd ambled down from the stands where he'd been ogling the women and eating Fritos—not in that order. "You're not gonna sleep, are you?"

"What I do in bed is no business of yours, Shotgun. But for the record, yes."

"Beauty rest," said Doc.

"I can understand that," said Shotgun.

Trace reared back and decked him.

Some things a boy has to learn on his own.

The rest of my evening passed uneventfully. The ambassador invited me over to the residence for a nightcap. I actually began to like him by the end of the night; he was one of the rare diplomats I've met with an actual brain. Whether he was allowed to use it or not was a separate question entirely.

These hours were the storied interlude, the downtime in between action that never makes it into books, not even (and especially not) mine. The truth is, most of war is two percent of high octane terror separated into tiny slivers by ninety-eight percent sheer boredom. Even in your typical Specwar operation, there may be only a few hours of "fun" amid days and days of monotony.

You do start to look forward to the calm moments though. The trick is to not be seduced by them into thinking there's no more fun and games left.

One thing happened that evening that actually didn't mean all that much to me at the time. In fact, it was kind of background noise in the midst of everything else. It did turn out to be somewhat critical, but damned if I realized it then.

As we just heard, Shunt still had access to the Special Squadron files and records. I set him to trolling through the various intel reports to see what he could come up with. Among other loose ends I was interested in tying up was the question of whether there was a traitor in the Special Squadron ranks.

At this point, we couldn't even be sure, one way or the other. It would have explained how People's Islam had such an easy time getting their people out of detention at the barracks. On the other hand, the alternative explanations—having planted the information about their rivals, all they really had to do was watch the base—made sense as well.

The data showed a tight connection between India for Islam and a member of the Pakistani intelligence service;[32] Shunt theorized that this was how India for Islam had gotten the information about the nukes. He kept pushing the string in that direction to try to find other connections and details, though by the time he reported in via an encrypted e-mail, he hadn't put anything together.

"A little more background on the two tangos who you brought back to India," he wrote. "One of them, Yusef, went to RPI in the States and got a degree in chemical engineering. Other guy—Arjun—also studied chemistry in Great Britain. Pretty brainy—good grades. Even had a job for a while."

I dismissed the information as something we already knew, even though Shunt supplied slightly more details. Neither man had a criminal record, though the one who had gone to RPI had run into trouble on campus for posting nude pictures of some sorority girls on a fake Facebook page. Apparently one of the young women had spurned his advances, and he was trying to get back at her.

Shunt's notes were included in a list of other general information and updates, and at the time, the only thing I wondered was why Yusef hadn't just drowned his sorrows in a couple of kegs of beer like the rest of us.

---

[32] He seems to have met with an unfortunate accident some weeks after I left India. I never met him, but I'm sure it was a great loss to humanity.

Trace did go to bed—and yes, for the record, by herself. She slept well, and didn't even need the alarm to get up at quarter to five.

That was because she was woken five minutes before that by two gorillas standing over her bed with AK47s.

[V]

Trace's first thought was that this was another drill. It would have been just like me—and therefore, she reasoned, Special Squadron Zero—to pull a last-second move like this to keep the security people on their toes.

"Up! Up!" barked one of the men.

"Into the hall," said the other.

They went out quickly, not even bothering to peek at her jammies. (Oversize sweatshirt and flannel shorts. Sorry to disappoint.)

Trace shuffled out into the hallway, probably a little groggy-eyed. Most of the other athletes were already there, more annoyed than scared—they'd been through this just a few days before.

There were two tangos at the far end of the hall, to Trace's left as she came out the door. Like the men who had come into her room, they were wearing scarves across their faces. Dressed in coveralls that looked as if they belonged to the local sanitation crew, each had an AK47 in his hands, with a double bandolier of bullets strapped across their chests. She glanced at them, and immediately realized this wasn't a drill. They were moving more than the men the other days had, jerking their shoulders and heads—nervous twitching was her interpretation.

For most of us, that wouldn't be much to go on, but Trace has always completely trusted her instincts. You can blame women's intuition or her Native American genes, whatever.

At the other end of the hall, several terrorists were trying to herd the athletes into the cafeteria—sound familiar? One of the women started mouthing off, advising the terrorist what he could do with his weapon.

Her suggestion would have been anatomically difficult. Rather than following it, he swung the butt end of the gun into her face, sending her to the floor. The terrorist next to him then raised his gun and fired a few rounds through the ceiling.

We all know that Trace sleeps with her teddy bear tucked under her pillow—teddy bear being her pet name for Kimber Compact 45, as cuddly a little piece of machinery as you'll ever find. It was now under her sweatshirt.

Trace thought about taking it out, but the way the tangos were aligned, she would only have been able to remove half the problem before the other half began firing—not an acceptable situation under the circumstances. So she did as we had planned she would do: she looked at her watch.

"Running a little slow," she muttered, pressing the buttons to adjust it.

And at the same time, sending me a signal that she had just been kidnapped.

Doc was upstairs with the rest of the coaches and trainers when the gunfire shook him out of bed. He jumped into his shoes, grabbed his own weapon—a classic Colt automatic, probably older than he was—then went out to find out what was going on. By the time he reached the hall, the face on his watch had lit up, set off by the system Trace had alerted.

It's not clear whether the tangos intended on taking everyone in the building hostage and changed their plans when the girl acted up, or if they simply figured the women on the team were all they needed. In any event, when Doc reached the stairs, he found them filled with smoke. One of the tangos had tossed a smoke grenade below and the stairwell was now thick with it.

Doc covered his mouth and nose with a handkerchief, slowly coming down the steps. The first-floor door was locked. He could hear people moving in the hall, then a few gruff shouts. Not knowing what the situation was, he retreated upstairs and had just reached his floor when I got him on the phone.

"Trace pushed her alarm," he said. "I heard gunshots. I don't know what's going on. The door to that level is locked."

"I'll meet you at the shaft to the service elevator," I told him. "We're a few minutes away."

You're wondering where all the extra guards are that the team brought in following our little demonstration.

Two are lying in the front foyer, dead. One is bleeding pretty heavily from his stomach near the back stairs; if someone doesn't reach him in the next ten minutes or so, he'll bleed to death.

And the fourth didn't show for work.

What? After your little demonstration they barely doubled the guard?

Plus ça change, plus c'est la même chose.

The tangos collected cell phones. Trace handed hers over grudgingly—covering for the gun, which of course she wasn't about to give up. Then with the others she moved down the hall to the stairs, watching and assessing the terrorists from the corner of her eye.

There were a total of five men in the corridor, all armed with submachine guns. Their faces were covered, so she couldn't really judge their ages, but the way their eyes darted and the way they moved and waved their arms and guns around reinforced her initial impression that they were young and scared.

In a way, that made them more dangerous than professional soldiers. They were much more likely to lose their heads and start shooting.

She suspected that there were more people involved; she would have run the operation with at least eight, and been happier with ten or twelve. But she didn't spot any as the group made their way down to the cafeteria.

By now the rest of the athletes had realized this wasn't a drill or a game. They moved sullenly, complying with the few barked orders directing them downstairs. One or two of the young women glanced at Trace, expecting her to do something. She made the slightest movement with her head, indicating that they should bide their time.

There was one other terrorist in the cafeteria. He wore an ill-fitting red-checkered Arab-style headdress. He seemed a little older—his mustache was visible beneath the scarf, and it was speckled with gray. But the person in charge seemed to be the man who had fired his gun downstairs. He spoke to the others in Arabic, giving quick, terse commands.

Trace's immediate problem was the pistol—she needed to hide it in case they were searched, yet she wanted it available in case she got an opportunity to use it. The only thing she could think of was to hide it in the restroom when she got downstairs.

At first, the guards made no move to search anyone, and Trace considered keeping the gun. If the risk was strictly hers, she certainly would have. But with the other women there and the men spread out around the room, she felt she was risking too much to leave it beneath her waist.

The kidnappers began to confer. They stayed in small groups, no more than three together—an attack was still far too risky.

Trace went over to Colina, the young woman whose head had been bashed. She was bleeding lightly from the mouth, and of course her head hurt.

Trace checked her eyes, trying to see if she had a concussion. There weren't obvious signs—her pupils both reacted to the light, though the eyes don't always tell all.

"Let's get you cleaned up," she said, gently helping Colina from her chair.

"You! Stop!" said the man who had bashed the girl's head in.

"She's hurt," said Trace. "She needs to be cleaned."

"No!"

"We're only going into the restroom."

Trace took a step in that direction. One of the guards moved over to block her.

The one who had said no fired a burst from his gun.

Trace's instincts screamed—pull out your gun and shoot the bastards.

One—two—she could get the men closest to her, and someone else might grab the rifle.

Might.

Might wasn't good enough. The gun stayed under her sweatshirt.

"She needs help," said Trace firmly. She looked at the man with the mustache, then at the one whom she had determined was the leader.

"In the name of Allah, who is the one just and holy God, praise and honor to Him," she said, using a common Muslim formula, "you must show mercy on the injured and sick."

He stared at her for a moment, then turned and barked something in Arabic to the man near the door. Apparently it meant step aside, for he did.

Trace put her shoulder under the other woman's arm and started for the door. The leader barked something else—the man by the restroom stiffened, frowned, then went and opened the restroom door.

"You will wait," the leader said. "He will check the room."

Trace stopped.

The gunman went inside and stepped back out quickly, the briefest inspection of a room ever conducted. Clearly he didn't want to be contaminated by female cooties.

The leader said something else in Arabic. The guard frowned again, and started to shake his head. The leader repeated what he said more forcefully.

"He will go in with you," said the leader.

"Into the ladies' room?" said Trace, summoning her most indignant tone.

"He will go with you."

Trace turned to the man, who was standing by the door, shifting his legs up and down, almost as if running in place.

"Well if you enjoy watching women pee, then I suppose you'll have a fun time," Trace said to him.

Another of the men started to cross the room, but the leader made it clear that Ahmed—what he called the man by the door—was the one who was to go in. The little drama was all about him proving his position as leader; the women were, at best, secondary.

Which was just fine, as far as Trace was concerned.

She helped Colina inside. The room was spartan; aside from a small stool pushed against the wall at the far end of the washbasins and an open metal waste container, there were only fixtures and commodes set off in standard metal cubicles. The window was a narrow slit near the ceiling at the far end; Trace could have jumped and reached it, but the space was so slim she would have had a hard time squeezing through.

"Colina, here, sit on the stool," said Trace, leading her across the room.

Trace sat her down and began running the water. The tango stayed by the door. He wasn't particularly tall—maybe two or three inches taller than Trace, who on her tiptoes in her best high heels I don't think tops five-four.

She had no doubt she could take him quickly. The problem was to do it quietly, and away from the door.

And then what?

After hanging up with me, Doc went to the freight elevator, making sure it was locked on to the top floor, where it was supposed to be parked every evening. Then he went and organized the rest of the staff, telling them to escape to the roof.

Automatically alerted by our alarm system, Indian police and military units were already on their way. Still waiting for me, Doc decided to call several of their officials personally and tell them this wasn't a drill. That was probably a good move, though the local police department had already sent two cars over. One of the men got out of the car and ran up to the front steps, pulling open the front door—a serious mistake, as he discovered when the booby trap the tangos had placed there went off.

Shotgun and I were two or three blocks away, thick in the middle of traffic, when I heard the explosion.

"Urdu, we're getting out," I told the driver, opening the door. "Take the car and head to the far end of the field. Wait there in case we need you."

We jumped out and started running toward the building. Cars up ahead had abruptly stopped. A tight circle of smoke rose from the school.

Wouldn't you know it? My sat phone began ringing precisely at that moment. I pulled it out, expecting that it was Doc. But instead, I found myself talking to Shunt.

"Hey, Dick. Got a minute?"

"I'm a little busy right now," I told him. I was about to click it off when he shouted at me.

"I found some more information out about those guys you rescued," he said. "One of them did an internship at W.R. and D. Chemical."

"That's real nice, Shunt."

"Here's the thing about W.R. & D.—the account that paid for those cars that came down from Delhi also funded the purchase of two railroad cars full of ethanol, which were parked on the siding leading to the factory two days ago."

"Shunt, I really don't need to know about a gasoline additive right now."

"You ever hear of transester process?" he asked. "Abban did a paper on it in undergrad. You use a precursor to a complicated compound, combining it with something like ethanol to finish your chemical off. Oh, yeah, I figured out their real names. They're not only on India's watch list, but about twenty others, including ours and Pakistan's. Those nom de guerre things they called themselves when they were caught weren't even among their known aliases. Did I tell you that already? I got student IDs and shit. Shunar was the intern . . ."

Shunt prattled on, but I wasn't listening anymore. I'd finally realized what the hell was going on.

I stopped so quickly Shotgun nearly bowed me over.

"Go help Doc get the hostages out," I told him. "Then find out where the hell W.R. and D. Chemical is and meet me there."

[1]

Let me be honest—to this day, I have no idea what a transester process is, or how it involves ethanol—which, besides being Iowa's own personal stimulus package, is your basic woodgrain alcohol, aka white lightning.

Shunt's detective work had just filled in the blanks in the middle of my essay question: why had People's Islam used Special Squadron Zero to transport its two thugs south of the border?

Answer: because even Pakistan would have arrested the SOBs.

Bonus question: what could possibly make them so valuable?

Answer: their chemistry skills were in great demand.

"What are they going to do, Shunt?" I asked as I ran. "Is this going to be a fertilizer bomb?"

Shunt straightened me out, filling me in on his theory as I ran.

"If only. Fertilizer bombs are bad, but this is bigger. Big, big, big. W.R. and D. Chemical makes a bunch of stuff," he said, "including these lighter things and matches and fungicides. They used to make gunpowder—"

"Keep it relevant, Shunt," I said.

"You sound like you're hyperventilating."

"I'm running."

"Oh. You ought to pace yourself a little better."

"Shunt! Explain what the hell you're talking about."

A long technical discussion followed. I'll give you the executive summary:

Between the factory and the chemists, People's Islam had the knowhow and key ingredients to manufacture VX gas[33]—and quite a lot of it.

VX is a nerve agent, the common name for Ethyl ([2-[di(propan-2-yl) amino] ethylsulfanyl) methylphosphinate or S-[2-(diisopropylamino)

---

[33] After considerable debate with the publisher's legal brain trust—such as it is—we decided to go ahead and name the chemical involved. Chemists will understand if we leave out a few critical details regarding the synthesis.

Yes, the chemicals are not difficult to obtain, the process is relatively well understood though not easy for amateurs, and this could happen in the U.S.

ethyl]-O-ethyl methylphosphonothioate. It is among the most potent chemical warfare agents known to man. It was first discovered in the 1950s in the United Kingdom. Among other qualities, it acts a lot like motor oil—it's slippery, sticky, and very hard to get rid of.

It's fatal in extremely small doses—touch it, and ten milligrams will kill you. No one appears to be one hundred percent sure how much you can breathe before permanently keeling over, but it ain't much. (A milligram is one thousandth of a gram. That's the weight of less than half a penny.)

There ain't too much of the stuff around—both the U.S. and Russia are believed to have relatively small quantities in storage—but back in 1998 the U.S. wiped out a supposed Sudanese drug factory after soil tests nearby showed it was being produced there.[34] It's dangerous but not extremely difficult to make, and once used, can contaminate an area for years.

The perfect terror weapon.

I hung up and continued running, turning up along the long block paralleling the side of the athletic complex. My lungs were starting to complain and both thighs had stitches in them as I took the gentle hill toward the spot where I'd told Urdu to wait. He'd already parked and was starting to wax up the hood of his taxi as I ran up.

"Mr. Dick—you should have called me," he said.

"W.R. and D. Chemical," I told him. "Drop me off near the railroad tracks."

"This is part of the operation against the Games?"

"It's a lot bigger than the Games," I told him. "Let's get moving."

---

[34] Well, that or a competitor to Green Gro Perfect Anti-Magot Grass Fertilizer, which I'm sure there's a lot of call for in the deserts of Sudan.

(II)

By the time Shotgun got to the school building where Trace and the others had been taken captive, more police had arrived. The explosion had made them wary; they were hunkered down behind their patrol cars, guns drawn, covering the front door. The body of the man who had made the fatal mistake of trying to get in lay on the front step.

Most of him, anyway.

Flashing the ID the ministry had given us for Special Squadron Zero, Shotgun ran in an arc behind the cars to the end of building, hunkered down, and crawled to the back. Looking in the window that covered the hall, he saw that it was empty. Then he stepped to the side, pulled down the ladder to the fire escape, and started climbing up.

Somewhere around the second floor, a policeman came over and yelled at him, telling him to get down.

"Cover me!" answered Shotgun.

That's what he claims he said, anyway. The policeman may have heard a slightly different verb.

Shotgun made his way up to the roof, pausing on each floor to look through the windows. By that time, the Scottish coaches and other personnel had all reached the roof.

"Go down," he told them. "Get away from the building quickly. It may be wired to blow."

If they needed any encouragement, his suggestion that there might be explosives inside was more than enough. They started moving down. As they did, two or three police officers came up to help.

Shotgun took a quick look around the roof, then went down a flight and entered the hallway window off the fire escape landing.

"Doc!"

"About time you got your ass over here. What the hell are you doing? Buying snacks?"

"No, Dick said there wasn't time," said Shotgun, trotting to the opening for the freight elevator. Doc had already opened it.

"Go ahead," said Shotgun. "I'm right behind you."

"Bullshit on that," answered Doc. "You fall, you're taking me with you."

"I ain't fallin'." Shotgun grinned and leaned inside, grabbing the rung of the work ladder that ran up the side of the elevator. He swung out, Tarzan-like, then began making his way down to the basement.

Doc followed, a little more slowly. He caught up with Shotgun between the second and third floors, where we had stashed a locker with gear.

There was a good selection of weapons. Shotgun opted for an M110 Semi-Automatic Sniper System—overkill in the situation, though you couldn't fault the choice.

For those of you not familiar with the U.S. Army's next generation precision killing tool, the M110 is an American-made semiautomatic manufactured by the good people at Knight Armament. It fires 7.62×51 mm NATO rounds and is as accurate as a computer calculating pi.

Reed Knight, friend and owner, did "special" work for me when I was outfitting SEAL Six. Now his son runs the show and we see each other at the trade shows where I show off my knives and other Rogue Warrior and Red Cell toys.

Toys—remember, the difference between men and boys is the price of their toys. But I digress.

Being a sniper rifle, the M110 has a fairly serious barrel, potentially a hindrance if you're climbing down an elevator shaft like Shotgun was. But he's a big boy, and big toys go with big boys—he strapped that sucker on his back, and looked just like Natty Bumppo setting off to fetch himself some deer meat.

Doc pulled the ever-reliable MP5 submachine out of the box, along with some extra magazines. Then he grabbed a small rucksack that held tear gas canisters and some masks and resumed his downward climb.

The elevator opened into a small hallway between the pantry and the kitchen. Rather than risking that, Doc and Shotgun slipped out an access door into the pantry.

We'd had a low voltage red light system installed in the pantry as part of our security preparations, arranging the lights so that the front part of the room was evenly lit while the entrance to the shaft was shadowed. Doc and Shotgun made sure they were alone, then crawled down along the first row of the shelves, stopping to pull out a box of equipment stashed there. They pulled on a pair of headsets with throat mikes. Their short-range radio signal was virtually undetectable, and the sensitive mikes would keep them from having to speak too loudly.

Doc then took an iPod Touch from the box and fired it up. The handheld computer was loaded with special apps designed by some friends of ours at Apple. Doc tapped an icon that brought up a new screen; after entering a password, the command unit for the school's video surveillance network came on screen. He selected one of the two cafeteria cameras, squinting a bit at the small screen. Shotgun, meanwhile, had taken a small video periscope from the box and was using it to check the hall.

"How the hell do I get the damn audio on this Walkman thing?" Doc growled.

"It's that slider on the bottom," said Shotgun.

"No, not that. I can't get it to feed into our radios."

"You gotta tap the little mouth that looks purple."

"Who's the asshole who decided it should be a purple mouth?" grumbled Doc. "Purple. Hard to see the damn thing in the dark."

That would be Shunt. He's a hell of a programmer, but not much on colors.

"Hall's clear," whispered Shotgun. "Moving to the kitchen."

"Hold up until I figure out where they are. Goddamn little screen. Why do they make these damn things so tiny?"

Trace, meanwhile, was in the ladies' room, calculating her next move. She could slip the pistol behind the commode easily enough, but the tango's presence in the restroom presented a huge temptation—if she overpowered him, she would not only have his rifle but one less asshole to deal with.

She knew that by now Doc and the rest of us would be on our way. We had hidden a radio unit in the ladies' room under the commode. Trace knew she could use it to talk to Doc, but the asshole with the rifle would almost certainly hear her mumbling.

Another argument in favor of taking him down. But once she did that, she was committed. It would also commit everyone outside; there'd be no playing for time while they got into position.

We had discussed several different scenarios before planting her on the team. My basic instruction to her was not to risk anyone's life, including and especially her own. That's an easy thing to say, but in practice, what does it really mean?

It means make a judgment based on the situation and your instincts. It also means that only the on-scene personnel—Trace in this case—can make the call. It's why we spend so much time and money training leaders, and training SEALs and other SpecWare people for that matter. You can't foresee every permutation of a situation beforehand—and you can't micromanage a war from a bunker in Washington, D.C., no matter how many hi-rez feeds you're getting from Predators and Global Hawks and whatever sleek creation is UAV[35] of the month.

Or to use more direct language: only the person up to his nose in a clusterfuck can find a way out of it.

Or *her* nose, as the case may be.

"Are you all right?" Trace whispered to Colina, the girl who'd been smashed in the head.

"Yeah."

Trace wet some paper towels and held them to the side of her head. Colina played defense on the team, and was used to mixing it up on the playing field.

"Can you see OK?" Trace asked, holding up a finger. "How many?"

"One."

"Good," she said. Then in a lower voice, she added, "Pretend you're really hurting. Moan a bit."

"Oh," said Colina.

"That's it. Louder."

"Oh."

The tango at the door was shifting around nervously.

"Can you handle a rifle?" Trace whispered to Colina.

"I could try."

Not the answer Trace wanted. In her experience, "I can try" is even worse than "maybe."

She shifted around, pretending to look over Colina's head.

"She's very hurt," Trace told the tango.

"You do," he said, waving his hand. "Do."

"I'm doing," said Trace. She knelt down in front of Colina and whispered, "Help is on the way. Can you stay in the restroom awhile?"

Colina nodded.

Trace rose.

"I need a med kit," she told the guard. "I need to get her some gauze and a wrap."

---

[35] UAV = unmanned aerial vehicle. I told you that already.

"You do," he said again, gesturing. He hadn't understood what she'd said.

"See what I need is a compress," said Trace, walking toward him.

She gestured with her hands, as if mimicking a very large bandage—an extremely large bandage. The motion brought her hands in front of her body, roughly even with the rifle, though she was still a few feet from the barrel.

"You do," he said firmly. He swung the gun up in his left hand. "You do."

"I will," she said.

And with that, she grabbed the barrel of the gun and jerked it from his hand.

"Trace isn't in the big room," said Doc, settling in behind Shotgun in the kitchen. They were behind the large window separating it from the eating area.

"Maybe she's still upstairs," said Shotgun. He was deeper in the room, moving to a spot where he could set up with the sniper rifle and not be seen.

"She'd've checked in by now."

"Maybe you're just missing her."

Doc stared at the screen. There was a zoom feature, but it didn't help all that much. Next time, we use the iPad.

"We got two guys at the far end," he told Shotgun. "Another near the door. Two close to us on the wall to our left. Total of five."

"I can get the guys at the far end," said Shotgun. "No other shots."

Outside, the police and SWAT teams had secured the street and the north side of the building. The team officials had been helped down, and soldiers were on the roof, waiting for a specially trained unit to arrive and begin working their way down the building. It was all textbook stuff—and all so terribly slow that a group of suicidal maniacs could have blown up the building three or four times by now.

Doc could hook into the police network using the iPod and another of Shunt's specially modified apps. But he decided not to for the time being; he wanted to know exactly where Trace was before proceeding. (The app alerted them that we were on the line; they tended not to use English over the radio so just monitoring the conversations wouldn't have been as useful as it was in the States.)

We had considered making the video feeds available to the police, but decided it was too much of a security risk; unless hardwired, it was possible the tangos would intercept the signal, and even if they couldn't read it they might be able to guess someone was in the building. There was also the fact that we worried there would be a traitor among the various police forces, or that word would leak about the setup.

"I got a good shot on two at the far end," said Shotgun. "They're close together."

"That's not going to work," said Doc. "We need to find Trace before we do anything."

Trace at that very moment was pulling the rifle from the tango's hand in the restroom, simultaneously kicking him where it would do the most good.

Her intention was to pull this off silently. In her mind, it went something like this: caught off guard as he lost the rifle, the man would have his breath as well as his ego stripped by the blow to his manhood. Gasping for air, he would be a vulnerable target for her next move—a smash with the rifle to his head. He'd fold. She'd gag him with his shirt, then move on to phase two.

But Murphy was lurking nearby. Being the perverse sort, he'd sprinkled a few drops of liquid soap on the floor the evening before, making the tiles just a little slippery. Trace hit one of them as she kicked, which threw off her timing. She managed to get her foot in the right place, but she tumbled to the side as she did. In the process, the gun flew across the room.

Colina tried to grab it midair but couldn't manage it. The weapon clattered to the floor.

Trace hopped to her feet, stomped on the tango's head—he hadn't managed more than a whimper in the meantime—then pushed him aside, unconscious.

"Get the gun. Stay in here," she hissed to her teammate. Then she pushed open the door into the cafeteria.

"Something's going on," said Doc when he heard the noise of the rifle falling.

"I still have two. The guys on the far end."

Doc looked at his screen. He calculated that he could get the two tangos to his left with his submachine gun—he'd jump up and spray, catching them by surprise. But that would leave the man on the right. And lots of women in between.

Something moved on the right side of the video screen.

"Door to the ladies' is opening," Doc told Shotgun.

Trace took a deep breath and walked into the cafeteria. The man closest to the door stared at her. He'd heard the commotion, but hadn't known what to make of it.

"We need a medical kit," said Trace loudly. "She's bleeding pretty bad and I need something to stop it with."

The leader yelled at her in Arabic. Possibly he was comparing her favorably to Florence Nightingale, but I doubt it.

"I need to stop the bleeding," said Trace emphatically. "Do we have a medical kit? Or at least a towel?"

"Where is Ahmed?" he demanded, this time in English.

"He's watching her."

The leader said something to the other tangos. Two started across the room toward her.

"Do you have a med kit?" she asked them.

One of the men slapped her across the face. Trace just barely controlled herself, falling back toward the ladies' room door.

The man yelled something at her—this was probably a comparison to Mother Teresa—then hit her again. Trace fell back, this time through the door into the ladies' room.

The tangos followed.

"What do you have?" Doc asked Shotgun.

"Just the two. Left and right. They're close."

Trace ducked to her right as she "fell" into the restroom. As she did, she pulled the pistol from the back of her waistband.

The tango who had hit her threw open the door, pushing it so hard that it flew against the wall and rebounded back, smacking him in the side. This made him even madder. He threw it back again and pushed into the restroom, quickly followed by the other terrorist, who was trying to restrain him.

Trace put a bullet into the second man's temple, then fired one into the side of the first tango's head as he turned.

"Go! Go! Go!" yelled Doc as he heard the shot.

Shotgun had already squeezed the trigger, firing on the gun blast. His bullet took the tango closest to the windows in the head. The next shot grazed the scalp of the second man as he ducked. The terrorist—he was the leader of the group—fell backward, his gun slipping from his hand.

Doc leapt upright. Hesitating a moment before completely sure of his bearings, he found the fifth terrorist against the wall and shot a half-dozen bullets into him.

"Down! Down!" he yelled as he fired. "Down! Everyone down! *Stay down!*"

In the restroom, Trace pulled the rifles away from the dead men. She grabbed one, then slid the other across the floor to Colina, who now had one for each hand. She spun around, gun pointed at the door.

"We're clear," Doc was yelling. Behind him, Shotgun was sweeping his sight across the room, looking for another terrorist.

Heart pumping, Doc leaned up and got himself through the window of the kitchen.

"Trace! Trace!"

"In here!" she yelled.

"Stay there!"

The athletes had thrown themselves to the floor and stayed there, frozen by the gunfire. But as Doc started walking toward the man he had shot to make sure he was dead, the women looked up. One, then another and another, jumped on the man who had been only grazed by Shotgun's bullet. One of the athletes grabbed his rifle from the ground. Another leaned down and punched him the face. Within moments, the entire team was gathered around him, pummeling him with feet and fists. In seconds his face was a pulp of blood and split flesh.

"Whoa, ladies, ladies, relax now," said Doc, trying to wade into the crowd. "Leave him to us."

The women were in no mood for that. Doc had to step back and let them spend their fury.

Shotgun, meanwhile, raced to the restroom and rapped on the door.

"Trace, it's me—you decent?"

She pulled open the door.

"What the hell took you so long?" she asked.

Shotgun looked in, saw the dead bodies, and whistled. He helped Colina out, then joined Trace in herding the women toward the ladder in the elevator shaft.

"Get everyone up to the roof," Doc told them, punching into the police network. "I'll call the police teams outside. When everyone's out of the building, we'll send the squad in and start the floor-by-floor search."

Shotgun cast a hungry eye toward the kitchen.

"Think there's time for a snack?" he asked.

[IV]

Hearing the shots, the police outside had started to rush the building. Doc convinced them to back off in case there were booby traps, assuring them that the hostages were already safe.

Evacuating the women from the building took another twenty minutes. The SWAT teams had to follow standard protocol, searching the women before taking them to safety.

Shotgun naturally volunteered to handle this personally, but the job was taken by a pair of matrons specially trained in the delicate art of female searches. He did, however, manage to find a bag of Twinkies in his vest, which was a partial consolation.

Meanwhile, Doc stayed in the cafeteria with the beaten tango. He tried questioning him, but between the shot that had grazed the man's head and the pummeling he'd received, he was too groggy to respond. Doc searched him and found only two things in his pockets—a cell phone and a small radio detonator.

The tangos had set charges to blow the building before waking the women.

"Better send the bomb squad in first," Doc told the police. "And evacuate the block. These guys aren't known for skimping on the explosives."

By this point, I'd reached the chemical plant.

You're probably expecting to see armed men all over the building, holding workers at bay, preparing some sort of megabomb to devastate all of Delhi.

So was I.

Imagine my surprise then when I found the guards on duty, and no report of anything amiss.

Not to seem too disappointed at the lack of a catastrophe that would potentially match that of Hiroshima, but WTF?

My first thought was that Shunt had gotten the location wrong. I walked back along the tracks, following the siding right to the building—it wasn't even blocked off by a fence. The two tank cars were there, sitting close to the building. Glancing at them, I saw no obvious sign that they'd been tampered with.

I'd been sure that the attack on the school would be a diversion—while India's security people scurried to help the hostages, the tangos would take over the chemical factory and turn it into a giant nerve gas bomb. The amount of alcohol they'd procured made that seem only logical.

But now another thought occurred to me. Maybe the two events weren't related at all. Maybe the tangos had already finished making their gas, and had in fact shipped it out, not in train cars but in jugs and small sealed containers, distributing it through Delhi or worse, through India or the world. A gallon or two of the gas released simultaneously in a dozen office buildings, dropped into air circulators in a few high-rises or indoor arenas, several shopping malls—the effect might not be quite as dramatic as 9/11, but it would certainly produce a similar level of terror.

That's the problem with this business. Hang around it for any length of time and all sorts of evil possibilities occur to you. I pity people in the profession who need more than two or three hours' sleep, because I doubt they can get it.

I was considering my next move—in other words, staring at the train cars with a dumbshit look on my face—when the sat phone rang. It was Doc, telling me they'd freed the hostages and were securing the building.

"Looks like they set some charges," he said. "The lead tango had a detonator device and a cell phone."

"What sort of numbers are on the cell?" I asked.

"I don't want to turn it on, in case it's a backup for the detonator."

That's Doc. Always thinking.

"What I figure is, they're waiting for an external signal to blow themselves up," he told me. "Now where the hell are you and what are you doing?"

At least I think that's what he said. I was too busy adding two and two together to pay much attention to what he was saying.

Why would the tangos inside the school need to wait for a signal to blow themselves up?

Obviously, something else had to happen.

A VX attack?

Had to be.

Actually, it didn't. But all the other information had led me here, and I was convinced that there must be a connection. Call it Rogue intuition.

And then I saw the two guys climbing the smokestack.

[V]

ccording to Doc, I told him to get his butt up to the chemical plant before hanging up. That may be true. I don't remember saying anything, or even hanging up. All I know is I started for the smokestack, then reversed course, running into the building.

I'd had it right in the beginning; I was just wrong about how far along they were, and what specifically they planned to do.

The men climbing the building were wearing backpacks. They were either intending to blow off the sensors at the top of the stack that shut down the plant when toxic chemicals were detected, or more likely simply wanted to make sure that the gas was released low enough to spread with maximum effect in Delhi.[36]

For all intents and purposes, the factory was operating normally, and as safely as ever: Day Number 1,643 without an accident, as the sign in the front lobby proclaimed.

That was about to change.

"My name is Richard Marcinko," I told the guards at the front desk. "I'm working for the Defense Ministry. I need to speak to the head of security right away."

A little white lie in the heat of the battle never hurt anyone.

The guard looked at my ID, looked at my beady little eyes, then nodded and ducked into the office behind him.

I started to follow. He met me inside the reception room.

"The director is waiting," he said, stepping out of my way.

I pushed into the room.

"I'm sorry to barge in like this, but you have a serious emergency. The building back by the train siding. There's something going on inside that has to be che—"

I stopped short. The director had leveled a .44 Magnum revolver at my stomach.

My editor suggested a cool scene here where Junior and Mongoose, having rested up down south, "borrowed" the advanced attack helicopter and

---

[36] We found it necessary to censor some information here. Sorry.

flew north with it. Realizing that I was being held hostage, they would crash through the windows of the plant, chain gun blazing, and proceed to fly around the interior, laying waste to the pack of dirty rotten scumbags who were trying literally to get on Delhi's nerves. The final climax would be a scene of fiery death, with their bullets igniting a series of flames. I would jump on the wheel and we would burst out of the building, glass and wood flying, moments before it blew up.

Then we'd land, I'd kiss a pretty young thing, and we'd all retire to the local bar for drinks.

Great ending.

Things didn't quite go that way, though.

"We are going for a little walk," the security director told me.

"I'm ready when you are," I told him.

"You will remove your weapons," he said. "And very slowly."

I took the PK out.

"Drop it on the floor."

"That's not a very safe thing to do," I said.

"Drop the gun."

I complied.

"No backup weapon?" he asked.

"Do I look like someone who would need a backup?"

Apparently I do, because he had me pull up my shirt and then lower my drawers, demonstrating that I was not, in fact, carrying another gun.

"Shoes come off, and socks," he demanded. "Roll up your pant legs."

I had to give up the Rogue Warrior knives. Some people will do anything to get them at a discount.

I looked down at my watch, pressing the button on the dial.

"What are you doing?"

"Checking the time."

"Give me the watch."

"It's just a watch."

"Give it to me."

I handed it over. He frowned at it, and started to throw it into the wastebasket.

"It's a Rogue Warrior watch," I told him. "Limited edition."

He looked at it again.

"Worth quite a bit of money," I added.

"Let's go," he said, pocketing it.

"Sure."

I turned and started out the door slowly. It was a classic takedown situation—as I passed through the door, I would slide to the side, grab the hand with the gun, push down and then push up, keeping control of the weapon while kicking him with my feet.

That was my plan, and it wouldn't have been a bad one, had not one of the director's guards appeared in front of me, his own gun drawn.

"The director is a traitor," I said, throwing myself to the right.

The guard smacked me on the side of the head with his gun, then took a quick step back.

He was a traitor as well. As a matter of fact, the tangos had taken over the entire security shift.

Doom on Dickie.

Doom on Delhi.

The watch *was* a Rogue Warrior watch. But it was rigged exactly as Trace's was. When I pushed the buttons in, Doc got an immediate alert.

"Dick needs us," he told the others. And within thirty seconds they were on their way.

Getting pistol-whipped is not my idea of a fun time, but I've certainly been hit much harder. I never blanked out. One of the goons kicked at me and got me to my feet.

They walked me down a long corridor. There were people working in the offices, but the guards had holstered their guns and I imagine that we didn't look too out of place. I worked out various permutations of how I might escape, what to do if someone came, but the right opportunity didn't present itself.

There was a door at the end of the hall. We went through it and entered a small courtyard paved in concrete. We continued to an older gray building on the left, entering a long gray hallway, dimly lit.

"All the way to the end," said the director, a few paces behind me.

There were no doors along the corridor—it was as if we were walking through a mine shaft. The door at the end led to an open area covered with broken macadam, pebbles, and debris. I was barefoot, and I used that as an excuse to duck back and forth, thinking it might give me a chance to turn and run. But they quickly grew tired of the game; the guards started pushing me forward in the direction of a large building. They were on to my game. These guys were a lot better trained and several times more wary than any of the tangos I'd dealt with before.

Several stories tall, the building was made of cinder blocks and steel panels. The blocks were on the bottom, about eight or nine feet high. They were worn down by the weather, though not so much that you could see through them. Rust poked through the seams of the steel panels above the bricks. Here and there splotches of brown covered vast parts of the panels, looking like giant blood clots that had burst against the wall.

The smell of a thousand Chinese laundries hit me as we moved through the door. A few steps later, the scent turned to something closer to the odor you get in a pool store, accented by a delicate bouquet of roasted metal. This was quickly replaced by a sweeter smell, almost like lilac water, if you can imagine it being boiled in the middle of your high school chemistry lab right after Dopey Joey burned a beaker's worth of sulfur onto his Bunsen burner.

The building, one of the older ones on the site, was used to mix chemicals in bulk. Old steel vats stood along the wall on my left. Each vat was at least ten feet in diameter; some looked considerably bigger, maybe thirty or forty feet across. Serpentine metal ladders ran around the sides, with a wide spiderweb of grates and walkways over and across the top.

A veritable pipe organ of tubing was mounted behind each of the vats; there were assorted gauges and crank wheels sprinkled randomly through the gear. A few glass tubes ran in and out of one of the large vats, but for the most part everything was metal, and not particularly new metal at that. I have no idea how old the equipment was, but it gave every impression of having been there since before India became independent.

That contrasted sharply with the right side of the room, where triangular stainless-steel containers gleamed amid a tangled weave of glass, black plastic, and steel pipes. Digital displays and thick fists of valves sat at regular intervals in the piping. At the base there was a control unit with several keyboard and display screens.

The floor—which was mostly where my eyes were aimed—was smooth, epoxy-covered concrete, recently applied. Toward the back of the room, a pair of railroad tracks bisected the concrete. They led to a large barnlike door; it wasn't hard to guess that the train cars I'd seen sat somewhere on the other side of the door.

Which put the smokestack to my left, above the large brick room punctured by metal octopus arms. Thick wires hung out the side of the arms, dangling like so many severed strands of muscle or, to make a more appropriate metaphor, nerve endings. They led to sensors and feedback controls, part of a monitoring and emergency shutdown system designed to keep toxic materials from entering the smokestack.

As I walked, I heard a clap of thunder followed by heavy rain—the top eighty or ninety feet of the smokestack had just been blown off.

Two men in lab coats were bent over the control station, talking in hushed tones. I recognized them both—our chemistry students, so conveniently deposited into the heart of India by Special Squadron Zero and yours truly. Three or four other men in white coveralls were working in the spiderwork above, checking different wheel handles and working on the pipes.

Two men dressed in security garb, both armed with AK47s, were standing in the middle of the room, watching us come in.

What does that add up to? Counting the guys who'd gone up the chimney, the guards that I knew about, the supervisor—a baker's dozen to kill or maim hundreds of thousands. Their productivity statistics were out of sight.

One of the men at the control board turned and shouted something in Arabic. Two of the men on the spiderwork above the old equipment began furiously turning cranks, while a third took what looked like a fire hose from the side and put it on the top of one of the tanks. The air started to smell like really bad eggs, or the kind of farts Shotgun emits the morning after killer chili.

I'd love to stay to chat, but really I must be going . . .

It was past time to make my escape, but there didn't seem to be an opening. I was surrounded by guys with guns, and it looked like I was the star attraction in an Indian clusterfuck.

My only option was to delay. Sooner or later, I figured, Doc was going to see the signal from my watch and realize what was going on. Of course, the fact that he and the rest of the team were involved in a hostage situation made later considerably more likely than sooner.

"So what's the overall plan here?" I asked my captors.

"How stupid do you think we are?" said the security director.

"You probably don't want an honest answer."

"A wiseass to the end."

I would have complimented him on his command of American slang, but at that precise moment I was hit across the back of the head with a thick black chain. I went down like a sailor cold-cocked by a marine in a bar fight.

My mind blinked dark for a moment or two; it came back online with a surge of pain—exactly what the sailor felt the next day, waking up in his rack with the ship a few hours out of port.

In heavy weather, I might add.

My hands and legs had been bound in chains, and I'd been lifted hand and foot by two goons. They were carrying me up one of the serpentine metal stairways to the top of the old vats.

The Sharkman was about to become a sulfur chaser.

The smell was even more intense here than below, and I felt myself starting to gag. The two goons carrying me were having trouble as well, shaking their heads and making sounds very similar to those that the sailor I was talking about would make en route to the head.

The guy holding my feet finally let go and turned, leaning over the side and letting loose. The one on my hands yelled at him—then dropped me unceremoniously to the grate.

And why not? I wasn't going anywhere—roll off and I was in a vat of some putrid-smelling plop that for all I know was acid. If I were Houdini, it would have been the perfect setup for an escape. But the only magic I've ever practiced has come between the sheets.

Still, this was about as close to a chance to escape as I'd ever get. I wiggled around, pushing to my knees and then awkwardly to my feet.

Which left me tottering dangerously close to the edge of the grate, right over a vat of brown-colored puke juice.

The director started yelling. I spun—to the extent you can spin while wrapped in chains—then lurched toward a small collection of wires and hoses. I was hoping to do my best Tarzan imitation and swing down off the catwalk. But the wires and hoses weren't nearly as strong as they looked. They gave way immediately and I fell feetfirst to the floor, bouncing against the side of the vat as I dropped.

Liquid began squirting everywhere. Steam, gas, foul odors—it was like the reception area of hell, or at least the kitchen of the worst Korean restaurant you've ever eaten in.

I reached down, pulling at the chains to unwrap them. As I did, one of the goons leapt off the stairway above me, aiming for my head. He hit my shoulder instead, sending me tumbling off balance against the wall. I swung my arms, flinging the chain into his face.

There was a fire hose and an alarm a few feet away. I waddled to the alarm, my feet still tangled in the chain, and pulled it.

Nothing happened.

Breaking the glass on the door to the hose, I pulled out the nozzle and punched the lever around, pressurizing it.

But I had no target. I was behind the vats of chemicals, out of view of the others. The guard who'd jumped was on the ground nearby, his head looking a little like a smashed mango.

I got the chain off my feet a few seconds before bullets began spraying in my direction. I looked up, pointing the hose in the direction of ricochets. Water spurt out, then died—they'd shut off the water to the building after taking it over.

There wasn't time to curse. Flopping down, I crawled toward the gap between the two vats for better cover. There I managed to pull the last chain from my hands. I started to throw it down, then realized it was the only weapon I had. Draping it around my neck, I grabbed a metal pipe that ran up the nearby vat and climbed King-Kong-with-Fay-Wray style to the top. Except I didn't have a pretty girl under my arm.

The tango who'd been shooting came down the narrow space behind the vats, looking for me. He reached the space a few seconds after I got to the top of the vat. I curled my knees against the piping then threw the chain at his head.

Bull's-eye!

But not on him. Murphy had chosen that moment to have a few pipes burst. One sprang out from its restraints and intercepted the chain, snagging it like the neck of a roadrunner caught by a bola.

If I could get a running start, I could jump on the bastard, I thought. I reared back, then promptly slipped on the top grating of the vat and fell inside.

It was a long way down. My life flashed before my eyes, and it wasn't pretty.

Closing my eyes tight, I held my breath and plunged through the surface of the liquid back-first. Instantly I tried to swim upward and get out of whatever I was in. Part of me kept waiting to feel the burning sensation that I was sure was my fate; the rest just acted instinctually, pushing me from the vat.

There wasn't all that much liquid in the container; in fact, all I had to do was stand to reach the surface. The liquid came just to my chest.

I wasn't burning at all. The smell was strong but not overwhelming. In fact, it was rather pleasant.

I'd fallen into a vat of alcohol.

Head swimming, I made my way to the side and climbed up to the top, just in time to see my pursuer's feet come over the edge of the rim. I pushed against the side of the vat and waited until he crouched down. Then I pulled him in.

Diving on top of him, I held him under until he had no more fight. Then I grabbed his gun from the liquid and climbed back up the side of the vat.

They were shouting in the big room, moving hoses and pipes around. Inadvertently I'd disturbed the mechanism they'd set up to finalize their creation of the gas, and they were working to get it back together.

I caught my breath, unsure what to do. Shoot the controls? Would that stop the process—or set it in motion?

Before I could decide, there was a loud crash at the far end of the building. I turned and saw the train cars rolling through the still closed door.

The cavalry had arrived.

(VI)

Cavalry is a figure of speech, of course. What actually had arrived was the engine from the 8:07 local, borrowed by Doc, Trace, and Shotgun as they rode to my rescue. Homing in on the watch, they'd realized where I was being held, and with Shunt's help, figured out that the terrorists must be mixing their magic elixir inside. They'd borrowed the engine and used it to push the cars into the barn, intending to disrupt the chemical production and rescue me at the same time.

It was an excellent plan, but the tangos had foreseen the possibility that they might be attacked during the home stretch of their project. As three different SWAT teams followed the train cars into the building, one of the chemists jumped from his chair at the mixing station and ran in the direction of the door where I'd come in.

I thought he was running away, but when he slowed and raised his hand toward the fire alarm, I realized it must have been rewired for something else.

Lucky these guys use the same MO. Then again, once you've come up with a clever plan, why change it?

I fired the AK47.

And missed.

(1)

Hell of a time to fail my basic rifle proficiency, eh?

In my defense, the shot was a little over two hundred feet in a relatively dark room. The gun was sopping wet. And, and, and . . . aw hell, I just missed the damn bastard.

The tango pulled the alarm.

What happened next can be described in a single word:

Nothing.

The terrorists had rigged a doomsday device and connected it to the fire alarms throughout the building, very much like they had intended to do at the stadium. The wires were connected to blasting caps, which would blow a number of the vats and send the chemicals that were already prepared out into the atmosphere.

But the setup was complicated, and the key detonation wires had been done in series not in parallel. Break the wire in one place, and none of the others would work.

I'd done that inadvertently when I'd fallen. That's why nothing happened when I set off the fire alarm.

What?

Am I saying that, if not for my clumsy escape and subsequent fall, the building would have blown up when I hit the alarm?

Yes.

And the explosions would have released several hundred gallons (as opposed to several thousand) of VX gas?

Yes.

And so I, Richard Marcinko, Demo Dick, the Sharkman, sometime defender of the free world, and Rogue Warrior par excellence, would have been responsible for the death of thousands of innocent Indians?

Check.

Sometimes it's better to be lucky than smart.

II

The SWAT teams took care of the tangos in short order. One tried to hang himself on some of the wiring above one of the vats, but the wire gave way and all he ended up doing was breaking his legs. The others, wounded in the melee or killed by me, were taken into custody.

They told me later that the terrorists were about fifteen minutes from finishing the process and creating VX gas. They'd already created the precursor—something called transesterified N-N di-something or other—and were getting ready to react it with the sulfur. That's why the place smelled like rotten eggs.

Or as Shotgun put it after he helped me down off the vat, "Who the hell had chili for dinner?"

All's well that ends well, right?

The Games, which were just getting under way across town with a massive welcoming parade, had been saved. We'd saved the stadium, of course, and now thwarted the kidnapping. With the exception of Colina, whose injuries were relatively minor, no athletes had been hurt in the attempted kidnapping. More importantly, the attempt to douse the entire city with VX gas had been smashed. In the process, People's Islam had been tripped up and depleted of its most devious members.

Add the helicopters and the action against India for Islam, and on the whole it hadn't been a bad few weeks for Red Cell International.

There were, however, two large loose ends that needed to be tied up.

Loose end number 1: the source of several leaks from Special Squadron Zero.

Who was the traitor?

Loose end number 2: who was responsible for the weak-assed attack on the nuke warehouse?

Would 1 lead to 2? Were they related, or not?

Too many questions—time for a beer.

Or it would have been, had Shunt not called as we were on our way over to Dublin.

After we'd set up the keylogger in the Squadron Zero computers, Shunt decided to insert a virus so he could get copies of instant messages and Internet access logs on the different computers. The results had been a snooze fest—until now.

"Whoever is using the computer right now," he told me when I answered the phone, "has got to be the spy."

Whoever it was had just gotten a text message from a cell phone, then logged into the Indian intelligence network.

"What are they looking for?" I asked.

"Bulletins."

"Maybe they heard about the hostage situation."

"Maybe. But the phone isn't one of the ones the members of Special Squadron Zero use. And I ran a quick reverse directory search—no known number. I think it's part of the batch that came out of that store you visited. Same company. I'm trying to break into their computers now."

I had Urdu change course and head to the old air base where Special Squadron Zero was headquartered.

"We're at least fifteen minutes away," I told Shunt. "Is there any way you can keep him on the computer?"

"That's not going to be a problem," he said.

Exactly twelve minutes later—Urdu used every shortcut he knew, and would have made Jimmy Johnson proud weaving his way through traffic—I walked into the commander's office and found Corporal Nadar in the middle of a marathon porn session, delivered free courtesy of Shunt's machinations.

He exhibited more than passing interest in breasts tied grotesquely with string. Not that I looked at the screen.

"Pleasure time's over, Corporal," I said in a loud voice. I had to talk loud to be heard over the screams on the screen.

The corporal jumped up.

"Commander Rick."

"Time for you to take a little ride with me."

He reached for the computer.

"You can let that play," I said. "And it's no use erasing the history on the browser."

"I just—just a little entertainment." He tried winking, but was too nervous to pull it off.

So to speak.

"I'm not interested in the porn," I told him. "Did you do it for money?"

He tried to curl his eyebrows down, as if he didn't understand what I was saying—but that didn't work either.

"It's no good, Corporal. I know you accessed the intelligence network. And I know you've been dealing with People's Islam. You'll do a lot better if you just admit it and cooperate."

"With who, cooperate?"

That was actually a good question—the people I trusted in the Indian intelligence service could be counted on the hand of an armless man.

"I have some friends in the navy," I told him, thinking of Admiral Yamuna, who could be trusted. "They'll take good care of you."

"I don't think that will be necessary," said Sergeant Phurem, walking in behind me. "This is an internal matter."

I turned and saw Phurem. He'd unholstered his service pistol.

"It's beyond Special Squadron Zero," I told him.

"No, I think it is internal. We are family."

I frowned, then grabbed the corporal's arm.

"I'll deal with him."

"You will release him," said Sergeant Phurem, moving the gun so that it was level with my chest.

Why was he being such a prick?

Oh, duh.

"He's working for you?" I said.

"For a man with an international reputation, you are very slow-witted," said the sergeant.

Not something I could argue with at the moment, to be honest.

"You're the source," I said belatedly. "Or you set it up. You're not stupid enough to be F5 himself."

The sergeant smiled a little. Obviously I was guessing, but it seemed logical—he'd arranged for the information from People's Islam, and made sure we'd grab their guys. In exchange, we got everything we got on India for Islam.

I guess I could understand horse trading, but afterward?

"So you were feeding information to the enemy?" I said. "Why?"

"India has many enemies," said the sergeant. "It is a matter of perspective."

"One of those enemies nearly killed thousands if not millions of people today."

"And then, you know what would have happened?" Sergeant Phurem asked. "Then Hindus would have realized who their real enemy was. We would have dealt with Pakistan the way it should be dealt with. Not shaking their hand."

It sounded almost noble the way he put it—a justification for helping terrorists kill innocent civilians.

"They gave you no money?" I said.

He gave me a crooked smile.

"You will keep your hands up and come with me quietly, or your death will be painfully slow."

"And yours will be fast and furious," said Doc, stepping out from behind the desk. He had a twelve gauge in his hands; the barrel was about a foot from Sergeant Phurem's head.

I suppose if the sergeant had been a brave or misguided man dedicated to a cause, he might have shot me in the chest before he died. That would have sucked—at that range, even my Miguel Caballero vest would have bruised me taking the bullet.

But he wasn't brave, and the only cause he was really dedicated to was enriching himself. He dropped the gun.

III

The person I really had to talk to about the sergeant and corporal was Minister Dharma, who after all was still the titular head of the unit.

Heh.

As it happened, I had arranged to meet the well-endowed minister that very evening, at one of the galas celebrating the opening of the Games.

It meant donning a tux and wearing an actual tie, but we all make sacrifices in the line of duty.

The event was sponsored by the Brits, and took place in a large hotel that they'd taken over for the Games. As I said earlier, the British really know how to do imperial decadence. The queen wasn't there, but one of the young princes and his entourage were the official hosts, and the place teemed with diplomats, government officials, international celebrities, and Bollywood stars. It was the perfect place to get a parking ticket fixed.

Trace was my date, and let me say she looked as lovely in floor-length chiffon as she did in tartan shorts.

She'd returned to the athletic field earlier in the day just in time to help the Scots to a 15 – 0 trouncing of Australia in the opening round. The bookmakers were no longer accepting bets on her team.

We bypassed the paparazzi, gliding into the hotel ballroom through a side door. We were maybe two paces from the bar when a short, gnarly-looking man turned to me and practically spit. Before I could react, the woman he was with turned and gave me a death stare.

"Madam Secretary of State," I said, nodding.

"Don't Madam me," she said, lips tight. "You screwed up a peace process I've been working on for months."

"*Moi?*" I wish I could have had a good comeback there, but I was actually taken by surprise.

"You publicized the attack on the weapons site to make yourself look good," she said.

"I publicized nothing. My lips were sealed."

I made a motion with my hand across my lips. I may or may not have used only one finger to do so.

She shook her head, then turned and walked away.

I heard a loud sigh behind me and turned to find my friend from State Department intelligence.

"Why'd you piss her off?" he asked.

"Why do I piss anyone off?" I said. It was a rhetorical question, because honestly, I didn't quite know *how* I had pissed her off.

"The Indians used the attack to back out of the talks," he told me. "They've moved all their nukes."

"They shouldn't have gathered them in one place to begin with."

"You think I don't know that?" he said.

"Does she know that?" I gestured toward the secretary of State. How many fingers I used—again, I'd rather not say.

"Of course she does," said my friend.

"Why'd she propose it?"

"Who said she proposed it?"

"Why did she go along with it then?" I asked. "If it was a dumb idea—why endorse it?"

"You don't understand diplomacy." He shook his head sadly, as if that was a major loss, like I'd spilled my drink or something.

The band started up at the other side of the room.

"Want to dance?" Trace asked.

"I'm here on business," I said.

"I'm not talking to you."

She smiled at my friend. They went off to trip the light fantastic. I slipped over to the bar—my motivations were purely medicinal, I assure you—then went in search of my prey.

Minister Dharma was holding court not far from the prince. The prince had a large group of admirers; hers was bigger. But her face lit up as soon as she saw me.

"The Rogue Warrior in the flesh," she said. She raised her arms, as if parting the Red Sea. "You made it. My hero."

Her attention was intoxicating . . . or maybe it was just the double helping of gin on an empty stomach. I offered my cheeks to her air kisses. Then I took her in my arms, bent her back, and showed her how a SEAL kisses.

A hundred pairs of eyes stabbed me in every body part. The minister caught her breath.

"Let's talk out on the veranda," I said, taking her hand.

"I need a drink," she said.

"Take this one," I told her, snatching a glass from one of her admirers.

He started to object. A frown persuaded him that wasn't a good idea.

Minister Dharma and I walked arm in arm through a pair of French doors to the patio. Two members of the prince's entourage were copping a smoke there.

"The prince hates smoking," I said.

Somehow, that convinced them that they were done. They left us alone. I took the minister in my arms.

"Oh, not here, not now," said Dharma. "We should wait."

"Wait? Why wait?"

"We'll get a room upstairs. I'm sure there are plenty."

"I think here is fine."

I ran my hands down her back, exploring the delicate curves of her buttocks, then up the sides and around the front. They are doing wonderful things with wire these days.

"Take me then," she said, pressing her lips into mine.

We tangled tongues. Then I stepped back, done frisking her.

OK, the kiss was just a bonus.

"The only thing I'm unsure of was how much you planned from the beginning," I said.

"To seduce you? From the moment I saw you."

"Clearly you didn't want peace between Pakistan and India. But did you suggest putting the warheads all in one place?"

She frowned. "Oh, we really shouldn't talk business tonight."

I bent her back and took a kiss long enough to empty her lungs.

"It was such a bad idea, that it couldn't have come from the Defense Ministry," I whispered, letting her breathe.

"I may have suggested it to the prime minister," she said, practically gasping for air. "Who remembers details?"

"You were always planning a fake attack? Or did you help India for Islam yourself?"

"I didn't help them. Of course not."

"Putting the bombs in one place would have helped them succeed."

"Why do you think I suggested they be the target?"

She curled her arms around me, ready for another kiss. I obliged, bending her backward. Sometimes the job is too dangerous for words.

"You take my breath away," she said when I let her up.

"So you were always planning some sort of fake attack on the nukes so you could break off the negotiations. You don't want to disarm Pakistan."

"They're all liars. We could never trust them. And who wants to?"

"Why trust anyone?" I asked, hugging her close.

"That is the problem exactly."

"Like Sergeant Phurem."

"Phurem?"

"Was he one of the people you wanted on Special Squadron Zero?"

"Someone from Transport Ministry asked for him. He was a cousin. But he had a good background."

"You checked it personally?"

"Oh, Dick, is that your gun?"

"Not exactly," I whispered.

"Very nice," she said.

"So you picked people for the squadron based on political connections, rather than ability."

"I didn't have time to check them all. Not like you."

She kissed me this time. She wasn't a bad kisser, I have to admit.

"Did you know that Phurem was selling information to People's Islam?" I asked. "That he'd dealt with the Maoists for years?"

Actually, I suspected that she didn't, but it's always nice to get people's ignorance on the record. She took a deep breath and drew back.

"This is too much business tonight," she said. "We have other . . . affairs to concentrate on."

"You may not have known that he was a traitor, but it was because of him that half a million people in Delhi nearly died today. People's Islam had a plot to flood the air with VX gas."

"*What?*"

"I guess I didn't tell you about that, did I?" I put my finger on my chin, kind of like Shirley Temple, except maybe she used a different finger. "So your political decision could have led to a lot of innocent deaths."

"The terrorists would have been responsible."

"You would have, too. You used Special Squadron Zero for political gain. Because of that, you were negligent setting it up. The people weren't vetted properly, and politics, not intelligence, was used to make the decisions. You're as responsible as Phurem."

She folded her arms in front of her breasts. A shame, really.

"I don't believe that he was a traitor," she said.

"He helped People's Islam. I'm not saying he was in charge or even knew of the VX attack, though he must have suspected something. He was in contact with them right after the attack. You know what he said?"

"What?"

"He said all those deaths wouldn't have mattered. They would have been a wake-up call for India."

"That is true," she said. "The Muslim bastards are a severe threat."

Cursing with lips I had just kissed? My, my.

Dharma picked up the nearby glass.

"You of all people should know the dangers of dealing with your enemies," said Dharma. "To accept peace with the Muslims? On what terms? They're radicals, maniacs. Maybe not all—but just one in their midst. That's all it takes."

"Fake attacks on nuclear sites aren't the best way to push your agenda. And letting terrorists kill thousands of your own people?"

"And what is it that you did with Special Squadron Zero? Were those not fake attacks? Did they not serve a greater purpose? My action helped our security—can you say the same even about your celebrated Red Cell antics?"

"Absolutely. And none of my people died. And I didn't wipe out half of Washington, D.C., or New York—if it weren't for Red Cell International, a lot of Delhi would be a graveyard right now."

"I don't like the direction this is taking," she said, sipping from her drink. "I have nothing more to say."

"You've said quite enough."

The booming voice didn't come from me; it came from the man standing in the doorway behind me: the Indian prime minister.

Next to him was the U.S. Secretary of State, who looked like she had swallowed a cat.

I know, she always looks that way. But this time it was a really big cat.

Trace was next to her. Among the other dozen or so people were several members of the Indian government, the British prince, and my friend from the State Department, all crowded behind the prime minister. They'd seen everything through the mirrored window.

The other three or four hundred guests had to settle for the broadcast I had arranged with Trace's help: my pillow talk with Minister Dharma had been piped through the band's PA system.

That hadn't been my gun, it had been my microphone.

"Let me explain," said Minister Dharma.

"You will have to explain to the Indian people," sputtered the prime minister. "Mr. Marcinko had this broadcast over the Internet on the *Delhi Delhi Times'* Web site."

Yes, the little runt behind Trace was my friend Kenyon Ganesh. Don't you just hate those media people?

I gave Dharma a big smile. As I was about to turn away, she tried throwing her drink at me. But she'd drank all but the tiniest sip. A few drops of wine flew through the air . . . followed by a cigarette butt. She'd been sipping out of the drink the prince's retainers had used to put out their cigarettes.

A shame, really. I would have gone in for one more kiss if that hadn't been the case.

(IV)

I left India the next morning, flying back to the States with Junior and Shotgun. They headed off to whatever it is young bucks do when they have a few weeks of well deserved R & R—I'll leave that to your imagination.

I'll also leave to your imagination my homecoming with Karen, who met me at the airport. Let's just say our arrival at Rogue Manor was pleasantly delayed.

Sean stayed in Karachi a few days longer, working on an interesting project that may have some promise in the future. He'd developed a little more information about Pakistan intelligence and its connections to India for Islam; I've integrated them all into the story.

Doc, Mongoose, and Trace made it back a few days later, after the field hockey competition ended. Mongoose had stayed to further relations with Argentina, or rather one Argentinean, Vina. What comes of that, only the future knows.

Scotland—well, I suppose you read about how they did in the press reports. Trace has her own side of the story, and is threatening to write an expose-all story someday. But at least the controversy seems to have cured her of her desire to whack balls with sticks, at least for a while.

As for Doc, his wife St. Donna has him well in hand—he won't be giving out massages except to her for quite a while.

The secretary of State has called several times to apologize, but I haven't been quite able to reach the phone. And the less said about the Games themselves, the better.

Omar was recalled not long after my return. He and I had some words on account of that. But that's a story for another day, as is Admiral Jones's officially unofficial comments on my relationship with the secretary of State.

I will give Ken this much—he does pay for his drinks. One way or another.